HOW COULD SUCH A LOVE
END LIKE THIS?

Gwenaseth watched the king with concern. Maelgwn had not rested in the long hours since Aurora had been brought to the tower room. He sat by the bed, holding his wife's hand and staring at her pale, still face. His handsome profile was ravaged by fatigue and worry. Maelgwn looked worse than Aurora. Her face wore a look of eerie peace, while Maelgwn looked like a man who had been tortured for hours. Gwenaseth could see that he was beside himself with worry, punishing himself with remorse.

Then there was the sound of moaning, an awful sound, and Gwenaseth's heart leaped in her throat. The queen thrashed about the bed as if in pain. As she struggled frantically in her sleep, she called out in a faint anguished voice.

"Help me! Help me, Marcus!"

"Who is he?"

The king's pain was etched deeply in those few words, and Gwenaseth felt her heart sink. Maelgwn had heard clearly enough—he knew that Aurora was calling for another man.

"You must not hold it against her," Gwenaseth said anxiously.

"She calls for him, instead of me . . . now . . . when her spirit is so near death."

"You must remember," Gwenaseth spoke softly, her voice little more than a whisper in the darkness. "When she left here last night, she was very afraid of you."

"How can I forget?"

The raw suffering in his voice was unbearable . . . .

Dragon
of the
Island

Mary Gillgannon

PINNACLE BOOKS
WINDSOR PUBLISHING CORP.

PINNACLE BOOKS are published by

Windsor Publishing Corp.
850 Third Avenue
New York, NY 10022

The P logo Reg U.S. & TM off. Pinnacle is a trademark of
Windsor Publishing Corp.

First Printing: November, 1994

Printed in the United States of America

To my Irish lover, Patrick

One

The Dragon had come.

Aurora pressed against the stone wall of the gate tower, watching the advancing army spill over the green hills and march toward the town. The warriors' war cloaks and armor glinted and flashed in the afternoon sun like the scales of a huge beast. Its jaws were opening, preparing to swallow them up.

The Dragon of the Island, they called him. Maelgwn the Great had risen out of the west like a thundercloud, killing his own kin in his brutal bid for power. After forcing all the other princes of Gwynedd to recognize him as overking, the Dragon had left his fortress in the mountains of Wales and pressed east. The old Roman town of Viroconium lay directly in his path.

Aurora turned her eyes to her father's troops, gathered staunchly between Maelgwn's army and the gates of the city. The defenders were clearly outnumbered. The invading army had dozens of archers and a huge cavalry force. Even if Constantine's army could survive the head-on charge, they could not hold them off long. Aurora could imagine the invaders swarming the city gates—just as the Saxons had, nearly a half a century before. They would kill . . . and rape . . . and burn . . .

Aurora gritted her teeth, wishing for the thousandth time that she were a man. Then she would not be so defenseless. Then she would have a weapon to fight with when the enemy arrived.

"My God, what are they waiting for?"

Aurora was startled from her thoughts by the impatient voice of her sister Julia. Her mother, two sisters and their ladies were crowded next to her in the tower. The other women had ceased their frantic praying and were watching the scene below intently. A puzzling stillness lingered over the battlefield. The invading army was almost upon them, but there had been no battle cry sent up, no drawing of swords or engagement of weapons. Aurora saw Constantine and a handful of men riding out to meet the enemy. It seemed they meant to talk before they fought.

Not even a whisper of breeze eased the oppressive heat. Aurora imagined the agonized tension of the soldiers below. The sweat would be dripping down their faces and pooling beneath their heavy leather tunics, the fat, bright flies tormenting the horses. In the tower, the women shifted awkwardly as the minutes dragged on.

Aurora struggled to get a better view of the battlefield, her thoughts turning hopeful. Her father—called Constantine after the emperor—was a shrewd, persuasive man. He might be able to talk Maelgwn the Great out of destroying the city. The rich lands around Viroconium produced a bounty of grain and livestock which were traded in Gaul for luxuries such as wine, oil, furniture—even gold. There was a chance they could use their wealth to bribe the enemy into leaving them alone.

The angry voice of Julia jolted Aurora from her thoughts.

"Even if Maelgwn agrees to a truce, how can we trust him? He is a madman, a barbarian. They say he once burned a whole fortress in a rage, killing everyone inside. How do we know that he won't do the same to us? How do we know he won't just take our gold and then kill us?"

"Hush, Julia!" whispered Aurora's mother, Lady Cordelia, in a voice harsh with anxiety. "There is no point in making everyone more frightened than they already are. That's just talk—we don't even know if it's true."

"Of course it's true. I overheard Papa. He wouldn't have repeated the story if it weren't true!"

Julia's words rekindled Aurora's fears. The invaders weren't civilized men. Even if her father made a truce, the enemy couldn't be trusted not to destroy the town.

There was movement on the battlefield. A portion of the enemy army broke away from the main force and slowly began to follow Constantine and his men toward the town gate. The soldiers were moving nearer, and Aurora could almost make out individual men. She searched for Maelgwn—the ruthless man who controlled the savage beast which waited below them, ready to tear the heart out of her beloved Viroconium. She spotted a crimson banner marked with a golden dragon. Right below it was a dark-haired man riding a black stallion.

No wonder he was called "Maelgwn the Great," Aurora thought in awe. Even from a distance she could sense the power which seemed to radiate from the foreign warlord as he handled the massive charger with ease. She stared at his long black hair. She had not guessed that the enemy was dark—somehow she had imagined Maelgwn as a blond giant like Hengist or Horsa, the legendary Saxon warriors who had nearly crushed the Roman Britains a generation ago.

As the enemy leader approached, Aurora suppressed a shiver. In one of the old stone buildings in the town there was a crumbling mosaic that depicted the god Dionysus. The god was portrayed riding a panther, his long wavy hair swirling around his shoulders, his eyes savage and exultant. The Welsh warrior looked like the mosaic come to life!

There was a shout from one of the soldiers guarding the gate below.

"Constantine is going to make a truce. All the women and unarmed men should go to the great hall to await the announcement there."

The women looked around in confusion. None of them had expected that Constantine would welcome the enemy into the city. Several of the women, including Carina, Aurora's other sister, began to pray again. Aurora reached out to touch her mother's shoulder.

"Mama, what are we going to do?"

Lady Cordelia's voice was calm and steady, her expression determined. "If Constantine brings Maelgwn and his men into the city, then they are our guests. We will treat them accordingly."

"I won't play hostess to those . . . those barbarians!" Julia sputtered.

"Indeed you will," her mother answered. "You will not dishonor your father by being rude to our guests. Come, we must go down and make ready for them."

The women watched numbly as Lady Cordelia gathered up her skirts and began to climb briskly down the ladder to the ground. Aurora was nearly the last to escape the hot tower, and in the few moments of waiting, she considered her mother's words carefully. If Constantine was bringing the enemy into the city, he must have some plan. A crude barbarian would be no match for her clever, well-educated father. Aurora hurried down as fast as she could, anxious to see what her father had in store for the foreign warlord and his men.

She raced ahead of her mother and the other women, determined to reach her father's feasting hall before everyone else. The great hall stood in the center of the town, looking cool and welcoming in the afternoon heat. The timber structure was built along the same lines as the Roman basilica it had replaced, with steps leading to a porticoed facade. Aurora ran lightly up the steps and across the scarred mosaic floor of the entryway. She found a place near one of the carved supporting beams and pressed her body tightly against the slippery wood, determined to keep her vantage point as the crowd increased.

People poured in around her, filling every inch of space—first the townspeople and the soldiers, then the enemy troops. The room was surprisingly quiet, and Aurora was reminded of two groups of dogs, meeting for the first time and sniffing the air, testing it for the sharp scent of danger. Just when Aurora decided she could not endure the tension a moment longer, Constantine moved to the end of the room, climbed the dais and gestured for quiet.

"People of Viroconium," he began. "Today we have avoided a great battle and the destruction of our town and homes." Constantine's voice was rich and melodic, and Aurora felt a surge of pride for her father.

"But there is a price for our continued peace. As your leader, I feel that it is only fair that I tell you what has come to pass."

The leader of the invaders stepped forward impatiently. The man was so tall he did not even need to climb the dais to be seen, and his voice—despite the strange accent—was deep and commanding.

"I am Maelgwn of Gwynedd," the man began. "Your leader"—Maelgwn nodded curtly to Constantine—"has seen the wisdom of surrendering to me. Because of that, we will be generous. We will let you live."

There were smiles from the bold warriors who accompanied Maelgwn, and angry looks among the townspeople. Aurora felt her anger rising as well. Who was this man to speak so arrogantly? The people of Viroconium were not defeated yet. The enemy commander had no cause to gloat.

Maelgwn began to recite a long list of the tribute he expected. He demanded gold and precious metals of course, but also grain, cattle, sheep and other produce. Surprisingly, he also asked for craftsmen—men skilled in masonry, carpentry, enamelware and pottery-making.

Aurora listened to the list intently. Maelgwn's terms were harsh, but not unbearable. She knew that the people of Viroconium would gladly part with some of their wealth if it meant they would be left in peace.

"Finally, in as much as you will be a subject people, submitting to my authority as your overlord, I would seal the alliance by taking one of Constantine's daughters as my wife."

Maelgwn's last words drew a sharp sound of surprise from the crowd, and Aurora felt her throat tighten in fury. How dare he? She and her sisters were not mere possessions to be bartered off to keep the peace. Constantine would never hear of such a thing, he would not allow it! She looked toward her father, still standing on the dais. Constantine's head was bowed slightly, his face furrowed with lines. Aurora wanted to run to him, to throw her arms around him and beg him to refuse this outrageous request. She was held back by the people packed tightly around her, and she could only watch in dismay as Constantine lifted his head and faced his conqueror.

"Maelgwn of Gwynedd," he said slowly. "We do agree to your terms."

Maelgwn nodded curtly, then faced the crowd again.

"Now we will feast with you, and after we have satisfied ourselves, I will choose my queen."

Aurora's chest was tight with shock. Her father couldn't possibly mean to go through with this agreement. Surely he had another plan, some plot to defy this madman!

Aurora pushed her way frantically through the crowd, trying to reach her mother. As she struggled by, she heard the relieved comments of the townspeople.

"Well, he was hard, but at least we can live with his demands."

"Aye, live with them, we can. I thought it would come to war, and I am too old to fight those young, well-drilled devils. It is too bad about Constantine's daughter though."

"He will choose Julia, I'm sure. She is the oldest and quite a beauty."

"All the girls are fair," countered another man. "That

must be the hardest part for Constantine to swallow—imagine having to give your child to that brute!"

The words affected Aurora like a blow, and she struggled even more furiously against the crowd. At last she was able to break away and reach the kitchen. It was crowded and chaotic. Servants hurried to and fro, trying frantically to prepare the unexpected meal. Aurora asked one of them about her mother, and the man gestured to a small anteroom that was used for storage of wine and oil. Aurora found her mother and Julia there, arguing. Julia's blue-green eyes flashed with fury, and her fair skin was flushed scarlet.

"He can't do this! Father can't possibly agree. We are not cattle to be sent off to pay a war debt." Julia grabbed a small knife from the nearby table and waved it menacingly. "Why, if that beast of a Welshman tries to touch me, I'll kill him myself!"

Aurora felt a surge of pride at her sister's defiant words. Julia was right—their conqueror was an uncouth monster. No Cornovii princess should have to marry him!

Her mother's next words reminded Aurora of the grim truth.

"I'll not have you blaming your father and bringing shame upon him," Lady Cordelia said firmly, taking the knife from Julia's trembling hand. "He has done the best he could to protect his people. He cannot refuse Maelgwn's demand without risking our lives."

Aurora's mother's face softened. She reached out for Julia and gathered her into her arms. "Would that he could spare you, Julia, but your father is king. He must do what is best for his people, and you must obey him."

Aurora felt her own heart sink, and she turned away quickly, unable to face Julia's tears. Her hope that her father had some plan to defy Maelgwn was completely dashed. It was likely that her oldest sister would be forced to wed Maelgwn, and there did not seem to be anything that anyone could do about it.

On the way out of the kitchen Aurora met her other sister.

"Carina! Where have you been?"

"I have been praying." Carina reached out and clasped Aurora's hand gently in her own. "Are you all right, little one?"

"Aye—except that I am so angry. It is not right that one of us should be forced to marry that arrogant savage."

"Right or not, it is the way of the world. We are all destined to marry foreign chieftains. The bond of our blood will forge alliances for the future of Viroconium."

Aurora stared at her sister's calm blue eyes. "You mean you are not afraid? What if Maelgwn chooses you?"

Carina sighed faintly. "If it be God's will that I marry this man, then God will be with me to bear it."

Aurora felt the anger in her bubbling up and spilling out. No one seemed willing to fight Maelgwn. It made her furious.

"It is lucky that I am the youngest and unlikely to be the bride. I do not think I could endure it!"

Carina shook her head reprovingly. "Come, Aurora, we must go back to the villa and change before the feast."

"No," Aurora answered, pulling away. "I have no intention of dressing up to impress that tyrant. The rest of you may be willing to grovel before Maelgwn the Great, but I am not."

Two

Aurora left the great hall and took off at a run, darting down the old Roman streets until she was breathless and sweating. Near the edge of the town, she paused to gaze up at the towering ruins of the old baths, silhouetted in the fading sunlight. Even cracked and half-shattered, the vast archways and proud pillars of the once-magnificent building stirred Aurora's pride. She squinted and tried to imagine what Viroconium must have been like in the old days, when the buildings were all of stone, the streets fine and smooth, and the town filled with the color and pride of the legions.

She sighed and continued on until she reached the town wall. Walking along it for a short distance, she came to a place where it had begun to tumble down. Hiking up her skirts, she climbed the crumbling wall and jumped down to the other side.

In the distance she could see the white stone walls and red tile roof of her father's villa. The sight lifted her spirits and calmed her nerves. The villa was home—she knew every fragrant corner of the orchard and garden, every secret nook around the sprawling house, every horse in the stables, every hound in the kennel.

Aurora hurried down the dusty road and through the

villa's gate. As she crossed the paved courtyard, she picked up speed. Marcus, a slave in her father's stables, was her best friend and closest companion, and she could hardly wait to tell him the news of the Welsh army's arrival. Inside the stables, she squinted in the dim light and made her way past the stalls until she found Marcus below the hayloft, repairing some harnesses with studied nonchalance. The white boarhound puppy she had given him in the spring wagged its tail in greeting and ran to meet her. Marcus only looked up and then went back to his work.

His indifference irritated Aurora's jangled nerves past endurance.

"Aren't you glad to see me?" she demanded. "Maelgwn and his men might have sacked the city and killed us all, and yet you stay here and go about your chores as if you had not a care in the world."

"You forget that I am a slave and cannot bear arms," Marcus answered slowly. "What use would I be to you if I went into town?" His gray eyes narrowed. "Besides, I didn't really think Constantine would fight."

Aurora gasped with annoyance. "You knew my father was going to surrender?"

Marcus shrugged. "What else could he do? He could not stand against an army such as Maelgwn's. I assumed that Constantine would meet the Welshman's terms."

It was Aurora's turn to be bitter. "Aye, he has done that. My father agreed to everything Maelgwn demanded—including that one of his daughters is to become Maelgwn's wife."

There was a flicker of interest in Marcus's eyes.

"Will it be Julia?"

Aurora avoided his probing look. "Maelgwn has not chosen yet," she said coolly. "He will select one of us as his queen tonight after the feast."

Marcus seemed to grow white beneath his tanned skin. "He will not choose you!"

Marcus said the words so fiercely, Aurora took pity on him and told him the truth.

"No, it is not likely. It is traditional that the eldest daughter be married first. Julia and Carina's dowries are much greater than mine, and most people think they are much more beautiful, too." Aurora thought ruefully of her sisters' lovely fair hair and elegant manners. Next to them, she always felt plain and awkward.

Marcus gave a contemptuous snort. "I am glad, for once, that most men seem to be blind to true beauty." He met Aurora's eyes, his face bright with an adoring smile. "If I were to have the chance to choose, there is no doubt which one I would find most beautiful."

Aurora smiled back, distracted. She was still puzzling over how to find a way to thwart Maelgwn's plans. If only Marcus would be her ally.

"It doesn't matter who will be the bride," she insisted. "We must think of some way to prevent this shameful marriage."

"How? Your father has already agreed to it."

"He could change his mind."

"And do what? The enemy is already within the gates of the city."

"What if Maelgwn were poisoned at the feast?"

Marcus looked aghast. "Your father would never plot to kill one of his guests—it would be dishonorable! Even if he did agree to such treachery, it would not succeed.

Maelgwn's men would likely retaliate by slaughtering all of you."

"Perhaps that would be better. At least we would die fighting!"

Marcus smiled faintly. "Brave words for a little lass— you put them all to shame. But remember, Aurora, the people of Viroconium have already shown their unwillingness to fight. I imagine they are comfortably resigned to giving up one of the royal princesses in exchange for their lives. Besides . . ." Marcus's face grew grim again, ". . . need I remind you that there are worse things than death. You might be made a slave."

Aurora shuddered. The fate of Marcus's family never ceased to horrify her. His grandmother had been a Saxon princess who was captured by the Roman army and sold into slavery. His mother was a house slave, his father a Roman nobleman. All Marcus had to show for his blood-line of lost nobility were his extraordinary good looks. Aurora never tired of admiring his thick golden hair, slate gray eyes and finely sculpted features.

Aurora sighed, struggling to deal with the truth of Marcus's words. What could one young woman do against the might of Maelgwn the Great? He was a despicable tyrant, but this was an age of tyrants. The fortunes of the Roman British nobility were on the wane, and ruthless chieftains like Maelgwn would soon rule the whole country. It seemed likely that someday her beloved Viroconium would go the way of the other ruined cities of the crumbling Roman empire.

Marcus touched her cheek tentatively, and his eyes glowed with longing. "Don't fret, Aurora. I cannot bear to see you so sad."

Aurora sighed again and allowed Marcus to embrace her. She nestled softly against his warmth, feeling his work-hardened arms tighten around her.

"Aurora!"

They both stiffened at the sound of Lady Cordelia's voice.

"You'd better go," Marcus said, releasing her reluctantly.

"No doubt she wants me to dress and do my hair before the feast," Aurora complained. She looked down at her dirty, sweat-stained gown and the tangle of unruly curls around her shoulders. "I won't heed her wishes this time! Maelgwn the Great is nothing but a barbarian, and he deserves no better than this."

Aurora gave Marcus a quick kiss and hurried out the back way. She slipped through the apple orchard and the woods, retraced her path over the town wall and through the darkening streets. When she reached the great hall, she went directly to the kitchen and offered her services. The cook looked at her askance a moment and then nodded. Picking up an urn of wine, Aurora left the kitchen triumphantly. It was perfect—it was completely appropriate for the host's daughter to wait on important guests, and by posing as a serving wench she would have a chance to observe the enemy up close without being detected.

Aurora walked briskly to the table where Maelgwn and his men were seated. They still wore their swords and battle attire, and Aurora doubted seriously if they had even washed. She suppressed the urge to pour the contents of the urn in Maelgwn's lap, and went around the table, neatly pouring wine in each finely wrought bronze cup.

The Cymry—as Maelgwn's men called themselves—talked quietly, their manner cautious and wary. Except for Maelgwn, the foreigners were not tall, but they were powerfully built. They had dark, rather deep-set eyes and long curly hair. Like the men of Viroconium, they shaved their faces, although a few wore mustaches.

Aurora returned to the kitchen for a tray of food, and carried it back to the head table. This time she dared to linger close to Maelgwn, and even ask if he would like more wine. He looked up, noting her vaguely, and then shook his head. Aurora moved on, trembling slightly. Even from a few inches away, Maelgwn looked very intense and dangerous. What might he do to her if he discovered that she was not really a serving girl?

As Aurora headed for another plate of food, she saw her parents and sisters entering the hall. Julia shot Aurora a look of horror, and her mother's eyes grew wide. Lady Cordelia leaned over to whisper to Constantine, and his eyes met Aurora's with a frightened stare. Aurora realized abruptly that her impulsive urge to play spy might well cause trouble between her father and his new ally. If Maelgwn found out who she was, he would undoubtedly think Aurora's father had put her up to the disguise, and blame Constantine for deceiving him. Aurora swallowed hard, cursing her own foolishness. When would she learn to think before she acted?

Aurora ducked into the kitchen and stayed there during the rest of the meal. Only when people finished eating, and the crowded hall grew silent with expectation, did she dare to slip out the doorway and take her place near the carved supporting beam. She watched as Constantine led her sisters to stand before Maelgwn. They looked beautiful in their finest gowns, their golden hair elaborately braided. Aurora's bitter resentment returned. The enemy Welshman did not deserve either of her sisters, not even quarrelsome Julia!

Maelgwn watched as Constantine led his two daughters to the dais. There was a soft sound of satisfaction from the room, for both girls were quite comely. The eldest, whom Constantine introduced first, had hair of a burnished gold color, rich and shining like the sun. Lady Julia's skin was a flawless ivory, her eyes a brilliant blue green. She was small, but rather buxom, showing a tendency toward plumpness.

The other girl's beauty was, if anything, even more arresting. Although Lady Carina's hair was a plainer, darker blond, her features were exquisitely perfect. Long dark lashes hid her soft blue eyes, and her mouth was a delicious rosebud.

But Maelgwn was unmoved by Constantine's daughters' loveliness, for he could find no satisfaction in what he sensed beneath the exterior of heart-stopping beauty. It was obvious that the eldest daughter despised him. Her brilliant cat eyes glared like daggers, and her fine features were contorted with contempt. If a part of him was amused by her spirit, his mind told him that she would likely make a shrewish, difficult wife.

In contrast, the younger princess seemed calm and accepting. Too calm, Maelgwn thought. He noticed that her hands grasped a prayer necklace and her lips moved as if praying. Maelgwn felt a twinge of uneasiness. Most of his people still honored the pagan gods of hill, stream and forest. He did not need an overly devout queen to cause dissension in his court.

Maelgwn turned away from the two girls and addressed Constantine impatiently: "I was told there were three daughters—I would like to see the third."

Constantine looked flustered. "Maelgwn, my lord. Either of my older daughters would make an excellent wife. Perhaps you don't appreciate . . . my wife has trained them herself in all the skills of running a fine household. They can both read and write and sing like nightingales. No finer needlework is done by any woman in Viroconium . . ."

Maelgwn interrupted Constantine's recitation of the wifely virtues of his daughters with a cold, mirthless laugh.

"Constantine, I see before me two quite lovely women—except that one looks like she would like to scratch out my eyes and the other belongs more in a convent than a marriage bed. Since I don't fancy having to take my sword to bed or having my soul prayed for daily, I would like to see the third daughter ere I choose."

Constantine flushed and looked around the hall with an odd expression. Finally, after glancing at Maelgwn uneasily, he motioned to a young woman who stood half-hidden behind one of the hall supports. As the woman walked forward, Maelgwn frowned in puzzlement. What was this—some well-favored servant girl Constantine sought to pass off as his daughter? The woman's wavy dark hair was disheveled, her plain gown faded and stained, and there was even a smudge of dirt on her cheek. With a start, Maelgwn realized that she had served him his wine before dinner.

"My youngest daughter, Aurora." Constantine's voice was stiff, his face grim.

Maelgwn stared at the young woman intently. On second glance, she did not look like a serving wench at all. She was quite tall, and her straight, proud bearing bespoke noble blood. Her dirt-streaked face was provocatively foreign, and her elegant cheekbones and finely-arched brows clearly bore the stamp of some Roman ancestor. Maelgwn suppressed a smile. Constantine had tried to be clever, but his cleverness had given him away. By dressing the youngest princess as a raggedy child and not even presenting her, Constantine had revealed his true feelings—this daughter was obviously his favorite.

Maelgwn allowed his eyes to linger on the woman's sensuous features and the supple curves of her body. A warm flush of arousal was spreading through his loins, and his mind met it with a vague sense of unease. This daughter was definitely beguiling, perhaps too much so. He sensed pride and keen intelligence in the enigmatic blue-gray eyes which met his own. His unease deepened, but only for a moment. This exotic-looking woman might not make the most docile of wives, but there was no doubt that she was the one he should choose. Constantine obviously held this daughter dear. What better hold could he hope to have on his unwilling ally's heart than to marry his most beloved child?

Maelgwn hardly glanced at the other daughters. "This one," he said, pointing at Aurora. "I will marry this daughter, Constantine. You may ready your household for a wedding tomorrow."

"How could you?" Julia asked Aurora peevishly as soon as they reached the privacy of the villa. "Acting like a loathsome table wench—Maelgwn might have thought Papa was trying to deceive him. Your behavior could have ruined the truce and gotten us all killed."

"I noticed that you were not so anxious to preserve the truce when it appeared that Maelgwn might choose you," Aurora retorted. "Perhaps I was foolish, but at least I will bear the blame for it."

"Don't say that," Carina implored. "You are not to blame. I think that Maelgwn chose you out of spite, to hurt Papa. It makes me wonder what kind of man he is."

"Don't be silly. We know what kind of man he is," Julia argued. "Maelgwn is ruthless, scheming, wicked . . ."

"Julia!" Lady Cordelia's voice was harsh. "It's time you went to bed. I want to talk to Aurora alone."

Aurora allowed her mother to lead her to her bedchamber and help her undress. Her bed was in a little alcove set off from the main room where her sisters slept, and she could hear their whispers through the separating curtain. For once she did not strain to hear their talk. She was too shocked, too numb to deal with anything but her own thoughts. Never had she imagined that Maelgwn would chose her. It was a complete breach of good manners to select the youngest daughter when she had two older, marriageable sisters available. Why had Maelgwn done it? Did he think that Constantine had deliberately hidden her away? If so, his choosing her was, as Carina suggested, an act of obvious spite.

Aurora tried to muster the energy to renew her fury toward her future husband. He was so arrogant, so brazen. She could not forget his probing look before he chose her, the way his eyes lingered on her body where the gown pulled tight. The memory of his look made her shiver with fear . . . and something else.

"Aurora," Lady Cordelia's voice was soft and tender as she brushed Aurora's tangled dark hair. "Don't be frightened. Despite what Julia says, we don't really know what kind of man Maelgwn is. There are plenty of leaders who deal ruthlessly with their enemies, but that does not mean that they are not decent or respectable people. Your father, for example—he has ruled Viroconium strongly and well for nearly a score of years, but no one could ask for a more devoted husband and father."

Lady Cordelia paused, reluctant to suggest that Maelgwn might be a doting husband. She didn't really know what to say to Aurora. She had never discussed the realities of marriage with her youngest daughter. She must try quickly to impart some of what she had learned in twenty years of being a wife.

"A man like Maelgwn will undoubtedly expect your complete obedience," Lady Cordelia began. "But making him care for you is another matter. If you can learn to anticipate his needs and meet them eagerly, your husband will soon come to depend upon you for comfort and security in his life. Over time you may become his partner, his consort as well as his wife."

Aurora gaped at her mother. "You mean you expect me to try and please Maelgwn, to make him happy?"

"Of course! I know little of Cymry practices, but among our people, the Cornovii, a man has complete authority over everyone in his household, including his wife. A wife's place is not to question her husband's authority, but to influence it."

Aurora looked distinctly displeased by these words, and Lady Cordelia felt a stirring of apprehension. She and Constantine had spoiled Aurora and failed to prepare her for her future as a nobleman's wife. Her daughter's fiery temper and headstrong nature would not endear her to a grim, hardened man like Maelgwn. Still, Lady Cordelia did not think even Maelgwn the Great could be immune to Aurora's beauty and innocent charm. Which brought her to another subject she needed to discuss with her daughter.

"Aurora, you do know of a wife's duties in the marriage bed, don't you?"

Aurora blushed and nodded. Lady Cordelia touched her daughter's cheek reassuringly.

"Lovemaking can be a great joy, Aurora, and forge a strong bond between you and your husband. It need not be an unpleasant duty, although much depends on the man . . ." She stopped short. Maelgwn did not seem like someone who would have patience with a frightened, inexperienced girl. She could only hope that her first impression of him was overly harsh.

Lady Cordelia smoothed the blankets around her daughter's slender form. There seemed little more to say. Aurora was marrying an unknown, rather uncivilized man. She could only pray that things turned out well for her.

After her mother left, Aurora lay in bed, too tense to

sleep. She listened to the villa's night sounds that floated in through the unglazed windows: the lowing of cattle, the bark of her father's hounds, the murmur of muffled voices through the plaster and stone walls. Her mind worked feverishly, slowly forming a plan. She might be doomed to marry Maelgwn and leave Viroconium behind, but that did not mean she must abandon everything she cared about. Despite her future husband's vile reputation, there were advantages to marrying a powerful and wealthy man. She would likely have her own chambers and her own servants to wait upon her. There would be nothing unusual in bringing along a manservant to take care of her horse and serve her in ways a maid could not. If Marcus could come with her, her lot would not be so bitter, nor her loss so great.

Aurora was flooded with relief as the idea unfolded. Maelgwn was a busy, important man and would probably be away on campaign much of the time. She would have plenty of time to be with Marcus, to ride and talk. It would be almost like things were now. Aurora lay back on the bed and began to relax. She would go to Marcus first thing in the morning and tell him her wonderful plan.

Three

The shoals and rapids of the river shimmered in the afternoon sun, nearly blinding him. Maelgwn looked away, focusing his eyes on the fishing line he was baiting. Sweat trickled down his forehead, but he was as oblivious to the heat as he was to the gnats that circled around him in iridescent clouds.

"Maelgwn!"

He turned, startled, and saw his sister Esylt coming down the pathway. His first reaction was anger—at her for surprising him and making him jump, and at himself for letting her sneak up on him. His anger lasted only briefly, for he saw something in Esylt's face that made his pulse quicken with expectation. Her deep blue eyes were bright as flames and her face flushed beyond the exertion of hurrying down the steep, rocky path. She reached out and placed a small tanned hand upon his own.

"Father is dead."

Her words sank in slowly as Maelgwn stared at the silvery-brown texture of Esylt's fingers. The contentment of the summer's day drained away, and he felt empty and cold. He forced himself to speak, cringing as his voice came out in an anguished, adolescent croak.

"How?"

"A sickness of the stomach." Esylt's voice was matter-of-fact. "It felled him at Cowyn and he died two days later. He suffered fiercely, but the end came quickly enough. Not a warrior's death—still, they say he was brave."

Dead. How could his father be dead? Maelgwn shook his head, as if trying to deny Esylt's words. Cadwallon had always seemed invincible. As far as Maelgwn knew, his father had never been beaten in battle. Now he was dead, just like any other man—except that he was not like any other man. No chieftain before him had ever been able to unite the warring tribes of Gwynedd into one kingdom, one people. Cadwallon's strong rule had brought the country years of peace. Maelgwn shuddered slightly, thinking about the future. Who could take his father's place? Who would carry on after him?

Maelgwn struggled to clear his throat and ask his sister the fateful question, already dreading her answer.

"What will happen now? Who will be king?"

Esylt's brilliant blue eyes sparkled with excitement. "There will be war," she answered. "Llewen and Owen have already begun recruiting men. Maelfawr will not be far behind."

"They mean to fight each other for the kingship?"

Esylt nodded. "What did you expect? There can be only one king, one leader. Whoever is strongest will take everything."

Maelgwn opened his mouth to protest, but the words wouldn't come. His throat seemed choked with dust. He reached out to Esylt, trying to communicate his fear to her, but her image seemed to fade before his eyes. Her blue eyes diminished to points of light, and then the river, the summer's day—everything vanished.

The soft linen sheets were tangled around Maelgwn's limbs, and he struggled to free himself, throwing off the blankets so the cool evening air could soothe his sweat-soaked skin. Moonlight poured into the room, illuminating the figure of a man opposite the bed who regarded Maelgwn with cold, angry eyes. For a moment, Maelgwn's breathing quickened again, and then he relaxed, shaking his head at his own foolishless. He was in Constantine's guest chamber. The fierce man was nothing more than a picture, a mosaic portraying the god Neptune as he rode the roiling waves. It was the moonlight that made the god's eyes glint with life and the six dolphins which surrounded him seem to leap in the room.

Maelgwn leaned back, trying to recover himself. The rich food, the spiced wine, the strange surroundings—all had addled his mind and caused this panicky mood. After weeks on campaign, his body could not adapt to the soft bed, the enticing atmosphere of luxury and comfort.

Maelgwn got up and poured himself a cup of wine. He took a gulp and grimaced with distaste at its rich, cloying flavor. He would rather be drinking water—the clear, sweet mountain water of Gwynedd. His mind turned back to the dream. Even now, over ten years later, the memory of the day he learned of his father's death still haunted him. He could not forget his own fear and shock, nor Esylt's gloating excitement.

As Esylt had predicted, his brothers had fought bitterly for the next three years, rending apart the kingdom that their father had united. Owen had been killed early on, but neither Llewen nor Maelfawr could defeat the other. Maelgwn had tried to avoid entering the struggle, but it was not to be. When there were rumors of plots against Maelgwn's life, Esylt convinced their Uncle Pascent to provide him with arms and men. She had saved his life, Maelgwn thought bitterly, and now she would never let him forget it.

Still, he had done the hard part—molding his men into an army, devising clever tactics to make up for his disadvantage in numbers. He would never forget the thrill of seeing the respect in the eyes of the old greybeards after Betws-y-coed. They had once followed his father, now they followed him. That victory had been very sweet, and yet afterwards he had faced the horror of looking down upon the glassy-eyed corpse of his brother Llewen. He should have known then how dark the heart of war was.

Maelgwn sighed and walked to the window, peering out at the flat, white moon which was caught in a tree in Constantine's orchard. Dinas Brenin, "king's fort"— he would never forget that name, that place. After Betws-y-coed, Maelfawr and his men took refuge there. They were joined by Maelgwn's mother, Rhiannon. From the beginning, she had encouraged the strife between her sons. At Dinas Brenin she took a stand with Maelfawr— her oldest living child—against Maelgwn, the unwanted babe of her autumn years.

Maelgwn forced back the pain. His mother had not loved him—never. And yet, he had not meant for her life to end that way.

He had planned to besiege the fortress and starve them

out. But Esylt had intervened with her subtle plan and not-so-subtle taunts. A siege would take time, she warned him. He might lose his men if he waited too long. A strategically set fire would burn Maelfawr and his men out and force them to fight much sooner.

He resisted until his men began to drift away, anxious to get home before the harvest. Even then he was reluctant. He wanted a pitched battle, an even contest. It was only when Esylt began her wicked taunts that he even considered a fire. She called him a coward and a fool. She sneered at him, warning that he was about to let it all slip away.

Maelgwn shook his head. How could he have listened to her? Even before the first sparks caught he had known that it was a mistake. The old timber walls of Dinas Brenin had gone up like kindling. His brother, his mother—all those people inside—they had never had a chance.

He turned from the window, the bile rising in his throat. He could never forget the part Esylt had played in the tragedy. He had never trusted his sister since that day. Perhaps that was why he was apprehensive about his impending marriage. Esylt was bound to resent any woman he chose to marry. A queen at Caer Eryri would lessen Esylt's importance and challenge her authority to run the fortress as she wished. She was bound to cause trouble.

The thought that he needed to consider Esylt's wishes made him furious. He was king—he had the right to marry any woman he chose. What better match could he make than this lovely, well-dowered princess?

Maelgwn lay down on the bed again, thinking of Lady

Aurora's sensuous beauty. So young and luscious she was, like a warm summer's day. His anxiety and anger eased, pushed aside by arousal. He wanted this intriguing princess. He would not let anyone deter him from taking his prize. Tomorrow he would wed Lady Aurora and annex her father's rich lands to his own. He was the Dragon, and no one could stop him. Not even Esylt.

A few paces away across the courtyard, Aurora stirred in her fitful sleep. Several times she woke and crept across her sisters' room to the unglazed window and peeped out, trying to decide if Marcus would be awake yet. When the glow of a lamp in the wing where her parents slept convinced her that it was near morning, she hurried back to her sleeping place and quickly dressed.

The villa was quiet. Aurora's sandals made a soft slapping sound on the paving stones of the courtyard as she ran past the garden. She inhaled the rich scent of summer flowers hovering in the darkness, and choked back a pang of longing. Even with Marcus beside her, she would miss her home painfully.

The familiar warm darkness of the stables affected her even more profoundly. She had spent hours in these comforting corridors—it did not seem possible she would never come here again. She hurried from stall to stall, searching desperately for Marcus. She had to speak to him now, before it was too late, before her mother and sisters came to dress her for the wedding and her life spun completely from her control.

"Marcus?"

He was brushing down one of her father's matching

chestnut geldings, and he did not turn when she called to him. In exasperation she made her voice as sharp and scolding as her mother's.

"Marcus!"

He faced her with eyes so full of bitterness and hatred that Aurora's heart pounded in her chest. She had hoped that he had not heard that she was to be a bride—she wanted to tell him herself when she explained her plan to him. Obviously Marcus already knew. He looked wild and hopeless, as if she had died and he was grieving for her.

She moved slowly toward him, extending her hand, as if he were a skittish horse she was trying to gentle.

"I know it is awful, Marcus, but I have a plan. I'm going to ask if I can . . . if I can bring you with me!"

Marcus did not reach for her hand, nor did his face change, except to grow even more desperate.

Aurora began to talk rapidly:

"I will be taking a maid, of course, so it wouldn't be that strange for me to bring a manservant as well. You could take care of my horse and wait on me. The important thing is that we would be together. Why, we might even go riding sometimes." She paused, out of breath and dreading the terrible look in his eyes.

"Please, Marcus," she begged. "Please come with me!"

The struggle between his pride and his feelings for her showed clearly on Marcus's handsome countenance. Aurora watched him in agony, pleading silently.

Marcus let out a painful sigh. "Aurora, I can't. I couldn't stand to watch you with him, to watch him possess you. He has no right to you."

Marcus turned away, unwilling for her to see his anguish. Aurora made no move to comfort him. She stood still and stiff, consumed by the sense of utter loss that washed over her. Marcus had been her last hope. Now there was nothing ahead of her, nothing except the unknown, frightening future.

"Maelgwn!"

He jerked awake and was fumbling for his sword when he recognized the voice outside the door. Maelgwn let his scabbard fall with a clatter and went to let in his first officer, Balyn ap Rhyderch. Balyn greeted Maelgwn with a cheery smile. His eyes grew wide as he glanced around the room.

"Truly it is a room fit for a king," Balyn said in a hushed, appreciative voice.

"Aye," Maelgwn agreed as he leaned down to pull on his boots. "Still, it is not a room I would want to spend another night in."

"All this beauty and luxury doesn't please you?"

Maelgwn shook his head and gestured to the lush bed and rich furnishings. "Comforts such as these make men soft and weak. It seems no wonder to me that Constantine cannot field a decent army. You would have thought he would have learned from his Roman forebears that an easy life leads to easy defeat."

"Harsh words from a man who is benefiting greatly from a Roman British leader's weakness," Balyn noted wryly. "Tell me, my lord, did you not sleep well?"

Maelgwn shook his head, then turned away from his officer's concerned brown eyes. Balyn had been at his side since the beginnings of his struggle for the kingship, and he trusted him implicitly. Still, Maelgwn was unwilling to share his doubts with his first officer. He did not want anyone to know that he had been awake half the night, troubled by thoughts of Esylt and memories of Dinas Brenin.

Balyn changed the subject with graceful swiftness:

"From the scornful way you speak of Roman ways, I suspect my discovery of the Baths would be lost on you."

"Baths?"

Balyn nodded. "I'm sure you have heard of the Roman passion for daily bathing. Constantine has his own private bathhouse. There is both hot and cold water and a room where they use hot rocks to make steam. I must confess that I have already enjoyed their invigorating pleasures this morning. You might try it, Maelgwn. It would be one way to prove to your lovely young bride that you are a civilized man."

Maelgwn's incredulous look quickly turned to an amused grin. "Aye, the girl did seem appalled to be wedding me, didn't she?"

Balyn shrugged. "Your reputation precedes you, my lord. No doubt the Lady Aurora thinks she is about to marry a terrible ogre."

"And yet she was brazen enough to pose as a serving girl at my table, a common spy." Maelgwn pointed out, raising his dark brows.

"Surely her father put her up to that!"

"No doubt," Maelgwn agreed. "But she had the nerve to carry off the disguise—which many women would not." He stroked his whisker-roughed chin thoughtfully. "I must admit the girl puzzles me. I can't say that I know what kind of woman I have agreed to wed. I intend to ask Constantine to have her brought to me before the wedding so I can see what my princess is like when she does not have a roomful of people staring at her."

"You're not regretting your choice, are you?"

"No, I have no doubt that Lady Aurora is the one I should wed. Believe me, I did not choose her for her fair face alone. As soon as I guessed that she was Constantine's favorite, I knew. What better hold can you think to have upon a man than to possess his dearest daughter?"

"You talk as if she is to be a hostage, not your queen."

"It won't come to that," Maelgwn answered emphatically. "The peace will hold, at least long enough for me to strengthen my other borders. In the meantime I may well beget an heir, and a child of our shared blood would solidify my alliance with Constantine for good."

Balyn nodded. "It is a clever plan, my lord. Let's hope that you are able to convince Esylt of the wisdom of your marriage."

Maelgwn scowled. "Esylt has no say in whom I marry. She will have to accept my decision as best she can."

Balyn nodded agreeably and then rose from the finely worked wooden chair. "If you wish to meet with your bride before the wedding, you'd best be seeking her. The morning is already half over."

Aurora paced in the garden, listening to the hum of the bees and trying to relax. The heavy scent of roses filled the air, and their vivid colors of coral, mauve, wine and yellow seemed to make Aurora dizzy. The heat was making her breathless anyway, or maybe it was the tight dress which made it so hard for her to catch her breath. She was dressed in a gown of thin, almost transparent blue-green fabric called "silk." Her mother said the dress came from Constantinople, and Aurora could not help wondering how the women stayed warm there—not only was the gown sheer, it was also embarrassingly skimpy— though it pinched tightly at her waist, it left her arms, shoulders and the tops of her breasts nearly bare.

Her discomfort was increased by her elaborate hair- style and ornate jewelry. Aurora's sisters had carefully braided her hair and piled it on the top of her head. Al- though Julia had assured her that she looked like a Ro- man goddess, Aurora's neck already ached from the weight of her heavy tresses. Her wedding costume was completed with massive gold earrings that pinched her ears, bands of gold and onyx around her wrists and a large, egg-shaped pendant of amber that dangled between her breasts, banging into her every time she tried to move quickly. As if Aurora were not uncomfortable enough, she had just found out from her father that Maelgwn had requested to meet alone with her in the garden.

Aurora straightened her spine and threw back her shoulders, listening to the jingle of her earbobs. If only Maelgwn would come. She could not stand this waiting. After Marcus's refusal to accompany her to her new home, her mood had sharply gone from despair to anger. The longer Maelgwn made her wait, the more her pain receded and her hostility grew. When she tried to remem- ber her future husband, all she could think of was his mocking half-smile as he chose her. It was infuriating!

What was she—a prize filly thrown in with the rest of the livestock he had insisted upon as tribute?

Aurora heard a soft sound behind her and turned. Her heart seemed to jump into her throat. Maelgwn was even bigger than she remembered. No man she knew was near to Maelgwn's height, and his broad shoulders, long limbs and lean, muscular body gave him an aura of power that was frightening. He wore a jewel-studded sword at his side and a dagger in his belt, as if ready to do battle instantly. Aurora was reminded of a wildcat ready to spring at its prey.

"Lady Aurora." He bowed politely.

"My lord," she breathed back, reluctant to curtsy and give him an even more immodest view of the cleft between her breasts, that the low neckline exposed. His eyes fixed there with an obvious interest that both embarrassed and angered her. In retaliation, she gave him a brazen, probing look.

In the bright sunlight Maelgwn's hair did not look black, but a very deep shade of brown, and his piercing deep-set eyes were a stormy blue. His freshly shaved tanned skin was smooth and fine-textured, and Aurora realized with surprise that Maelgwn was rather young, no more than a score and a handful of years. She was wondering how he had come to power at such an early age, when her thoughts were interrupted by Maelgwn's low, rumbling, rather musical voice.

"What do you think, Aurora, of your bridegroom?"

She flushed crimson. How foolish she was—sizing him up, trying to decide if he pleased her. It hardly mattered if he appealed to her or not. She was stuck with him.

He fixed her with a sly smile. "I had not thought you to be so shy—not after your turn as a serving girl yesterday. What did you hope to gain by spying on me?"

"I was not spying," she answered indignantly. "It is not unusual for a young woman to wait upon her father's guests!"

"Perhaps not. But unintroduced and dressed in rags?" Maelgwn shook his head. "Your behavior suggests deceit, but it could well be that you are not to blame. I do not doubt that your father put you up to it."

"No! My father had nothing to do with it! It was my idea, mine alone," Aurora answered, anxious to avoid any impugning of her father's honor. "I defied him and did not dress for dinner but offered my services in the kitchen instead."

"Why?"

Maelgwn was looking at her with a studied interest that made her throat go dry.

"I don't know—I guess I was curious."

"Curious?" Maelgwn raised his eyebrows slightly. "That is an acceptable answer I suppose. I must admit that I am curious about you as well. Perhaps we should sit down and get to know one another better." He gestured toward a bench beneath an old apple tree. Aurora nodded and followed him to the bench, listening almost hypnotized to the soft sound of his sword shifting beside him as he walked.

She sat beside him awkwardly, and he turned and put his fingers under her chin, lifting her face so he gazed directly into her eyes.

"It is important that you know, Aurora, that I hate deceit. I won't tolerate lying and manipulation."

She nodded, sure that the lump of fear in her throat would choke her if she tried to speak. His eyes bored into her with deadly intensity, as if seeking to probe her very soul. As much as she wanted to look away, she held his gaze. She had done nothing wrong, and she wouldn't yield to his shameless attempt to intimidate her.

After a moment, Maelgwn smiled again, his hard features thawing.

"But other than that, I see no reason we should not enjoy one another. You are a beautiful woman, and I, despite my reputation, am not unappreciative of beauty." His hand left her neck and moved up to lightly caress her cheek. Aurora suppressed a shiver. It was unnerving to have this man touch her so delicately. She could not forget the raw power, the ironlike strength she sensed in his lithe, graceful body. She had never been so close to a man like this—a hard, taut-muscled warrior.

His fingers moved to her hair, deftly unpinning one of the thick, coiled braids.

"What are you doing?"

"I prefer your hair long and loose—as it was yesterday."

Aurora pushed his hand away in exasperation. Her sisters had gone to a great deal of trouble to fix her hair as befitted a Roman British princess, and now he was ruining it. She paused when she looked at Maelgwn's face. His eyes were rapt, his lips slightly parted. She could sense his desire, and it ignited something in her— some proud attempt to bedazzle him. She reached up with trembling fingers and undid her hair herself, smiling in gratification as his eyes grew dark with emotion.

"There, is that better?"

"Aye, much."

His lips came down on hers. His mouth was soft and moist and insistent. She was startled when Maelgwn licked her lips lightly and then pushed his tongue into her mouth. No one had ever kissed her like this before. It felt strange, but not unpleasant. A little shiver ran down her body, and Maelgwn used the movement to pull her closer to him. Now she could feel not only his mouth upon hers, but his strong arms around her. He gripped her tightly, possessively. He was much bigger than Marcus, but smelled faintly the same—the masculine odor of leather and horses.

It was odd how she could feel his kisses through her whole body. She could not get close enough to him, and she was almost relieved when he pulled her awkwardly on his lap. She found herself kissing him back, opening her mouth and touching his probing tongue with her own.

She was intensely aware of his hard thighs beneath her and his chest pressing against her shoulders. The world was swimming around and around. She could not seem to think of anything except the burning ache in her belly. It was spreading, gradually moving up to her breasts. Maelgwn seemed to know it was there, for he reached his hand down her dress to touch her tender, swollen nipples—first one and then the other.

"That is enough!" Constantine's furious voice finally penetrated Aurora's dazed state, and she looked up to see her father's face ablaze with fury.

"I have agreed to give you my daughter for a wife, Maelgwn, not a concubine."

"We were just finding out how we pleased each other." Maelgwn smiled his mocking smile and slowly helped

Aurora up. She was near choked with humiliation, and indignant tears stung her eyes. What could she have been thinking of, to let Maelgwn touch her so intimately? Her father's viselike grip on her arm as he led her from the garden reinforced her shame. During their first private moments together, Maelgwn had not treated her as a princess at all, but instead pawed her for all to see—as if she were a harlot.

Despite her shame, Aurora could not resist one backwards glance. Maelgwn was still standing there, watching her, and on his face was a look that sent another hot thrill down her body.

Four

It was late afternoon when Aurora and her father led the procession to the open meadow where the wedding was to be held. Maelgwn had insisted that all the soldiers and townspeople be allowed to attend the ceremony, and the unused battlefield had been converted into a makeshift chapel to accommodate the crowd. The marble altar from the town church was disassembled and transported to the field, along with a large bronze standing cross. Around the area where the ceremony was to take place, posts were driven into the ground and decorated with banners, and twined with summer flowers.

A gay and festive-looking parade rode out from Viroconium. Constantine and his family were decked in all their wealth, with Lady Cordelia and Aurora's sisters resplendent in bright summer gowns, their necks and wrists gleaming with gold and jewels. They rode in wagons drawn by Constantine's best horses, whose harnesses were adorned with ribbons and flowers. Behind Constantine's household followed the other noble families of Viroconium. At the end of the procession came the townspeople, farmers and other freeman. Only servants, slaves and those too old or infirm to make the journey to the wedding site remained behind in the town.

Although Constantine would no doubt have given him permission to attend, Marcus was one of those who did not join the procession. Aurora had one last glimpse of her friend, watching her as they left the villa, and the look Marcus gave her showed such pain, it seemed to enter her heart like a sword. She turned away, sick with longing, and her father reached over and pulled on her horse's bridle to urge her along.

The journey to the field seemed to take no time at all, and with frightening swiftness they were beyond the town's gates and heading for open country. Aurora caught sight of the deep green of the forest at the edge of the field and repressed the urge to spur her horse and bolt into the nearby woods. She was leaving behind forever the innocence and freedom of her childhood, and something inside her rebelled at her new and uncertain life. The sight of Maelgwn's soldiers spread out over the field, waiting for them, unnerved her further. For the last few paces to the wedding site, Aurora closed her eyes, set her jaw and allowed her horse to follow her father's gray stallion.

In moments, the pony halted and Aurora's father called her name. She opened her eyes to see Maelgwn standing a few feet away. He looked magnificent. He wore a dark blue tunic that matched his dramatic eyes and turned them a cold lovely blue—like sapphires. Around his neck was a glittering gold torque, and his wrists shone with the ceremonial jewelry of a high king of one of the ancient tribes of Britain. He smiled at her warmly.

Aurora's father helped her off her horse and presented her to her bridegroom. Maelgwn's strong, hard fingers closed over Aurora's, and he led her to where the priest stood. The ceremony was a blur, but somehow she responded at the appropriate moments. Soon it was over, and Maelgwn was looking at her with a triumphant, self-satisfied grin. She allowed him a kiss, but could not find it in herself to respond. Now that it was over and she belonged to him, her thoughts were even more mutinous. It was bad enough that her father had given her away like a possession, but that Maelgwn had chosen to have the whole town and all his men present to witness her humiliation rankled sorely.

They rode back to town for the wedding feast. Maelgwn's black stallion set a brisk, impatient pace, but Aurora had little difficulty keeping up with him, for instead of her brown pony, she rode a graceful mare of smoky gray. Pathui, as the horse was called, was a wedding gift from Maelgwn. The mare had a lovely, silky gait and seemed trained to please.

The wedding feast was lavish. Whole roast oxen were carved, as well as several pigs, accompanied by tender fowl, wheat and barley bread dripping with honey, summer vegetables in sauces, spiced cakes and colorful pastries. The wine flowed freely, and despite a few tense confrontations between the soldiers of Viroconium and the Cymry the atmosphere was mainly festive and cheerful.

Aurora sat beside Maelgwn, too angry to look at her husband. She had learned soon after arriving at the great hall that Maelgwn was not going to allow her to bring even a maid with her to Gwynedd. Her father told her that he had begged Maelgwn to reconsider, but he had refused. Aurora was furious. It was going to be hard enough for her to adjust to her new country—to deny

her the companionship and assistance of a servant from
her homeland seemed pointlessly cruel.

Fortunately, Aurora was able to hide her anger from
Maelgwn with little difficulty. The constant procession of
people to their table—friends of her parents coming to
say good-bye and soldiers begging kisses—made it almost
impossible for the newly married couple to do more than
exchange the most banal pleasantries. Maelgwn glanced
curiously at her from time to time, but Aurora kept her
eyes averted, hoping that he would assume that her silence
was the result of shyness rather than hostility.

Aurora was so careful to ignore Maelgwn that she was
never really sure when he left the feast. Sometime late
in the evening she turned to ask her husband when they
would be leaving in the morning and realized he was no
longer at her side. Looking around the room, she was
startled to find that there was not a Cymry soldier left
in the place. Her first reaction was fear—had Maelgwn
changed his mind about wanting her as his wife? Did he
mean to leave her behind when he returned to homeland?
The thought panicked her. Where only a few hours ago
she would have been relieved to be left behind, now the
idea mortified her. It was bad enough to be forced into
marriage with her father's enemy, worse yet to be rejected
afterwards.

Aurora's mother saw her confusion and was beside her
daughter immediately.

"Come dear, we must finish packing your things."

"But Maelgwn . . ."

"He has gone to prepare to leave tomorrow. You will
be taken to his tent when all your things are ready."

Aurora's fury returned with a vengeance. Maelgwn

had not taken leave of her or said good-bye. Instead, he had left instructions for her to be brought to him—as if she were a servant or one of his possessions!

Aurora's mother led her to a waiting wagon, and Constantine and the rest of her family rode back with her to the villa. There, while servants gathered Aurora's possessions for the journey to Gwynedd, she said her tearful good-byes. Her sisters were weeping openly, and when her father pulled her aside, his face was a rigid mask.

"Aurora, my little one," he whispered. Aurora looked at her father, trying to be brave. Constantine was not a handsome man, and with his thinning hair and hawkish Roman nose he looked every one of his forty years. Still, his regal dignity made Aurora's heart soar with pride. Her father was a king, as great a man as Maelgwn.

Constantine smoothed a lock of unruly hair back from her forehead and spoke.

"This is not the marriage that I would have wished for you, Aurora, but it cannot be helped. I know that you will remember who you are—a princess of the Cornovii and a descendant of the great emperor Theodosius. I expect you to conduct yourself as a noble lady and bring honor to your people." He paused and the formality left his face. His eyes glittered with tears.

"I have asked Maelgwn to take care of you, and he has promised me he will. But I want you to know—should he mistreat you in any way, send me a word, and I will avenge you—even if I must sacrifice my own life and the lives of my people to do it!"

Aurora nodded and blinked back her tears. Her father had done what he had to do, but he still loved her. He was asking her to do her part, to honor her husband and do nothing to endanger the treaty. She must forget her anger at Maelgwn and attempt to be a good wife.

Maelgwn's men had arrived at the villa gate, and Aurora gave her father a quick kiss and mounted her new mare. As she rode out the villa gate for the second time that day, Aurora realized what a beautiful summer night it was, full of the soft sounds of insects and the bright shimmer of moonlight. They traveled past the town and then out into the open field. Before them lay Maelgwn's army camp. The many campfires and torches seemed to reflect the multitude of stars in the sky above, and the thought of so many soldiers out there on the plain filled Aurora with awe.

Aurora's resolution to be a dutiful, obedient wife took on new meaning. She had married a king, with hundreds of men at his command. Who was she to demand anything of him? Instead of concerning herself with how he treated her, she should be devoting her efforts to pleasing him. It was not just a matter of honor, but of self-preservation. Her father's bold words notwithstanding, once they were out of sight of her homeland, Maelgwn could ignore her or abuse her as he wished, and no one would care. She was at her husband's mercy.

Perhaps the soldier who helped her off her horse when they reached the king's tent sensed her foreboding, for he spoke as if to reassure her.

"The king is still making preparations for tomorrow, but I'm sure he will be here shortly. In the meantime, is there anything I may get for you, my lady?"

The man's accent was strange, but that was not all that intrigued Aurora. From his smooth, beardless face and soft hazel eyes she guessed him to be much younger than the hardened soldiers who made up the rest of Maelgwn's personal bodyguard.

"Nothing, thank you," she answered, trying not to stare at him. There was something about his sweetly handsome face and deferential manner that reminded her of Marcus.

The young soldier moved ahead of her and lifted the tent flap for her to enter. She saw with relief that there had been some attempt to prepare for her arrival. There was no bed in the tent, but a mattress of sheepskins on the ground was comfortably spread with blankets. There was also a low table with a lamp—and an urn of water and a chamber pot had been placed discreetly in the corner. Maelgwn's men unloaded the baskets and chests that contained her clothes and personal items and stacked them neatly in the corner of the tent. Then they left her—bowing quickly as they took their leave.

Aurora sank down on the blankets, tired to the bone. As she fumbled awkwardly with the tie of her wedding dress, she thought again how unfair it was that Maelgwn had not let her bring a maid to help her with her clothes and hair. She forced the thought away, realizing that she must not dwell on her resentments. Having made up her mind to try and please her husband, she dared not think about the things he had done so far to anger her.

Aurora crawled into bed wearing the thin, linen tunic she had worn under her wedding gown. She shivered slightly, remembering the possessive, demanding way Maelgwn had kissed her in the garden. She did not like to remember the way he had made her feel, so weak and out-of-control. Tonight she would have to submit to him, but that was all she would do. This time she had no intention of letting his kisses turn her into a gasping idiot.

Aurora listened intently to the night sounds of the camp, expecting to hear Maelgwn's footsteps or deep voice at any minute. When he did not come, she sighed and shifted restlessly. It had been a long day, and it was bliss to lie down and relax. Her last thought was that if Maelgwn did not come soon, she would be asleep.

As Maelgwn made his way to his tent, he met Balyn and Evrawc, another of his officers.

"She's here, settling in by now I imagine," said Balyn, motioning toward the torches which burned near the king's tent.

"All went well—she is comfortable?"

Balyn shrugged. "As comfortable as we could make her. I really think you should have let her bring a maid, Maelgwn. It's not right that a lady of her background have no female servant to attend her."

Maelgwn's mouth set in a hard line. "Aurora must adapt to her new life as a Cymraes. I thought that a companion from her homeland would make it harder for her to set aside the past and accept her lot as my wife."

"You expect a great deal from someone so young, especially a woman who has obviously been sheltered and protected all her life," Balyn said with a shake of his head. "She is bound to be homesick, perhaps miserably so."

"I disagree," put in Evrawc. "You are right to make Lady Aurora accept the terms of her new life right away. Too many women get the idea that they rule the household instead of their husband."

Maelgwn and Balyn looked at each other and shared

a faint smile. It was no secret that Evrawc's wife was an acid-tongued shrew who made him miserable. Perhaps that accounted for Evrawc's dour outlook on life. Like Balyn, Evrawc had been with Maelgwn almost from the beginning of his struggle for kingship, but there could hardly be two men more unlike than his two chief officers. Balyn was big, powerful, good-natured and always joking. Evrawc was small and wiry, with a disposition that was as gloomy as Balyn's was sunny. Maelgwn felt they made a nice balance in his life—one cheering him up and the other advising him with shrewd pessimism.

"I'll consider your advice—both of you," Maelgwn answered. "Good night. I'll see you both on the morrow."

Maelgwn walked briskly to his tent. Balyn's words troubled him. He did not mean to be cruel to his wife, but he was uneasy with the idea of coddling her. From Constantine's obvious affection for his daughter, it seemed likely that the girl had been pampered—spoiled by her easy life and doting family. If she was to be his queen, she must be toughen up and learn to think of others, as well as of herself.

Still, he did not want to hurt her or make her hate him. He was looking forward to their lovemaking, and he wanted more than her acquiescence in bed. Maelgwn recalled Aurora's ardent response in the garden. Aye, he might well be willing to spoil her a little himself if she were to display some of that passionate enthusiasm again.

Maelgwn pulled aside the flap and entered his tent. The lamp still burned, but it appeared that Aurora was asleep. She was curled up on the bedplace, her face turned away from him. Maelgwn dropped his heavy sword and scabbard on the ground. Aurora did not stir.

He climbed over the clutter of boxes and baskets at the foot of the bed to get a better look at her. Asleep, his wife looked exquisitely enticing. Her soft, rosy mouth was slightly open, and her hair tumbled in wild curls around her face. Maelgwn leaned over and took a lock of it in his hand, feeling the silky weight of it, thinking how good it would feel against his naked body.

Then he sighed deeply. He could not take her now. It would be near rape to wake her out of this peaceful sleep to have his way with her. His body ached with unfulfilled desire as Maelgwn blew out the lamp and lay down beside his new wife. There would be time enough, he told himself. He would possess this beautiful young woman yet. She was his wife, and she would soon know that Maelgwn the Great commanded her.

Five

Aurora woke and looked around. Although there was evidence that Maelgwn had come to the tent during the night, he was gone now. Aurora felt a strange disappointment. Last night had been her wedding night, and nothing had happened, nothing at all. Was it possible that Maelgwn did not really want her—that he had married her only to humiliate her father?

Shouts and noise came from outside the tent, and Aurora hurried to dress. In one of the chests at the end of the bedplace she found her traveling clothes and other personal items. Tears came to her eyes when she saw Julia's favorite bronze comb carefully packed away among her things. She and Julia had not been close—it seemed that she could never please her critical older sister. It was especially touching that Julia had chosen to give her one of her most prized possessions.

Aurora began the frustrating process of trying to untangle her hair. The day was hot, and she was soon sweaty and very thirsty from her struggle with her obstinate curls. The urn of water on the table looked stale and unappetizing, and Aurora thought with longing of the spring in the nearby forest. She could almost taste the cold, sparkling water. Why not? she thought impulsively. The spring was only a short distance away—there was no reason she could not help herself to a drink. She finished combing her hair quickly.

The day was brilliant with sunshine, promising great heat by midday. As she left the tent, Aurora was amazed at how much Maelgwn's soldiers had already accomplished. The night before, a large camp had been spread, and this morning there was just a cluttered, muddy field. The grass was trampled, and dotted with bare wet patches and a few smoldering fires. Most of the men were ahead of them, grouped to march, and only a few lingered behind to finish up.

The young soldier who had escorted her the night before was stationed near the tent. He nodded courteously and bade her good morning.

"Do I have time to go for a short walk? I would like to wash, and there is a spring I know of just a few paces within the forest." She pointed across the ruined meadow.

"Of course, my lady," he answered politely.

Aurora immediately set out for the dark line of forest. The thought of the cool spring water drew her on, and she felt the need to escape the oppressive mass of the army crowded so near. She was disconcerted when she saw that the young soldier was following her.

"I *do* know the way; I'll not get lost," she said over her shoulder.

"Aye, my lady," he answered, but continued to follow her.

"I'll not try to escape," she added, turning to face the soldier with flashing eyes.

"Of course not, my lady," he said with an awkward

look on his face. "But you are the queen and must be guarded. Maelgwn commanded it."

Aurora turned and continued walking. She felt badly that she had snapped at the man. Clearly he was only doing his duty, and it was some consolation to learn that Maelgwn was protective of her. Still, surely the soldier would let her walk alone when she came to the forest.

They walked on, neither speaking, her escort following a few steps behind her. Aurora had been carefully picking her way through the mud and garbage, but as they reached the portion of the camp where the horses were kept, it seemed impossible for her to continue without ruining her sandals. She paused, close to tears. She had only wanted to spend a last few quiet moments in the woods, but here she was, a grown-up, married woman, no longer the young girl who could run wild and free, heedless of her clothes and shoes.

"My lady," his voice came softly from behind her. "May I help you across?"

At first Aurora was startled by the suggestion, but then she nodded her assent and allowed the young soldier to pick her up and carry her over the sodden ground. He was surprisingly strong, despite his youth and slender build, and he carried her with little effort. His face was very close to hers, and Aurora glanced at him shyly and saw that he was watching her.

They were not yet to the open meadow when they were both surprised by the sound of horse hooves. Maelgwn, mounted on his black stallion, rode up rapidly, nearly running them down.

"I bade you look after my wife, and here I find you carrying her off."

"She wished to wash at a spring near here; I am taking her there."

The young man's answer, so calm and precise, relieved Aurora. For a moment even she could have believed that this gallant young soldier was abducting her, and she had been a little frightened by what Maelgwn would think.

Maelgwn shifted his horse so that the sun did not shine on them so brightly. Aurora could see that he was smiling.

"Well, if my wife needs assistance, it is only proper that I give it myself. Lift her up, Elwyn."

Maelgwn caught her about the waist and helped her up to sit in front of him on the horse. Her position was awkward, and she felt that all that held her on the huge horse was Maelgwn's firm grip about her waist. The pressure of his arm made it seem that she could barely breathe—or was it the excitement of having him so close? She could feel his warm breath upon her hair, and the power of his taut muscles as they guided the horse, sent thrills along her body.

Aurora pointed the way, and Maelgwn directed the horse to the edge of the forest. They reached it in a few massive strides, and Maelgwn released Aurora so that she slid gently off. He dismounted after her. For a moment their bodies were very close, and there was a surge of feeling between them. Aurora pulled away in embarrassment, filled with unease. She could not forget Maelgwn's frightening effect on her in the garden—she did not want to risk having Maelgwn paw her in public again.

Aurora entered the forest quickly. Maelgwn followed right behind her, and she had a start as she realized that he meant to escort her to the spring. The idea upset her. She was looking forward to being alone one last time in this sanctuary of her childhood. She glanced back at Maelgwn. He was watching her intently. She looked away and hurried down the path ahead of him.

"Aurora."

"Aye, my lord."

"This place you are taking me to—do you go there often?"

The nerve of him! What right had he to pry into her life—except he had every right, after all, he was her husband.

"Aye, 'tis a pretty place, and one that soothes my spirit."

"It is lovely country here. Different from Gwynedd, but very green and fertile. I imagine that it is only a matter of clearing the trees, and near anything would grow here."

Aurora did not answer him. She had no heart for talk of land and farming. She had come to the forest to find the peace and contentment that usually awaited her here among the tangled green thickets and misty air. This place was a refuge from the tensions of her father's household, the clatter and bustle of the town. How many times had her mother scolded her for shirking her chores to escape to the woods to while away the hours daydreaming?

Aurora stepped lightly on the soft, cushiony undergrowth, and Maelgwn followed behind her more noisily. She felt another stab of irritation at his presence. He seemed too big and loud to belong to this secret world. She could almost feel the forest creatures warning of his approach, like a whisper on the wind. To them, Maelgwn was an intruder—the hunter, who brought fear and death to the forest.

Maelgwn felt the subtle shift in Aurora's mood as soon as they entered the forest. A moment before, they had been close, their bodies pressed together and her quick desire echoing his own. Now Aurora was silent and withdrawn, and she hurried down the narrow path as if she wished to leave him behind. Her coolness infuriated him. Didn't she realize that she was his wife now? Didn't she know that she could not run away from the bargain her father had made? He quickened his pace, puzzling over her frustrating behavior. She was obviously very familiar with the forest—she said she came here often. Had she come alone or with another man? The very thought enraged him.

Maelgwn stared at the woman ahead of him. Her step was light and graceful. Her long, nearly hip-length hair swung back and forth, keeping provocative rhythm with the sway of her hips. Desire ignited in him with painful urgency. He would not wait any longer to claim his haughty royal bride. These quiet woods would serve as well as any place.

They reached a ravine and made their way carefully down the mossy, emerald green slope. Snowdrops and wood anemones grew in the moist soil near a tumble of rocks, and hidden among them was a small spring that dribbled clear cool water. Aurora knelt down and cupped her hand for a drink. She had barely begun to quench her thirst when she turned to find Maelgwn very close to her. He looked strange—his face was flushed, his blue eyes intensely bright.

"Would you like a drink, my lord?"

Maelgwn shook his head. He pulled her up and kissed her—hard. Aurora slipped on the damp ground and found herself thrown against him. A flicker of panic flashed in her mind. They were alone. Maelgwn appeared determined. This time her father would not come to rescue her.

"We should go back. Your men are waiting for us."

Maelgwn said nothing. He continued to stare at her with his impossibly deep blue eyes. Aurora edged away, feeling the fear throbbing in her veins. She had imagined that Maelgwn would consummate the marriage eventually, but not like this. There was no bed, no darkness to hide in. What if someone came upon them? She glanced at Maelgwn. There was no way out unless she fled. She wondered if she could outrun him. Maelgwn was weighed down by his heavy clothes and weapons, and she knew the forest much better than he.

She turned and stumbled directly into a small birch tree.

"You—you are so beautiful."

His eyes held hers, filled with longing, the fire of desire. Aurora closed her eyes, waiting, trembling. She could feel his warmth close to her, then his arms around her. His mouth came down on hers hungrily, and his hands moved over her body. It was too much—Aurora squirmed slightly, trying to get away from his strong fingers. Her chest heaved, struggling for breath, struggling to remember to breathe. Maelgwn's hands were everywhere, sending exquisite shivers down her body. She parted her lips slightly and was invaded, possessed by

Maelgwn's insatiable mouth. Her thoughts dissolved into the wet, dizzy darkness.

How good she felt—soft and warm and quivering. Maelgwn could feel the heat of her, the pulsing desire he had first awakened in her father's garden. He tangled his fingers in the rich, dark spill of her hair, feeling the softness of it flowing down her back. He slid his hands farther down Aurora's spine to the luxurious curve of her hips, cupping the soft swell of her buttocks. Her mouth grew greedier as he gradually pulled up her long skirt and ripped off her linen undergarment. He touched her silken nakedness and sighed in satisfaction.

She could not move. She was firmly trapped between Maelgwn's body and the tree behind her. She did not want to move. The sensations moving through her body were terrifyingly pleasurable. She could feel Maelgwn's broad, warm chest through his tunic, his tongue thrust achingly between her lips, and his rough fingers moving along the bare skin of her hips. Her whole body was shaking and shuddering, and she felt weak, as if she might fall down. She reached up to put her arms around Maelgwn's neck, feeling his long hair tickle her skin. He was stroking her softly, gently. Aurora could feel the spill of moisture between her legs, the aching need there. She wanted him to touch her—aye, like that!

She nearly swooned with the indescribable pleasure that surged through her. A darkness raged in her body— she could not see or think, only feel. A hunger, raw and demanding, took possession of her, and she moaned in ecstasy.

Abruptly, the pleasure turned to discomfort. Maelgwn

was forcing his finger inside her. It hurt! Her body stiffened as the pressure increased.

"Maelgwn, stop. Please don't hurt me!"

He stopped kissing her and looked down at her with a soft faint smile. She could hardly bear to look at him. She felt humiliated as she thought of her unseemly moaning. He made her feel so helpless, so out of control—just as he had in the garden. Aurora leaned against the tree, trembling and ashamed. Through half-lowered eyelids she watched as Maelgwn took off his sword, spread his cloak on the ground and began to undress. She wanted to stop him, to protest that it was not the right time nor place, but she did not. She was afraid of him, afraid of his powerful body and devouring blue eyes. Most of all, she was afraid of the way he made her feel, turning her will to water.

"We must finish," he said hoarsely as he saw her watching him. The black of his eyes was huge—almost blotting out their deep blue.

"Take off your dress."

She did not know how to resist him. Aurora loosened the tie at her waist and pulled her gown over her head. Then she slid off the linen tunic she wore beneath it, shivering even though the day was hot. His eyes were everywhere, examining every inch of her. She flushed, and tried not to look at him, at the proud naked body that stalked her. Maelgwn moved close and put his hands on her, stroking her skin with an unnervingly light touch.

"My darling," he whispered.

Aurora kept her head down. Maelgwn pushed the hair back from her neck and began to kiss her, his lips floating over her skin. The tingling, burning fire grew inside her.

His arms went tight around her while his head bent down to bring his mouth to her shoulders. His lips were rough, nibbling and sucking at the soft skin with a harsh rhythm.

She was near faint with desire. Maelgwn pushed her down upon the ground, parting her legs with his knees as she fell. The soft mossy ground cushioned her landing but the sensation of Maelgwn's naked body on hers went through Aurora with a jolt. She gasped. He was so warm, so big, so alive. The hardness of his manhood pressed excruciatingly against her thighs, and an unbearable ache radiated from a spot between her legs throughout her whole being. She longed for him to touch her again in that wet, burning place between her legs, but he was busy kissing her, his tongue teasing her with a langorous, teasing lightness. His mouth grazed her neck and moved lower, licking the hollow between her breasts. Slowly his lips circled one nipple, moving closer and closer, finally closing in upon the taut, sensitive skin. She cried out as he suckled her, thrashing wildly and whipping them both with her long hair. She pushed her hips against him desperately. Her body was on fire! She would fly apart if Maelgwn did not do something to comfort the raging need deep within her. She wanted more of him, more and more!

She reached for his shoulders and pulled him up for a kiss, her fingers cradling his hot face. He kissed her savagely, his mouth crushing her lips. Then, abruptly, he pulled away, his eyes sweeping her face. Seemingly satisfied, he maneuvered his body over hers and pushed into her with a sharp stabbing thrust.

Aurora bit her lips and dug her fingernails into the smooth skin on Maelgwn's back, trying not to cry out.

She had not expected it to hurt! He was so big—she felt like she was going to break apart. Maelgwn moaned deeply and began to move within her slowly and rhythmically. He was deep inside her, touching her innermost being. Aurora held her breath, feeling the tears squeezing at her eyelids. She had wanted him, she had wanted this, but she had not expected it to be so uncomfortable.

Maelgwn moaned again and moved within her more rapidly. The pain subsided, weakening to a dull throb. It almost felt good—almost. Aurora pressed her face against Maelgwn's sweaty neck, and Maelgwn began to kiss her again, his tongue thrusts matching the rhythm of the ones below. Aurora took him in, her thoughts forgotten.

Maelgwn shuddered violently, groaned and lay still. Aurora savored the weight of him spread across her, pressing her into the soft, fragrant earth. She was still breathless from exertion and surprise. So this was what it was like to be so close to a man that you could not get any closer, she thought in wonderment. She had not expected to feel like this, so fragile, so exhilarated. She listened to the heavy rhythm of Maelgwn's heart. She stroked his damp skin. Their bodies were twined together tightly, their breathing a rapid duet of sound.

It seemed that only seconds had passed when Maelgwn pulled away and stood up. Aurora watched him, startled and confused. She wanted to reach out and touch the vibrant aliveness of her husband, but it was too late. He was dressing. Her eyes lingered on him, taking in his sleek, square shoulders, long, well-muscled back and solid, but narrow hips. His strong lovely body disappeared into his clothes. His face changed—once more becoming hard, determined, unreachable.

Aurora closed her eyes. She knew Maelgwn would be impatient for her to dress, but she continued to lie there stubbornly. Her mind was a turmoil of fury and disbelief. Maelgwn did not love her or care for her feelings at all. His whispered endearments meant nothing. He had only wanted her body, the final payment of tribute from her father. Now that he had taken what he wanted from her, he was done with her. She despised him.

Maelgwn looked down at his wife as he dressed. Her face looked sad and desolate. He had the urge to kiss her, to tell her again how beautiful she was, how sweet, but he held back his tender words. It was in the quiet moments after lovemaking that a woman could most easily manipulate a man and make him pay for the pleasure she had just given him. He did not know this woman well enough yet to trust her.

"Aurora, you must get up and dress. My men will come looking for us eventually. I do not think you want them to find you like this."

Spurred by the fear of Maelgwn's men finding her naked, Aurora washed herself in the spring and dressed quickly while Maelgwn stood a discreet distance away. Her body was still stiff and sore, but she managed to follow his rapid pace back through the forest. She was shocked to find Elwyn waiting for them, and she wondered immediately if he guessed what they had been doing. His disciplined soldier's face showed no emotion as he led her to her horse, which was saddled and ready for her. Only when she found her seat on the mare with a gasp of pain, did he blush and look away from her.

Maelgwn reached up to give her a light kiss. Then he rode away. Aurora sensed that it would be a long time before she saw him again. She would have hours alone to sort out her confusing feelings toward her husband.

Six

It was late morning when Maelgwn's army began their slow march back to their homes in Gwynedd. Maelgwn rode at the head of the column of soldiers, while Aurora and her escort brought up the rear with the wagons and battle equipment. For a while Aurora was able to follow Maelgwn's dark figure far ahead of them, but eventually he was swallowed up by the green hills. It did not matter, for with every jolt of her horse, she was reminded of him by the soreness between her legs. Despite her discomfort, Aurora felt a lingering desire which embarrassed her.

As the verdant landscape spread out before them, Aurora's thoughts turned to the place they traveled to, the land beyond her father's domain. She knew almost nothing of her new home, of how she would live and what would be expected of her. She turned to the young soldier who had helped her earlier.

"Elwyn—that is your name, is it not?"

"Aye. How may I serve you my lady?"

"I wish to know how far . . . how long we will be riding."

"Seven days, my lady. On horseback by myself, I

could ride it in but four, but with the army it takes much longer."

Aurora nodded. She had never been more than half a day's ride from her home. Gwynedd might as well be across the sea or even in Rome itself for all she knew of it.

As if reading her thoughts, Elwyn asked kindly, "Have you ever been away from home before?"

"No. I have read about many places in my lessons, but I have never left Viroconium."

"You can read?"

"Aye," she answered proudly. "For a while we had a Greek teacher who taught us. My writing is poor,"—she thought of Arion's despair over her scribbling—"But I do like to read."

She glanced over to see Elwyn staring at her with a look of awe.

"Is it so odd? My sisters and I were raised to be noblewomen, and it is a very useful skill to have when running a household." She stopped, thinking of how her lessons had ended, with her father's friend, Antillus, warning Constantine that no man wanted a woman who was more learned than he. Aurora looked at the young soldier next to her with apprehension. Would her learning be held against her in her new home?

Elwyn's reassurance came quickly. "Truly, it is wonderful that you can read and write. I have often wished that I could learn."

"It is not hard. Perhaps I could teach you . . ." Aurora bit off the words in midsentence. What was she thinking of? She barely knew this young soldier. It was just that he reminded her so much of Marcus.

Elwyn stared at Aurora for a moment and then turned away, moving his horse slightly behind her again. Aurora felt her isolation anew. Oh, let him be my friend, she thought desperately—she needed one so badly now.

They rode in silence as the sun grew hotter and Aurora felt the sweat dripping off of her, staining her new dress. She pulled her veil more closely around her face to shield it from the sun. Despite her Roman blood, she burned easily, and she remembered how Marcus had always admired her smooth, creamy skin.

The landscape was changing slightly, becoming hillier—pasture instead of cropland. Stands of grayish white sheep frosted the hills, with the dark figures of shepherds moving among them. The shepherds stopped to watch the huge army passing by them. Even from far away, Aurora could sense their awe and fear. For the common people, soldiers and armies meant death and destruction, and they avoided their path as much as possible.

Aurora wondered again what Gwynedd was like. She had heard it was wild and mountainous, but she did not know if it was forested or open pasture. Her curiosity slowly overcame her fear of embarrassing Elwyn further.

"Is Gwynedd anything like this?" she asked him, gesturing toward the rich green landscape.

"No, tis not much like this," he answered gravely. "It is rocky and high, wetter and cooler than your land, too. But it is beautiful," he added loyally. "There are waterfalls and green meadows, lakes and high overlooks where it seems you can see forever—when the sun shines, the colors are so bright they hurt your eyes."

Aurora tried to imagine it, but could not. Already she was homesick for the lazy, tranquil beauty of her home.

Still, the land was not as important as whether she would be accepted by Maelgwn's people. Aurora had heard her father speaking of a place called Caer Eryri, Maelgwn's headquarters. The name sounded forbidding, and Aurora wondered if it was a huge army camp or a town like Viroconium.

Aurora turned to face her escort. "Please, Elwyn, tell me of Caer Eryri."

"What would you like to know?"

"What it looks like, how many people live there."

Elwyn thought a moment. "Caer Eryri has a long history," he began. "The name means "fortress of eagles," and the Cymry have lived there since before the Romans came. A part of it dates from ancient times—such as the walls and towers where Maelgwn and his sister have their sleeping chambers."

"His sister?" Aurora interrupted. "I thought the rest of Maelgwn's family were dead."

"No, he has an older sister named Esylt," answered Elwyn. "She has been at Maelgwn's side since they were children."

A sister. Aurora was both intrigued and disturbed by this new insight. It would be nice to have another royal woman to talk to—Aurora had been fond of her sisters and she knew she would miss them sorely. Still, she was unprepared to find another woman in Maelgwn's life. It might make it harder for her to be accepted.

"His sister, what is she like?"

"She looks very much like Maelgwn. She is tall for a woman and has dark hair and blue eyes."

Aurora frowned in concentration. Somehow it was hard to imagine a woman looking like Maelgwn—there was something so cold and forbidding about his appearance. Did that mean her children would look like him, too? Aurora had always imagined her children as blond and adorable, with fine delicate features such as Marcus had.

"Esylt is a very capable woman," Elwyn continued. "She runs Maelgwn's household. All the servants and craftsmen answer to her when he is away."

"Does she rule with him?" Aurora asked hesitantly. She had not planned on competing with another woman who was already established as queen—it might make it harder for her to be accepted in Maelgwn's household.

"No, she has no real authority in the rule of Gwynedd."

Aurora sensed Elwyn's hesitancy and her curiosity was piqued. "Does he listen to her counsel in private then?"

Elwyn laughed nervously. "Nah, nah, not if he can help it. Maelgwn often seems to be trying to avoid her for fear she will bend his ear on some subject."

Aurora got the distinct feeling that Elwyn was very uncomfortable talking about Esylt. She turned back to questions of her new home.

"You were telling me of Caer Eryri. Please continue."

"Aye. As I was saying, the fort itself is old, but when the Romans made it a garrison for their troops, they built barracks and many other buildings which are still used. Maelgwn's officers, as well as the craftsmen and freemen of the tribe, live within the fortress walls."

"Is it a town then, like Viroconium?"

"Not exactly. There is a village down by the river, where the farmers grow their crops. The fortress is more of a military headquarters. Most of the people who live there aren't farmers or herdsmen, but warriors who serve in Maelgwn's army and help protect Gwynedd."

"Do all these soldiers live there?" Aurora asked, gesturing to the mass of troops ahead of them.

Elwyn shook his head. "No, most of these men will go back to their homes—scattered throughout the hills—until they are needed again. There are not a lot of people in Gwynedd. It is a poor land in some ways, and makes for a hard living. But while our people work hard, the Cymry are a hearty, merry people who love music and tales." Elwyn continued. "There are festivals and celebrations during the summer, and feasts during the winter when everyone gathers to hear the bards tell of the past."

"Do you observe the rituals of the old gods?" Aurora asked. While her family had converted to the new faith of the Christ, many other gods were still worshiped by the people of Viroconium.

"Aye, feasts are held at Beltaine, Lughnasa, Samhain and Imbolc. And you—you are a Christian, aren't you?"

"I suppose so," Aurora answered, feeling uncomfortable. She was not really sure *what* she believed.

"I have heard that the Christian god is jealous of all others, and that is why the Christian holy men are so intolerant."

"So it would seem. I am not very devout. Not like my sister, Carina, who is always in prayer. I think my father and the priest spoke to Maelgwn of raising our children as Christians, but I am not sure he agreed."

Elwyn nodded. "I'm sure you could go to the priory in the valley if you wish to worship."

"The priory?" Aurora asked in surprise.

"Aye, some holy brothers have begun a settlement at

the other end of the valley that Caer Eryri overlooks—
they have a chapel there."

"And Maelgwn permits this?" Aurora asked in amazement. People had led her to believe that Maelgwn was
a backward heathen.

"I am not sure of his personal beliefs, but Maelgwn
has always permitted the worship of all gods in
Gwynedd—even the practices of the druids."

Aurora's eyebrows went up in shock. She had been
raised to believe that the druids were a hideous cult
which practiced human sacrifice. She knew they had settled in the west after the Romans drove them out of the
rest of Britain, but she did not realize that the sect still
had followers.

"But how can he tolerate their barbaric rites?" she
asked hotly. "It is not decent!"

"It is true that some of their cults go too far in carrying out the old rituals, but druids have much knowledge and power, too. Many of them are physicians and
bards. It is even said that Esylt, Maelgwn's sister, knows
some of the old magic arts."

"She is a sorceress?" Aurora asked in horror.

Elwyn smiled nervously. "I am sure if she had any
real power, she would have used it against her enemies
long ago. No doubt it is just a story told by the common
people."

They rode in silence for a while. Although she sensed
his reticence to talk further, Aurora finally dared to ask
the young man beside her the question that had been troubling her all along: "Elwyn, I must ask you, and you must
be honest for my sake—will the people of Gwynedd accept me as queen?"

The young man looked distinctly uncomfortable, and Aurora sensed that he did not want to answer her. He looked away and then back at her. "You do not look much like a Cymraes," he said softly. "But certainly we could not hope to have a more lovely queen."

The compliment made Aurora blush, but she was not satisfied with his flattering answer. He seemed to be avoiding the intent of her question completely.

"But will they . . ." Aurora searched for a dignified way of asking if she would ever be treated as anything other than a war trophy, "Will they respect me?"

Elwyn sighed. "I don't know. The Cymry are not over-fond of outsiders, but Maelgwn is a strong king and you are his wife, so no one will dare mistreat you or show you disrespect."

The young man's face seemed very earnest and sincere, and Aurora knew he did not mean to upset her, but Elwyn's words did little to reassure her. There was something in his manner that led her to believe that her reception at Caer Eryri would not be pleasant.

"And Maelgwn's sister?" she asked Elwyn, thinking out loud. "Will she accept me?"

Elwyn looked startled, and Aurora's uneasiness grew. After a moment, Elwyn regained his composure, and when he spoke, she sensed that he was choosing his words with the utmost care.

"You must remember that Maelgwn has never had a wife or a consort before, and his sister has always managed his household. It will be a change for her, and she is a woman who loves power. I . . . I am afraid Esylt may not greet you graciously."

Aurora could not stop the chill that ran through her at

Elwyn's words. Her place at Maelgwn's side seemed very much in doubt. It was quite possible that Maelgwn would continue to regard his sister as the most important woman in his household. Aurora might well be relegated to being nothing more than his bed partner.

They stopped to eat, well past midday. Elwyn brought Aurora soldier's rations of dried meat and coarse bread and some disgusting heather beer. She sat on the sheepskins he had spread on the ground for her and ate the dry, tasteless food, feeling uncomfortable and very lonely. Elwyn ate with the other soldiers a few paces away, and the sound of their quiet, comfortable talk increased Aurora's misery and sense of isolation.

Although she tried to quell it, her seething resentment of Maelgwn was returning. Why had he not let her bring a maid to wait upon her? How was she to manage with only a group of embarrassed soldiers for assistance? She thought she would die of humiliation when she had to walk to a secluded grove of trees to relieve herself and several of the soldiers began to follow her. Fortunately, Elwyn guessed her mission and called them back, but Aurora still fumed at Maelgwn's lack of consideration. As she returned to the soldiers, something inside of her seemed to snap. She was hot and dirty, miserable and lonely. She decided that Maelgwn obviously deserved his reputation as a barbarian—certainly he had no idea how to treat a decent woman. She had to change that. When she saw him tonight she must make his responsibilities to her very clear. He had to do something to improve her situation while they traveled, and while she was at it, she would also speak to him about her role in his life when they arrived at Caer Eryri.

All day Maelgwn's mind had turned irresistibly to the thought of Aurora's soft, yielding body beneath his. To his delight, his new wife had turned out to be a wildly passionate woman. Their lovemaking this morning had been intoxicating, and it made Maelgwn smile just to think of it. The eagerness he had sensed in Aurora in the garden had been real enough, and she had unfolded to him like a flower blooming—a lush, perfect flower. She was so beautiful and smelled so wonderful, he could hardly believe that she was his.

It had disturbed him to see how sad and desolate she looked when their lovemaking was over, but perhaps that was normal—he had always heard that it was not so good for women the first time. But from now on it would get better. He would do all the things he knew to please her. If only night would come, so he could go to her. The day dragged on, hot and tedious. Maelgwn was glad he could occupy his mind with the details and problems of moving such a large army. More than once he thought of going back to see her, but he decided against it. The sight of Aurora would arouse too many delicious memories, and he would be uncomfortable the rest of the day.

At last it was sunset, and they were able to set up camp. Maelgwn ate quickly and saw to the few items that couldn't wait. Then, with the bawdy jests of his men echoing in his ears—was his eagerness that obvious?—

Maelgwn made his way to his tent. Elwyn was standing guard nearby.

"How does the queen?" he asked the young soldier.

Elwyn looked uncomfortable. "I do not think she is very happy—perhaps she is homesick."

Maelgwn lifted up the tent flap with a smile. He would make her happy now, he thought with satisfaction.

"Good evening, my lady," he greeted Aurora, bowing and smiling. He moved close for a kiss, but she backed away.

"Maelgwn, I must talk to you,"

"Talk to me?"

"I cannot stand it!" she said emphatically. "I will not travel this way—eating horrible food and always feeling dirty and uncomfortable."

"The food?" Maelgwn was puzzled. He had not thought of what his wife was to eat.

"I must have some cheese or fresh meat, some grains or vegetables. And I must have water to wash with . . . and I have no one to help me dress and take care of my clothes!"

Maelgwn shook his head slowly. "There is no woman in camp who could attend you. But I will try to get you better food, and water to wash with." He was confused. Why was she so angry with him over these little things that could be easily arranged? He took another step toward her, longing to quiet her angry mouth with a kiss, but she moved away from him and spoke accusingly.

"What of when we reach Caer Eryri? What do you intend to do with me then? They say you are a powerful, wealthy man—how can you expect me to live in some ancient fortress with no servants to attend me? I am a princess, after all!"

"Of course you will have a maid," Maelgwn said impatiently. "And my chambers are comfortable and well-appointed—even if they aren't Roman." He was growing tired of her accusations; she acted if he were a fiend who was going to keep her in a dungeon.

"But what kind of queen am I to be? Your sister runs your household—what am I to do with myself? Am I nothing more than a hostage for my father's goodwill?"

Maelgwn was startled. He was concerned as to how Aurora would be accepted by Esylt, but he had not really thought ahead to what she would do with her days, how she would spend her time. He had always assumed that the woman he chose as his wife would be busy sewing and having babies. He certainly didn't want to be discussing these things now, when his whole body was throbbingly eager for lovemaking.

"Your role in my household will be to please me, and you can begin right now by taking off your clothes and getting into to bed!" he answered harshly.

His crude order infuriated Aurora. She no longer cared about being a good wife, and she lashed out with the first angry words that came to mind.

"So, I am to be your concubine . . . your whore, after all. How do I even know if our children will be recognized as your heirs?"

Maelgwn took another step forward and Aurora's eyes flashed. "And what of your sister? Does she rule Gwynedd, too, as well as your household?"

Maelgwn's face turned as cold as ice, but he tried to control his voice. "My sister is no concern of yours. She is very skilled at managing things at Caer Eryri. You will have to find other ways of occupying yourself. I advise you to stay out of her way."

"You have no right to treat me like this!" Aurora said in a voice of muffled rage. "You made an agreement with my father to marry me, you cannot push me aside like a slave girl when we reach Gwynedd."

"I can do whatever I wish. Right now I command you to take off your clothes and lie down."

Maelgwn's eyes were dark and deadly, and he looked as if he might force her if she did not obey him. Aurora was desperate; if she backed down now he would never respect her, never treat her as a queen. She searched her mind frantically for a weapon to use against him.

"You are such a proud and mighty warrior," she sneered. "But it is clear you are afraid of your own sister. What power does she hold over you? What dark secrets does she know?"

Maelgwn's face went white. No one, *no one* had ever mentioned his relationship with his sister in such a way before. And her tone . . . so mocking, so sarcastic. He did not even remember lifting his hand to strike the blow, but suddenly Aurora was sprawled on the ground, holding her cheek and staring at him with bright tears in her eyes.

Maelgwn was shocked at himself, at what he had done. He had never struck a woman before, not even when Esylt provoked him to fury. Slowly, he made himself go to Aurora and help her gently onto the bedplace. He could not bear to look at her, to see her red, swollen cheek. She turned away from him, her body shuddering with silent sobs. He did not know what to say, how to comfort her, and so he left the tent.

The night was overcast and nearly starless. Maelgwn walked quickly past the guards and began to pace the perimeter of the camp, trying to steady his nerves.

In Lludd's name—what had gotten into him! He had gone to his new wife eager to pleasure her and make her sigh with delight. Instead they had quarreled and he had hit her, lashing out like an angry little boy. His loss of control appalled him. She was a woman, weak and defenseless. That he had seen fit to control her by using his fists made him appear a cowardly fool.

Maelgwn flexed his shoulders and tried to think. It was the taunt about Esylt that undid him. He had never gotten over being sensitive about the role that his sister had played in making him king. But how had Aurora known that, and what kind of woman was she that she dared push him to the point of violence? Maelgwn stopped pacing and stared out across the dark hills. His new wife had a defiant streak that disturbed him. It must be dealt with, and dealt with quickly. But how? If he punished her further for her mocking words she might hate him, and then he would never get to taste the delicious secrets of her lovely body again. Oh, she would submit—she had no choice. But it would not be the same. He could not forget the way she had melted in his arms. He did not want to lose that.

Damn—this was hard. He had never guessed that having a wife could be so difficult. He had planned to marry Aurora, enjoy her beauty, savor the hold she gave him over Constantine, and then go on with his plans and campaigns. But already this woman was disrupting his life, making him feel things he did not want to feel. He had meant to keep Aurora as a hostage, a bargaining tool, but she was more than that. Here he was, pacing sleeplessly in the darkness, worrying that she would hate him.

Seven

Aurora fumbled in the baskets around the bedplace, searching for a rag with which to blow her nose. She could not stop sobbing. Her cheek and jaw ached unbearably, but the wound to her pride stung more. No one had ever struck her before—not her parents nor her nurse—no one. But what could she expect from an evil-tempered brute like Maelgwn the Great!

Aurora cried harder, the anger and pain washing over her like waves. Only gradually did the nagging thought that she was partly to blame for her misfortune prevent her from wallowing in self-pity. She *had* meant her words to hurt. She had guessed that Esylt was a sore point with Maelgwn, and she had dared to use that knowledge to try and shame her husband into showing her more respect. If words could be weapons, she had chosen the most deadly ones she knew. It was not surprising that Maelgwn had retaliated—she was lucky that he had not beaten her instead of merely landing a quick blow.

Aurora sat up and stared at the tent entrance apprehensively. What a fool she had been. She had defied her husband and then mocked him. By now he had probably decided that she was a hopeless shrew, and he would be better off sending her back to her father. Her father had been depending on her to accept her lot as Maelgwn's wife, to fulfill his part of the agreement. And what had she done?—taunted her husband into a rage! Aurora suddenly felt sick. Even now Maelgwn might be planning to turn his troops around and vent his wrath on Viroconium.

It would be better if Maelgwn came back and punished her instead, Aurora thought grimly. At least then innocent people wouldn't suffer because of her reckless temper. Or perhaps she could make it up to Maelgwn. If her husband came back to bed, she would try to act eager and willing for lovemaking. Perhaps then he would forget her awful words.

Aurora hurried to undress. Her hands were trembling, and she realized how exhausted she was. Could she really convince Maelgwn that she wanted him? Could she appear eager and seductive, even though her insides were tight with fear and anger? Aurora sighed and crawled into the blankets. She had to try. She had to think of some way to win back her husband's goodwill. She waited—listening anxiously to the night sounds of the camp—but he did not come.

In the morning, Aurora spent a long time with her mirror and the few pots of cosmetics she owned, trying to fix her face before she left the tent. When she finally ventured out, there was no sign of Maelgwn.

Elwyn gasped when he saw her face. She mumbled something about falling into the table, but she was sure he did not believe her. Aurora drew her veil close to her face to cover her swollen cheek. She dreaded arriving at Maelgwn's fortress looking bruised and battered. From

what Elwyn had said, it was going to be hard enough to
win the respect of Maelgwn's people without this badge
of shame upon her cheek. That is, if Maelgwn still intended to take her home as his wife. Aurora listened
closely to the soldiers' talk. She heard no mention of a
change in plans. It appeared for now that Maelgwn had
not decided to send her home.

They set off and kept to a steady, if monotonous
pace. By late morning, Aurora noticed that the landscape was changing. Fierce outcroppings of dull gray
rock veined the land, and the hills around them grew
craggy and barren. The weather was changing, too. The
sky had turned a sullen gray, and the air had a damp,
slightly metallic scent. The track they followed narrowed and grew more rugged, finally winding into a
steep-sided valley.

Aurora shivered as they entered a silent world of mist
and shadow. Shapes sifted in and out of the hazy light,
and the gnarled, ancient trees around them reached out
like spirits beckoning. The stillness was broken only by
the echo of running water. The sound seemed to come
from below them, beneath the ground. Aurora recalled
that the poor farmers around Viroconium believed that
every rock and stream and hill had its own god. Here
she could almost believe it was true—the very air seemed
haunted.

As they rode slowly on, Aurora remembered a story
from her childhood about Pluto, the Roman god of the
underworld. He had carried off the beautiful princess
Persephone to his kingdom beneath the earth, and she
dwelt there still during the months when the land was
cold and barren. Looking around at this gloomy land, it

was easy for Aurora to imagine herself as the ill-fated princess, and Maelgwn as the god of darkness and death, come to carry her away from the beauty and tranquillity of Viroconium. Aurora shuddered and urged her horse closer to Elwyn's.

By afternoon they had climbed to higher ground, and the opressive atmosphere lifted to some degree. Despite the change, Aurora could not overcome her foreboding. Maelgwn still had not appeared, and she had no idea what he meant to do with her. The uncertainty tortured her. The longer he waited to confront her, the more she feared the worst. She looked at the young soldier riding beside her. Elwyn had been silent and grim all day, and she wondered what he was thinking. Maelgwn obviously trusted Elwyn, so he must have some idea what was to be done with her. Aurora hesitated for a few paces. Would it really be easier if she knew the truth? Aye, she had to know—anything would be better than this horrible waiting!

"Elwyn?"

He turned toward her abruptly, as if she had startled him from his thoughts.

"My lady?"

"I . . . I appreciate your kindness to me, Elwyn, truly I do. It has made this journey bearable."

Elwyn glanced at her quickly and then looked away.

Aurora plunged on, fearing that she would lose her nerve if she did not speak now.

"I need to know . . . it would ease my mind a great deal if you would tell me what . . . what is to be done with me when we reach Caer Eryri?"

"Done with you?" Elwyn's face was blank, as if he

had no idea what she meant. Aurora felt a stab of irritation. Surely he was not going to pretend that everything
was well between her and her husband! Anyone could
see from the angry bruise on her face that it was not.
She continued on more emphatically.

"I have angered my husband, and I wish to know what
he plans to do with me."

"I . . . I don't know."

Elwyn's voice was halting and thoughtful. Aurora grew
impatient.

"Well, does he usually beat his women?"

The young soldier gave her a look of horror.

"No, my lady! Why, I cannot remember a time that
the king has ever disciplined a servant, a slave—nay,
even a dog—with his fists!"

Aurora was not sure what to make of Elwyn's shocked
words. It was reassuring to learn that Maelgwn did not
have a reputation for violence, but that meant that her
words had provoked him even more deeply than she had
guessed.

Elwyn seemed to be thinking the same thing, for after
a moment, he questioned her hesitantly: "My lady, it is
none of my business, but . . . what *did* you say to the
king?"

He was right, it was none of his business, Aurora decided. Still, she needed some advice on how to deal with
her husband, and Elwyn obviously knew Maelgwn better
than she.

"I . . . I suggested that he was afraid of his sister."

Elwyn went white and uttered an oath. "Gods above—
you did not!"

"I did."

"My lady, I am sorry. It is my fault. I should never have told you about Esylt."

Aurora sighed.

"Nay, 'tis not your fault. It was I who taunted him. My mother often warned me that my sharp tongue would get me into trouble." She sighed again. "I only wish that it had not been so soon. I hardly know my husband; I do not want him to hate me!"

"Maelgwn's temper is legendary," Elwyn said sympathetically. "And Esylt . . ." Elwyn shook his head. "I do not know why, but she has the effect of a mite under the skin with Maelgwn. The mention of her makes his face grow hard and cold, and if he spends too long in her company he becomes a raving madman. I am not sure, but I suspect that it has something to do with Dinas Brenin."

"Dinas Brenin?"

"Aye, there was a great tragedy there. The fortress was burned in a battle, and everyone perished."

Aurora's eyes widened. "Aye, I have heard the story. They say Maelgwn burned his whole family to death."

Elwyn shook his head. "Not his whole family . . . just his brother and mother . . . enough, I suppose, to make men whisper dark, evil things about him."

"Is it true that Maelgwn ordered the fires set?"

Elwyn looked deeply at her, his hazel eyes murky with pain. "Aye, it is true, but you must remember, it was war. If Maelgwn's brother Maelfawr had been the one on the outside, he would have done the same thing."

"But his mother . . ."

"No. Maelgwn did not mean for her to die. The fire was set not to take lives, but to drive the soldiers out to fight. It was an accident that women and children were killed."

"An accident!" Aurora's voice was incredulous. "Why did Maelgwn not think of the risk before he ordered the fires set? I cannot help wondering if he is not as ruthless and savage as his enemies say!"

Elwyn shook his head. "Maelgwn has grieved deeply over Dinas Brenin for years. Despite what men say about him, Maelgwn is not a hard-hearted man. I know. I was sent to Maelgwn's father's household for fostering at the age of seven, and I have served the king as long as I can remember. There is not a better, more just king in Britain." His eyes returned to her face, soft and pleading. "If you will give him a chance, you will find my words are true."

Aurora was silent. She had been told that Maelgwn was a monster, a cruel, power-hungry man. But Elwyn did not seem to think so, and her own experience with her husband had not proven him to be entirely a brute. She could not help remembering the tender, provocative way Maelgwn had loved her in the forest. He had taken pains not to hurt her, to give her pleasure. If he were truly a barbarian he would not have given her feelings any consideration. Perhaps Elwyn was right—perhaps she should give Maelgwn a chance.

Aurora sighed. Her worry that Maelgwn meant to void the marriage and the alliance was leaving her, but another fear was replacing it. Now that he knew what a shrew she was, Maelgwn might well decide to ignore her, to use her body only to beget an heir and then leave her for a more agreeable woman. The idea made Aurora even more wretched. Maelgwn might not be the man she would have chosen to marry, but he was her husband now. She wanted to be his wife, his queen, not just a hostage to secure her father's loyalty.

Eight

Aurora stared at the brooding majesty of the violet-colored peaks. She wondered if she would ever feel at home in the formidable land called Gwynedd. When the sun shone, the deep green valleys, glistening rivers and sparkling waterfalls enchanted her, but more often it was overcast, and the land seemed untamed and desolate. In six days of traveling they had passed no towns nor villages. Only an occasional farmstead or shepherd's hut suggested that anyone inhabited the stark highlands and misty valleys—except the eagles and hawks who circled far above. How homesick she was. Maelgwn had not come near her since the first night, and she had begun to worry that he intended to shun her forever. When she questioned Elwyn, he shook his head sadly and told her that he didn't know Maelgwn's plans, but the king must be mad to reject such a beautiful woman.

Mad, aye, he might be, Aurora thought gloomily. Her husband's behavior so far had been baffling. He had avoided her since their fight, but his men had made sure that she had fresh food and water to wash with after every meal. Obviously Maelgwn had listened to her complaints and was trying to make her journey as pleasant as possible. Why then did he not come to her? Had she ruined things between them with her taunting words? Or was the truth that she had never been anything more to Maelgwn than a hostage to control her father?

No, he had wanted her once, Aurora thought stubbornly. She could still recall the thrilling eagerness in his kisses and the way he had moaned when he came inside her body. The memory made her shiver. Would Maelgwn ever touch her that way again? Surely he would have to, if he meant to beget a legitimate heir. She was his wife, and he had no choice but to share her bed occasionally. Ah, but a man did not need to give a woman satisfaction to plant his seed and make a baby grow, Aurora reminded herself. If Maelgwn hated her as much as he seemed to, he would make sure their coupling was quick and infrequent.

She sighed softly and glanced down at the valley below, searching for a glimpse of her husband. Despite the agonizing confusion that the sight of him stirred within her, she could not help watching for him. She squinted and saw him very far below, directing some soldiers as they forded a small river with one of the supply wagons. His long dark hair and the huge stallion he rode were unmistakable. Aurora's stomach convulsed with tension, although whether from anger or longing, she could not say.

She glanced quickly at Elwyn, hoping he did not guess. She had tried to guard her emotions carefully and not to let him know how upset she was. She did not want word of her distress to get back to Maelgwn—she certainly did not want her arrogant husband to think that she cared if he spoke to her or not.

She also did not want to worry Elwyn. He had been

so sweet to her, so kind and considerate. How wonderful it would have been to marry a man like Elwyn—someone who truly cared for her, someone whom she could talk to. No, she thought wistfully, a man like that was not likely to possess the wealth or the power needed to make a profitable alliance for her father. She was doomed to wed Maelgwn. If it had not been him, it would have been another foreign chieftain, perhaps one who was old and ugly, his belly thick with fat and his teeth rotten. Would that have been any better? Perhaps, Aurora thought ruefully—at least then she would not care if her husband ignored her.

"Aurora, you are so quiet. Are you feeling well?"

Elwyn's sympathetic words interrupted her thoughts, and she turned and forced herself to smile at him.

"Aye, I am well. I was just wondering how much longer we will be traveling—I am heartily sick of riding."

"It is not much further," Elwyn answered, smiling back. "Tonight we will camp at an old Roman fort called Tomen-y-Mur. From there the road leads straight to Caer Eryri. We should be there by midday tomorrow."

Aurora nodded, feeling the familiar anxiety twisting in her belly. Tomorrow she would meet Maelgwn's sister and the rest of his household. If they were anywhere as cold and cruel as Maelgwn, her future was grim indeed.

"Maelgwn!"

Balyn was coming toward him, moving quickly through the chaos of wagons, horses and men. It was almost sunset, and the damp air rang with shouts and curses as the army set up camp.

Balyn smiled broadly and held out a wineskin. "Mead from Constantine's private store—one of the serving girls gave it to me. She was ever so grateful that we did not burn the place down."

Maelgwn laughed. "Was she now? I imagine you led her to think the worst."

Balyn shrugged. "We have a reputation to uphold. I did not think it out of place to remind our hosts that we are rude savages. Anyway, it seems like fine stuff." He shook the wineskin gently. "If you join me around the campfire later, I'll make sure you get a share."

Maelgwn nodded distractedly. He did not feel much like celebrating. The memory of the fight with Aurora still gnawed at him.

Balyn at once detected his gloomy mood.

"What is it, Maelgwn? You're one day away from returning from the most successful campaign of your life, and yet you frown as if you had just lost a war." Balyn glanced over at the king's banner, flying above his tent at the center of the army camp. "It is Aurora? Has your quarrel with her brought on this morbid temper?"

Maelgwn nodded, his eyes distressed, his brow furrowed. "I don't know how to right things with her. I keep meaning to go to her, but I can't think what to say."

"That's easy—beg her pardon, tell her how beautiful she is and then insist that you can't live without her."

"I can't do that!" protested Maelgwn, looking aghast.

Balyn shrugged. "It's the easiest way—just ask any married man here." The twinkle left his eye as he forced himself to be serious. "But even if you can't make yourself grovel before your princess's feet, you'd still better work out some arrangement with her before we arrive home. At the very least you must negotiate a truce. Tell her that you'll forgive whatever it is she said to you if she will forgive your violent loss of temper. Remember, there is much to be gained in mending this rift between you. Esylt will make boiled mush of you both if she guesses you are already fighting!"

Maelgwn nodded and sighed. "I had not expected my marriage to be like a war bargaining table already."

"What did you expect?" Balyn asked pointedly.

"I thought . . . I thought she would want to please me, that she would would be eager to do my bidding. She seemed so sweet and lovely."

"Some young women are like that—but not, apparently, Cornovii princesses. You are going to have to change your strategy to suit your opponent. Although there is perhaps another consideration." Balyn smiled slightly. "Love."

"Love! Cease your jesting at my expense, Balyn. I am a king. I cannot afford to fall in love!"

Balyn shrugged. "Well then, the battle lines are drawn, and if you don't want to fight, you'd better sue for peace. At any rate, you'd be wise to make your move before we reach Caer Eryri, and Esylt changes the thrust of the battle altogether."

Maelgwn nodded, then walked off, still looking troubled.

Balyn shook his head as he watched the king go. Maelgwn was very astute in judging people, but he had obviously not realized that the rules were very different when it came to women—especially wives.

Maelgwn walked slowly, contemplating Balyn's words. The comparison to a battlefield had its merit. He had underestimated his opponent, and she had surprised him nastily. Now he must make concessions until he had the advantage again and could take *her* by surprise. Somehow the thought of subjugating his wife as if she were a rebellious chieftain, displeased him. He'd had enough of war in his life. With his wife he wanted peace and a safe haven from the brutal demands of being a battle commander.

When he entered the tent, Aurora was sitting cross-legged on the bedplace, combing her thick dark hair. The sight of her loose, luxuriant tresses aroused him to tongue-tied admiration. She jumped up quickly, as if frightened of him, and stared back at him with her soft, gray-blue eyes. He flinched at the sight of the deep purple bruise on her cheek and turned away, regarding the terra-cotta urn on the table with grave interest.

"Aurora—I've come to beg your pardon."

"There is no need," she whispered in a soft, relieved voice. "The fault was mine. I should not have . . . brought up subjects which displease you." She paused, seemingly as tense as he was. "I also want you to know that I am grateful for the better food and the other considerations you've given me."

Maelgwn nodded, unsure how to continue. He did not know how to talk to women. He felt comfortable with them only in bed, their bodies soft and yielding beneath his. That was what he wanted now with Aurora, but the sounds of soldiers laughing close by the tent reminded him of their lack of privacy. He could hardly take his pleasure with his wife in the midst of a bustling army camp. He looked at Aurora again, in awe of her beauty, her devastating desirability. Then he reached out for a lock of her wavy hair, twisting it idly in his fingers.

"I must join my men now. It's sort of a celebration—before we get home, before we have to deal with everything there."

She accepted his regrets gracefully, nodding her head and saying nothing. He leaned over and kissed her softly, lingered his lips lightly over her neck. She trembled.

He released her, went to the tent opening, then turned and permitted himself one last look at Aurora's lovely, exotic features.

"There's no need for you to wait up for me, Aurora. I'll wake you when I come to bed."

Aurora stood frozen for a moment, then hurried to the tent flap and stared after her husband as he strode away in the fading light. His walk was powerful, graceful, and as he disappeared into the purple twilight, she was helpless with longing. She sighed. She was relieved, but also a little angry. She had endured days of exhausting riding; she was lonely, tired and anxious. Did Maelgwn really think he had only to speak a few words of apology and everything would be right between them?

She sat down on the bed wearily, trying to collect her thoughts. Even if she hadn't forgiven Maelgwn, she was eager to welcome him back to her bed. As much as her husband infuriated her, there was something about him that made her as weak and helpless as a child. His dazzling blue eyes and passionate face unnerved her; his deep, rumbling voice made her knees weak.

But now he had left her again. She could hear the laughter of the soldiers outside the tent. There was an easy, careless ring to their outbursts that made Aurora think they would be up late tonight. She was exhausted, but she knew she would not rest—not until Maelgwn came to her bed—if ever he did.

"So, the king leaves the pleasures of a married man and joins his men tonight," Balyn said, flashing Maelgwn a warm smile and moving aside to make a place for him near the fire.

Maelgwn sat down, trying to shake thoughts of Aurora from his mind and join his men's exuberant mood. The soldiers' excitement was almost palpable. They were returning to their homes healthy and rich. Their wagons were loaded with valuables and foodstuffs, the men were weighed down with armor, jewels, and other booty. Now that they were deep in the high country, there was no way any army could follow them. Their campaign had been an unqualified success.

"I think many men will follow in the king's footsteps and marry at the summer festival of Lughnasa," spoke up Gareth, the commander of Maelgwn's cavalry.

"Indeed," agreed Balyn. "With all our plunder, almost every soldier can afford to marry his favorite maiden when we return home."

"Maybe Elwyn will finally ask for the Lady Gwenaseth's hand," said Evrawc. "It is clear he is in love with her, but he is too shy to propose. You should offer her to him as his bride, Maelgwn, he could not refuse the king's gift, and Gwenaseth is your ward."

"Aye, it would be good to see Elwyn married," agreed Balyn. "It would settle him down, perhaps knock some of those foolish fancies out of his head."

Many of the soldiers nodded knowingly. Despite his impeccable loyalty, Elwyn sometimes seemed too soft for a king's companion. Perhaps marriage would help him mature. Balyn had other reasons for wanting to see the young soldier married off. More than once when he went back to check on the wagons, he had found Elwyn deep in conversation with the queen and smiling delightedly. Balyn feared that Elwyn's kind heart and Aurora's obvious loneliness could prove to be a dangerous mixture.

Maelgwn spoke in the low, thoughtful voice he used when he was planning something.

"If many of our soldiers marry, we will need to expand our workshops. There will be an even greater demand for plows and harnesses, wool and pottery."

The men all nodded, and Balyn smiled enthusiastically.

"With the craftsmen of Viroconium, we could build more than workshops," he suggested. "We could even renovate the fortress itself. I would not mind adding some of the comforts we saw at Constantine's villa."

"Perhaps you would like a bath complex next to your hut, and a sloe-eyed servant girl to wash you," Maelgwn suggested with a sardonic smile. "With such treatment you would soon grow so fat and lazy I could not take you on campaign except in a litter."

Balyn laughed. "With such an easy life, I would have no desire to be a warrior at all. I would be content to stay at Caer Eryri and watch the hawks and kites float on the downdraft all day."

"You are speaking as though we had been at peace

for years," Evrawc said irritably. "There will always be war. The Irish raids are as inevitable as the tide, and the Cymry chieftains are always looking for an excuse to rebel. And Constantine—he was hardly a willing ally. Even now he may be joining forces with Gwyrtheryn to the south and plotting to regain control of his lands."

"Constantine wouldn't do something so foolish," scoffed Balyn. "Gwyrtheryn is well known as a treacherous liar. For all his weakness as a battle commander, Constantine seemed like a shrewd man and not one to enter into a dangerous alliance. Why, it would be a lamb making a pact with a wolf."

"Aye, Balyn, but Constantine has lost a great deal, and bitter men are prone to errors in judgment when they seek revenge," answered Maelgwn.

"But we were more than generous with Constantine's people," Gareth broke in indignantly. "Not a man was slain, and we asked only for tribute and an alliance sealed with a royal wedding."

"My marriage is the key," Maelgwn agreed thoughtfully. "It is what has angered Constantine and also what should stay his hand against us."

"You do not think that Constantine would risk an invasion of Gwynedd because of his daughter?" asked Evrawc.

"No, I do not. I am gambling on Constantine's love for Aurora. But I could be wrong too; we must always be ready for war."

"I do not understand a man who sets such store by a mere girl. Is she not a princess, born and bred to be married off in the best arrangement her father could make?" asked Evrawc.

"Aye. And it was not so bad an arrangement for Constantine—he got to stay alive," laughed Balyn.

There was laughter all around. Constantine's wounded pride seemed rather comical to them all.

"But what of the northern borders? Have you heard word from Cunedda regarding the Picts?" asked Rhys, a small intense man who often served as a messenger because he was able to read and write.

"No, no word," Maelgwn answered. "I expect to visit Cunedda before Lughnasa, but so far I have not heard of war. Perhaps this will be a peaceful summer after all. Even the coasts are quiet—the Irish raiders must be busy elsewhere."

"Another reason to celebrate!" said Balyn, lifting up the wineskin. "It is a bit late for a toast," he said, sadly shaking the nearly empty container. "But I will propose one anyway. To the Cymry—our loved ones and families, to our great king Maelgwn, and of course, to his new and lovely queen!"

It was late when Maelgwn made his way to his tent. On the way, he breathed the cool mountain air deeply, hoping it would clear his head. He had imbibed the mead sparingly, but it was potent stuff, and he was tired. The torch by his tent flickered, but there was no light inside. Was she asleep? He ducked into the tent and paused a moment, trying to see. There was no sound, no movement. He undressed, and eased himself slowly onto the bedplace. He could smell her—the rich, hypnotic perfume he had first noticed when in her father's garden. He had thought then that it was the roses. He inhaled deeply, feeling the rush of desire in his body.

She still had not moved. He rolled toward her and

touched first her hair and then a silken shoulder. How
soft her skin was. In the daylight he had been so aware
of her beauty he had not really noticed the exquisite
smoothness of her flesh. Now that he could not see her,
he could savor the scent and feel of her even better. His
fingers drifted down her back. She did not stir or turn
toward him, and he wondered again if she were asleep.
His fingers touched her naked hips. There would be no
fumbling with clothes tonight, no heavy fabric in the way
of his caresses.

He played with the soft curves of her bottom and nuzzled her neck. Aurora stirred slightly. He rolled her over
and began to mouth her breasts. Deliciously round and
firm they were—he could not help kissing them greedily
and taking the taut, swollen nipples in his mouth one at
a time to suck. Was it his imagination or did she suppress
a moan? His mouth moved down, slowly licking and
kissing the way down her belly. She tensed slightly when
he reached the soft hair, but he pushed her thighs apart
abruptly, exposing the warm, wet opening there to the
cool night air.

A pity it was so dark—he would have liked to see the
expression on her face. He did not think she was asleep
now. He breathed on her gently and felt her whole body
quiver. Then he plunged in, his mouth buried in the hot,
sweet wetness of her. She cried out—a light, airy moan
of surprise. Aye, he had her now. He could feel the rip-
ples of pleasure coursing through her body. He was overcome, himself. She was so wet, so soft, so dizzyingly
female. He could wait no longer. He raised himself over
her and pushed in, penetrating deeply.

Ahhhh! The gods help him! Such sweet oblivion! Their

bodies matched so perfectly . . . his hardness within her softness. Aye, this it what he had wanted all along. This was the way to deal with a woman.

Aurora stared into the darkness. Her body felt wonderful, achingly satisfied. She had never dreamed that a man could make her feel like that—Maelgwn's mouth had been magic, licking waves of fire through her body. The convulsive vibrations still seemed to come from deep inside of her. Her breath was coming in long shudders, her heart still pounding. She was spent and weary, but her mind would not let her rest. What had this man done to her to make her feel so utterly, completely overcome? It was embarrassing—and frightening. It seemed he had only to touch her or kiss her and all thoughts fled from her mind. When she was with him she did not act like a princess or a queen—she was more like a slave girl submitting meekly to her master's wishes!

Aurora turned on her side, trying to relax. She could hear Maelgwn's breathing clearly—heavy, contented. The sound irritated her. He was so sure of her, so sure he could control her. No doubt he had only pretended to be sorry about their fight, cleverly placating her so she would welcome his lovemaking.

Aurora got up restlessly. She pulled on her shift and went outside. The night was cloudy, dark, silent. It seemed even the sentries dozed. She noticed a torch still burning on a stake by the tent, flickering faintly in the breeze. A thought came to her—born of frustration and curiosity. She pulled the torch from the rag that held it and entered the tent. She pulled back the blankets and shone the light upon the form of her husband.

In sleep—with the fierce, deep-set eyes closed in misty shadows and the hard jaw relaxed—Maelgwn's face looked surprisingly young. His nose was straight, with gently flaring nostrils. His mouth was slightly wide, drooping now with sweet sensuality. Aurora recalled that Maelgwn's mouth could also look brutal, as it had the first time she saw him. His jaw was square and strong, his finely muscled neck proud and royal.

Her eyes moved down his body to his smooth chest, darkened with only a scattering of hair. There was only one scar on it that she could see—it ran beneath his arm like a wild river—but his arms were crisscrossed with numerous smaller scars, healed to a silvery white on his tanned skin.

Her eyes went lower, drawn irresistably to his male organs. Despite their intimacy, she had not really gotten a good look at that part of him. His limp penis, curled up now like a soft, pink sleeping animal, bore little resemblance to the large organ which had impaled her earlier. It was fascinating, Aurora thought, how sleep robbed Maelgwn of his aura of power and danger. She smiled slightly. The dreaded Dragon of the Island was just a man, and really a rather young one at that. Maelgwn looked almost like a boy as he dreamed in the shadows, and she suppressed the urge to stroke his cheek—darkened now by a day's whiskers—as she would caress a sleeping child.

Maelgwn stirred slightly, as if disturbed by the glare of the torchlight or the cool air on his nakedness. Aurora hastily took the torch outside and tied it back on the stake. She crept back into the tent, her heart pounding as she settled down beside Maelgwn. He rolled over and wrapped a heavy arm around her. Aurora sighed and snuggled closer. She had almost fallen asleep when he whispered her name—soft and low—into the darkness.

Nine

The next morning, Aurora sensed—even before she opened her eyes—that the weather had changed. A clammy dampness coated her skin, and her thick hair, always unruly, was coiled into fat curls. There was almost a chill in the air too, even though it was summer.

She dressed quickly and went out to find a world thickly shrouded in silvery fog. Voices around her were heard with startling clarity in the mist, and Aurora was disoriented—unsure in which direction the rest of the camp lay. She was grateful to hear Elwyn's reassuring voice behind her.

"My lady?"

"The fog. It is so thick. Can we travel in this?"

"Aye, it will clear as the sun burns it off, and we are so close to home now the horses could find their way there without us to guide them."

Home. The word stuck in Aurora's throat like a bite she could not swallow. At least in this mist Elwyn could not see her cry. If only Maelgwn were near her now—his presence would have comforted her. But he was already gone.

With much confusion and swearing, the camp was packed away, and the army train set out. Aurora took her place on her gray horse and followed Elwyn closely as they moved like ghosts in the thick mist.

"Is weather like this common in your land?" she asked Elwyn.

"Aye, it is a very wet country, Gwynedd. That is what makes the land so lush and beautiful. But fog is less likely in summer, perhaps this comes from being so high in the mountains."

High—they were that. It seemed to Aurora that they climbed with every step, and she felt lightheaded and short of breath. She marveled at the horses and men who crossed these highlands so easily. The Cymry were a different kind of people—hardy and tenacious. No wonder the Romans had made few settlements in this wild land.

The stony track narrowed so that only one wagon or two horses could pass, and they finally climbed above the mist. Aurora was not sure that being able to see clearly was an advantage—on their left the track fell away so sharply it made her heart pound. Far below she could see a dramatic valley of lush forest and the flash of streams and lakes, but looking down made her dizzy with fear.

"No wonder it is called 'fortress of eagles,' " she said softly. "You have to be able to fly to get there."

Elwyn laughed. "It is not much farther, and the track gets better, truly it does."

They climbed and finally reached the summit. Aurora slowed her mare, transfixed. As the sun ate into the mist, it turned the air around them into a frothy dazzle. Where it had cleared completely, they could see a huge rainbow arcing majestically over the mountains. Below, the fog lingered, forming a steaming pathway across the valley.

It seemed to lead to a large fort in the distance, glowing bronze in the sun.

"It is so beautiful," gasped Aurora. "I feel as if we could step off the mountain and float away into fairyland."

Elwyn smiled back at her, intoxicated by the breathtaking scenery and Aurora's radiant smile. He had never seen any woman look as beautiful as the queen did now. Her long hair floated behind her like the waves of a dark sea, dancing with rich reddish lights. Her pale face was lit with wonder, and her blue eyes shone with a luminous, lavender light.

They could not stop long, with the rest of the baggage train pressing on behind them, and so they quickly descended into the valley. The world grew gloomy and forbidding again, and Aurora's elation vanished.

They reached the valley, where the track followed a river that wound through small stands of hawthorn and beech. They must be almost there, Aurora thought with a mixture of anticipation and dread. She noticed a cluster of rude brown huts scattered on the edge of the hill among the trees.

"Is this the village?" she asked.

Elwyn nodded. "The farmers here grow barley and rye in small fields along the river."

Aurora looked doubtfully at the narrow striplike fields along the river banks. It was a wonder that the people of Caer Eryri ever got enough to eat. There hardly seemed room to grow enough crops to feed a household the size of her father's, let alone an entire fortress, and the rest of the land in the valley was too rocky and rough for anything but pasture. No wonder the Cymry had to rob their wealthy neighbors.

At the edge of the valley, they met the track leading to the fortress and the going was easier. The path was wide and level, although growing soft and muddy from the many feet which had traveled it ahead of them.

Aurora stared up at Caer Eryri. With its high round towers and massive walls, the fortress seemed like a formidable, comfortless place. It reminded her of the burial mounds of the Old Ones. There was an air of antiquity about the crumbling walls, and Aurora imagined that she could already detect the sour, musty odor of ancient stones.

The track crossed fortified ditches on the way up the hill and then reached a massive wooden gate. Aurora and Elwyn were at the very end of the army train, and by the time they reached the fortress, almost everyone else was inside. The sounds of celebration echoed clearly through the thick fortress walls, and Aurora's heart sank as they entered.

Once inside, Aurora could make out the sturdy squareness of the old Roman buildings as well as a clutter of newer ones made of timber. She had never seen such commotion—children raced jubilantly in the mud, followed by eager barking dogs. Everywhere people were shouting, laughing, embracing. Servants ran to and fro, trying to care for the livestock and unload the wagons. In the noise and confusion, it seemed to Aurora that she would never find Maelgwn. She halted her horse just inside the gate, frozen with apprehension.

She might have waited there forever if Elwyn had not offered to help her dismount. He did not leave her as she expected, but stayed loyally at her side. Tears of gratefulness filled Aurora's eyes. What would she have done on this lonely, friendless trip without him?

A small, tawny-haired woman came running toward them.

"Elwyn," she cried. "I am so glad you are safe!" Aurora caught a glimpse of a girlish, freckled face before it was lost in Elwyn's exuberant embrace.

Elwyn was obviously very pleased to see the girl, but he did not forget his duty. Within moments he had released the young woman, and holding her arm, presented her to Aurora.

"Gwenaseth, I would like you to meet our new queen, Lady Aurora, daughter of King Constantine of Viroconium." He subtly pulled at Gwenaseth's hand as he spoke, and she dropped awkwardly into a curtsy, managing a breathless greeting of, "My lady."

It was clear the girl did not expect to meet her new queen under such circumstances. She gazed at Aurora with a startled expression as Elwyn explained how Maelgwn had come to be married.

The turmoil in the courtyard intensified, and it was a while before Aurora was able to locate Maelgwn. She finally caught sight of him surrounded by a large group of people. Even then Aurora did not have the nerve to approach her husband. Her relationship with him was too uncertain for her to be sure of her welcome. She stood miserably with Elwyn, hoping the young soldier did not pity her too much.

At last Maelgwn noticed her and gestured for her and Elwyn to come forward. Aurora glimpsed a dark-haired woman standing next to Maelgwn. Her brooding, deep-set eyes and proud features marked her unmistakably as Maelgwn's kin. Aurora noted critically that the woman's face was too fleshy for beauty, but her dark coloring and piercing blue eyes were striking. Her bearing was regal, almost haughty, and like Maelgwn, she made the other people around her seem small and insignificant.

The woman watched Aurora walking toward her as a cat might watch a mouse, stalking Aurora with cold interest. Aurora's heart sank with every step, and she could only look desperately at Maelgwn, hoping that he would give her a welcome that would make her place at Caer Eryri clear. Elwyn walked behind her protectively, and Aurora vowed to repay his kindness someday.

Maelgwn smiled at her as she neared him, but his warm expression did little to soothe Aurora's nerves. She could not forgive him for leaving her alone and overlooked for so long. She felt her face harden into a rigid mask.

"Aurora, I would like you to meet my sister, Lady Esylt."

Aurora acknowledged the other woman with a cool stare and a light dip of her head. She would not curtsy or bow, she thought disdainfully—she was Esylt's equal.

Esylt inspected Aurora. An icy smile played upon her lips, and then she spoke in a low, cruel voice:

"Brother, you said you had taken a Cornovii princess for a bride, but I see before me only a frightened, simpering child. Is this the best those soft-headed, Romanized fools can do for royalty?"

Aurora heard Elwyn suck in his breath sharply behind her. Maelgwn's jaw muscles twitched dangerously. She herself felt stunned, as if she had been slapped in the face. She could think of nothing at all to say in retort, and she turned helplessly to Maelgwn, begging him with silent, pleading eyes to defend her.

Maelgwn's face was full of the white-hot fury she had seen before, but when he spoke, Aurora thought his response was ridiculously weak and concilatory.

"I have made a most advantageous alliance with this match, Esylt. I expect you to honor my decision."

Without another word, Maelgwn walked off, leaving Aurora to face Esylt alone, with only the faithful Elwyn behind her. Esylt grinned maliciously at her, and Aurora tried in vain to meet her flashing eyes with a calm, confident stare.

"Does your father count you among his precious things, little one?" Esylt purred. "If so, you would be wise to go back to him. There is no place in Gwynedd for you, and you'll soon find that there is no room in Maelgwn's heart for a weak, spoiled girl."

She gestured to Aurora's cheek, still bruised and swollen from Maelgwn's blow. "Why, I see he has begun to tire of you already."

Aurora was so breathless with outrage and fury, she could not speak. Esylt walked away contemptuously, and Aurora leaned gratefully against Elwyn's strong arm.

"Come, my lady," he said gently. "Let me take you to the king's chambers."

Aurora's anger helped her hold her head high while Elwyn led her across the courtyard. They climbed the dark, narrow stairs to Maelgwn's sleeping chamber. The stairway had a musty, oppressive smell, but the tower room seemed fresh and airy. Soft breezes blew through the narrow open windows, bringing in the scent of dar~

pine. The round room was small, but well-furnished and comfortable, and the furniture—though obviously old—was of a well-made, Roman style. There was a chair, a stool by the fireplace, a small table and large wooden bed covered with a soft purple blanket.

Aurora sat down wearily on the bed, trying to collect her thoughts. Elwyn stood beside her for a moment and then moved toward the door.

"I will have someone come and help you dress for the feast." He paused, and his voice grew softer and less formal. "Do not let Lady Esylt trouble you. She is an evil, vicious woman. No one at Caer Eryri cares a fig for what she thinks."

After Elwyn left, Aurora sank back on the bed, trembling with rage. Her arrival in her new home had been disastrous. She would never forgive Maelgwn for letting his sister say those terrible things to her, and the thought of him touching her filled her with fury. He did not deserve her! He was a brute and a savage! How could her father have made her marry him? Helpless tears began to flow down Aurora's cheeks, and she buried her face in the soft blanket that covered Maelgwn's bed.

Ten

Elwyn hurried across the courtyard to Maelgwn. "I have taken the queen to your chambers, and she is resting there," he announced breathlessly.

Maelgwn favored the young soldier with a warm smile. "I owe you a debt of gratitude for escorting her on this journey. Your loyalty and service will not be forgotten." Maelgwn turned to leave, but Elwyn stopped him.

"My lord," he said awkwardly, staring at his commander. "I am very concerned about the queen. I think Lady Esylt upset her greatly."

"My sister is a meddling fool. Aurora will have to learn to ignore her."

"Aurora deserves better than to be left alone with no defense against Esylt's sharp tongue. She is a princess—and your wife—you must take more of an interest in her feelings."

Maelgwn looked at Elwyn in surprise, and there was a mocking, hostile edge to his voice: "You seem to know quite well what my duty is to my wife. Bear in mind, though, that she *is* my wife, and I don't need your advice on how to deal with her."

Elwyn's heart leaped into his throat as he realized how

he had spoken to his king, but he pressed on as tactfully as he could.

"Of course, Maelgwn, I would not presume to interfere. But it does seem to me that a lady must be found to wait on the queen; she does not even have a servant to help her dress."

Maelgwn nodded. He had promised Aurora a maid. She would have a slave to see to her basic needs, but she also needed a woman to help her with her hair and attire and to serve as a companion. Maelgwn wrinkled his brow in thought. It was difficult. Most of the noble women of Caer Eryri either had families or were too closely tied to Esylt to risk asking one of them to serve his queen.

Just then, Gwenaseth came looking for Elwyn. She stopped when she saw him talking to Maelgwn, but Maelgwn motioned for her to approach.

"My lord," she said to Maelgwn, bowing low. Then she turned to Elwyn. "Your father and brother are here for the victory feast. I thought you might wish to speak to them."

"Of course. I will come shortly," Elwyn answered, feeling embarrassed. He had been so involved in Aurora's problems that he had not thought of anything else, including his own family.

"Gwenaseth." Maelgwn spoke her name gently, and the girl looked up at him in awe. "Your father has sent you to me to see that you learn all the arts of running a noble household."

Gwenaseth nodded, looking slightly puzzled. It was common enough for the sons and daughters of noble families to be sent for fosterage when they were of an age. She was not sure what Maelgwn was leading up to.

"My wife . . ." Maelgwn paused and his forehead creased slightly. ". . . she is from a fine Cornovii household. Now that she has come to Caer Eryri, she needs a woman to assist her and keep her company. I think you could learn much from her, and I am asking you if you would be willing to serve as her lady's maid and companion."

Gwenaseth smiled broadly. "I would be most honored to serve the queen."

"Of course, we will have to make other arrangements after you marry and have a family," Maelgwn added quickly. "And speaking of that matter—I was thinking of asking your father if he had any objection to a match with young Elwyn," he nodded slightly in Elwyn's direction. "I can certainly ask him, if you would like me to."

"Of course I would." Gwenaseth smiled luminously at Elwyn. "I would like nothing better."

"Good," Maelgwn said heartily. "As soon as I can get away to the coast, it will be done. Now I think it is time you went to the queen."

After Gwenaseth hurried off, Maelgwn turned back to Elwyn, looking pleased with himself. "I hope you are satisfied with this arrangement, Elwyn. I have given you your bride and her a place of honor in my court. Now perhaps you can turn your attentions back to being a good soldier."

Elwyn nodded stiffly. "Thank you, my lord."

Maelgwn walked away, and Elwyn stood still for a moment, feeling let down. He loved Gwenaseth, he was sure of that, but his feelings were not quite the same since he had met Aurora. Even now, he felt responsible for the young queen, and it angered him that Maelgwn had so obviously relieved him of his duties toward her. If Maelgwn continued to be so indifferent to Aurora's feelings, she would need him more than ever.

Gwenaseth climbed the steep stairs to the tower room and paused at the door. She was embarrassed and shy to be attending Maelgwn's new wife. It was obvious that Lady Aurora was from a refined and wealthy background, and Gwenaseth hoped she would know how to please her. Gwenaseth had grown up on the coast where a brisk trade with Gaul and even Greece and Rome still flourished, and she was accustomed to fine and expensive things. But in the many years since her mother had died, she had been around few women who could really be called 'noble-women.' Despite her nervousness, Gwenaseth was looking forward to serving this elegant foreign princess that Maelgwn had so unexpectedly brought home. She took a deep breath and knocked.

"Come in." Aurora looked up, expecting to see Elwyn or one of the other soldiers bringing up her things. She gazed in surprise as the small, slim figure of Gwenaseth entered and bowed low before her.

"I am to be your lady-in-waiting," Gwenaseth said carefully, suddenly aware of her lilting, coastal accent. "How may I serve you?"

"Elwyn sent you?"

"No, King Maelgwn. I am to be married to Elwyn, though, so we will both serve you," she added, blushing prettily.

Aurora found herself rather taken back. For all her haughty demands of Maelgwn, she had never had her own maid before. She was uncertain how to treat the dainty creature who stood before her, waiting for instructions. Elwyn had told Aurora a little about his betrothed, and he had not exaggerated Gwenaseth's beauty. She was as tiny as a bird, with graceful arms and neck, and a pert, pretty face lit up by warm, melting eyes. Only her rather wispy hair was anything but perfect.

"Well, most of all, I would like to bathe," Aurora said quickly. "Can you show me to the baths?"

It was Gwenaseth's turn to stare at Aurora in startled confusion. "The baths?" she asked hollowly.

"Aye, surely you have baths here—it was a Roman garrison after all."

"Why, I'm sure there was once a bathhouse outside the fort, but it has been years . . ."

"What do you do to get clean?" Aurora asked impatiently. "Surely you don't go without bathing!"

Gwenaseth was bewildered and a little embarrassed. "Well, in the summer we go bathing in the river—or we get water from the spring and wash with that."

"I don't understand. How can you get clean without heated water?" Aurora was beginning to feel the first pricklings of alarm. Surely, the people of Gwynedd washed regularly. She had noticed a certain stale smell among the soldiers, but she thought that was because they had no way to wash while traveling.

Gwenaseth hung her head, looking dismal. "I know the Romans believed in taking their daily baths—there was an old bathhouse near my father's house at Llanfaglon I used to play in as a child. But here in the hills . . ." she looked doubtful, ". . . it is too cold much of the year to bathe everyday, and people have given up the practice."

Aurora tried to suppress the stab of homesickness that went through her—she must, after all, try to adapt to her husband's people and their customs. "I understand, I guess, but I have been traveling and there is to be a great feast of celebration tonight . . . I sorely need to bathe and to wash my hair."

"Of course," Gwenaseth said briskly. "I did not mean to suggest we could not accommodate you. I will send for a slave to bring some water, and I believe there must be a tub somewhere you could wash in."

Gwenaseth was all quiet efficiency then, giving orders to a plain, brown-haired slave boy—with an authority Aurora could never have managed. It was only a matter of time before a large bronze caldron was found and filled with a mixture of cold and heated water to form a tepid mixture for Aurora's bath. Even chilled, Aurora found a luxurious contentment in being clean. After they had washed and rinsed her hair, and the grime of the road filled the bottom of the caldron, Aurora sat upon the bed and relaxed as Gwenaseth expertly untangled her damp tresses.

"What will you wear to the feast?" Gwenaseth asked.

"I guess the dress I wore for my wedding. It is a lovely color, and it is made of a special kind of cloth, called 'silk.' "

Gwenaseth nodded. "I have heard of silk—it is very rare and valuable. You will look beautiful," Gwenaseth added warmly. "You have such lovely, thick hair, and I truly envy your coloring."

"My coloring?" Aurora exclaimed doubtfully. "Surely it is better for a woman to have light hair like yours."

"Ah, but you have no freckles, Lady Aurora, and I envy you your smooth, creamy skin. Anyway, I think Maelgwn must have chosen you because of your unique beauty—I'm sure there is no other woman in Gwynedd who looks like you."

"I have no illusions as to my charms for Maelgwn—he chose me because my father is rich and he wanted to control him. Anyway, it doesn't matter, Maelgwn has made a bargain with my father, and now he will have to live with it. It matters little to me if I please him."

"You must not say things like that—he is your husband!" Gwenaseth looked at Aurora with a shocked expression. "Do you mean you did not want to marry Maelgwn?"

Aurora laughed grimly. "No, I did not want to marry him. I think perhaps I hate him."

Gwenaseth stopped combing Aurora's hair and looked absently at her own hands. "You should not be telling me these things, Aurora," she chided softly. "It is disloyal."

"I don't care! I do hate him. He has no concern for my feelings at all. He let his sister humiliate me and spoke no word to stop her. He treats me like a slave girl, seeks only my body in bed . . ." Tears were filling Aurora's eyes, and she stopped to catch her breath, sniffing slightly and looking away from Gwenaseth's awestruck face.

"Hush," Gwenaseth whispered, putting an awkward, consoling arm around Aurora. "I am sure you are mistaken about Maelgwn. He seemed so proud of you when he spoke to me. You must remember that the king has never had a wife before, or even a woman he was close to. I'm sure he just does not know how to show his feelings for you."

Aurora shook her head. She dared not speak, or the humiliating tears would come.

"At any rate," Gwenaseth said briskly as she stood up. "I must go get ready myself. I will return in a little while to help you dress." She turned at the door and gazed at Aurora with a thoughtful, rather calculating look.

"Remember, Aurora, you must go to the feast with your head held high and proud. It would never do for Esylt to know she had succeeded in hurting you."

Aurora nodded to herself as Gwenaseth left. Aye, Gwenaseth was right. She could not give her enemy the pleasure of knowing how deeply her words had cut. She crossed the small room and began to search among the tumble of baskets and chests until she found a bronze mirror. She held it up and gazed at her reflection critically.

For most of her life, she had cared little how she looked. It was too much trouble, and she never felt as though she could compete with her beautiful older sisters. But now she did care. Tonight, she was going to meet the people of her new land for the first time, and she wanted them to be impressed. She frowned as she looked at her reflection. Her eyebrows were striking, her eyelashes long and dark, her skin smooth and glowing. But her lips were clearly too full and her nostrils flared too much. Her newly washed hair seemed wild and messy, and she did not know how to fix it, except to wear it long and loose. Still, with her bright dress and her best jewelry, she thought she could do it—tonight she must pass for a princess, an elegant royal princess of the Cornovii.

Eleven

If he did not have to pay this visit to his sister, Maelgwn thought, he would have been in a very good mood. His army was home, safe and successful. His people were content—and he had even found a maid for his wife. But there was this one last bit of unpleasantness left to attend to.

Maelgwn braced himself for the confrontation. He was tired of Esylt's interference, but he had to remember that she was just a woman. She had no other way to make herself important, and so she caused these petty problems which he was left to resolve. But this rudeness to Aurora—he could not allow that. Esylt would have to realize that she must leave Aurora alone.

He found Esylt supervising in the large kitchen behind the great hall. He motioned to her, and she followed him to a secluded corner so they could talk privately.

She was still a good-looking woman, and he knew that she easily found lovers from among the unmarried soldiers. He had tried to arrange advantageous marriages for her, but she had always refused. She said she did not want any foul-breathed, grunting old man as her master. Now she faced him with her head held high, her jaw set with determination.

"Esylt," Maelgwn began sternly. "I won't tolerate it if you harass Aurora or frighten her."

She sniffed contemptuously. "Why should you care? After all, she is just a hostage to keep Constantine under control."

"No. She is not just a hostage. She is my queen, and I expect everyone at Caer Eryri to treat her with the respect due my wife—and that includes you!"

"Are you serious? You intend to keep her at your side and share your bed with that sniveling little bitch?"

"Indeed, I must lie with her if I am to have an heir someday," answered Maelgwn dryly.

"You plan to have children with her? You would dilute the ancient royal line of Cunedag with her mongrel blood. What is she—part Roman, part Saxon whore?"

"She is as British as any of us," Maelgwn answered coldly. "I could hardly wed a Cymry girl—as king, I had to marry a woman who brought a dowry of wealth and power to Gwynedd. Through this marriage I gained control of the rich lowlands to the east with very little trouble."

"You could have burned Viroconium to the ground and taken your precious wife as a slave, according to many of the soldiers I talked to. Constantine is so weak he could not raise an army to fight off a group of children!"

Esylt's voice was heavy with sarcasm, and her arrogant features were contorted in scorn. "There was no need to make this lopsided match. With Constantine's loyalty you get his kingdom to plunder, but you must also protect a weak and ineffectual ruler from others who would seek his wealth too."

Maelgwn's eyes were dangerous as he faced his sister down. "Did you think I could just burn Viroconium and take their gold and jewels? What good would that do me? We have no people to settle the lands or rebuild the town. The rich green fields would lie empty for want of people to tend them, the shops decay for lack of craftsmen to use them. The Cymry can't eat gold. Constantine's wealth is in the rich harvest that his people reap and the craftsmen I have brought back who still know the old techniques of the Romans. I need Constantine's loyalty if this campaign is to do more than enrich us for a single season."

Esylt's full lips curled into an ugly snarl. "You always avoided fighting, Maelgwn, even as a child. There is always some excuse to seek peace, compromise, alliances. They call you the Dragon of the Island—what a joke that is! If only they knew that Maelgwn the Great has about as much courage as a newt in a hilltop puddle!"

Maelgwn had had enough. He stormed out of the kitchen, terrifying the servants and slaves who had the ill luck to be in his pathway. The walk across the courtyard cooled his temper some, but as he climbed the stairs to his chamber, he was still shaking with anger. Esylt had a way of twisting his successes around and making them seem like failures. She had always done it—at least since Dinas Brenin. It was obviously her way of getting back at him for no longer being the uncertain boy she could control. Still, her nasty taunts haunted him. Had he been too generous with Constantine? He was counting on his marriage to Aurora to keep Constantine from turning traitor as soon as his troops left, and he had left his new ally without even a garrison to make certain of his loyalty. Was it a mistake? Showing weakness might make his enemies decide that the time was right to take him down.

Maelgwn was so preoccupied, he almost ran into Aurora as she came out the door of the tower chamber. The queen looked exquisite, and the scent of her freshly perfumed skin distracted Maelgwn from his worries. Gwenaseth was sorting things and putting them away in the room, and she looked up in time to warn him away.

"Nah, nah. You must not muss her dress or hair," she chided, "Does she not look like a vision though?"

"Aye," Maelgwn said with a smile. "Would that the feast were over, and I could really enjoy her."

Aurora returned his glance coldly, but Maelgwn decided not to worry about it. There would be plenty of time to win back her favor once they were alone together.

Laughter and the buzz of voices filled the great hall as Aurora entered with Maelgwn. A hush moved through the room as people looked up to see their king with his queen, and then the crowd broke into cheers and jubilant shouts. The hearty, dusky-skinned Cymry—dressed in gaudy colors and brilliant jewelry—seemed to fill the hall until there was no air to breathe. Aurora was so nervous she was almost faint, and she leaned gratefully on Maelgwn's strong arm as he led her to their table. With a sigh of relief she took her place between Maelgwn and his first officer, Balyn. Perhaps now everyone would stop staring at her and go back to their normal talk.

Food was brought for them—heavy, rich dishes that

turned Aurora's nervous stomach. She looked with distaste at the heaping trencher she shared with Maelgwn.

"Have some wine." Balyn suggested. "It will help you relax."

Aurora looked at him sharply, but saw no malice in his broad face. Balyn's brown eyes looked sympathetic, and his smile sincere. "Thank you," she answered, trying to hide the trembling of her hands as she picked up the heavy gold goblet.

"What do you think of your new home?"

"I . . . I have not had a chance to see much of it yet."

"It has its good and bad, as does any place," Balyn said agreeably. "It would be most surprising if you were not homesick. I hope Lady Gwenaseth will be a good friend to you and ease your loneliness. She is a newcomer to Caer Eryri as well."

Aurora's face brightened with interest. "Is that why she speaks a little differently?"

"Aye. Gwenaseth is from along the coast of Gwynedd. Her father is an ally of Maelgwn, and he sent her here to Caer Eryri for fostering."

"She is very kind," agreed Aurora. "I am most grateful for her help."

"You look very lovely tonight, Aurora," Balyn said admiringly. "Maelgwn is a lucky man."

Aurora blushed and glanced at her husband. He seemed to be deep in conversation with Evrawc, and for once she was glad he was ignoring her. She could not have hidden her anger toward him if he had tried to speak with her just then. She looked back at Balyn and caught him watching her with curiosity. She wondered with embarrassment how much he knew of her relationship with Maelgwn.

When the meal was finished, Maelgwn rose to speak. Aurora found it hard to pay attention; she was looking around the room, staring at the unknown people who were now to be her subjects. Their clothes were unashamedly bright and garish—no man in Viroconium would ever wear such wild shades of red, saffron, blue, and purple—and there was not a toga to be seen. The men wore short tunics, leather trousers and vividly patterned shawls over their shoulders. The women wore loose gowns gathered at the neck and waist. The colors they used were softer and more subdued than those of the men's clothes, but their necks and wrists were adorned with bright enamel and bronze jewelry, their hair elaborately braided and decorated with gold threads, pearls and precious stones.

Maelgwn was still speaking, describing the events which led up to Constantine's surrender. He seemed to be emphasizing the ease with which they had frightened the Cornovii, and there were occasional derisive shouts of laughter as he painted the picture of Constantine cowering before the superior Cymry forces. Aurora felt herself flush as she realized that Maelgwn was portraying her father as a fool. It was so unfair! What had he expected her father to do? Fight and get them all killed?

When he had finished with his fun of ridiculing the Cornovii army, Maelgwn began a long recitation of the livestock, grain and other property which Constantine had paid for the truce. The crowd grew more exuberant with each item. It would be an easy winter in Gwynedd no matter how the harvest fared.

After he listed the tribute, Maelgwn paused, and the crowd held their breath expectantly. Aurora could not help turning with the others and staring at Maelgwn. Her husband was an imposing man, and he looked especially dramatic this night. Dressed in his best dark tunic, with a deep red mantle draped over his shoulder and his long dark mane of hair framing his masculine face—even Aurora felt a stirring of awe as she looked at him. Then he began to speak in his arrogant voice, and her hatred returned.

"As a symbol of his complete loyalty, Constantine has given us another gift."

Maelgwn glanced almost imperceptibly at Aurora, and she wished she could disappear into the floor.

"I know that I speak of one of Constantine's most prized possessions, and that it pained him greatly to give her up."

Maelgwn's slight smile broadened into what seemed to Aurora to be a gloating grin, and she felt the blood creeping into her face. She was being presented as a trophy prize, part of the spoils of Maelgwn's victory over her father!

"As a gesture of his fealty, Constantine of Viroconium has given me his fairest daughter in marriage."

His silly compliments counted for nought, thought Aurora bitterly. He chose me not because he found me fair!

The spectators crowded around, red-faced and loud, staring at Aurora. Maelgwn turned to her, and taking her hand, helped her stand and face the room.

"I present to you, my new queen, Lady Aurora." The playfulness was gone from Maelgwn's manner, and he faced the room with a commanding air, his eyes daring any man to show a hint of disrespect.

Aurora stood as tall as possible and tried to pretend she was her mother—calm, regal, in control—but her hand gripped Maelgwn's in white-knuckled fear. The room was hushed, and Aurora looked out at a sea of faces—some leering, some hostile, some smiling, all curious.

Balyn broke the silence with a confident shout. "A toast, a toast to our beautiful Queen Aurora!"

Other voices followed and soon the hall rang with exuberant cheers. Glancing nervously at the room full of excited faces, Aurora's eyes rested for a moment upon Esylt, seated near the king's table with a group of raucous soldiers. Their eyes met, and Aurora felt the force of Esylt's hatred. She stepped back instinctively, just as Maelgwn gave a full-throated laugh and grabbed her for a lusty kiss. The onlookers roared with appreciative delight. Aurora tried to smile, but her face felt frozen; she could not forget the malice she had seen in her sister-in-law's eyes.

Gradually the hall began to settle down, and tables were moved away from the center of the room. Aurora's nerves steadied and she grew curious as to what would come next. A lone man, robed in the plain, nondescript wool of a bard and carrying a huge, graceful harp, moved to the center of the room in front of the king's table. The crowd grew quiet as he dangled his hand across the silken strings, sending a ripple of silvery notes into the hushed room.

His voice was beautiful, low and vibrant, but Aurora was disappointed. The man's accent was so strong that between that and his lyrical delivery, Aurora was unable to understand most of what he was singing about. It seemed to be the story of Maelgwn and all the battles he had fought, but many other kings and heroes were mentioned, and Aurora grew weary of his recitation.

At last it was over. People began to get up and move into informal groups. Aurora spied Gwenaseth holding Elwyn's hand and smiled uncertainly at them. To her delight, the young woman hurried over to her. Gwenaseth was wearing a beautiful saffron-colored dress with a brilliant purple shawl. Her necklace and earrings of gleaming amber rivaled even Aurora's costly jewels.

"You look beautiful, Gwenaseth," Aurora said softly, reaching out to touch the shawl. "I have never seen such a rich purple."

"It is dyed with a special dye made only in Tyre," Gwenaseth answered proudly. "It is said to be the same color used by Roman senators for their state robes."

"Aye, I have heard of it—royal purple, it is called," Aurora said, feeling slightly envious. She wondered if Gwenaseth did not look more striking than she. But if she did, Aurora could not tell by the way Elwyn looked at her. The young soldier was staring at her with a dazed expression of near worship.

"Next there will be dancing," Gwenaseth said enthusiastically. I don't think Maelgwn will join in, but you can stay with us," she added kindly.

Aurora nodded, feeling ashamed of her less than generous thoughts. Gwenaseth seemed as loyal and kind as Elwyn.

The pulsing beat of drums and pipes began, and groups of people stepped out of the crowd and began to circle and twirl with abandon. The spirit of celebration was contagious, and it was not long before Aurora's body longed to move freely to the stirring rhythm. The ritual feasts at Viroconium—now held in conjunction with Christian holidays instead of the ancient celebrations of harvest, sun and fire—suddenly seemed very dull compared to the primitive throb of life that filled the great hall of Caer Eryri.

Laughing, Elwyn and Gwenaseth pulled Aurora into the swirling, sweaty crowd. At first, Aurora was uncertain, wondering if she would know what to do, but gradually she surrendered to the hypnotic beat and followed the instinctive rhythm of her feet. She was soon exhilarated and sweating, and a warm glow spread throughout her body, making her feel weightless and full of life. She gradually lost track of Gwenaseth and Elwyn and moved along with the flow of the crowd. As she clasped hands with flushed, smiling strangers, the barriers Aurora had felt earlier as a foreigner in Gwynedd were gone, and the Cymry suddenly seemed to be the handsomest people she had ever known. She admired their glossy dark hair and the flash of strong white teeth in their dusky faces. The Cymry were not savages after all, she decided, but a dynamic, fun-loving people!

As she moved around the room, admiring eyes followed Aurora, and the bolder men shouted bawdy compliments. Aurora could not help blushing, but deep down she was pleased. It was nice to be treated as a desirable woman. She was no longer the raggedy little sister, but the king's wife. It was hard to believe that the flashing confidence she felt had come so quickly.

Aurora stopped to catch her breath and gulp some watered wine, and Gwenaseth joined her.

"It is a wonderful celebration, is it not, my lady?" Gwenaseth's eyes glowed with soft fire as she followed Elwyn's graceful figure as he moved with the other dancers.

Aurora nodded, but she felt a sharp pang of jealousy, too. Elwyn was sweet, but he belonged to Gwenaseth. Why could she not have a kind, considerate husband like him, instead of cold, arrogant Maelgwn? She looked around the smoky room for Maelgwn's tall figure. He had not joined the dancers but was standing with his men, a jeweled cup in his hand. He caught her watching him and smiled.

Aurora looked away quickly, a tingle of unease coursing through her. It would not be easy to avoid Maelgwn's unwelcome embraces tonight. She had found him watching her more than once with a rather drunken, possessive stare. She could only hope that he would drink so much he would not be able to stay awake for lovemaking.

Twelve

Maelgwn watched, mesmerized, as his wife danced. His eyes followed the sweep of her long dark hair—glinting russet, almost wine-colored in the dim light—and the sinuous lines of her body in the bright gown.

"Many a man is envying his king tonight." Balyn commented as his eyes were drawn to the vivid figure of the queen.

"Aye," conceded Evrawc. "I thought her sisters fairer myself, but there is no doubt that the queen is a beauty."

"The people seem to like her," added Maelgwn. "Perhaps despite being a foreigner, she will be a popular queen."

Balyn smiled at the king. "The main thing is that she pleases you, my lord," he said, gulping contentedly from his cup. "Perhaps this will be the start of a love match as well as a strong alliance."

Maelgwn looked up sharply. "I warned you before not to jest about my feelings for Aurora. She will serve well as my queen, but that is as much as I want from her."

"Of course, Maelgwn," Balyn said with a small smile. "I should have known that kings were above such frailties and foolishness as love."

"Do not mock me, Balyn," Maelgwn said with a

frown. "Kings cannot afford to fall in love, and I am a king first of all and a man second."

Rhys interrupted with a lewd laugh. "Well, I do not envy the king then, but ah, the man . . . would that I would ever have such a beauteous creature to grace my bed."

"Are you sure you would know what to do with a woman like that?" asked Balyn with a laugh. "Tell us, Maelgwn, are Cornovii princesses the same as other women in bed . . . or do they have some special charm all their own?"

The king's deep-set eyes drooped dangerously, and his low voice was thick and indistinct. "Aye, she is different," he said after a moment. "Never have I had a woman whose skin was so soft, who smelled so sweet. Her body is like swan's down scented with the flowers of spring."

Maelgwn's men looked at him with surprise. It was unusual for the king be so open with them—usually he ignored their indiscreet jesting and retreated behind a wall of impenetrable reserve. It was obvious he was getting very drunk.

Balyn was especially concerned by Maelgwn's mood. Despite his enthusiastic speech, the king seemed edgy tonight, and it was uncharacteristic of him to drink imprudently. They would have to keep a watchful eye on his cup. Maelgwn was a heavy man to carry, and the tower stairs were steep.

Aurora was dancing ecstatically when Maelgwn came and grabbed her tightly around the waist.

"It is late, my love," he said softly. "Come to bed."

Aurora was in no mood to leave the dancing, and she wrinkled her nose in distaste at Maelgwn's state. He was drunk and leaned heavily on her, breathing his hot, sour breath in her face.

"You go," she said, trying to disentangle herself from his strong arms. "I will be there soon."

"Ah, so already you prefer the company of other men to mine. It does not matter, for they cannot touch you, you are mine alone," he whispered as he tightened his possessive embrace.

Aurora was suddenly anxious—there seemed to be no way to escape Maelgwn's unwanted attentions. "It is not that," she answered nervously. "As host and hostess of the feast, one of us should stay until the festivities are over."

"I care not what people think," Maelgwn said loudly. "Tonight I intend to consider my own needs first, and right now I need you naked beneath me."

Aurora glanced around in embarrassment. People were watching them, only halfway containing their curiosity, and the way Maelgwn was touching her was lewd and humiliating. His hands had insinuated themselves below her waist to stroke the curve of her hips familiarly.

"All right," Aurora hissed under her breath. "I will go with you. But please . . . stop holding me so tightly and touching me so. Everyone is watching . . . it is unseemly."

Maelgwn grunted and released her. As they made their way through the room, people moved aside to let them pass, smiling and murmuring delightedly. Aurora's happy mood quickly evaporated, and she felt shamed and humiliated, imagining that everyone was commenting on her body and Maelgwn's sexual prowess. Why did he have to make such a spectacle of his power over her? Whatever warm desire the wine had aroused in her was gone, and Aurora was more determined than ever to get out of making love with her husband.

They left the feasting hall. Outside, it was a lovely summer evening, and under different circumstances, Aurora might have enjoyed the amorous atmosphere of moonlight and fresh mountain air. But tonight she was concerned only with stalling Maelgwn and keeping his big strong hands off of her. Perhaps she could divert his attentions and tire him out by walking.

"Maelgwn, please, show me around the fortress," she coaxed as he led her toward the tower.

"You mean tonight?"

"Aye, it is so pretty out, and I know you won't have time in the morning."

"It is beautiful here in the highlands, isn't it?" Maelgwn said expansively, stopping and leaning heavily on her.

"And the fortress is very impressive—tell me, what is that building?"

"Nah, nah, I do not want to talk about buildings tonight," Maelgwn protested, nuzzling her neck. "Now is the time for bed . . . but we could go somewhere else, if you don't want to go back to the tower."

"Where?"

"Like my office in the barracks or outside in the grass."

Aurora shuddered. It would serve no purpose to have him bed her on the damp ground and ruin her dress. Maelgwn was being very persistent, and he was probably not drunk enough to fall asleep without having his way with her. She must think of some other tack to distract him.

"No, let us go back to the tower," she said resignedly.

"It was a good celebration, was it not, Aurora?" Maelgwn began again, seemingly talkative.

"Aye," Aurora replied sullenly.

"So, we are not such monsters after all, are we?"

"Who?"

"The Cymry—the wild savages of the west that your people fear, that even the Romans could not conquer."

"I do not know yet," Aurora said sulkily. "It is true that your people know how to wage war and how to dance and make merry, but whether they can do anything else, I have not seen."

"And make love," Maelgwn added. "You know, don't you, that the Cymry are great lovers?"

"Hah, I have seen none of that. You are just crude rutting pigs like all men!"

"Do not talk to me that way! You have liked to feel my hands upon you since that first day in your father's garden."

The memory of that hot, dizzy afternoon invoked shameful memories for Aurora. How could she have let Maelgwn fondle her in public? No wonder he had no respect for her and treated her like his private slut.

"That is not true." Aurora said, trying to pull away from Maelgwn's fierce hold. "You think that because you are a man and stronger than me that you can use my body any way you wish, but it does not matter—you cannot make me care for you!"

Maelgwn laughed coldly. "It is not your heart I desire tonight—it is your body—and I will have it."

They reached the tower door, and as Maelgwn paused to open it, Aurora twisted away from him and ran up the stairs. Despite her head start, Maelgwn caught her halfway up and pushed her painfully against the rough stone wall. He began to kiss her sloppily, breathing his wine-stained breath upon her, shoving his hand down her dress.

"Maelgwn, please," she cried. "You will ruin my gown."

"I care not," he answered, slurring his words. "Why did you run away from me just now?"

"Because I don't want you tonight! You are stupid with wine—you reek of it."

"What makes you think it matters what you want?" he asked in a voice so cold it made Aurora shiver with fear. She pulled herself up regally, pushed him away, and answered him in a voice just as cruel and cold.

"So, I see you as you really are—not the civilized commander who bargained for peace with my father, but the ruthless warlord who takes what he wants by force. You are like a greedy little boy who grabs for what he wants but has no right to. I have nothing but contempt for you!"

Maelgwn answered her by leaning over to suck noisily on her neck. Panic surged in Aurora. He was going to win—he was so strong, even drunk as he was now she could not hope to fight him off. For a moment, Aurora considered trying to push him down the steep stairs. Something held her back. Maelgwn was her husband, and she did not want to hurt him. There must be some other way!

Maelgwn stopped his caresses to unfasten his sword. Aurora saw her chance and pulled away, escaping into the tower chamber and struggling to shut the door behind her. Maelgwn lurched after her and forced his shoulder against the door. She could not hold it—she gave up and Maelgwn crashed into the room, sprawling awkwardly on the floor. He picked himself up and moved steadily toward Aurora, who crouched near the bed.

"You do not want me?" Maelgwn growled.

Aurora shook her head. Her voice had deserted her, and her eyes were fixed upon Maelgwn's murderous-looking face looming closer and closer in the flickering lamplight.

"Why?" Maelgwn asked, pausing a few feet away from her. "What have I done to you?"

"Your sister . . ." Aurora choked out. "You let her humilate me . . . you said nothing to defend me."

"That is not true," Maelgwn argued. "I told her that you were no concern of hers."

"You walked away," Aurora reminded him, her voice shaking with rage. "You left me to face her alone."

"It does not matter," Maelgwn answered. He realized how tired he was, his head had already begun to throb. But he felt there was a point to be made. "You are my wife, Aurora. It is my right to have my way with you."

Maelgwn's voice was quiet, but he moved toward her steadily. Aurora climbed over the bed so that it lay between them and faced Maelgwn recklessly. There was fire in her blue eyes and her body was tense and alert.

With a sudden lunge, Maelgwn grabbed for her, nearly jumping across the bed, but Aurora was quicker. Her head was clear now, and she realized just how dangerous her situation was. Should Maelgwn catch her, she did not know what he would do—from his angry, bloodshot eyes and grim mouth, she feared that rape was the least of his intentions.

She flew around the bed nimbly, always keeping just out of reach. Enraged, Maelgwn lunged for her, once, twice . . . the second time his foot caught on a small chest Aurora had left carelessly strewn on the floor. He stumbled. His reflexes were slow and clumsy from drinking, and he did not have time to put out his arms to cushion his landing. Maelgwn hit the hard stone floor with his forehead, groaned once and lay still.

Aurora stood frozen. She could hear the violent thud of her heart and the throb of blood in her ears. At any moment she expected Maelgwn to get up and begin his pursuit again. But he did not, and she cautiously ventured over to where he lay face down upon the floor.

Staring at Maelgwn's slack, motionless body, a new fear overwhelmed Aurora. What if her husband were dead or badly injured? Aurora could scarcely breathe at the thought—if Maelgwn was dead, her own life was over. She would surely be killed, perhaps horribly so.

Still holding her breath, Aurora bent over Maelgwn. She caught the rasping sound of his breathing and sighed in relief. He was not dead after all, and she was very glad. She had never wanted him to die or even be hurt, only to leave her alone for one night. She was exhausted and confused. What should she do? If she tried to get him into the bed, Maelgwn might wake and start his shameful advances against her again. No. Better to leave him there. He seemed to be breathing normally—he was snoring now. With luck he would sleep until morning.

Aurora shivered as the cool night air blew through the narrow windows. She was numb with fatigue, and she walked stiffly back to the table by the bed and quenched the lamp. With leaden fingers she took off her gown—now badly soiled and torn at the neck—and climbed into bed. By the time her body had begun to warm the blankets, she was asleep.

Thirteen

Maelgwn woke with a horrible taste in his mouth and a fierce ache in his head. The pain was much worse than the usual dull throb that too much wine left, and as he lifted his head, the agony intensified. He opened his eyes and looked around. There were strange square patterns next to his face, marked with uneven patches of sunlight. He blinked, feeling dizzy, and realized that he was lying face down on the floor of his bedchamber.

His body was stiff and cold, and Maelgwn raised himself with painful slowness, trying to remember how he had come to be there. He glanced around the room, noticing the messy tumble of clothes and baskets and the disarray of blankets on the empty bed. Aurora—it was morning, and she was gone.

Maelgwn struggled to organize a confusion of memories from the night before. His recollections were misty, almost dreamlike, but the events seemed clear—he had fought with Aurora . . . chased her . . . fallen. He recalled his own drunken desire, his rage and humiliation at Aurora's rejection. He could even remember her cold, mocking words.

Maelgwn put a hand to his head, feeling the lump on his forehead that spread hot fingers of pain into his eye and scalp. He had fallen hard. No doubt he already had the beginnings of a black eye—he could feel the healing blood filling the swollen soreness on that side of his face. Carefully, rather unsteadily, Maelgwn straightened his clothes and picked up his fallen dagger from the floor. He badly needed a drink of fresh water and some food. Aurora, wherever she was, could wait.

The courtyard was quiet this morning. Few of the soldiers were up after the night of revelry, and the women and servants who went about their business only nodded at him politely and then looked away. Maelgwn was relieved not to have to face his men yet. The bruise on his face was nothing to be ashamed of—many men had fallen at one time or another when the wine muddled their brain and left them as clumsy and ungainly as a new-born colt. It was Aurora's rejection of him that truly stung. He might be the king, but his wife had turned him out of her bed like a callow boy. Worse yet, she had left him lying on the floor all night!

Maelgwn found that his anger made his head hurt, and he tried to control it. He must eat and have the bruise tended to before he did anything else.

The old Irish cook in the kitchen gasped when she saw him.

"Nah, nah, Maelgwn, what foolishness have you been up to?" she clucked at him solicitiously.

"The same as many a man last night," he answered as heartily as he could. "It seems the floor got the best of me."

"You fell then?"

"Aye, it seems so, though I hardly remember."

"And where was your new wife?"

Maelgwn smiled weakly. "She was in no condition to help me."

"Let me call Torawc," the old woman said as she stood on tiptoe to wipe his face with a damp rag. "A blow to the head can be dangerous."

"No, 'tis nothing." Maelgwn said impatiently. "Just get me something to eat and have someone find Balyn. If I'm going to be awake and miserable, I want him to suffer as well—it was Balyn who kept pouring the wine last night."

"Of course, my lord," the cook answered. She motioned angrily at the young servant who had stopped his work and was staring dumbly at Maelgwn.

While he waited for his breakfast to cook, Maelgwn closed his eyes and leaned his head on the heavy battered table. No wonder he drank so seldom, he thought miserably. The price the next day was much too high. He longed desperately to go back to bed. The peaceful kitchen sounds seemed to lull him into a half-waking doze, and he scarcely heard Balyn's footsteps when he returned with the servant.

"By the gods, Maelgwn, what happened?" Balyn exclaimed when Maelgwn lifted his head.

"I fell."

"We were worried about you last night, but I thought surely with Aurora to help you . . ." Balyn's voice trailed off. He felt very guilty for not paying more attention to his king. He, too, had drunk too much—he hardly even remembered Maelgwn leaving the feast.

"Aye. Aurora—my loving wife," Maelgwn answered sarcastically.

Balyn's eyebrows rose in surprise at the king's scathing

tone. "She did not . . ." Balyn gestured toward Maelgwn's battered face.

"Nah, nah, I fell through my own clumsiness. I do think though, that she wished me dead last night. It seems she considers me—now what was it—a filthy rutting pig I believe she called me."

Balyn stared at Maelgwn incredulously. "She said that to *you?*"

"Aye, when she was not pushing me away and telling me she did not want me—that I was a stinking drunk and a brute because I did not defend her honor against Esylt."

Balyn made a choked sound, and tears were gathering in his eyes. "I'm sorry, Maelgwn," he said between muffled sobs. "I know it is not funny, but I cannot help it—I can just see her taking you on—Maelgwn the Great, bested by a mere girl. Oh Jupiter, we can't let Evrawc find out about this—he'd lose his place as most abused husband in Gwynedd!"

"You think it is funny?" Maelgwn was trying hard to be stern and commanding, but a grin was forming painfully on his own face. "You should try it sometime, if you think it is so amusing."

Balyn turned away, struggling to compose himself.

The smile quickly faded from Maelgwn's face. "You see, don't you, that I can't tolerate her defiance?"

Balyn turned sober, too. "It is a tricky situation. You may have been in the wrong, but now she's made it so you can't easily apologize to her and make up."

"Apologize! I have nothing to apologize for!"

"Begging your pardon again, Maelgwn, but it does seem to me that your behavior wasn't the best. My wife made sure to tell me this morning that your attentions toward Aurora were crude last night—more than a few women wondered why you didn't wait until you got to the bedchamber to fondle your wife. I also heard that Esylt insulted Aurora quite publicly yesterday when you introduced them. You should have done something about that."

"I did! I went to Esylt afterwards and was very clear about how she must treat Aurora from now on."

Balyn shook his head. "I'm afraid it was too late for Aurora. It is obvious that Aurora is a woman with more than a little pride. You must bear in mind that she was raised as a princess."

"But she *is* just a woman, and my wife. Perhaps I have different ideas of what a marriage should be like than you, Balyn," Maelgwn said coldly. "I intend to command my wife and have her obey!"

Balyn shook his head. "You are the king and perhaps you can have things the way you wish, but I can tell you that it is not like that in most marriages."

"Well, it will be that way in mine," Maelgwn said emphatically. "As soon as I am done eating and begin to feel better, I am going to make that clear to her."

Aurora tried to proudly meet the faces of the people she met in the courtyard, but she could feel her legs quivering like water beneath her.

It had all started when she woke up. Even before she was fully aware of things, she had been gripped by a grim foreboding, and as she stirred, her anxiety grew and grew. Slowly, terribly, the events of the night before had come back to her, like a bad dream that lingered even upon waking. Her worst fears were confirmed when she opened her eyes and saw Maelgwn lying face-down on the floor. Shaking with panic, she had dressed and left the tower room as soon as she could.

Her first few minutes in the courtyard had been spent staring at the sprawling clutter of the fortress. Even the old, rebuilt town of Viroconium was not as bad as this. The neatly laid out streets of a Roman garrison were barely visible, indeed all that Aurora could see that looked Roman at all was the great hall which had been the garrison's headquarters and two large L-shaped buildings which could only have been barracks. The rest of the complex was a jumble of square timber buildings and round huts like the ones she had seen in the village.

As Aurora walked along the dusty, unpaved pathways—which undoubtedly turned into masses of mud when it rained—she tried to guess the purposes of the buildings: there would be storerooms and granaries, stables, a smithy, an armory, a creamery and bakehouse, and sheds for housing animals. Elwyn had told her that Caer Eryri was a nearly self-sufficient settlement. If they had to, the people here could get along without trading for anything except wine, spices—and judging from the poor farmland along the river—grain.

Self-sufficient or not, the fortress was nothing like her father's villa. There were no gardens, no orchards, no paved courtyards or walkways. The windows of all the buildings, including the tower, were unglazed and open to the elements or covered with animal hides. There were no mosaics, no statues, indeed, Aurora had seen almost no ornamentation on anything except the clothes and jewels the Cymry wore and the weapons the men carried.

Continuing to look around at the rough, rather dirty settlement, Aurora heaved a deep sigh. She felt more homesick than ever. The memory of her awful fight with Maelgwn would not leave her, and a cold dull fear throbbed in her empty stomach. She had insulted her husband, mocked him and rejected his sexual advances. Everything bad that a woman could do to her husband— except for being unfaithful to him—she had done. Soon Maelgwn would wake up on the cold floor of the bedchamber and remember, and then he would come looking for her—to punish her.

She touched her cheek, remembering the dizzying pain when Maelgwn had hit her before. The spot was still tender; it had not even healed yet. Maelgwn was so strong—he could easily kill her if he did not check his blows. Last time he had acted impulsively, this time he would have time to think over how she had wronged him. Would that make him temper the pain he caused her, or spur him on to real cruelty?

Aurora shuddered. Her knees felt weak. She could try to run, but she could not get far without her horse, and she was not sure where Paithu was kept. If she tried to escape and Maelgwn caught her, it would go even worse with her. There was also her father's gentle admonition to consider. He expected her to fulfill her part of the marriage agreement. Refusing her husband his marital rights might be grounds for Maelgwn to break the marriage contract. If that happened there would likely be war.

Aurora sighed as she reached what appeared to be a spring, bubbling up from a crick in the rocks on the far end of the fortress. No doubt this convenient source of fresh water was the reason this site had been chosen for the fort. A slave girl with brilliant red hair was collecting water from the spring in a large gray pottery vessel. She looked up at Aurora, uneasily, almost hostilely, and then stepped aside to let Aurora help herself first. Aurora nodded politely at the girl—admiring her vivid hair—and then bent down to cup some water in her hands.

"Here, my lady, use *my* cup."

Aurora turned to see the smiling face of a soldier she recognized from the feast.

"You should not be waiting upon yourself," he said softly, his clear blue eyes looking into hers. "Do you not have a maid to draw water for you?"

"I did not want to bother anyone so early," Aurora said shyly. "It seems many people are sleeping late today."

"I would be sleeping too, if I did not have to leave to go back to my home," the young man answered wearily. "The excitement of being a soldier is over for now; it is time for me to go home and see if we have a herd left to keep us through the winter."

"Are you a shepherd?"

"Aye, and we have cattle too." The young man smiled shyly at her; he seemed surprised to be talking so casually to his new queen.

Aurora drank gratefully from the soldier's cup and then looked at him appraisingly. "I need to wash—could you get me a rag or something I could use."

The soldier looked doubtful. It was clear he was not used to such requests. Then his face brightened. "I will be back," he said as he ran toward the old barracks.

In a few moments he returned, waving a scrap of cloth triumphantly. "Will this do?"

"What is it?" Aurora asked as she looked at the torn, but clean piece of fabric.

"A bandage," the soldier answered cheerfully. "We suffered few wounds in this last campaign; there are plenty left."

Aurora smiled back, and bent down to soak the rag in the icy water. It was not as good as a real bath, but at least her face felt refreshed. It was nice, too, to have a man wait upon her and smile at her.

"Thank you," she said to the young man as she turned to go. "I hope you find everything is well when you return to your home."

As she walked back toward the tower, Aurora found that some of her confidence was returning. The young soldier had treated her like a queen—she *was* a queen—although for a moment she had forgotten.

For some reason the story of Marcus's grandmother flashed into her mind. Grimelda had been a queen too, and when the Romans defeated her people, she had gone to her captors proudly. From the way Marcus told the story, she must have been an impressive sight—her white skin gleaming with gold, silver and amethyst, her silvery blond hair shining and her blue eyes as cold and regal as Egyptian facience beads. No wonder Marcus's grandfather had fallen in love with her and made her his private concubine against the orders of Rome!

Aurora decided that she, too, would go to her judgment with her head held high and looking her best. She might not be able to make Maelgwn forgive her, but at least he would not pity her. She would act like a queen.

Aurora hurried back to the tower room. The door was slightly ajar, and it opened with a creaking sound as Aurora pushed it. With relief, she saw that Maelgwn was gone. Aurora walked in and surveyed the cluttered room with dismay. She was looking for her comb and hair ornaments when Gwenaseth knocked softly and entered the half-open door.

"Good morning," Gwenaseth said cheerfully. "How do you feel? Has the wine given you a headache?"

"Aye, a little one."

Gwenaseth shook her head. "This room looks as if the feasting and merrymaking had been held in here."

Aurora said nothing. She did not want Gwenaseth to guess how badly things had gone with Maelgwn. Gwenaseth had been so shocked by Aurora's anger the day before—she would never understand the frustration which had driven Aurora to treat Maelgwn so hatefully last night.

Gwenaseth noticed Aurora's pale face and subdued manner.

"What is wrong?" she asked. "You do not seem very happy this morning, Aurora."

"I . . . Maelgwn and I quarreled last night."

To Aurora's surprise, Gwenaseth did not seem disturbed.

"It is not unexpected that you quarreled. I saw how Maelgwn was grabbing you. I am not surprised that you were offended by his crude behavior. Why, if Elwyn were to ever touch me so . . . I am afraid I would slap his face in front of everyone!"

Aurora looked at her maid uneasily. It was nice that Gwenaseth was sympathetic, but she had no illusions as

to how far that sympathy went. Gwenaseth had no idea
how she had defied and insulted Maelgwn.

"Gwenaseth," she said softly. "Please stop straighten-
ing the room and come help me. I want to look my best
when Maelgwn returns."

Maelgwn walked to the tower with his long, restless
stride. He felt much better after a breakfast of sausages,
barley bread, goat's cheese and figs, and he could almost
forget the nagging ache in his head.

But his anger toward Aurora was still keen. He nursed
it—thinking about her cutting words, imagining how
foolish she had made him look as he chased her drunk-
enly around the small tower room. Aye, she would have
to be made to understand—finally—just how little power
she had as a woman. If he did not thwart her independent
ways now, she might end up like Esylt, always trying to
manipulate him and sometimes succeeding.

Yet, even as he climbed the tower stairs, some of
Aurora's words stirred doubts in Maelgwn's mind. She
had ridiculed his lovemaking. Was it really true that she
had found his caresses crude and disgusting? No woman
had ever complained about his way in bed before, but
what did that mean? It was not likely that any other
woman would be brave enough to challenge the king's
sexual prowess. Maelgwn pushed the disturbing thoughts
away. He knew Aurora had wanted him, more than once.
He could still recall the feel of her fine-boned, silky body
melting at his touch, the way she pushed her slender hips
up to meet him eagerly. She had only said those things
to hurt him, he was sure of it. Maelgwn set his mouth

grimly. Aurora was nothing but a defiant, spoiled little minx, and she badly needed to be frightened into realizing her place as his wife.

When he opened the door Aurora was waiting for him in a creamy white dress Maelgwn had not seen before. Her hair was arranged in the long braids the Cymry wore, and her neck and wrists were loaded with jewelry. When she saw his face, all the blood seemed to drain out of her cheeks, and she brought her hand to her mouth as if to smother a gasp.

"My lord," she said in a stricken whisper.

Despite himself, Maelgwn was touched. It was clear that Aurora had not guessed how hard he had fallen, and she was obviously concerned for him. All at once, he could see their fight differently. He *had* been drunk and crude, and part of Aurora's rejection might have been out of fear of him. Damn Esylt! She had done it again. If she had not taunted him into such a rage, he would have never gotten drunk and behaved so badly.

Maelgwn hesitated, trying to decide what to do. Should he beg Aurora's pardon and let their fight be forgotten? Or should he teach her a lesson as he warned Balyn he would do? Instinct warred with his soldier's training, but in the end, the memory of his mother and sister's mocking words about weak men won out.

Maelgwn moved toward Aurora, keeping his face stern. He stopped in front of her and reached down and pulled her head up by the hair. Aurora gasped.

"Aye," he said softly. "You would do well to be afraid of me. There are many men who would punish your insolent tongue with their fists."

Aurora held her breath, and Maelgwn reached out to stroke her cheek idly with a callused finger.

"Do not think that I check my blows out of pity or kindness, Aurora," he warned. "It is true that I cannot afford rumors that I abuse you to reach your father, nor do I like the idea of talk within Gwynedd that the king has trouble with his new foreign wife. But if I thought beating you would make you understand, I would do it."

Aurora flinched, and Maelgwn continued grimly. "I have found that mercy can be a more potent weapon than violence, especially with women. I will only warn you this time, and I will choose to forget the things that went on between us last night, but do not be mistaken—from now on you must obey me and honor me as your husband in all ways."

Aurora nodded slowly, letting her pent-up breath escape in a gasp. She had the feeling of coming face-to-face with some deadly force and then having it move on, passing her by.

But Maelgwn was not done. He reached to touch her dress. It was gathered at the neck, and he fumbled to loosen the tie that held it there. The dress slid down on one shoulder and partially revealed her breasts while Maelgwn watched with a cool possessive gaze.

"You have said you do not desire me, Aurora. So be it. But do not forget that I am the only man who is allowed to touch you . . . ever." Maelgwn pulled the dress tight so that the fabric dug into Aurora's shoulder. "Do not think of betraying me, Aurora, or you will find me not so forgiving."

Maelgwn released her and began to undress. "Now,"

he said in a whisper. "Now we will make up for last night."

Aurora hastened to undo her clothes and take off the cumbersome jewelry. She wondered with a spasm of fear if he would be rough, taking forcefully what had been denied him the night before, but he approached her slowly, almost tentatively, and began to kiss her with a light teasing pressure. His fingers touched her throat very gently, caressing the graceful hollows there, playing with her earlobes and the downy nape of her neck. He was stroking her as one would a pet dog, finding the sensitive, secret parts of her he had not taken time with before. He nibbled at her ear, penetrating the whispering darkness there with his tongue. Aurora's chest heaved convulsively and she bit her lips to keep from crying out. She had not expected this delicious tenderness. Her whole body was weak with desire.

Maelgwn was patient, agonizingly so. His hands moved down her body, testing the fine ridge of bones along her spine and the light, fragile framework of her ribs. Only gradually did he begin to stroke her breasts, making slow circles around her nipples until Aurora reached for him feverishly.

Maelgwn held himself away from her hungry mouth, finally grasping a thick braid to hold her still while he caressed her nipples with his other hand. He explored her body like a blind man, and Aurora sighed and shivered under his studied, expert touch. After a while he lifted her across the bed and lay down next to her. Still, he did not enter her, but went on kissing her slowly and languidly, as if tasting her. He had one hand firmly tangled in her hair, holding her down.

Aurora was gasping and frantic with desire, but Maelgwn was not finished with foreplay yet. He straddled her, pushing her legs apart with his knees, and knelt to bring his mouth to one sensitive, swollen nipple. He was rougher now, almost hurting her with the hard pressure of his mouth and the slight, sharp prick of his strong teeth as he sucked and nuzzled.

Aurora moaned and arched her back, forgetting her fear and their angry words, forgetting everything except the fierce, gnawing need of her body. She was dizzy, blind from lack of air as she forgot to breathe and sank into the dark red void of pleasure.

At last Maelgwn moved his hand between her legs, and Aurora almost jumped from the jolt of sensation that flowed through her. Even now, Maelgwn was slow and controlled, feeling the quivers of ecstasy which ran through Aurora's body at his touch.

"Ahhhhhh!" she cried with a groan. "Ahhhhhhhhhhh!"

Maelgwn moved his face close to hers so that his hot breath covered her. "So, you do like it, you do want it from me after all," he whispered harshly.

Aurora opened her eyes and nodded, almost insensible. It did not matter—giving in did not matter.

"Well, you shall have it!"

Maelgwn plunged into her savagely, penetrating her so deeply that Aurora screamed at the unendurable ecstasy. She could only surrender to Maelgwn's violent rhythm as he thrust within her over and over, until they were both shaking and drenched with sweat. It was like being caught in a raging river and being drawn on helplessly in the seething, irresistible current. His arms were around her tightly, painfully, and Aurora caught the wild, violent scent of him like a mist over both of them. She struggled to breathe, to think. There was mindless rapture, a vivid brilliant shiver down her spine . . . and then darkness.

It was over. Aurora was drained, exhausted, her thoughts spinning in small calm circles. She opened her eyes and looked at Maelgwn. He looked spent as well, his hair black with sweat, his skin flushed and hot. Aurora reached out a tender caressing hand to touch his face. He opened his eyes, startled, but he did not move as she tentatively examined his wounded face. He did not flinch, but watched her with dazed staring eyes. After a moment he reached up and pulled her hand down to his mouth and kissed it.

Fourteen

"What are you doing?" Aurora asked as Maelgwn dug through the pile of baskets and clothing which covered the large chest at the end of the bed.

"I am trying to get to *my* clothes. Can't you get Gwenaseth to put all these things somewhere else?"

"But I use them," Aurora protested.

"How can you? All these jars and bags and baubles . . . it is a good thing you had my whole army there to carry your possessions home when you left Viroconium!" He picked up a bracelet of silver strung with blue beads and flung it across the room for emphasis.

"What are you looking for?" Aurora asked again, hurrying to help him lest he start throwing her things out the window.

"My good tunic—I have not had it since we arrived."

"I am sure Gwenaseth put it away in the chest," Aurora said, scrambling to retrieve a bronze pot of rose oil that Maelgwn had thrown aside. "Why do you need it?"

"I am going to visit my holdings along the coast."

Aurora stopped her frantic rescue of her possessions and stared at her husband anxiously. "Will I be going with you?"

"No."

Maelgwn did not look up as he opened the large wooden chest bound with strips of hammered bronze.

"How long will you be gone?"

"A few weeks at most."

Aurora's heart sank. It had barely been a week since they had arrived at Caer Eryri and already Maelgwn was leaving. She did not like to think of staying in this lonely, foreign place without him.

Maelgwn glanced up and saw her worried face.

"Is there no way I could go?" she pleaded.

"No. We will be traveling fast and light, we cannot be slowed down to worry about a woman."

Maelgwn's face was hard and determined, and Aurora knew that there was no point in arguing. Anyway, how could she explain the sense of desolation that came over her at the thought of being left alone at Caer Eryri? It was more than missing her family and the familiar surroundings of home. She felt a nameless dread—as if something terrible was going to happen.

Maelgwn found his tunic and was looking at her with warmth in his eyes. "If you will miss me, come and show me how much," he said huskily.

Aurora went to him willingly, surprised by her need for him. Since the day after their fight, things between them had been very good.

Maelgwn left early the next morning, and Aurora soon decided she had never been so miserable and bored in her whole life. There was nothing for her to do at Caer Eryri. Esylt was in charge of everything, and whenever Aurora ventured into the bakehouse or the creamery or the dye-room, she was met with stares of curiosity and sometimes outright hostility. The acceptance she had felt the night of the homecoming feast was gone, as if it had been an illusion conjured up out of the music, the wine and the smoky fire. Most of the Cymry had gone off to the far corners of Gwynedd, and those left behind had no intention of giving Aurora a chance.

The women especially seemed wary and disapproving. They seldom spoke more than a few words to her, and often when she entered a room or passed by an open door, all conversation stopped, as if she was intruding. The women of Caer Eryri met in the great hall nearly every afternoon—to spin and sew and gossip. Aurora had joined them several times, taking some embroidery to work on while trying to make friends. The women never made an effort to include her in the conversation, and Aurora soon grew bored with their talk of babies and dyes and stitches.

Her suspicion that they were only tolerating her was confirmed by an incident with one of Sewan's children. The chubby youngster ventured near to Aurora one day, and with childish curiosity, reached out to touch her long, unbound hair. Sewan immediately rushed over and snatched the child away. Although she explained that she did not want the child to bother Aurora, Sewan's stiff face told Aurora the truth—the women of Caer Eryri did not want their children near the strange, foreign woman Maelgwn had chosen for his queen.

"Why would Sewan act like that?" Aurora asked in a wounded voice when she related the incident to Gwenaseth afterwards.

"I don't know," Gwenaseth answered gently. "I think you must be patient and give them time to accept you."

Aurora frowned. "Could it be Esylt's doing?" she

asked, suddenly suspicious. "Perhaps she has poisoned their minds against me."

Gwenaseth shook her head. "No, I don't think so. They treated me much the same at first, and while Esylt is no friend of mine, she had no reason to turn people against me. I'm afraid that it's just their way. The Cymry of the hills are a very tight-knit, clannish people."

"It seems so . . . so stupid," Aurora said in frustration. "How do they know what kind of person I am if they don't give me a chance?"

Gwenaseth tried to soothe her. "Caer Eryri is not like my home, along the coast, where strangers come every few weeks bringing goods and news. The people here live in the same valley where their great-grandparents grew up. The men go off to fight and learn of new things that way, but many of the women will never be out of this valley in their lives. Their days are filled with small worries of their children, their households and their husbands. A woman like you . . ." Gwenaseth glanced at Aurora's rich gown, the shimmer of jewelry at her slender neck and fine-boned wrists. "You threaten them, make them feel the dullness of their lives."

Aurora sighed. "What of the dullness of my life? Maelgwn will always go off without me. I hate sewing and spinning, and Esylt will not allow me any part of the responsibilities I was trained for by my mother. What am I to do to fill my days?"

"Well, eventually, God willing, you will have children to care for." Gwenaseth smiled dreamily at the thought. "As for now, you must learn to entertain yourself somehow—tell me, what did you do with your time when you were growing up?"

Aurora frowned, remembering the idle hours she had spent with Marcus. "Well, I did have certain responsibilities—it was my job to see to the butter-making each week and to help my mother with the inventory of all household supplies. Of course, we all took turns spinning and weaving, and for a long time I had lessons with Arian. I complained about it then, but now I miss it. And here . . . here there are no books to read nor anyone to teach me."

Homesickness was creeping over Aurora again, and her voice began to quaver slightly. "But most of all, when the weather was fine, I went riding. It was wonderful to feel the wind blow in my hair and smell the sticky fragrance of honeysuckle and apple blossoms in my father's orchards, or to go into the woods and hear the warblers and green plovers calling."

"Why can't you go riding here?" Gwenaseth asked.

"I suppose I could," Aurora said thoughtfully. "But who would go with me? You've already told me that you hate riding and none of the other women would willingly consent to spend time with me."

Gwenaseth had to agree. No woman she knew would choose to tramp about on a horse for pleasure. Esylt had her own horse and sometimes went riding, but then she, too, was royalty and far removed from the average woman's lot.

"I could send Elwyn," Gwenaseth said with a bright smile. "After all, Maelgwn told him to look after you while he was away."

Aurora was uneasy with Gwenaseth's suggestion. She liked Elwyn very much, too much considering that she was married already and he was betrothed to Gwenaseth.

She was also afraid that going riding with him would bring back the memories of Marcus that she had tried to put out of her mind.

"I don't think Maelgwn would like it if I took Elwyn away from his work. Maybe I should just go by myself. I'm sure it is safe if I do not venture out of the valley."

Gwenaseth looked doubtful, but eventually went along with the idea.

It was not as easy to persuade Flavian in the stables. Paithu had been let out to pasture near the fortress, and one of the slave boys would have to go and fetch her. But Aurora used her warm smile and soft voice to its best advantage, and soon the lovely gray mare was ready to depart.

It was a warm, sunny day, with only a slight breeze to ripple the silvery green leaves of the trees in the valley. Aurora wore her old, stained dress from Viroconium, and her hair was done up in braids. Her thick hair was especially cumbersome outdoors, and since Maelgwn was not here to care how she wore it, she had decided that the long braids the Cymry women wore would be both practical and comfortable.

It felt good to be riding again, and Aurora wondered why she had not thought of it before. She gave Paithu free rein and headed down the track at a gallop. Aurora's heart soared in her chest, filling her with a warm happiness. She had already learned that clear sunny days were a rarity in Gwynedd—more often it was rainy and overcast. She marveled now at the vivid colors that the sunshine revealed. There was every shade of green imaginable shading the wide sweep of the valley, and the verdant loveliness was highlighted with the sparkle of silvery rocks and the fleeting color of wildflowers scattered over the rugged terrain. Farther down the valley, the glitter of two quiet, gray-blue lakes caught her eye.

Aurora followed the pathway down to the river and skirted the squalid village on her way to the largest of the lakes. The soft light turned the lake waters a pale blue that contrasted prettily with the green of the reeds and grasses around it. As she paused at the edge of the lake, a slight breeze ruffled the loose strands of hair at the base of Aurora's neck and cooled her sweaty skin. Paithu tossed her head suddenly, and Aurora realized that her horse was sweaty and thirsty. The bright green and blue flies had already discovered the mare's delicious, salty skin, and Aurora decided to allow the horse to walk eagerly into the shallows to drink and drive away her tormenters.

When the mare had drunk her fill, Aurora rode on looking for a dry spot—away from the damp marshes with their hordes of insects. She finally found a small cove surrounded by boulders where she could dismount and sit comfortably on the gravelly shore. Clasping her arms around her knees, Aurora leaned back and watched the wheeling circles of the birds overhead. A strange languid calm filled her. The lake water was glassy and still, and only the call of the water birds—fishers and black-backed gulls—broke the peaceful spell of the place. Aurora closed her eyes and breathed deeply. It seemed she could smell the salty scent of the sea, which she knew was only a few dozen miles away. She inhaled the strange, exotic fragrance deeply. The warmth of the sun and the humid air enveloped her, and she grew sleepy and content.

The jangle of Paithu's bridle as the mare shook off the tormenting flies startled Aurora awake. She had barely dozed, but it seemed she dreamed. Marcus's name was on her lips, as if she had just been with him. This was the sort of place he would have enjoyed, she thought as she began to throw pebbles idly into the water. An important man like Maelgwn would never take time to linger on this peaceful shore. Aurora felt the bitter sting of tears in her eyes.

Her tears blurred her vision, and Aurora looked out onto the water, staring unseeingly at the scum of petals and insects that coated the oily surface. She gasped in surprise when she caught sight of a large, creamy white bird floating into the inlet. It was a swan—as silvery white as a summer cloud—followed by her smoky gray cygnets. Aurora held her breath, entranced by the scene of grace and tenderness.

"I thought I would find you here," a voice said from behind her.

Aurora was so startled, she jumped. Then she turned to smile at the familiar tanned face of Elwyn.

"How did you know I would be here?" she asked, still a little breathless with surprise.

"You admired this lake when we first came to the valley, and I guessed you might come here. Gwenaseth sent me to find you."

"I told her that it wasn't necessary to take you away from your other responsibilities."

"I don't mind, and Maelgwn told me to look after you." Elwyn's eyes were grave and admiring, and Aurora pulled her glance away with difficulty.

"Look," she said, pointing to the swan and her brood. "Are they not beautiful?"

"And I had not the presence of mind to bring my bow."

"You would not!" Aurora whirled to face him again. "They are so beautiful; how could you want to kill them?"

"They are beautiful, but they make fine eating, too," Elwyn said with the glimmer of a smile. "I can see you are from a place where food is plentiful, or you would not be so quick to dismiss an easy meal. But no . . ." he continued more seriously. "I would not kill a female with young. Now the cob—I would not hesitate to pursue him for the supper table."

"It is strange that females are held cheaply among men, when they are so valued among animals," Aurora mused.

"Cheaply is a poor choice of word," said Elwyn. "At least for a woman like you. I'm sure Maelgwn would fight very hard to keep you, and clearly your father set great store by his youngest daughter."

"Women are hardly considered important by the Cymry," Aurora said irritably. "We are left behind, forgotten, while men do the important things."

"I hardly think 'forgotten' is fitting either. I'm sure Maelgwn thinks of you while he is away, and I . . . I could never hope to forget you."

Aurora blushed at his compliment, suddenly uncomfortable. She had not been fishing for kind words, and she hoped he did not think so. She took a stick and began to dig in the soft gravel on the shoreline.

"I don't wonder that you wish to linger here," Elwyn said with a soft sigh of satisfaction. "It's so peaceful, and except for the mountains all around us, it must re-mind you of the gentle landscape of the lowlands."

"It's funny, I had almost forgotten the mountains. I am not used to them yet, they seem somehow to crowd me."

"You will grow used to them in time," Elwyn an-swered. "Come on, let us walk awhile, our horses will wait for us."

Aurora put her sandals on, and then, because the shore was slippery, took the arm that Elwyn reached out to steady her with. They did not speak as they walked. It was as if they both wanted nothing to interrupt the dreamlike quality of the day.

They walked back to the marshy edge of the lake. When Elwyn made a move to lead her to drier ground, Aurora let her arm slip out of his. "I want to pick some of those," she said, motioning toward a clump of purple flowers blooming among the reeds. She took off her san-dals and stepped gingerly on the marshy ground, holding her dress up to her knees.

"Be careful," Elwyn warned.

The lake edge was slicker than she thought, and Aurora stepped awkwardly on the slimy surface. All at once, a blackbird, surprised to find danger so close, flew up, calling out an angry alert. The sudden motion sur-prised Aurora, and she lost her balance and slipped into the water with a little cry.

"Aurora!" Elwyn called as he waded in after her, shoes and all.

"I am all right," Aurora said, laughing. "Oh, look at you!" She laughed helplessly at the sight of Elwyn stand-ing knee deep in the muddied water.

"Here, let me help you," he said, reaching out to her. Aurora grasped his hand and stood up carefully. Then she began to slip again, almost dragging Elwyn down. Her eyes were full of playful mirth, and Elwyn thought for a moment that she meant to pull him in.

"Oh no, you don't!" he cried, scooping her up in his arms. Aurora giggled happily as Elwyn sloshed through the water toward the dry ground. She glanced tentatively at Elwyn's face, now so close to hers. How different his face was from Maelgwn's—it was still as smooth and soft as a boy's. She could see the flecks of gold in his hazel eyes. What beautiful children he will have with Gwenaseth, she thought—babies with eyes of gold and green.

Elwyn did not dare look down at the radiant face watching him. He concentrated on his footing, but his heart pounded unnaturally and when he finally put Aurora down, his hands were trembling.

"There," he said at last, releasing her. "I hope you are satisfied. You've ruined my shoes as well as your dress."

"It is an old dress," Aurora answered. "Anyway, was it not a small price to pay to make your queen smile?"

"Queen! You look more like a dirty village girl fishing barefoot in the river!" Elwyn answered gaily. He could not believe the bold, teasing tone he was using. There was something about Aurora that made him feel so comfortable, so at ease, he completely forgot that she was the king's wife.

Aurora did not seem to mind his jesting. Her cheeks were flushed with pleasure, and she smiled broadly at him. For a moment, Elwyn could scarcely take his eyes away. They dwelt lingeringly on the delicate bones of her face, the haunting blue eyes and the irresistible curve of her lips.

It was Aurora who broke the trance with a cracked whisper. "We must be getting back." Then more lightly she added, "While I have no one who awaits me, Gwenaseth will be impatient for her beloved Elwyn to return."

Without speaking, they walked back to their horses. The same somber mood infected them both. They could sense danger in their friendship. As enjoyable as this quiet afternoon had been, they dared not do it again.

Fifteen

The next day, Aurora dressed to go riding again. It was overcast, and the valley seemed bleaker and more desolate. Aurora glanced at the dull, opaque sky and decided to take her cloak—it would most certainly rain before the day was over.

As she left the fortress and guided the horse down the hill, Aurora felt the familiar ache of homesickness. Still, she was determined to go riding alone. The special time she had spent with Elwyn the day before made her uneasy. She had begun to suspect that Maelgwn was a fiercely possessive man. He might not be pleased by her friendship with one of his men.

She set her course for the nearer lake and took her time following the track by the river, pausing to admire scattered bunches of flowers releasing pollen and scent into the breeze. The trees in the valley reminded her of her father's orchards, so spicy rich in the fall, sweet and fragrant in the spring. How much she missed her home—the sight of white stones in the sun, the urgent buzz of the black and yellow bees, the fruity, hypnotic odor of ripening apricots and pears. Here there was no orchard and nothing that could be called a garden either.

When Aurora reached the lake, she was disappointed

by how different it seemed from the day before. The water was a cold greenish-blue, and the cry of the gulls sounded lonesome. Impulsively, she turned away from the water and headed toward the spill of forest on the west edge of the valley. Full of curiosity, she entered the tangle of vegetation. This was a different sort of forest than that of the lowlands. Much of it was made up of dark green pines and the stunted, twisted sessile oaks. The rocky ground was cushioned everywhere with damp, blackish mosses, and the echo of running water was never far away. The sound seemed to come from under-ground—a vague, uncanny gurgle that reminded her of spirits whispering beneath the earth.

Aurora continued into the forest, searching for the wa-terfall that Gwenaseth had mentioned. The dense, dark trees let in little light, and Aurora's eyes struggled to adjust to the dim environment. She felt a tingle of apprehension. The strange sense of bewitchment was back—as she had felt it when she had first entered the mountains. The oak was sacred to the druids, and here the ancient gnarled trees seemed to be everywhere. Aurora thought of the blood sacrifices of the druids and shivered. Had human blood been spilled in these dank shrouded groves?

Aurora's dread weighed so heavily upon her that she finally decided to turn back. She guided the horse in a circle, trying to return to the pathway she had just taken. The damp leaves left no mark of her passing, and Aurora was not sure of the trail. She rode along, growing more and more frightened by the eerie stillness and the twist-ing, confusing pathway. For a moment she thought some-one was following her, but when she turned back to look, she saw no one.

Her apprehension must have spooked the horse, for when a small frightened creature hurried in front of them across the darkness of the forest floor, Paithu shied away.

"It is all right, girl," Aurora whispered soothingly, patting the mare's neck.

But Aurora was not sure. The hair on the back of her neck prickled strangely and her heart was beating fast. She dismounted for a moment to lead the horse over a fallen log that was crusted with ancient lichen and moss, and she heard something more than the rustle of her sandals on damp leaves. She turned back the way she had come and gasped—Esylt stood a few paces away, staring at her.

For a moment Aurora could not find her voice. Coming face to face with her enemy in this dark, spooky place unnerved her. She wondered how long Esylt had been following her.

"What are you doing here?" Aurora asked when her nerves had steadied.

"What are *you* doing trespassing on the king's lands?" Esylt retorted. Even in the shadows of the forest her face shone white against the dark of her hair and the blue blaze of her eyes.

Aurora felt herself filling with rage. "I am the queen!" she answered hotly. "By rights these lands are mine, too."

"Queen!" Esylt spat out the word contemptuously, her full mouth twisting in scorn. "You are no more than my brother's slut. I hope you please him well."

"He would not wish to hear you speak so of me."

"Ah, and would he wish to know that his wife spends

her time in the arms of one of his officers while he is away?"

Aurora sucked in her breath and answered in a low, frightened voice. "How can you say such a thing? Elwyn is only a friend. He is completely loyal to Maelgwn."

"And you . . . are you completely loyal to Maelgwn?" Esylt asked with a mocking laugh. "No. I daresay if you could find a way out of this marriage, you would take it. My brother is a fool." Her face brightened with the threat of malice. "Would you like me to tell him what kind of fool he is? Would you like me to tell him exactly how you spend your time when he is away?"

"There is nothing to tell," Aurora answered as calmly as she could. "Elwyn and I have shared nothing other than friendship, and Elwyn will tell Maelgwn that himself."

"Aye, Elwyn is betrothed to Lady Gwenaseth, whose father rules the rich lands along the coast. It would be awkward for him if everyone at Caer Eryri knew of his lack of loyalty to Maelgwn."

"No one would believe it—why Gwenaseth herself sent Elwyn after me."

"No one?" Esylt looked at Aurora consideringly. "I think there are many at Caer Eryri who would like to believe the worst of you. They might well think both Gwenaseth and Elwyn were protecting you."

Aurora tried to shake off her rising panic. Esylt was twisting things so wickedly. She could not understand why this woman hated her so much.

"What do you want from me? Why are you threatening me?"

Esylt moved toward her slowly, until Aurora had

backed into Paithu and had nowhere to go. Her sister-in-law's blue eyes glittered like ice, and Aurora found she could not look away.

"Want from you?" Esylt asked haughtily. "I want nothing from you . . . except to have you away from Caer Eryri and out of my brother's life."

"I . . . it is not up to me," Aurora answered haltingly. "It is between Maelgwn and my father. The peace between our two lands depends on this marriage."

"Peace! Do you think I care about peace? If Maelgwn had any sense he would have burned Viroconium to the ground and killed all of you!"

Aurora flinched, keenly aware of the hatred, the madness that flowed from Esylt's eyes to hers. She was deathly afraid of her sister-in-law. She did not want to fight with Esylt—she wanted only to get away.

Esylt seemed to have spent her anger. She gave Aurora one last cold, hostile look and then turned away, disappearing into the forest as quickly as she had come.

Aurora stood frozen for a moment, sweating and breathing hard. Never had she faced such raw hatred, and it made her almost ill. She tried frantically to sort out her thoughts. What should she do? She wanted to tell Maelgwn of Esylt's threats, but a shadowy fear held her back. Would he believe her, or would Esylt's clever insinuations about Elwyn make him too angry to listen?

Aurora shivered as she mounted Paithu again and began riding anxiously in the direction Esylt had taken. She urged the horse on carelessly, seeking to escape the sinister gloom of the forest as fast as possible.

Aurora thought back to the idyllic afternoon she had spent with Elwyn. Aye, she had to admit that there was just enough truth in Esylt's taunts to make it hard to face her husband. Although they had done nothing disloyal, there was something special about her relationship with Elwyn, a closeness that might make Maelgwn jealous. No, she did not think she could depend on Maelgwn to believe her over Esylt. She would have to hope that Esylt would not carry out her threat. But how could she stand it, to stay at Caer Eryri while Esylt plotted against her? She had to think of a plan before Maelgwn returned from the coast.

The coast! Maelgwn had forts all up and down the coast—as well as scattered among the hills. As soon as he returned to the fortress, she would ask him if she could live at another of his strongholds. She would speak to him right away—before Esylt had a chance to tell him her lies.

Sixteen

"That finished them!" Maelgwn shouted gleefully.

Abelgirth let out a yell in response, and then raised his sword threateningly at the retreating soldiers. The Irish raiders had given up the battle and were fleeing toward the sea, scrambling to get back in their boats as fast as they could.

"Take that, you Irish curs!" Abelgirth shouted. "That will teach you to attack the Cymry."

"You know they'll be back," Maelgwn said as he walked over to the big chieftain.

Abelgirth was still holding a cowering Irishman in one hand while he wiped off his sword on his blood-soaked tunic with the other.

"Aye, I know they'll be back, but today we gave them a reason to delay a few years."

Abelgirth gestured toward the beach littered with Irish dead, and then to the handful of enemy survivors who were being rounded up and put in chains.

"A good day's work, I'd say."

Maelgwn nodded. The Irish raiders barely had time to set the little fishing village afire before Abelgirth and his men were upon them. When it came to repelling coastal raids, Abelgirth was a superb commander, and

Maelgwn was well pleased by what he had seen on this visit to Llanfaglon. The string of forts along the coast of Gwynedd was solid and well-supplied. The defenses were so good, in fact, that the Irish raids had dwindled to almost nothing. He was lucky to have hit this one on his visit.

Abelgirth released his captive to be chained with the rest, and then the two men walked among the dead, looking for armor and weapons that could be salvaged.

"I believe we've seen more action here than you have in your campaign to the east, Maelgwn. I hear you took the town of Viroconium without so much as a sword being drawn."

"You heard the truth. We marched in and made an alliance with Constantine. I took one of his daughters as my wife to seal the bargain. It was the easiest victory I've ever had."

"A wife, eh?" Abelgirth commented with a sly grin. "You are probably anxious to get back to her."

Maelgwn smiled and then shrugged. "No need for that. She must get used to me being gone for weeks. I have a country to look after. Anyway, I believe that men who hold themselves too close to their womenfolk grow soft and weak."

"Ah, but you smile at the mere mention of her. It is clear that this woman has more to recommend her than just the dowry of Viroconium."

"Aye, she is a beauty," Maelgwn said proudly. "Even I did not know what wealth I had stolen until I bedded her." His face grew more serious. "But she can be difficult. I don't know if the Romans breed particularly stubborn, willful women, or if it is just that she is spoiled, but Aurora tries my patience regularly."

Abelgirth laughed. "Surely that is not Roman blood, but the Celtic strain which makes British women as fierce as their men. Anyway Maelgwn, there is a price for everything worth having. My own Gwenamore—God rest her soul." Abelgirth crossed himself with his huge hand, for he had recently become a Christian. "She was a beauty indeed, as bright and graceful as the sea foam. But I paid a high price for her loveliness—she was too small a woman to bear children easily, my children at least. I lost her and my only son when she died in child-birth."

"I had forgotten, Abelgirth. I am sorry."

"It is no matter now," Abelgirth said dismissingly. "I have my lovely Gwenaseth, and God willing, she will soon give me a brood of healthy grandchildren. I am glad that Elwyn has finally asked for her hand. The boy does not have overmuch spirit, but he is as loyal as a faithful old hound, and he makes her happy."

"It is good you are pleased with the match your daughter has made," Maelgwn said. "I have always felt a little guilty that I did not ask her to be my queen."

"You!" Abelgirth gave a deep rumbling laugh. "You would swallow up my sweet little Gwen like a cormorant devours a minnow. At any rate, the ties between us did not need strengthening. You had to make a match such as you did—one that expands your lands and power."

"If not me, why not another prince? There are many chieftains who would have paid well for the privilege of being your son-in-law."

Abelgirth's broad, ruddy face softened. "I may be a

foolish old man, but I could not see my only child bargained off to the man with the most gold. No, I wanted Gwenaseth to be happy, to be with a man who will cherish her for herself and not her dowry."

"You can sympathize with Constantine, I guess," Maelgwn said with a smile. "I am sure I was not the man he would have chosen to marry his dearest daughter."

"He could have done much worse. Why, from the way your face changes when you speak of her, it would seem you are falling in love with this Cornovii princess."

Maelgwn looked startled. "No," he protested. "I don't want to be in love with any woman. It is only that she pleases me well."

Abelgirth frowned, and his face grew unusually somber.

"I believe it is good for a man to have a trusting, loving relationship with his wife. Myself—I never appreciated Gwenamore until it was too late. I was always out wenching and enjoying myself." He sighed. "And then one day, she was gone. I can tell you, if I had a chance, I would go back and do things differently."

Maelgwn considered his friend's words. It was not uncommon for a man to look back on his past and be tortured by the decisions he made when young. Abelgirth, for all his formidable bulk and fierce demeanor, was an exceptionally kind-hearted man.

"I wonder how my kinsman Arthur is doing in his efforts to keep the Saxon sea wolves at bay along the eastern shores?" asked Maelgwn, changing the subject.

Abelgirth shook his head. "Arthur is a great soldier, but he cannot prevail forever. There are too many Saxons, no matter how many he kills, there will always be more arriving from across the sea." His deep voice was brooding and cold. "I'm afraid someday they will invade as far as Viroconium, and Constantine—if he survives—will finally appreciate how civilized and generous a conqueror you were."

Abelgirth unclasped a wineskin from his horse's saddle and took a drink.

"We can only hope to hold them back in the west. The Saxon curs have no use for the highlands, so your settlements will survive. And here, along the coast, we have been fighting invaders for so long we know of nothing else."

Maelgwn nodded solemnly at his host's grim assessment. Arthur was a valiant warrior, but now that the legions of Rome were gone, it was only a matter of time before the riches of Britain were plundered, and the Roman forts and towns sacked and ruined by the blind greed of the Saxons. The important thing was Gwynedd—he was determined that his beautiful wild hills should remain safe. The coastal forts were the key to their safety, but his heart was in the highlands. Even now he ached for the lonely valleys hidden with in the embrace of Yr Wyddfa's majestic shadow.

"So, what do we do, now that we have kept the coasts safe for another day?" Maelgwn asked, taking the wineskin that Abelgirth offered.

"Back to my feasting hall, of course," Abelgirth answered with a smile. "My cooks are preparing a special meal in your honor. What do you say to roast salmon and eels boiled in wine and butter?"

"I say—what are we waiting for!" Maelgwn replied as he mounted his horse.

The slight breeze stirred Aurora's hair as she sat on her high lookout on the side of the steep hill that guarded Caer Eryri. She had come to this spot almost daily since her encounter with Esylt. It was close enough to the fort to be under the watchful eyes of the guard at the gate, and yet far enough away for her to escape the oppressiveness of life in the fortress.

There was nowhere in the fortress where she could be comfortable. The tower chamber was hot and stuffy during the day, and everywhere else there was the bustle of people going about their business to remind her of how purposeless her own life was. Unlike at Viroconium, she had no desire to spend time around the stables or the other farm buildings. They were not so clean as the ones at home, and in the enclosed space they gave off unpleasant odors. Anyway, Aurora mused, she was a queen now, and she could not go dragging her skirts through the dirt to chase a stray cat or play with a puppy as she once had.

In her loneliness and boredom she had wandered to this spot, taking her sewing with her to keep up the pretense of being busy like everyone else. It was a pleasant place. She could see the horses grazing nearby and hear the soft call of the ringdoves that nested in the nooks and crannies of the fortress walls. From behind her came the sounds of mock battle as the soldiers trained in the open space behind the fortress. From her vantage spot she had a stunning view of the whole valley, and she could watch the farmers and villagers below go about their business like so many busy ants. On clear days she could even see the small cluster of buildings that made up the priory farther down the valley.

Aurora did little sewing in her lookout spot. She brooded and made chains of the white starflowers that grew in profusion on the hill. She was preoccupied with worry over her encounter with Esylt. She had not told anyone—even Gwenaseth—of Esylt's threats. Her plan was to get Maelgwn to take her to live somewhere else in his kingdom, someplace away from Esylt's treachery.

But how could she ask her husband without arousing his suspicions, she wondered? She must be very clever and subtle, and convince Maelgwn of her unhappiness with other things at Caer Eryri besides his sister. Aurora both looked forward to and dreaded Maelgwn's return to Caer Eryri. She had missed him, in truth, but she also feared him. What would happen to her if Esylt told him her lies and he believed her?

Aurora was seated there, watching the valley, when she saw the black shapes of horses and riders moving near the river—Maelgwn was back. Before the lookout had even announced the king's arrival, Aurora hurried into the fortress to wash and change her dress. She wanted to meet with Maelgwn alone as soon as she could, and she intended to look her best.

Aurora met the king at the gate with the others. Maelgwn's eyes alighted on her with glowing pleasure, and after he dismounted he pulled her to him for an eager and very public kiss. Aurora's relief at her husband's warm greeting was marred by Esylt's presence. Knowing that her wicked sister-in-law was so near seemed to send a chill down her spine.

A dozen things commanded Maelgwn's attention, and Aurora did not see her husband again until the evening meal. The atmosphere in the great hall that night was cheerful and relaxed, and Aurora could almost forget the cold loneliness that had haunted her while the men were gone. Balyn was joking and playful, and even Evrawc smiled politely at her. Aurora wondered if she was beginning to be accepted, at least by Maelgwn's men.

After the meal, Maelgwn made no pretense of lingering, but eagerly led Aurora to their bedchamber. She could not seem to put Esylt's threats out of her mind, and her unease obviously conveyed itself to Maelgwn. After a few probing kisses, he pulled back and looked at her with a puzzled expression.

"Aurora, what is wrong?"

She shrugged, uncertain how to begin.

"Obviously there is something wrong," Maelgwn said with a touch of impatience. "You do not even seem glad to see me."

"It is not that," Aurora protested, pressing herself against him.

"Speak woman," he said more softly. "Tell me what is troubling you."

"Is it true you have many holdings in Gwynedd besides Caer Eryri?"

Maelgwn nodded.

"Do you dwell then at Caer Eryri most of the year or do you travel from fort to fort?"

"Why both—I stay at Caer Eryri as much as I can, but I must visit all my holdings every few months."

Maelgwn's puzzlement was turning to irritation. Why must she ask him these things right now?

"And what of me?" Aurora's voice was plaintive, tinged with unhappiness.

"Why, I had planned for you to remain here at Caer Eryri—it is safe and has many comforts." Maelgwn frowned. "Surely you do not expect to go with me on my travels; it is no life for a woman."

"I have no wish to be left behind in this unfriendly place all year!"

"What is it about Caer Eryri that displeases you?"

"The women here hate me; they will never accept me. There is nothing for me to do here. I have no say in the running of your household, and I am tired of sewing and spinning!"

Maelgwn paused and looked at his wife's face searchingly. She seemed genuinely unhappy, but he could not help suspecting that Esylt was behind it.

"Where would you like to live?"

"Why, anywhere else. Along the coast, at another mountain fort—anywhere I can be more than your despised, pampered bed partner!"

Maelgwn considered. It was not as easy as she thought to find another place for his queen to dwell, and he did not like the idea of catering to Aurora's whims. On the other hand, he was anxious to make her happy so she would be willing and enthusiastic for lovemaking. He decided to put her off. He touched Aurora's cheek with a warm lingering caress.

"I will think on it, Aurora, I promise. But for now . . . can we not continue what we were doing?"

Despite her anxiety, Aurora forced herself to respond

to her husband with all the passion she could muster. Now it was more important than ever that she keep Maelgwn satisfied.

Balyn asked Maelgwn the next day: "How are things with you and Aurora?"

Maelgwn shook his head. "As soon as we were alone together, Aurora surprised me with a request that I find her some other place to live. I know that her unhappiness here is real enough, but do I dare give in, especially since it will be considerable trouble to move her elsewhere?"

"Why is she unhappy?"

"Well, for one thing, she says the other women are cold and unfriendly to her."

"I'm not surprised," Balyn said thoughtfully. "As much as I have tried to get Sewan to befriend her, my wife steadfastly refuses to give Aurora a chance."

"Do the women have real grievances against her, or is it just the petty jealousy of their sex?"

"Oh, their grievances about Aurora are quite damning," Balyn answered with a smile. "They think she is vain and proud, too proud to speak to them or make the first gesture of friendship. I have tried to make Sewan see that Aurora is really shy, not haughty and rude, but as usual she does not see my point of view."

"She says I know nothing of women," he continued. "Actually, I think I understand them all too well—they are jealous of Aurora—jealous of her many gowns and elegant appearance. Beauty such as Aurora's does not endear her to other women. They see their husbands watching Aurora, their eyes lingering on her body and the graceful sweep of her unbound hair."

"Aurora is my queen," Maelgwn said stiffly. "Her beauty pleases me—should I have her wear rough gowns and bind up her hair so she does not outshine the plainer women?"

Balyn shrugged. "You see the problem it causes. If she were a Cymraes the problems might be lessened some, but with her odd accent, her foreign ways of dress and manner . . ."

"And if I take her elsewhere . . . to one of my lesser holdings, will that make it easier? No, I think not. The women there would be even more in awe of her." Maelgwn groaned in frustration. "I had no idea that having a wife would cause so much difficulty."

"Are there other reasons she does not like Caer Eryri?"

"Aye," Maelgwn answered wearily. "She does not like it that Esylt runs my household, and not she."

"I am not surprised. Esylt would be hard for any woman to take."

Maelgwn's face stiffened with determination. "Aurora will have to learn to ignore Esylt and the other women. There is only so much I am willing to do to keep her happy."

"You will refuse her?"

"I must. She has to learn to adjust to her new life—she is only a woman after all."

Aurora waited impatiently for Maelgwn. The barley bannock she had eaten for breakfast sat heavily in her stomach, and her thoughts churned in restless circles. She had tried to please her husband well last night, but there was no telling what he would do, if he would listen to her. If he did not . . . Aurora shuddered. How would she endure life with Esylt breathing her foul, evil breath upon her back?

Maelgwn came at last to the tower room. He looked at her with warmth and then leaned down and kissed her.

"Let us go for a walk," he suggested. Maelgwn played with her fingers distractedly as they walked through the fortress, testing the sharpness of her nails against his callused palm.

Aurora was not sure about this gentle, thoughtful mood of Maelgwn's, and as they left the gate and he had still not spoken, her anxiety grew. They walked down the track for a while, and finally Maelgwn led her off into the grass. When they were near the place where Aurora had been coming to watch the valley, Maelgwn stopped and turned to her.

Aurora searched her husband's handsome face—the deep-set, moody eyes, the sensual mouth. Even now, so close to him, she could not guess his thoughts, and her heart pounded in her chest.

"I told you I would think on your request to live elsewhere than Caer Eryri—and I have," he said softly. "I'm sorry, Aurora, but the answer is no."

Aurora gave a little gasp and began to protest, but Maelgwn silenced her with a curt shake of his head. "Hear me out. There is nowhere else you could go, nowhere you would be safe, not to mention live comfortably."

"I don't care about safety!" Aurora cried. "What does it matter if I am safe, but alone and miserable!"

"Your safety matters a good deal to me. You could be taken hostage, and I could be forced into an unwanted war because I failed to guard you properly. I will not let your foolishness compromise Gwynedd's security."

"But what of Llanfaglan? Surely I would be safe at Abelgirth's stronghold."

Maelgwn shook his head grimly. "There are the politics of where my queen lives to consider. Already there are chieftains who think I am much too tight with Abelgirth. To lodge you at Llanfaglan would give substance to their grumbling that I favor him over others."

Aurora's face was full of dismay, desperation even, and for a moment Maelgwn regretted his refusal of her. "I am sorry Aurora," he said as gently as he could. "It is not an arbitrary decision. If I could think of a safe place that would not upset the balance of power among my princes—I would consider it."

Harsh words came to Aurora's tongue, but she held them back. To mention the conflict between herself and Esylt was too dangerous. So far Esylt had not gone to Maelgwn with her lies, but Aurora dared not risk forcing Maelgwn into a confrontation with his sister. Still, it seemed to her that Maelgwn was condemning her to a life of misery and fear.

The sun shone brightly, turning Aurora's tears to glittering ribbons on her cheeks. Maelgwn was torn—he wanted to comfort her, but he was also determined not to let her affect him deeply. Suddenly he thought of a way to make his decision seem less harsh.

"Would it help if you could go away from here for a little while?"

Aurora nodded.

"I have to visit Cunedda in the north to talk with him of the Pictish raids. It is a long hard journey, Aurora," he cautioned. "It would mean being tired, dirty, eating traveling food . . ."

"I don't care," Aurora said defiantly, her tears forgotten. "I do not want to be left behind again. When will we leave?"

"Tomorrow. That is, if Gwenaseth can get you ready in time."

"Who is going with us?"

"Balyn, Evrawc, Rhys, Gareth . . . and Esylt will no doubt bring her latest bed partner."

"Esylt!" Aurora almost choked.

"Aye. Cunedda is a distant kinsman of ours, and he and Esylt have been close since they were like puppies playing together at the same hearth." Maelgwn read the dread in Aurora's eyes. "Have you changed your mind about going?"

Aurora considered. Esylt would have long hours on the journey to tell Maelgwn her hateful lies. No, as much as she loathed the thought of being near Esylt for so long, she needed to be with Maelgwn—to remind him that he desired her and that she knew how to make him happy.

"I . . . I still wish to go."

"Good." Maelgwn gave her a satisfied smile. "Why don't you go tell Gwenaseth the news."

Seventeen

"I do not know if you will like Cunedda's people," Gwenaseth said skeptically when Aurora told her of the journey. "The Brigantes are wild and uncivilized—they make the Cymry look like proper Roman townspeople by comparison."

"It will be exciting. I like to ride, and I will see many new things."

"I will never understand your desire to go roaming about on horseback. I would just as soon stay on my own two legs and by my own hearth all my days," Gwenaseth said with a shudder.

"I have never been anywhere except Viroconium and Caer Eryri," Aurora answered. "On my trip here, I was so nervous and homesick I hardly noticed anything except whether Maelgwn smiled at me or frowned."

"Well, it seems Maelgwn smiles at you now," Gwenaseth observed happily.

"It is not so certain as that. I have learned better how to please him, but he is still capable of dealing with me very coldly."

"You will see just how considerate and civilized a man Maelgwn is when you meet Cunedda. He is a brute!"

We've got your authors!

If you seek out the latest historical romances by today's bestselling authors, our new reader's service, KENSINGTON CHOICE, is the club for you.

KENSINGTON CHOICE is the only club where you can find authors like Janelle Taylor, Shannon Drake, Rosanne Bittner, Sylvie Sommerfield, Penelope Neri and Phoebe Conn all in one place...

...and the only service that will deliver their romances direct to your home as soon as they are published—even before they reach the bookstores.

KENSINGTON CHOICE is also the only service that will give you a substantial guaranteed discount off the publisher's prices on every one of those romances.

That's right: Every month, the Editors at Zebra and Pinnacle select four of the newest novels by our bestselling authors and rush them straight to you, usually *before they reach the bookstores.* The publisher's prices for these romances range from $4.99 to $5.99—but they are always yours for the guaranteed low price of just *$3.95!*

That means you'll always save over $1.00...often as much as *$2.00*...off the publisher's prices on every new novel you get from KENSINGTON CHOICE!

All books are sent on a 10-day free examination basis, and there is no minimum number of books to buy. (A postage and handling charge of $1.50 is added to each shipment.)

As your introduction to the convenience and value of this new service, we invite you to accept

4 BOOKS FREE

The 4 books, worth up to $23.96, are our welcoming gift. You pay only $1 to help cover postage and handling.

To start your subscription to KENSINGTON CHOICE and receive your introductory package of 4 FREE romances, detach and mail the postpaid card at right *today.*

We have 4 FREE BOOKS for you as your introduction to KENSINGTON CHOICE

To get your FREE BOOKS, worth up to $23.96, mail the card below.

FREE BOOK CERTIFICATE

As my introduction to your new KENSINGTON CHOICE reader's service, please send me 4 FREE historical romances (worth up to $23.96), billing me just $1 to help cover postage and handling. As a KENSINGTON CHOICE subscriber, I will then receive 4 brand-new romances to preview each month for 10 days FREE. I can return any books I decide not to keep and owe nothing. The publisher's prices for the KENSINGTON CHOICE romances range from $4.99 to $5.99, but as a subscriber I will be entitled to get them for just $3.95 per book or $15.80 for all four titles. There is no minimum number of books to buy, and I can cancel my subscription at any time. A $1.50 postage and handling charge is added to each shipment.

Name _____

Address _____ Apt. _____

City _____ State _____ Zip _____

Telephone ( ) _____

Signature _____

(If under 18, parent or guardian must sign)

Subscription subject to acceptance. Terms and prices subject to change.

KC1194

We have
4
FREE
Historical
Romances
for you!

(worth up
to $23.96!)

Details inside!

KENSINGTON CHOICE
Reader's Service
120 Brighton Road
P.O. Box 5214
Clifton, NJ 07015-5214

Gwenaseth shuddered again. "It is hard to believe that they are distant cousins."

"It is not so hard to believe," Aurora said with a smile. "Why just today Maelgwn was telling me of your father. From his description, I can hardly believe such a man sired you."

"My father is big and loud and crude sometimes, but he is also good-natured and loyal," Gwenaseth answered defensively. "I know Maelgwn counts him among his strongest supporters."

"I just teasing. I am sure Abelgirth is a good friend to Maelgwn . . . just as you are to me," she said, looking at Gwenaseth fondly. "Now, help me decide what to take."

Maelgwn and Balyn sat in a corner of the great hall, discussing gifts to take to Cunedda. "By the way," Maelgwn said as an afterthought. "I have decided to bring Aurora with us."

Balyn looked surprised. "It is a long ride, Maelgwn, and not one for a woman like Aurora."

Maelgwn shrugged. "She rode to Gwynedd well enough . . . and she wants to go. She complains she has nothing to do here at Caer Eryri."

"But what of her and Esylt? Can you hope to keep them from being at each others' throats when they are together for days?"

"Perhaps it will be good for them. Being forced to be together might make them more tolerant."

Balyn shook his head. "I don't know, Maelgwn. It seems ill-advised to take two women on such a long jour-

ney." He looked at Maelgwn suspiciously: "Why *really,*
are you taking her?"

"Do you suspect that I have become so infatuated with
my wife's lovely body that I cannot bear to leave her
behind?" Maelgwn asked with a smile. "No, I do have
other reasons. Aurora is proof of my easy victory over
Constantine—Cunedda cannot boast of having such a
woman."

"You think it is time to remind Cunedda of the might
of your army?"

"It may be . . . I cannot tell. Despite our shared blood,
Cunedda and I have never been easy with each other. He
wants my help with the Picts, but I fear he would betray
me if he thought it would benefit his people."

Balyn nodded. He wondered if Maelgwn's decision to
take Aurora was really wise. Maelgwn seemed very
much like a little boy, eager to show off a new plaything
to a rival. Had his gloating over his beautiful wife
clouded his judgment? Aurora was lovely and charming,
but she was also unpredictable, naive and headstrong—
hardly the sort of person most leaders would want to
take on a peaceful visit to an uneasy ally.

As he lay sleepless in his bed that night, Maelgwn,
too, had second thoughts about his decision. Aurora had
been passionate and eager when they made love, and his
body felt exquisitely satiated. But his mind was crowded
with doubts. How well did he really know this woman
who lay beside him, sleeping in the silvery moonlight?
Esylt had warned him that Aurora was weak and untrustworthy—was his sister blind with jealousy or was *he* the
one who was in thrall to his own desires?

Maelgwn watched Aurora sleep, tracing the delicate

curve of her cheek with his fingers. He had never before felt for a woman as he did for this one. It worried him. His whole future was bound up with this mysterious, foreign woman and he did not really know her—no, not at all.

They left at dawn. Aurora wore a pair of Elwyn's trousers and an old tunic. Her hair was braided to keep it out of her face, and she wore a veil to protect her fair skin.

Maelgwn was used to riding next to Balyn, but Aurora's horse trotted beside him now, and Balyn had dropped back next to Rhys and Gareth. Maelgwn had to admire Aurora's skill on a horse, but it was strange to see her dressed in men's clothes. If anything, the close-fitting garments emphasized her feminine charms, and Maelgwn tantalized himself with the thought of sliding down the awkward trousers to reveal the creamy naked curves of her hips.

Esylt rode at the end of the caravan near the wagon full of gifts for Cunedda. Next to her rode a lean, swarthy man named Grimerwyn, who appeared to be her most recent lover. A single slave drove the wagon, and from his vivid red hair, Aurora was sure he was kin of the Irish slave girl she recalled from her first morning at Caer Eryri.

Aurora was happy and excited. Riding next to Maelgwn reminded her of the times she had gone riding with Marcus. Although she was not entirely comfortable with Maelgwn, it was nice to feel as if he were her companion.

As usual, Maelgwn said little. Aurora had found him to be a quiet man, despite his ability to speak well before a crowded feasting hall or to make his men comfortable with a friendly word or jest. Even though they were married, Aurora seldom saw Maelgwn alone, except when they were in bed together, and then he was usually too busy—doing other things with his mouth—to talk! She was looking forward to a chance to converse at length with him.

"Maelgwn," she began. "Tell me about Cunedda's people—what are they like?"

"Cunedda's grandsire, and mine, were brothers, but there was little influence of the Romans in the north, and the Brigantes still keep the old ways. The land they live in is too wild and densely forested for farming. They hunt the red deer and the wild boar, and herd their cattle. Cunedda's army is undisciplined, and they have no cavalry, but they are excellent bowmen and fierce fighters."

Aurora considered this wealth of information carefully. "What of the women of the Brigantes? Does Cunedda have a wife?"

"I believe he has several."

"Why, that is . . . barbaric!"

Maelgwn looked at her with a mocking, amused stare. "That may be, but it is his people's way."

Aurora looked back at him in agitation. "Do the Cymry . . . Would you ever . . . ?"

Maelgwn laughed. "Me? I have enough trouble with the one wife I have," he answered wryly. "At any rate, Cunedda's wives may be of noble blood, but none of them have brought him the wealth of Viroconium."

"That is it then?" Aurora asked, her eyes flashing. "I bring you power and wealth, so I am valuable to you?"

"What do you want me to say?" Maelgwn asked, the edge of frustration creeping into his voice. "I cannot say that I would have married you if you were a poor free-man's daughter."

Aurora bit her lips silently. How could she admit to her husband that she longed for something more than respect—that she dreamed of love and tenderness, laughter and companionship?

"So, you go to meet with Cunedda to discuss his problems with the Picts and the Irish?" Aurora asked when her irritation had begun to cool.

Maelgwn nodded.

"If you help him, send him warriors and supplies for battle, what will he do for you in return?"

Maelgwn smiled at his wife. For all her innocent face, her mind was sharp—she knew the right questions to ask. "Perhaps someday I will need Cunedda's help and perhaps he will help me."

"Perhaps? You doubt him?"

Maelgwn looked appraisingly at his wife. He was used to guarding his tongue carefully around all but his officers and closest counselors. Was it wise to trust his new wife with doubts regarding his allies? She could have little understanding of the heritage of conflict that haunted the tribes of north Britain. Blood was no proof against treachery—you had only to look at the deadly rivalry that had destroyed his family to know that.

"What interest do these subjects have for you, Aurora?"

"If I am to be your wife and queen, it would seem

wise to know a little of who are your true enemies and allies."

"You need not trouble yourself on that account. I have advisers and officers enough to deal with those problems. I only expect you to be appropriately beautiful and charming when we get to Manau Gotodin."

Aurora could feel her rebellious temper rising again. It had obviously been too much to hope that Maelgwn would ever treat her as his equal, or even trust her as much as he did his soldiers. Hot anger flashed through Aurora; now the day did not seem so fine nor the journey so exciting.

Maelgwn looked regretfully at the tense set of his wife's mouth. He had not meant to hurt her, but why was she interested in these things anyway? It reminded him too much of Esylt. He wanted his wife to spend her time pleasing him, not worrying about politics.

They rode in silence for a while—Aurora, angry and hurt, and Maelgwn regretful but stubborn. As usual, Aurora could not hold onto her anger, and it disappeared as quickly as it had come. Before they reached the shadow of another hill, she found herself full of eager questions again.

"Do you rule over all this land?" she asked her husband, gesturing to the vast gray, blue and russet slopes which surrounded them.

"Aye, though 'rule' is an extravagant word to use. The tribes that live here have a simple life, herding their cattle and sheep over the moors as their grandfathers did. I act as their protector, and they give me homage, but truly the eagles that fly above these high peaks are as much lords of the hills as I."

Aurora was immediately struck by the image of the majestic eagle looking down on his wild, forbiddingly beautiful kingdom. How much Maelgwn was like those lords of the air—powerful, solitary, ruthless. No wonder he felt so at home in his mountain fortress.

"Why do they need a protector?" Aurora asked after her thoughts had run their course. "It would seem that no one would disturb them here."

"Perhaps they don't," Maelgwn said slowly. "The Irish, the Picts, even the Romans—no invaders have ever really penetrated these wild lands. It is too much work to bring an army here, and there is too little wealth to seize to make it worthwhile. But even here the people have a sense of what it means to be Cymry, and they fear what would happen if that were lost."

Aurora shook her head in confusion. "Cymry—what does it mean?"

Maelgwn smiled, and his eyes grew misty with a softness Aurora seldom saw there. "It means 'the people' but it is more than a name. We have been here so long, we are part of the land. Already the barrows and magic places are ancient, and my people's heritage goes back even before that time. Our bards sing of heroes dead for centuries, gods that have inspired awe for a thousand years."

"And you hate all who came after you—like the Romans," Aurora said resentfully.

Maelgwn answered sharply, "I cannot hate the Romans. I'm sure that my people hated them—the Deceangli fought them most bitterly. You could say the Romans never really conquered us. They just built their forts and lived side-by-side with our settlements. But by now most people can see that the Romans gave us many good things—warhorses, Samian ware, wine. They taught us how to fight wars with discipline and strategy—otherwise we would never be able to hold our own against the Saxons, the Picts, the Irish.

"While I cannot live like your father—wearing a fine white toga, living in a boxlike house with patterned floors, statues and fountains, I can appreciate the beauty and wealth that the Romans made possible." He paused and a half-smile played upon his lips. "Everything I sought at Viroconium was there because of the Romans—even you."

"Do you appreciate *me?*"

"What makes you think I do not?"

Aurora was silent. It was humiliating to try and get a word of tenderness from this man. She would not beg for it. He seemed determined to see her as just another of Constantine's fine possessions he had stolen.

The silence weighed heavily between them, and they were both grateful when Balyn pulled up to discuss where they would make camp that night. Aurora let her horse fall behind the men, keeping to her own thoughts. Behind her she could hear Esylt's husky voice as she spoke to her companion. Despite Maelgwn's presence, Aurora felt uneasy at the thought of having to look at Esylt's face across the campfire. The hate that ran between them was so strong, it seemed to move in the air like a living thing. Esylt still had not said anything to Maelgwn about Aurora and Elwyn, but that did not mean she never planned to. As little trust as she had with her husband, Aurora did not want to see that little bit destroyed.

The rugged hills and marshy valleys made for hard riding, and Aurora was glad when Maelgwn decided to make camp early in a narrow valley filled with alder and birch. The sun was still visible in the misty sky, but evening fell quickly in the shadowed hills and the purple curtain of night descended over them.

They had not taken time to hunt for game, and so they made a meal of barley bannock, hard white cheese flavored with wild garlic, and heather beer. Aurora had no taste for the beer, and they had no wine, so she drank water. There was a sweet spring near where they camped, and Aurora was able to wash her face and hands after supper.

For a while they all sat companionably around the fire—Aurora and Maelgwn, silent, Balyn, Gareth and Rhys arguing the merits of a certain type of bridle bit in battle. Esylt had made the Irish slave wait upon her since they stopped, and when he finally fell into an exhausted sleep in the back of the pack wagon, she called out angrily to him. "Get up, you useless cur of a boy, and get us some more beer!"

Aurora sucked in her breath and looked at Maelgwn, her eyes full of hatred, but he shook his head and warned her with his eyes against speaking. Aurora tried to keep calm, even though she was choking on her anger, but when Grimerwyn bent his head close to Esylt's face and began to kiss her noisily, Aurora could endure it no longer—she stood up and walked off into the darkness.

The wan light of a lean moon soothed her some, but her hands were still clenched into fists when Maelgwn came to find her.

"Why do you tolerate her disgusting behavior?"

"What harm is it? It is her own pride and self-respect she squanders, not mine."

"But she is your sister!"

"And a free woman. Esylt chooses her own companions, and the way she wishes to live. As long as she does not interfere with my life, why should I care?"

"And *I* am not a free woman?" Aurora asked suddenly.

Maelgwn's voice changed, and she could sense the tense set of his jaw in the half-darkness. "No," he answered.

"But why not? I am a princess, too, I have as much royal blood in my veins as she—more if you count my Roman great-grandfather, who was nephew to Emperor Theodosius."

"Because you are my wife," Maelgwn said firmly. "When your father chose to give you to me, all your rights passed into my hands."

"My father did not choose!" Aurora said indignantly. "He was forced."

"It is all the same now."

"So I have no rights?"

"You have rights. You will live a life of comfort and leisure because of me. People will defer to your wishes and honor you always."

"But I have no rights with you? Is that what you are saying?"

Maelgwn turned to face her, and she could see his face—hard, arrogant and as cold as a statue. "According to Cymry law, there are some things you could divorce me for."

"Such as?"

"Bringing another woman into our home . . . or if I am incapable in bed."

Aurora laughed mirthlessly. "And what of you? According to Cymry law, for what reasons can you divorce me?"

"A Cymry man can divorce his wife is she is unfaithful or if she mocks his manhood. But since I am king I have more reasons—if your father breaks his promise with me or if you fail to bear me a son, for example."

"But if my father keeps his part of the bargain, you can hardly afford to divorce me for any reason," Aurora suggested cagily.

"Isn't it odd," Maelgwn said coolly. "If I bring up my arrangement with your father, you fly into a rage, yet you use it whenever you are afraid."

"I am not afraid!" Aurora hissed in fury.

Maelgwn pulled her to him, and the touch of the cold metal of the dagger at his belt made her jump. His hands moved over her body intimidatingly, first stroking her roughly, lingering tantalizingly for a moment between her legs, and then finally moving up to hold her throat in a firm, but gentle grasp.

"I do not want you to be very afraid of me, Aurora," he whispered. "Just a little."

It was hopeless, Aurora thought as she began to respond to the sensations Maelgwn's strong fingers aroused in her. Maelgwn had years of experience in negotiating, testing his opponents, finding their weaknesses and measuring how to dominate them. After these few weeks of knowing Maelgwn, she still did not understand him, or know his vulnerable points—except for Esylt, and that was a weapon she dared not use.

Aurora gave in to her husband. It felt good, and she did not want to be fighting him in the lonely, whispering darkness. She let him find the tie to her trousers and impatiently pull the loose garment off of her. He rode her like a stallion then, standing up. His back arched against a tree as he pumped into her, and Aurora grabbed his strong shoulders and held on.

Eighteen

The rest of the journey was uneventful. They rode long hours over endless hills and valleys. The scent of the sea followed them, but they never set eyes on it—they were always a few miles inland. Despite her early eagerness for the journey, Aurora soon tired of riding. The pace they kept was more rapid than she had ever maintained for any length of time, and she was weary of the tasteless traveling food and of always being dirty.

They stopped occasionally at settlements of the local people, although they were hardly proper towns or even villages. The small, dark people stared at them wild-eyed. Although a few of them ventured to speak with Maelgwn and his men, they viewed Aurora with awe. In these desolate places, even the young women were hollow-eyed and careworn. Aurora realized how lucky she was to have been born into the comfort and security of her father's household. Beauty did not last long in this harsh place.

They reached the homeland of the Brigantes. The forest grew thicker and more impenetrable, and several times it seemed that they would not be able to get the wagon through. Maelgwn would consult with Rhys, and hours later the men would somehow cut a track through the dense undergrowth. The heavy moist air and the darkness of the forest oppressed Aurora, and she wondered what kind of people could stand to live in this dreary, spooky wilderness.

At last they reached the edge of the forest and looked out on a valley studded with gray-blue lakes. On one side of the valley there was a high, grassy hill, and on this natural lookout was built a low stone wall with a few dozen circular huts huddled inside. It appeared that Gwenaseth was right—the Brigantes did live like crude savages.

"This is it?" Aurora asked Maelgwn dubiously.

"Aye. It is only a summer camp. Their winter camp is further north and has better defenses."

As they rode toward the camp, people came out to greet them dressed in brightly woven cloaks and heavy jewelry. The Brigantes immediately reminded Aurora of the Cymry, although they were bigger and even more dramatic-looking. Many of the men were taller than Maelgwn, and the women would have towered over most Cymry men. Their coloring was striking, too. Reddish hair was common, although it was a deeper shade than Gwenaseth's and not so bright as the Irish slave's.

The biggest man came forward to meet them, and Aurora guessed that he must be the chief, Cunedda. Esylt spurred her horse ahead, dismounted, and threw herself into Cunedda's arms. The man picked her up as if she were a child and swung her around delightedly. Aurora heard his excited words of greeting but could not understand him. It seemed the Brigantes spoke a dialect different from that of Maelgwn's people.

The rest of them dismounted, and Maelgwn greeted Cunedda formally. Several men came up to Maelgwn, and Aurora guessed that they must be Cunedda's brothers. As Aurora moved close to Maelgwn, one of the men, who had hair the color of a fox's pelt and eyes of brilliant blue-green, stared at her in awe. Maelgwn saw his interest and pulled Aurora forward proudly, holding her arm possessively.

"Cunedda, king of the Brigantes, I would like to present my queen, Aurora, daughter of Constantine of Viroconium."

Maelgwn had spoken in the familiar British speech, and Cunedda answered him in a heavily-accented, but pleasing voice: "I had heard Maelgwn brought back much wealth from the Cornovii—now I see what riches he has plundered."

Cunedda smiled at Aurora in a leering, open-mouthed fashion that both pleased and dismayed her. His dark-blue eyes did not meet her gaze for long, but moved quickly down to assess her body appreciatively.

Aurora returned their host's probing look. Cunedda was not a handsome man—his reddish hair was thinning, and his eyes showed too much white, giving him a surprised, excited appearance—but he certainly was imposing. His body was as broad as a tree trunk and his huge hands and thick neck bespoke tremendous physical power.

Aurora bowed gracefully as Cunedda's eyes returned to her face. She still felt embarrassed. Esylt's ease with their host disturbed her, and she could not help wondering what lies her sister-in-law might tell Cunedda about her when she got him alone.

After their horses were taken care of, Maelgwn and Aurora were led to one of the round huts. The structure

was made of hides stretched over branches, with a smoke
hole in the center. It hardly looked to Aurora like a proper
dwelling in which to house guests, but the inside seemed
comfortable enough. A pile of furs and sheepskins in the
corner promised a good night's sleep at last, and on a
low table there was a bronze ewer of water for washing,
and a pottery urn.

When their escort had left them, Aurora gratefully
stripped off her grimy clothes and started to wash. She
had hardly begun to splash her face when she felt
Maelgwn's strong hands reach around to cup her breasts,
and felt his warm breath blowing in her ear.

"Not now, Maelgwn," she said with a shiver. "I am
all dirty and sweaty from traveling."

"I do not care. This is a raw, wild place, and I want
you as you are—salty and tangy like the sea," he added
as he began to lick her neck.

Aurora sighed passively, feeling his fingers reach for
the crack between her legs and rub her there. Slowly his
mouth moved down her body, leaving a wet pathway that
cooled in the air. At last he reached the tip of her pelvis,
and his hands pulled her thighs apart before he tasted
her with his tongue. Aurora stood unsteadily, with her
legs supported by Maelgwn's shoulders as he licked and
probed. This was something she must tell Gwenaseth
about, she thought dreamily. She was sure that not every
man was so wonderfully skilled at this sort of lovemaking.

Maelgwn knew her tolerance—Aurora could stand the
teasing, light touch of his tongue for only so long before
she wanted something more substantial within her. He always took her to the edge—left her gasping and weak—

and then he knew he could find his own satisfaction in any position he wished. Tonight he pushed her down on the cozy bedplace and lifted her legs up high, almost to his shoulders.

Aurora was overwhelmed—pushed to the edge of ecstasy and beyond. It was like sliding off a cliff as she surrendered to the dizzying, blind exhilaration of her body. When she returned to awareness again, she found that Maelgwn still thundered within her, and she held on, amazed that he could control his own climax for so long after she had lost herself in the radiant waves of her own.

At last Maelgwn moaned, and Aurora felt the hot, sweaty weight of him upon her. For a moment she wanted to cradle his burning face against her breast, but she did not. He was too heavy to move, and he seemed content.

"Did you bring your green dress?" he asked as he watched her wash in the firelight a few moments later.

"No. It would have been ruined after being squashed in a pack all this way."

"Uhhh," Maelgwn grunted, sounding disappointed.

"I brought this white one," she said quickly, pulling it out of the leather bag that she carried her things in. It was simple and showed off her figure well, but perhaps in Maelgwn's eyes it did not look rich enough to suit his queen. "Will this do?" she asked, suddenly doubtful.

"Put it on, I cannot tell like that," he said impatiently. "But wait, before you do, come here and let me look at you one more time."

Aurora thought they would never get to the feast—and

it was held in their honor. She had not even begun to dress when Maelgwn had pulled her down to the sheepskins again. There was something erotic about this strange alluring place, but Maelgwn's strenuous attentions had left her sore, and she had barely had time to dress and take out her braids.

Gwenaseth had been right, she decided, looking down at the dress. The simple style and creamy whiteness of the gown stood out dramatically from the clash of vivid colors the other women wore. With her hair smoothed into a thick wavy mane, she looked more elegant than any other woman in the thatched-roofed feasting hall. What would her mother and sisters think of her though, she thought with a smile. She looked like a Saxon, with all the jewelry, and married Roman women were never supposed to wear their hair down in public.

But then, her family would have been horrified by everything about the Brigantes. Even for this formal event, they dressed like savages. In the warmth of the hall, the men had taken off their furs and their cloaks, and Aurora saw that underneath they wore little—shawls woven of several different colors over one shoulder and short tunics that barely reached to their bare knees. In the flickering light their fair skin writhed with weird shapes and colors, for many of the men had pictures of beasts and patterns covering their arms and chests.

The men ate greedily, stabbing their knives into the barely cooked haunch of beef to tear off large chunks, which they washed down with great gulps of heather beer and mead. Aurora watched, appalled but fascinated by the crudeness of their hosts. The Brigante women ate separately from the men, and Aurora and Esylt were the

only women close to Maelgwn and Cunedda. They had
a place near the fireplace, and their food had been
brought to them in trenchers so that they did not have
to tear at the carcass like animals. Still, Aurora felt awkward, sitting on the floor, trying to balance her cup as
she took a bite.

The hall was smoky and full of menace, and Aurora
was glad to have Maelgwn's reassuring presence so near.
She watched her husband carefully. Maelgwn looked relaxed and at ease, but she knew that nothing escaped his
keen eyes. For once he was not the biggest man at the
gathering, but it did not matter—the aura of power and
kingship marked him as clearly as if he wore it as a
mantle.

Esylt, on the other hand, fit right in with the uncouth
Brigantes, Aurora noted with disgust. Her sister-in-law
was sharing a cup of mead and some ribald jest with
Cunedda. In the crowded atmosphere of the hall, Aurora
was only inches away from her enemy. She watched sur-
reptiously as Esylt moved her jeweled hands over
Cunedda's bulky body. The man obviously enjoyed her
lewd attentions, and in a moment, he began to return
them—sliding his reddish, raw-boned fingers into the
neck of Esylt's gown.

Aurora repelled, turned away, and glanced at Maelgwn,
who sat impassively, sipping his beer. His face looked
calm and imperturbable, but Aurora saw the slight twitch
in his jaw, and knew that he, too, was displeased by
Cunedda's and Esylt's familiarity. It was bad enough for
them to fondle each other so obviously in this public
place, but it was worse to know that Cunedda's wives—
and perhaps Esylt's lover—were watching, too. Aurora

hoped that Maelgwn would never be so crude as to caress another woman while she watched. She had a feeling he would end up with her eating knife in his gullet if he ever shamed her so!

Perhaps Cunedda tired of Esylt, too, for presently he turned to Maelgwn and began to converse politely with him. Aurora could not quite hear what they were saying, and she let her mind wander, glancing around the large room in curiosity. She picked out the figure of the young red-haired man she presumed to be Cunedda's brother as he stood near the wall with a group of other warriors. With his extravagant coloring he easily outshone the other Brigante men, and Aurora found it hard to pull her eyes away.

The young warrior was much younger than Cunedda, and it was likely he had a different mother. He was also leaner and more gracefully built, and the air of fierceness about him came not from brute strength, but from a fiery energy that burned in his sharp-boned face. He was handsome like a wild animal, Aurora thought, intrigued, and as she watched, he looked directly at her, catching her in the act of admiring him.

Aurora glanced away in embarrassment, realizing too late how inappropriate, even dangerous, her behavior was. As she stared down at her wine, shamefaced, she could feel the young warrior's magnetic eyes boring into her, and she anxiously hoped that no one else in the room had noticed their quick exchange of glances.

She looked over at Maelgwn and Cunedda and was relieved to find that the two men were still deep in their discussion. But her indiscretion had not gone completely unnoticed. Aurora realized that Esylt was staring at her intently. She kept her glance directed down, avoiding the venomous hatred in Esylt's glittering blue eyes. Her heart pounded ominously in her chest, and the chill of fear that moved into her bones deepened as she flicked her eyes up to see that Esylt had gotten up and was walking in the direction of the red-haired man.

Aurora almost jumped when Maelgwn put a hand on her knee to get her attention. She looked into his smiling face for a long moment before she figured out that he was explaining that the next part of the festivities—the gift giving—was about to begin. Within seconds, servants came to take the remains of the food away, and Cunedda stood to formally welcome the Cymry to Manau Gotodin.

Balyn and Gareth had long since left the hall, and now they returned with the red-haired slave. Each of them carried a heavy load, and one by one, the gifts of Maelgwn to his host were brought forward and displayed—baskets of grain, jars of wine and oil, and then the more luxurious items: a small box of pearls from the Gwynedd coast that was passed around among the delighted women, finely crafted iron tools, and the beautiful skin of a spotted cat, the snarling head still attached.

Then it was Cunedda's turn. Several women came forward to present the gifts, and for a moment Aurora's attention was focused on the women themselves.

In addition to their exceptional height, the Brigante women looked very strong, and to Aurora, they seemed almost as frightening as the men. They were beautiful, though, in a haughty, lurid way. Their skin was milky white, with blue veins that shone in their necks, and their hair was thick and heavy, in varying shades of red and reddish gold. They wore their hair in fat braids, fastened

with ornaments of gold and bronze. Aurora saw in awe
that one of the women had braids to her knees.

The women walked toward Maelgwn with stately, regal
grace. The first one brought forward a pile of beautifully
dressed hides and laid them at Maelgwn's feet. Another
carried a flash of gold in each hand. When she reached
Maelgwn, she kneeled down and placed a heavy gold
torque around his neck, where it flashed in the firelight.
Sitting as close as she was, Aurora could see that the
ends of the torque were formed into snarling wolf heads.

An identical, but smaller torque was placed around
Esylt's neck by the same woman. At first Aurora felt a
stab of anger that Esylt was deemed worthy of such a
royal gift, while she was not, but her disappointment
faded when she saw the necklace a third woman had
brought to place on *her* neck. It was made out of large
creamy white beads that looked like bone, but which had
a finer, more delicate texture. Each bead had been intri-
cately carved into a tiny figure, and as Aurora looked
down in awe, graceful birds and strange and fanciful
beasts seemed to dance around her neck. Many of the
animals depicted, she had never seen, but from her lessons with Arian, she suspected that one was a lion, another an elephant. There was even a dragon with a minute
arrowlike tail and forked tongue.

"It is beautiful!" Aurora gasped in delight, and then
looked up and saw that her pleasure was mirrored in
both Cunedda and Maelgwn's faces.

"It is a rare and beautiful gift for a rare and beautiful
woman," Cunedda said in his heavily accented voice.
Aurora smiled back at him, well-pleased with the extravagant compliment and gift.

The gift giving did not seem to be quite over. Aurora glanced up and saw that Cunedda's fox-haired brother stood in front of her.

He smiled as he knelt down to her, and Aurora smiled back, admiring his strong white teeth. He placed a soft leather bag gently in her lap and then stood and bowed gracefully. The round object within the bag had a familiar feel, and Aurora moved eagerly to open it.

The drawstring neck opened easily, and Aurora reached inside and pulled out the rather hairy object. It was a human head—dead for some time and beginning to rot. Blind, decaying eyes stared at her from the shrunken face, and Aurora screamed and dropped the head. It rolled slowly down to her feet, and as it rolled, Aurora caught the glimmer of gold lining the inside of the skull.

Aurora sat stunned, speechless, and looked around at the startled faces watching her. Maelgwn's face was a cold deadly mask. Cunedda and Esylt had begun to laugh, but the rest of the room was silent, and Aurora could sense their chilling disapproval.

Aurora moved her eyes up uneasily to face the young man who had presented her with the gift. The muscles of his neck were corded in rage and his whole handsome face was curdled with hatred. She shook her head pleadingly—she had not meant to offend him—but the gesture seemed to infuriate him even more, for he whirled and stomped off.

Aurora looked back imploringly at Maelgwn, but his eyes were hard, and she knew he would not help her. Even Balyn and Gareth, who had come to sit by Maelgwn, stared at her in open embarrassment. But it was the sound of Esylt's cackling laughter that unnerved her. Shaken and confused, Aurora jumped up and ran out of the hall.

No one moved or tried to stop her, but even out in the damp darkness, Aurora's panic did not subside. She had the feeling of having done something truly awful, and she expected at any minute to be punished for it. The sound of her own footsteps on the rough, rocky ground sent her heart up into her throat. She kept anticipating a knife in her ribs or a crushing hand on her throat, and for a few seconds she was too terrified to figure out the direction to the guest lodge.

Gradually the fresh air cleared her head, and her eyes adjusted to the darkness. It was a misty, heavily overcast night, and it took some time to locate the hut. When Aurora finally found it and looked inside to see the reassuring clutter of her clothes and possessions, she was so overcome with relief that she rushed in and sank down trembling on the skins near the dying fire.

As she closed her eyes, the image of the rotting trophy head flashed into her mind, and she gagged. How could the Brigantes even touch such things, she wondered in revulsion? Yet, it was obviously an important and precious gift—the gold that lined the skull must have been enough to make a torque as fine as the ones that had been given to Maelgwn and Esylt. The young man who gave her the head had meant to honor her, Aurora realized wretchedly, and she had managed to humiliate him—and to dishonor Maelgwn as well.

Aurora shuddered again in the cozy sheepskins. She felt almost too miserable to cry. She had done something terrible, and then had run cowardly away with Esylt's taunting laughter ringing in her ears.

Then it hit Aurora like a thunderbolt. She had seen Esylt talk to the young man after he had caught Aurora staring at him. That was right before the gift exchange began, and Aurora had not seen the red-haired man again until he walked up with his hideous gift. It all made sense now—no doubt Esylt had suggested the gift of the trophy head, knowing well what Aurora's probable reaction would be. Esylt had planned the whole thing; she had deliberately contrived to humiliate Aurora, to disgrace her before one of her husband's most important allies.

Consuming anger and hatred replaced Aurora's shame. She would not take all the blame for her mistake this time. Esylt had gone too far in her attempts to make Maelgwn reject her as his wife. This time Aurora intended to confront Maelgwn with Esylt's treachery and make him realize what a monster his sister was!

Maelgwn walked to the guest lodge wearily. His head was spinning with fatigue, mead and the unpleasant surprises of the last few hours. It was as if his worst fears had been realized. He had brought Aurora with him on this journey to impress his ally with her beauty and elegance, and she had ended up embarrassing him and perhaps endangering their future relationship with the Brigantes.

Still, he could not really blame Aurora for her behavior. Few women who were unfamiliar with the old Celtic custom of trophy heads would not have greeted the gift with some shock. If only she had made an effort to apologize, to smooth things over instead of running off like a distraught, frightened child.

Maelgwn sighed. He was disappointed, but he did not want to be too hard on Aurora. His wife was a spoiled, childish woman, but in a way, that was part of her charm. He could still see the radiant beauty of her face as she fingered the beautiful ivory necklace—she was a woman who was meant to be indulged, and somehow he could not help himself. Even now, tired and discouraged, he could not forget the thrill of watching her naked in the firelight—and the rapture of her silken skin and streaming hair covering him.

Maelgwn shook off the enticing image. He must be firm with Aurora. If she was to be his queen, she had to learn more self-control. Tomorrow she had to make a public apology for her behavior, especially to Ferdic. Did Aurora even realize that the young man was Cunedda's oldest son and that someday he would probably be leader of the Brigantes? Maelgwn hoped they could settle things amicably with the young prince. Surely Ferdic would not let something that happened with a mere woman affect an important trading relationship and alliance.

Maelgwn lifted the hide flap which covered the door of the guest lodge and went inside. He expected to find Aurora in bed, her face tear-streaked and miserable. Instead he found her staring grimly into the fire.

"About your behavior tonight . . ." he began, trying to be tactful.

"My behavior tonight—what of Esylt's?" Aurora snapped.

Maelgwn was almost too surprised to be angry. He had not expected her to attack him. "I have told you that

Esylt's behavior is no concern of yours. It hardly reflects on me the way your rudeness does."

"What if I told you that Esylt planned the whole incident with the . . . the head? That she deliberately arranged it to humiliate me." Aurora had jumped up and stood facing him, her eyes flashing in the firelight.

"I don't believe you," Maelgwn answered flatly. "She would not risk our relationship with Cunedda and his son Ferdic for such an absurd form of vengeance."

"His son?" Aurora stopped and her face grew still and thoughtful.

"Aye. That young man you offended so rudely is the man I may well have to deal with in years to come as the leader of the Brigantes."

"I didn't know. I thought he was Cunedda's younger brother."

"Well, that hardly excuses you!" Maelgwn continued angrily. "Aurora, you must admit that you have no one to blame but yourself for your foolish behavior. It is time you grew up and thought before you acted."

"I tell you, Esylt was behind it!" Aurora cried out in frustration. "I saw her talking to Ferdic right before the gift giving began. I know that she put the idea into his head. You saw how she laughed. She didn't care that her laughter humiliated Cunedda's son even further."

Maelgwn threw his cloak down irritably. "I am tired of your squabbling with Esylt. You blame her for everything that displeases you."

"And I am tired of you standing by while she insults me! Did you know that when you were gone to visit the coast, she followed me and threatened me? She warned me to return to Viroconium or she would tell you lies about me."

There was a flicker of interest in Maelgwn's eyes. "Why did you not come to me with this sooner? What lies did she mean to tell me?"

Aurora stopped, realizing too late how much she had said. "It was . . . she threatened to tell you that Elwyn and I . . . that I were unfaithful to you. It is not true, of course," she continued breathlessly. "Elwyn was just being kind to me—he would never dream of being disloyal to you or unfaithful to Gwenaseth."

Maelgwn's face was a mask—calm, unreadable. His voice was light and ironic. "It is not Elwyn that I worry about when it comes to loyalty . . . it is you. You have told me enough how unwillingly you came to this marriage. How do I know that I can trust *you?*"

Aurora tried to meet her husband's eyes levelly, but she could not. She was thinking of Esylt's taunting words.

"I would never be unfaithful to you Maelgwn," she said softly.

Maelgwn took a shaky breath. "No, I suppose you would not. You are probably too afraid of me." His voice was bitter and scornful, and Aurora wondered what she had done wrong.

Maelgwn tried to fight back the feelings of helpless jealousy that raged within him. How could he admit, even to himself, that he wanted more than Aurora's loyalty and fear of him? He wanted her to love him, wanted her feelings for him to be so strong that they erased from her mind the thought of every other man except him.

Aurora was frightened by her husband's stark, murderous face as he stared at her in the firelight, but even in her fear, her tongue seemed to form the resentful angry words: "You are a fine one to be jealous," she shouted. "What of me? You have always chosen to respect Esylt's feelings over mine. Someday you will find that you cannot have both of us—someday you will have to choose between us!"

Aurora's furious words gradually penetrated Maelgwn's fevered mind, and the rage and jealousy dropped away from him as quickly as they had come.

"Aye," he said softly, staring into the fire. "You are right, I suppose, I will have to choose after all."

He turned back to her, and Aurora saw that his face was once again controlled—the inscrutable mask.

"It does not matter. The important thing is to salvage what goodwill we have left with our hosts." Maelgwn's eyes bored into Aurora, and his voice was implacable, commanding. "Tomorrow, you will apologize . . . to everyone."

Aurora nodded. She knew that begging her hosts' pardon would be easier than making things right with Maelgwn.

Nineteen

The next day Aurora knelt before Cunedda and his son and spoke the words that Maelgwn had taught her. Cunedda smiled at her lustily, and she knew no harm was taken on his part, but of Ferdic she was not so sure. His beautiful blue-green eyes flicked over her face coolly, and she could not tell if the hurt had been soothed or aggravated. She worried that she had made a lifelong enemy.

After an awkward, rather gloomy meal, they set out for home. Aurora could barely stand the sight of Esylt and her crude escort, and she rode as far from them as she could. Maelgwn was moody and preoccupied, seldom speaking to anyone. Aurora found herself riding beside Balyn, and the big man remained friendly and cheerful despite the obvious tension between Aurora and the king. Balyn's warmth helped Aurora endure the long, exhausting days of traveling, but the nights were nearly unbearable. Aurora slept alone, nursing her anger toward Esylt, blaming her sister-in-law for ruining things with Maelgwn. Aurora's emotions were usually fleeting, but this time her anger did not ebb, but grew and grew. By the time they reached the valley below Caer Eryri, she was seething with hatred.

* * *

Elwyn and Gwenaseth waited arm in arm for Maelgwn and the other travelers to arrive. As he drew near to the fortress, Maelgwn smiled confidently and gestured in greeting to his people. Aurora remained grim and unsmiling, her face pale and tense. Gwenaseth and Elwyn looked at each other uneasily.

"Find out what is wrong with Aurora," Elwyn whispered. "Something has happened between her and Maelgwn."

Gwenaseth nodded.

Aurora and Gwenaseth climbed the tower stairs, neither of them speaking. The slave boy followed after them, carrying Aurora's things. As soon as he had left and the door shut behind him, Gwenaseth turned to Aurora.

"God in heaven, Aurora, what is wrong?"

"It is all Esylt's fault! I'm afraid Maelgwn will never forgive me!" Aurora burst into tears.

"Tell me what happened," Gwenaseth said, putting a comforting arm around Aurora's shoulders.

In a voice shaking with rage and frustration, Aurora told the story of Ferdic's gruesome gift and of her fight with Maelgwn afterwards.

"Well, I suppose you did act impolitely in rejecting the trophy head," Gwenaseth said when Aurora had finished. "But I am not sure I would have been able to do much better." She shuddered. "I told you that the Brigantes were not decent people."

"But it is not just Ferdic and the Brigantes. Once again Maelgwn has taken Esylt's side against me."

"You don't know that for sure," Gwenaseth pointed

out. "Perhaps Maelgwn is just worried about what will happen with the alliance."

Aurora shook her head grimly. "No, it is more than that. Maelgwn will not speak to me, will hardly even look at me."

"It wasn't appropriate for you to tell Maelgwn that he must choose between you and his sister. It is your place to yield to him, not the other way around. Perhaps that is why he is so angry."

"Why?" Aurora asked bitterly. "Why must I accept Esylt's influence in Maelgwn's life? She is evil! She is deliberately scheming to get rid of me."

"Then you are playing right into her hands," Gwenaseth noted grimly. "If you continue to make Maelgwn angry, she may well succeed in getting rid of you."

Aurora looked troubled. "You do not think . . . that Maelgwn would disavow the marriage . . . set me aside?"

Gwenaseth shook her head. "I don't know, but perhaps you had better consider that possibility and think of a way to make up with him."

Aurora looked down at her hands. "I don't know how to make things right with Maelgwn."

"It is easy. Just tell him that you are sorry and that you love him."

"Love! How can I love him? He doesn't care about me at all."

"Perhaps you don't know what love is. Many a young girl is disappointed when she discovers that marriage is different from the dreams and fancies she nurtured growing up."

"I *do* know what love is!" Aurora said defensively. "It

is trust . . . and tenderness . . . and companionship . . ." Her voice trailed off and she blushed.

Gwenaseth stared at Aurora suspiciously. "Who was he?"

Aurora could not meet Gwenaseth's eyes—she had said too much already. "He was . . . no one. No one I could ever marry," she answered with resignation.

"I had guessed there was someone else. How close were you? Did you and he . . . ?"

"No!" Aurora answered emphatically. "We were more like children playing together than lovers. I was a maiden when I married Maelgwn."

"Then there is no reason you cannot care for Maelgwn. He is your husband, Aurora. You must try to be a good wife. It seems you have found much pleasure in bed together—that is more than many women have."

"Perhaps I could care for him if it were not for Esylt. The sight of her burns like bile in my throat. Never will I forget that first day when she taunted me and ridiculed me and Maelgwn did nothing."

Gwenaseth shook her head at Aurora's flashing eyes and flushed face. "You cannot win your battle with Esylt by blaming Maelgwn. It is only if you win his trust that he will finally see his sister for what she is and take your side."

"But how do I do that?" Aurora asked imploringly. "He will barely even speak to me. It is humiliating to have everyone see how cold he is to me."

"He may be cold to you, but it is also clear he has a real weakness for your beauty," Gwenaseth said with a smile. "Leave it to me. We will find a way to get Maelgwn back in your bed."

* * *

Maelgwn was tired and irritable. He had gone over the visit with the Brigantes with his council, dealing lightly with the incident of Aurora and the trophy head. It served no purpose for his men to hold Aurora's mistake against her, and they might well question his judgment in choosing her as his wife.

Certainly *he* questioned his judgment. It was not just that Aurora was impulsive and emotional. He could forgive that in a woman—in many ways it was preferable to Esylt's cleverness. No, it was the effect she had on him that was frightening. Since he had first taken Aurora as his wife, he was either distracted and lovesick, or so angry he wanted to kill someone. And this jealousy he felt—he had always considered jealousy a poison, a sickness—and yet something about Aurora made him mad with it. If he had any sense he would probably send her back to her father. But if he did that, he would be admitting that he had made a mistake, that he was wrong to marry her. He did not want to give Esylt the satisfaction of gloating over his error in judgment.

Esylt. He still had to visit her today. Some of what Aurora said rang true. Esylt was certainly capable of the sort of mischief that Aurora had accused her of. It was unlikely that Esylt would ever admit to scheming against Aurora, but he had to question her.

Maelgwn rapped impatiently on Esylt's chamber door and waited. After a moment, she answered and greeted him with a lazy, sloe-eyed smile as she motioned him in.

"I am honored. After a week of traveling together, my brother has not yet tired of my company."

Maelgwn stepped into the room impatiently. "There is something I wish to discuss with you, and I could not talk freely with others around."

Esylt gestured disdainfully, bidding him speak.

"It is regarding the incident with Ferdic and the trophy head."

"Of course," Esylt smiled gleefully. "I'm sure you will want to take Aurora on all your diplomatic visits, since she has shown herself to be so tactful and quick-witted."

Maelgwn ignored her sarcasm. "I wish to know your part in that unfortunate event."

"My part?" Esylt's eyes were opaque and guileless.

"Aye, Aurora suggested that you put Ferdic up to presenting her with that gruesome gift to embarrass her."

"Why would I do that? I have no desire to make an enemy of Ferdic."

"Yet you joined Cunedda in laughing at Ferdic's humiliation."

Esylt shrugged. "It *was* funny. Aurora looked as if her eyes would pop out of her head. I don't think it was such bad manners to join our host in a joke. Cunedda rules the Brigantes—Ferdic will have to earn the kingship in his own time."

Maelgwn moved restlessly to the other side of Esylt's chamber. There was an odor here that always annoyed him—some sharp perfume that made his head ache and reminded him unhappily of his mother. If it had not been for Aurora, he would never have come here when he was already tired and short-tempered.

"Aurora also said that while I was visiting the coastal

forts this past moon cycle, you followed her and threatened her."

Esylt snorted derisively. "I have made no secret of my dislike for her—if she considers that a threat . . ."

Maelgwn broke in impatiently: "She said that you threatened to tell me lies about her if she did not return to Viroconium. Explain that to me."

Esylt's face was composed and serious for once.

"It would not be a lie to tell you that I saw her and Elwyn laughing and embracing alone by Lyn Fenydd, but the conclusions you draw from that are your own affair. It would not be a lie to tell you that Aurora was eyeing poor Ferdic quite eagerly that night while you talked with Cunedda. Has it ever occurred to you why Ferdic chose to give your wife such a costly gift? Can you honestly say that you trust your wife when you are away from her?"

Maelgwn struggled visibly to maintain his composure. He turned away from Esylt, trying to breathe normally. He did not want to give Esylt any more weapons for her cutting accusations.

He turned and spoke scornfully.

"You and Aurora are two of a kind. You both slyly seek to make me doubt the other, until I am trapped in your webs of deceit and malice and cannot find the truth. I am sick of you—both of you!"

Esylt laughed. "I am glad that you at last begin to see Aurora for what she is. Beware, Maelgwn. Your wife's pretty face hides a devious little mind, and her lush, young body is just a trap to make you weak and stupid."

Maelgwn walked up close to his sister and glared at her threateningly.

"I have had enough. I'm not going to listen to this anymore. I'll warn you again—leave Aurora alone!"

Maelgwn breathed a sigh of relief as he left Esylt's room. His head seemed to be spinning, and he took deep breaths of the fresh night air, trying to focus his thoughts. He walked impatiently, rather aimlessly in the fortress courtyard, struggling to work off the painful tension in his body.

Why had Esylt's words made him so angry? He was used to his sister's taunts, and usually he ignored her, but tonight her words had stung with the bite of truth. Could he, indeed, trust Aurora? There was something about her—a secretiveness and rebelliousness—that both tantalized him and frightened him.

"Maelgwn, my lord."

Maelgwn whirled violently at the sound of the soft voice behind him.

"Gwenaseth! By the light," he said, reverting to an old soldier's oath. "What is it?"

"It's Aurora," she answered shyly. "She bids you come to her. It's important."

"Is she ill?"

"Nay, it is not that, but she does have need of you."

Maelgwn stared doubtfully at the pale oval of Gwenaseth's face, half visible in the growing darkness. She was a sweet thing—his friend's daughter—and he suspected her of no scheming or manipulation.

"All right, I will go to her," he said quickly. "Just give me time to have something to eat."

Maelgwn finished eating hurriedly, and washed the last bites down with some old sour wine. Then he took off at a brisk walk toward the tower. He was troubled by this summons from his wife. What could she want? He certainly hoped that she was not going to complain to him about Esylt again.

Maelgwn climbed the tower stairs and pushed open the door without knocking. Then he stopped and stared dumbly at the sight that met him.

Aurora was lying naked on the bed. Her wavy hair was splayed out on the soft purple of the blanket like a mist around her face, and her skin glowed pink and smooth in the lamplight. He could see the graceful arch of her ribs below the soft mounds of her breasts. Her nipples were rosy and taut, and her slightly parted legs revealed the tantalizing pink moistness between them. Maelgwn had always thought Aurora was an exquisite woman, but tonight her beauty was heightened by the warm radiance of the lamplight and the unexpected thrill of her obvious readiness for him. As he watched, she ran her tongue over her parted lips and stared at him with a bold, seductive expression.

He moved toward her, drawn to her despite his fatigue.

"What is this?" he asked, abruptly motioning toward her enticing position, her obvious seductiveness.

"I want to make up for all the trouble I've caused you," she said, purring like a jewel-eyed cat. "You are my husband, and it is my responsibility to make you happy, not to burden you with my problems."

Maelgwn stood a few feet from the bed, undecided. He feared she was playing some game with him, but he was too aroused and confused to care.

He walked the few steps left to the bed, and Aurora moved smoothly to meet him. He stopped, and she reached up with fingers that trembled slightly and began to unfasten his scabbard. It dropped to the floor. She fumbled with the drawstring of his trousers until she had released them. She slid her cool, smooth hands down along his bare flesh.

Maelgwn groaned with desire. In all their time in bed, Aurora had never sought to touch him so boldly. At first, she stroked him clumsily, with an erratic, tentative touch. Gradually she responded to the feel of him, and her caresses became more sensual and rhythmic. Maelgwn watched her, enchanted by the sight of her rapt, lovely face as she caressed him. His arousal was intense, almost painful. Overcome, he leaned back and sighed; his mind was empty, his thoughts vacant swirls of pleasure.

He had grown used to the delicate stroke of her fingers when Aurora abruptly stopped. Maelgwn opened his eyes, ready to protest, but as he watched, Aurora moved her face toward him. He stared, fascinated, as she took him in her mouth, swallowing him with a quiver of her dainty chin. She had never looked so beautiful. Her eyes were closed in concentration and her hair streamed backward over the bed. He could watch no more; her ministrations left him blinded with rapture. As he neared climax, he pushed into her mouth roughly, and Aurora struggled for breath. Impatiently, Maelgwn raised her up and then pushed her down on the bed beneath him. He did not try to be gentle, but forced himself into her with brutal urgency. With only a few extravagant lunges, he found sweet release and collapsed, sweaty and spent, onto Aurora's cushioning flesh.

Maelgwn opened his eyes as Aurora twined her fingers in his hair with a luxuriant sigh. He was dull-headed and drowsy as if after too much wine, and he struggled against the grogginess that was overtaking him as he rolled off Aurora and stretched out next to her. Something nagged at him, despite his lethargy. He looked over at Aurora and pulled a tendril of curling hair away from her face, studying her closely. Her face was soft and blurred with sex and contentment, but her eyes watched him with a sharp, appraising look.

Maelgwn remembered Esylt's warning words. She had said something about Aurora using her body to make him weak and stupid. Ah, he thought—it was true. How skillfully his wife had manipulated him. She knew how much he desired her, and she had cleverly exploited his greedy lust.

The delicious flush of relaxation moving through Maelgwn's body changed to irritation. Did Aurora think that anytime she angered him, she could win him back with her expert, thrilling touch? For a moment Maelgwn stared at Aurora with narrowed eyes. Then he stood up brusquely and began to dress.

"What is it?" Aurora asked.

Maelgwn did not answer her but continued to pull on his clothes. He did not want to look at her. He knew her face would be confused and fearful, and he was afraid he would weaken and not be able to leave her. The power she had over him was terrifying—she was like a sorceress who could change her form to manipulate his pathetic heart. He had to get away. Now—while he still could!

Aurora stared in disbelief as the door to the tower chamber swung shut after Maelgwn. What had happened? A few moments ago Maelgwn had been sighing with satisfaction in her arms. The bed was still warm from his body, and her own body ached with the dull throb of gratified passion. But now he was gone, and without a word of farewell or tenderness.

Aurora pulled the blankets up protectively around her body, trying to figure out what had gone wrong. Maelgwn had wanted her; he had enjoyed their lovemaking. He had even reached out to stroke her hair when it was over. But then he had stared at her, hard, and a change had come over his face. For a moment he had looked as if he hated her.

A cold sweat was forming on Aurora's rapidly chilling skin, and her stomach churned with dread. She got up. She must find Maelgwn and speak to him. She must beg him—this time with words instead of caresses—to change his mind, to give her another chance.

Aurora groped for her clothes. As usual, they were strewn carelessly on the floor. She could not find one sandal, and she had to crawl awkwardly on the floor to look for it. At last she found everything and dressed with clumsy, shaking fingers. The clasp to her brooch eluded her, so she threw her cloak aside and left the room wearing only her loose gown.

The night was cloudy, and without a torch, the mazelike pathways of the fortress were dark and confusing. There were so many buildings past the great hall—the harness shop, the smithy, the stables, the kennels. Aurora was running, darting from one dark shape to the next. Surely the barracks were here, but no, she was too far, a freeman's hut showed its squat roundness to her right. She backtracked again, glancing up helplessly at the eerie starless sky that begrudged her any light.

At last she found the solid, square shape of the barracks and turned the corner, looking for the light of a lamp in the part of the building that Maelgwn used as an office and council room. Everything seemed black and formless, and Aurora felt the panic rising in her chest. It was not the damp, dark night which frightened her, but something else. It seemed somehow very urgent that she find Maelgwn and talk to him tonight.

In her confusion, Aurora nearly ran into Balyn as he stepped out of a doorway in front of her. Aurora gave a little yelp of fright, and Balyn reached out instinctively to steady her. He held the torch up to her face.

"My lady, what is it?" he asked worriedly.

"Maelgwn. I must find Maelgwn," she said breathlessly. "Where is he?"

"I'm sorry, he is gone," Balyn answered gently. "He left but a few minutes ago."

Aurora let out a small moan of dismay, and Balyn held the torch closer to see that she was all right. He noticed that her hair was unbound and disheveled, and she wore only a light gown with no jewelry or ornament.

"What is it?"

Aurora shook her head and looked away. After a moment she asked dully, "Where has he gone?"

"To the coast, to escort Abelgirth back for the wedding. I thought him crazed to set off so soon, with only Rhys to escort him, but he seemed determined, and I do not argue with Maelgwn when he is in that mood . . ."

Balyn's voice trailed off slightly, and he looked at Aurora in embarrassment. It seemed clear that Maelgwn and his wife had quarreled, and Maelgwn had been angry enough to ride off foolishly into the night, even though his legs were still stiff from his last journey. It must have been some fight, Balyn thought grimly. Aurora looked pale and anguished, and she trembled at his touch.

"Here, let me find Lady Gwenaseth," he suggested sympathetically. "She can help you to bed."

"Don't worry," he added after a moment. "Maelgwn will be back soon—Lughnasa is only six days away—he will be home by then."

Twenty

As the sound of his horse's footfalls fell into a steady rhythm, Maelgwn leaned back and inhaled the damp night air deeply. He felt better with Caer Eryri behind him, but he could not relax completely yet. Riding at night was treacherous—no matter how well you knew the country there were always hidden bogs and sharp ravines that could be deadly in the dark. Still, this was the kind of danger he had been trained to deal with since childhood, and it did not unsettle him—in fact, he relished the fear that cleared his mind and honed his senses to a keen edge.

Beside him rode Rhys, sleepily struggling to sit upright in the saddle. Maelgwn squinted in the darkness to see his companion's face. No doubt Rhys was confused and irritable to have been roused out of a comfortable bed for this journey. Maelgwn had abruptly ordered him to dress and be ready to ride, offering no explanation for their sudden departure.

How *could* he explain the panic that had risen in him—as if the very nearness of Aurora was enough to weaken and enslave him? He had been foolish to let Aurora get so close to him. Surely he should have learned from his mother and his sister that all women were trouble. For a while he had thought that Aurora was different, but now he knew that her soft loveliness made her even more dangerous. She would use him just as Esylt had, and the more he indulged himself in the pleasures of her body, the weaker and more helpless he would become. He needed to get away from her before her evil beguilement took hold completely and robbed him of his manhood forever.

The clouds shifted, and there was a faint glow of moonlight showing through the trees. Maelgwn's horse started as the ghostly paleness of a wood owl swept past them in the night, but his hands were sure on the reins. They were almost there—Maelgwn could see Abelgirth's stronghold in the distance—perched on a high cliff above the coast. The smell of the sea was in his nostrils, and he could almost ride blind—floating on the night air like a boat upon the seafoam.

Abelgirth was still abed when Maelgwn arrived at Llanfaglan and was escorted to his chambers. A dusky-skinned, raven-haired girl was with him, and she glared at Maelgwn coldly before stalking off naked, affording him a tantalizing view of her dainty heart-shaped buttocks as she walked away.

"I hope I did not interrupt anything," Maelgwn said coyly as Abelgirth grunted and began to to rouse himself.

"Nah, nah. It has been years since I felt the urge again in the morning." Abelgirth hauled his bulk out of the bed to sit on the edge of it and rub his eyes sleepily. "What is it Maelgwn? Is it war . . . my daughter . . . what . . . that you should ride here so early."

"It is none of that. I have just come to escort you back to Caer Eryri for the Lughnasa."

"And rode all night to do it, by the looks of you! Good God man, you could have sent one of your men, an escort wasn't even necessary. Besides . . ." he added as he stood and stretched. "I thought you were still visiting the Brigantes."

"Aye, I just returned from there yesterday."

Abelgirth stopped and stared at Maelgwn's dusty, weary face and bloodshot eyes. "Don't play games with me Maelgwn, clearly something is wrong. Did all not go well with Cunedda?"

Maelgwn shifted restlessly, the fatigue was catching up with him. "There was an unpleasant incident with Aurora, but I do not think it will have lasting damage."

"What happened?"

"Somehow Cunedda's son, Ferdic, got the idea to present Aurora with a trophy head—a gift worthier than gold they say. You can imagine her reaction."

"Can I not, though," Abelgirth chortled. "I know how my Gwenaseth would react to such a thing. Did your wife jump up and scream? You can hardly hold such behavior against a fair-born woman."

"Nay, I do not, and yet I am reminded again just how ill-chosen my new bride has turned out to be."

"What is this? The last time I saw you, you seemed besotted with the lass. For some men it might just mean the newness had worn off, but you—I counted you more loyal than that, even in the bedchamber."

Maelgwn laughed harshly. The glimmer of a smile was gone from his face, and he looked more tired than ever. "Make no mistake, Aurora still makes my blood run hot. Perhaps that is the problem—I do not like to be in thrall to a mere woman."

"What has she done to send you out into the darkness like a man fleeing an evil spirit?"

Maelgwn sat down heavily on a stool in the bedchamber.

"She quarrels with Esylt, defies me and then tries to win back my favor with her alluring body. I am tired of her manipulations."

"It seems to me that she is using the only weapons she has to make a place for herself at Caer Eryri. It cannot be easy for her with Esylt there."

"She is only a woman—it is not her place to make demands." Maelgwn retorted bitterly. "I'll not have my wife rule me!"

Abelgirth glanced at Maelgwn's flushed weary face—it seemed clear that the king was fooling himself. If he really cared so little for his wife's feelings, he would not be so distraught.

"Let us forget your troubles for now," Abelgirth soothed. "You need sleep. I'll have Cadwyl take you to the guest chambers."

Maelgwn woke up refreshed. The brisk sea air of Llanfaglan always invigorated him, and by daylight his long night ride seemed like a foolish whim. He wandered to the kitchen where the servants told him that Abelgirth was out hawking. After eating the hearty breakfast they brought him, Maelgwn set out on horseback to find his host.

The track he was directed to led straight down to the sea and out on a promontory. Here there was the constant cry of the gulls and cormorants, and the dull restless thrashing of the sea on the rocks far below. The land itself was barren and rough, with grass and sea pinks struggling for a foothold on the gray rocks. The country was very different from the highlands, even though it was not that far away. Maelgwn knew that if he turned east he would be able to see the misty rose peak of Yr Wyddfa in the distance, rising high above the coast.

Maelgwn rode quickly toward the figure of Abelgirth, who was ambling along with a large hawk perched on his shoulder. The bird and the man both seemed to be watching the rocks below, and with the din of the surf, Maelgwn was almost upon them before Abelgirth turned and smiled at him.

"Sleep well my friend? You look better for the rest."

"Aye, I feel much better. Thank you for your hospitality," Maelgwn said, dismounting.

Abelgirth shrugged. "No thanks necessary. I have as much interest as anyone in keeping the king of Gwynedd healthy and sharp-minded. The air and peacefulness here will do you good. I often come here when my mind is tangled about something."

"It is not the usual country for hawking," Maelgwn said, motioning to the elegant russet and cream-colored bird. "There seems little prey here to provide you with sport."

Abelgirth nodded, stroking the bird's sleek feathers tenderly. "Mostly I take them for company."

Maelgwn stared at the hawk's wicked-looking amber eye. He had always liked falconry, although it seemed he had little time for such entertainment. Still, he would not have thought of the birds as companions.

The two men walked together along the rocks, staring out at the sea while Maelgwn's stallion grazed.

"The sea gets in your blood just as the mountains do," Maelgwn mused after a few moments of silence. "I can see that it would be hard to leave this place if you grew up here."

"Aye, it would be hard for me, although Gwenaseth did not seem to find it wrenching. She wants only to be with her beloved Elwyn . . . I take it all goes well for their wedding?"

Maelgwn nodded. "The women have it in hand." Abelgirth watched the younger man carefully. He did not want to overstep the bounds of his friendship, but he wondered if Maelgwn had softened yet in his attitude toward Aurora.

"So, after a good night's sleep, are you more disposed to forgive your wife her terrible faults?"

Maelgwn shrugged. "It is nothing. I see now that I was overreacting. She is merely a woman—she can do nothing."

"You were quite distraught when you first came here. Are you sure that there isn't more to it than that?"

"Of course," Maelgwn answered briskly. "I have held myself close to Aurora for too long. One night with another woman, and I will be cured of my weakness for her."

Maelgwn smiled widely, showing his big, strong teeth. "Speaking of which, is that little dark-haired girl someone special, or would you be willing to share?"

The furrows in Abelgirth's broad forehead deepened. "Nah, nah, she is just an ambitious little fisherman's daughter. Really Maelgwn, I do not think you are taking the right approach with your wife. I, too, tried to run away from my feelings, and I have regretted it ever since."

"There is a difference," Maelgwn said rather sharply. "You said you were in love with your wife. Me . . . I cannot love any woman. What I feel for Aurora is no more than raw lust."

"We shall see," Abelgirth said softly, and for a moment his dark eyes looked as shrewd and sharp as the hawk's. "We shall see."

Twenty-one

Aurora was sewing quietly in the tower chamber. There was a soft knock, and Gwenaseth entered, breathing hard from her run up the stairs.

"I have good news, Aurora—the king and my father have been sighted in the valley."

Aurora tried to keep her face expressionless, but her breathing quickened. She could not help it—she had been counting the hours until Maelgwn returned.

"I can hardly wait," said Gwenaseth dreamily. "Tomorrow Elwyn and I will be married in the chapel and then handfast at the Lughnasa ceremony."

Lughnasa—the word intrigued Aurora. For as long as she could remember, the ancient festival had been shrouded in mystery and a sense of the forbidden. Perhaps it was time she found out what it meant.

"Gwenaseth, tell me—what do you do at Lughnasa?"

"We celebrate the coming harvest and the bounty of the earth. The celebration is named for Lugh—god of the sun. Here in Gwynedd we also worship Cerrunos—the god of the hunt. I do not know the exact meaning of the celebration, but it is very old. Have you never participated in a festival, Aurora?"

Aurora shook her head. "The people who live in the

hills around Viroconium still meet to honor the old gods, but my parents were Christians, and they considered such things immoral and blasphemous."

Gwenaseth looked startled. "My father and I are Christians, but we also observe the seasonal festivals. I do not understand how that can be wrong."

"Perhaps it is different here," Aurora said thoughtfully. "I can remember my sisters whispering about the hilltop festivals. They said that people took off their clothes and danced naked around the fires, and young women were sometimes dragged off and ravished. We had a maid who was found to be pregnant soon after attending a festival."

"If your maid went with a man, I'm sure it was willingly," Gwenaseth answered sharply. "It is not uncommon for couples to make love in celebration, but no woman is forced."

"So, there is lovemaking?" Aurora asked, her eyes wide.

"Of course. Lughnasa is a celebration of life and fertility. There is something special about making love around the sacred fires, and afterwards many women find themselves with child. It is also a time when a woman can couple with a man other than her husband, and no one will consider her unfaithful."

Aurora stared in disbelief, and Gwenaseth watched her closely. "Would you like to do that—go with another man besides Maelgwn?"

Aurora gave a grim, tense laugh. "It would be interesting to see if another man could want me for myself, instead of my father's lands and wealth." She sighed. "It doesn't matter. I'm sure Maelgwn wouldn't let any other man near me, no matter what the custom."

"Oh, even Maelgwn would not dare protest," Gwenaseth said confidently. "Lovemaking during Lughnasa is sacred, and even a king must accept what happens."

"All the same, it is unlikely. I cannot imagine any man willing to risk Maelgwn's wrath."

"Aurora," Gwenaseth asked carefully. "Are things still so bad between you and Maelgwn?"

Aurora looked away, trying to hide the tears that swam in her eyes. She didn't want anyone, even Gwenaseth, to know how much Maelgwn's abrupt departure had hurt her.

"Perhaps I should change clothes before our guests arrive," she answered. "Here, help me with the clasp on my necklace."

It was not going to be as easy as he thought, Maelgwn mused glumly, staring at the crowd of people celebrating in the great hall. He had returned to Caer Eryri determined to ignore Aurora and prove to her—and himself—how unimportant she was to his life. But things had not gone as he had planned. The first sight of Aurora hit him like a blow. She looked ravishing as she stood at the gate to greet their guests, and when she smiled her enchanting smile at Abelgirth, Maelgwn felt his stomach twist with jealousy. He had wanted to run away again, but he could not. He had been forced to stand beside Aurora and introduce her to all his guests and then sit next to her at the feast. It was torture to be so close to her and remember that he had vowed not to touch her.

He breathed a sigh of relief when she left to join the

dancing, but he soon found that this was no better. He could not help watching her as she twirled and swayed to the music, and he was sure that every other man in the room was watching and wanting her as well. The jealousy rose thick and choking in his throat, all the more bitter because Aurora's smile seemed to be meant for every man but him.

"What is wrong, Maelgwn?" Abelgirth asked, coming to stand beside his host. "You look as if you had been eating something that tasted bad."

"Did I? It must have been a passing thought that angered me . . . anyway, it is gone now."

"Your wife certainly seems to be enjoying herself," Abelgirth murmured, gesturing to Aurora. "Frankly, if I had a wife who looked like that, I would think about locking her away and keeping her for myself."

Maelgwn nearly choked on his wine, and then gave Abelgirth a long, cold stare. He walked away, leaving his friend to gape after him in surprise.

Maelgwn knew he had to get out of the hall, out of the smoky room filled with sweaty, happy people. He slipped out into the cool night and walked toward the gate. The moon had grown since he went to Llanfaglon, and there was plenty of light to show the way. The bored, weary guard looked down in surprise as Maelgwn's boots crunched on the gravel.

"Who goes . . . Maelgwn! Is something wrong?"

"Nah, nah. I am just out for a walk this fine night. I am going down to the village. If Balyn or any of my officers come looking for me—tell them."

The guard looked curious, but he nodded obediently. Maelgwn continued his leisurely pace down the hillside track. The air was faintly warm and filmy, and Maelgwn inhaled the sweetness of it. Some flower was in bloom, and it reminded him of being a boy and playing outside in the summer night. He sighed. It was so long ago. His childhood had been cut short so soon. If he ever had a son, he would want him to have a chance to be a boy longer, before he took up the weighty problems of being a man.

A cloud passed over the moon, but despite the shadow of darkness, Maelgwn had no trouble finding his way. It had been a long time—nearly three moon cycles—since he had followed this particular path, but the way was familiar, well-worn, comfortable. Maelgwn reached the village and paused where the pathway veered off. He knew what he would find when he came to the end of it: the rough, well-patched hut, the low fire banked for the night, the bed of sheepskins and furs, and the woman—Morganna—dark blond hair, placid brown eyes and a warm body smelling of smoke and earth.

Maelgwn sighed. How long could he go on pretending that it was another women he needed? He had tried that at Llanfaglon. When Abelgirth sent the dark-haired girl to him, Maelgwn had been tense with expectant desire. But after one look at the girl's shrewd, pretty face, he had sent her away. She was not Aurora, and there was no hope that she would satisfy the aching longing within him.

It was the same with Morganna. He cared for her, truly he did. But it was not love or desire that had first driven him to her bed, but pity. After what he had known with Aurora it was not enough.

He turned away. It seemed too late to return to the

fortress. He would have to sleep outdoors, under the stars. It was a perfect night—warm, soft and as gentle as a lover. Maelgwn found a sheltering tree on the hillside and lay down, cradling his head on a pile of dry leaves.

When he woke early in the morning, the mist was still gray upon the hills and the thrushes and plovers were calling softly through the growing light. He stood up, glancing toward Caer Eryri. The faded stones of the fortress beckoned to him. He watched as the high towers rose gleaming above the mists.

He sighed softly. It was no use—he wanted Aurora more than ever. No other woman would ever satisfy him. He wanted that dangerous passion that burned through his flesh through his very bones. He looked up longingly at the high tower. Aurora would be asleep. He longed to go to her, to feel her silken skin against his, to shiver beneath the soft curtain of her hair. But he dared not. He'd been cruel to his wife, greeted her with cold disdain and then ignored her at the feast. He could not expect her to welcome him back to her bed now, not a haughty, spoiled little princess like her. Why, he'd be lucky if she did not try to push him down the stairs again!

Maelgwn made his way to the river, still tense with desire and frustration. The sun was burning away the mist, and the morning chill was leaving him. He followed the worn pathway down to the water. The river was low this time of year, and the current ran swiftly but quietly. Maelgwn shed his grimy clothes—the worn wool tunic, the leather trousers, his loose hide boots with their soles reinforced with bronze studs—and waded into the water up to his hips. The water was cool, nearly cold, and it woke him up quickly.

He took a deep breath and plunged in, feeling the water wash away the sweat and dust from his skin. He wished he had brought some soap so he could wash his hair, but he could do that later when he shaved. He leaned back in the water, enjoying the buoyancy of his own body. Ah, this was way to bathe, not like the Romans with their warm water and tiled bathhouses. No perfumed oil could ever smell as sweet as the scent of mountain flowers warming in the sun, no tepid bath invigorate like these sparkling cool currents dancing over the rocks.

His mind turned to the Lughnasa festival, and Maelgwn felt a vague sense of unease. Tonight the spirit of the gods would be contagious. Many people would shed their clothes to escape the heat of the fires and dance more freely, and couples would go off into the shadows to honor the Old Ones with lovemaking. What if Aurora should go off with another man? Would he be able to endure it, knowing that someone else was touching her, enjoying her smooth, burning flesh?

Maelgwn shook off the image with a shiver. If it did happen, he dared not interfere. The ceremony belonged to the old gods, it honored the Lord and Lady. He must let things happen, feel the power of the night, the fires, the music. He must not let his jealousy interfere with the ancient tradition.

When he was done bathing, Maelgwn left the river and dressed on the bank. Despite his doubts, he felt better than he had in days, as if the quick dip had washed away some of his anger and frustration. It was no use denying that he cared for Aurora. He was almost willing to go to her and make amends—it would be worth it to have her back as his wife. He headed toward Caer Eryri, enjoying the feel of the earth beneath his boots, the sun on his damp back. He was always in awe of the way the light hit the walls of the fortress in the morning, turning the stones to gold. As he neared, the illusion faded, and the walls were gray and crumbling again.

As he entered the gate, Maelgwn nodded at the guard and then headed toward the kitchen. He was hungry, starved actually.

Aurora woke with a headache that began behind her eyes and spread throughout her body. She sat on the edge of the bed as the agony flickered through her. Why had she done this to herself? She had always been careful not to drink too much wine at feasts and festivals. Last night she had been working so hard to make Maelgwn jealous she had forgotten to be cautious.

Aurora rose from the bed unsteadily. Her plan had worked so well at first. The hall had been crowded with Maelgwn's soldiers. They'd come to Caer Eryri for the Lughnasa festival and left their women and children behind in the hills. They were eager to dance and flirt with the pretty new queen, and their attentions had certainly had the desired effect. The few times she allowed herself a glance in Maelgwn's direction, Aurora had been gratified by the glum, miserable look on his face. But then Maelgwn disappeared, and her game lost its charm. She continued to dance and flirt recklessly, but inside, her heart was sinking. She could not help wondering where

Maelgwn was, and why he did not return to the feast. She was relieved when Balyn came to see her to bed.

Aurora looked around the messy room, searching for her clothes. If only Gwenaseth would come to her. She badly needed a drink of fresh water, and her stomach burned with something like hunger. Then she remembered. It was Gwenaseth's wedding day, and she had told her to sleep as late as she wished. She would have to do without her help today.

Somehow she managed to put on her clothes and untangle her hair. She left the tower and set off across the courtyard toward the bakehouse. The courtyard was crowded with people this morning. Aurora saw several men she had danced with the night before, and they smiled sheepishly at her. Aurora felt too weak and miserable to smile back. She walked on, hoping that food would help her feel better.

When she reached the bakehouse, she entered and leaned against the rough stone walls. Unlike most new buildings at Caer Eryri, which were constructed of timber, the bakehouse was built of stone to lessen the hazard of fire. Even in summer the walls were cool. It felt good to rest her throbbing head and steady her queasy stomach before she went to find a fresh loaf for breakfast.

She was feeling better when she heard the wooden door open. She looked up, expecting to see one of the kitchen slaves, but instead, her eyes met Esylt's dark-browed face.

Esylt smiled. "I see our new queen has the common touch," she said delightedly. "Last night she mingled with the soldiers and freemen, and this morning she goes to fetch her own breakfast."

Aurora held her breath. It seemed best not to respond to Esylt, but to let her speak her hateful, venomous words so she would leave Aurora in peace.

"But it appears that my brother prefers common women," Esylt continued. "I don't suppose you wondered where Maelgwn slept last night?"

Aurora did not answer. It was clear that Esylt wanted only to taunt her.

"Of course, it is not the first night he has spent with the village whore. He has been going to her for a long time. It seems Morganna and you have much in common, although she does not dress so finely or hold herself so haughtily."

Aurora dared not meet Esylt's contemptuous stare. There was not enough air in the humid bakehouse to breathe. She leaned heavily against the wall, praying that Esylt would leave.

"Are you jealous, sweet Aurora?" Esylt asked mockingly. "I'm sure you can find a man to warm your cold bed—you have only to flash your little cat eyes at a man, and he comes running. Of course, Maelgwn will kill you if he finds out; he is very jealous. It seems to be a weakness you both share. So, perhaps it would be best if you went back to Viroconium."

Esylt glared at Aurora for a long moment, as if giving her one last measure of hatred. Then she turned and stalked out the door.

Aurora barely had time to move away from the wall and lean over before she began to retch, spilling out the sour remains of her stomach on the dirt floor of the bakehouse. When she was done, her stomach felt better, although her head was worse. Esylt's gleeful voice still rang in her ears. Was it true? Had Maelgwn really gone to a harlot last night?

Waves of shame washed over Aurora. She had to know if Maelgwn hated her so much that he preferred a woman like that to her. She had to find out.

Aurora tried to cover up the mess she had made, scuffing up the dust with her sandal. She hurried from the bakehouse and ran to the small daub-and-wattle house. Gwenaseth greeted her with a surprised smile. "Aurora, I did not think you would be up so soon." She looked closely at Aurora's white, strained face, and her smile disappeared. "Is something wrong? Are you ill?"

"Gwenaseth, I have to know the truth."

The desperation in Aurora's voice frightened Gwenaseth. "Know? Know what?"

"I must know if Maelgwn . . . if he went to a whore in the village last night."

"Who told you that?"

"Esylt. She said Maelgwn shares the bed of a common woman in the village, that he went to her last night."

"I'm sure she just said those things to hurt you," Gwenaseth soothed. "You must pay her no mind."

"Gwenaseth, I have to know! I order you to tell me if these things are true."

Gwenaseth looked doubtful. "Morganna is not exactly a whore—in a way you could say that she and Maelgwn are old friends."

"Morganna," Aurora hissed. "Who is she?"

"She is the wife of one of Maelgwn's men who was killed in battle several years ago." Gwenaseth's eyes were wary, almost frightened. "It's true that Maelgwn shares her company sometimes, but I don't believe it's what you think."

Aurora exhaled a long, shaky breath. "How could he? How could he shame me so?"

"You do not know if it's true," Gwenaseth protested. "Esylt could easily be lying."

Aurora shook her head miserably. "I don't think so. She knew . . . and she enjoyed telling me so much."

"Remember, Aurora, don't let your pride allow Esylt to win."

"It doesn't matter. I am tired of being hurt. Perhaps she is right—perhaps I should go back to Viroconium!"

"No!" Gwenaseth said sharply. "It could mean war. How would you feel if your father were killed trying to avenge you against Maelgwn?" Gwenaseth grabbed Aurora's arm and looked her fiercely in the eye. "How would you feel if Maelgwn were killed?"

Aurora's face was stubborn and hard. "Tell me what this Morganna is like," she asked coldly.

Gwenaseth released her grip on Aurora. "She is older than you, perhaps Maelgwn's age. Her hair is the color of oak leaves in the fall, her eyes dark. Her skin is dark too, almost darker than Rhys."

"Is she beautiful?"

"No, not what most men would call by that name. She has had a hard life and it shows in her face, but her body is plump and pleasing."

"Why?" Aurora asked bitterly. "Why would Maelgwn go to her?"

"I think at first he went to her because he felt sorry for her. She loved her dead husband a great deal. And now . . ." Gwenaseth paused, troubled. "It could be that he feels comfortable with her, safe."

"How unfair he is. He threatens me lest I let any other man touch me, yet he leaves his marriage bed for a common whore!"

"Perhaps Maelgwn is running away from his feelings for you," Gwenaseth suggested.

"He has shown me naught but cruelty and arrogance!"

"Aye, he has hid his love for you very well, even from himself."

"Love!" Aurora's voice was mocking. "Don't try to soothe me with that foolishness! Maelgwn loves grain and gold—the dowry of wealth and power I brought him. He cares nothing for *me!*"

Gwenaseth shook her head. "You are wrong, Aurora. Maelgwn does care. I have never seen the Dragon run before. He is afraid—afraid of his feelings for you."

Twenty-two

Aurora lay back and tried to sleep, but her thoughts tormented her. It was well enough to say that she hated Maelgwn, but that did not change how difficult it had been to be crowded next to him in the priory chapel for Gwenaseth and Elwyn's wedding ceremony. She had hardly heard the prior's droning words—her every sense was concentrated on Maelgwn's distressing presence. She could still smell the odor of the soap he had used to wash with, and she was painfully aware that he had cut his hair and been freshly shaved. Who was he trying to look nice for, she wondered? Was it for her or for his common slut in the village?

Aurora tossed restlessly, trying to find a comfortable position on the bed. Her head still ached from the wine, and sleep eluded her. The fortress was mostly quiet as everyone prepared for the Lughnasa, but the older children had gathered outside for games and races to pass the time, and their shouts and cheers always seemed to wake Aurora just as she began to drift toward sleep. She realized she was hungry, and she thought with regret of the rich stews and fresh fish she had passed up at the feast the night before. Today, there would be no evening meal at all—Gwenaseth had told Aurora that all the

Lughnasa participants had to fast for several hours before the ceremony.

A cramp of fear squeezed Aurora's empty stomach. Tonight she was going to participate in what many people in Viroconium considered an evil, disgusting ritual. Just being there was no doubt a sin. Yet she had to admit that she was intrigued—would the old gods walk the earth tonight, Aurora wondered? Were they out there now— waiting in the still mountain air?

Aurora finally dozed, and when she awoke it was almost time to leave for the ceremony. She dressed hastily, selecting a new gown of rose-colored silk that had come from Llanfaglan, and then turned her attentions to her hair. She quickly combed it out, letting it flow in masses of dark curls around her shoulders. Aurora looked around the room uneasily, wondering what she had forgotten; she felt naked without her jewelry, but Gwenaseth had warned that no metal was to be worn to the ceremony—it might interfere with supplications to the gods.

Aurora ran down the tower stairs and into the courtyard. It was getting late and many people had already left the fortress. She didn't bother looking for Gwenaseth and Elwyn—they had gone to prepare hours ago. Out of force of habit, she glanced around for Maelgwn. He was nowhere to be seen, and Aurora chided herself for thinking of him at all. Perhaps he already planned to go with one of the other women tonight, she thought angrily. Good. Then she would not have to worry about him.

The sun was rapidly sliding into the hills when Aurora joined the last stragglers leaving Caer Eryri. The ceremony would be held on the hilltop behind the fortress, and as they neared the open space, Aurora saw that many bonfires had been lit to form a large circle in the grass. The ring of fire glowed brilliantly in the fading light. As they approached, the flames seemed to gain brightness, as if stealing strength from the orange sun that floated in the sky of lavender and silver.

The mood of the people around her was quiet and solemn, very different from the atmosphere of fun and joviality that usually surrounded the Cymry. Aurora's tension grew; her throat felt dry and her body cold and rigid. She could almost feel the spirits watching them from the violet hills. As they neared the fires, Aurora heard the pounding of a drum, echoing the beating of her own heart.

Once she was within the circle, Aurora saw that there was a large fire in the very center. A group of people formed a ring around it, their hands clasped together, standing very still. The people were naked, and their bodies were painted with strange dark designs—as if serpents were slithering over their skin. As the pounding of the drum quickened, they began to chant and dance around the fire. Gwenaseth had explained that circling the fire in the same direction as the sun moved through the sky, invoked Lugh's protection and helped to bring his spirit among them. The movements of the dancers were lithe and graceful, and Aurora was reminded of salmon, spawning in an invisible river.

The drum stopped and the chanting ended. The people in the center turned to face the rest of the crowd gathered around, and Aurora was surprised to see that Gwenaseth and Elwyn were among the participants. She also recognized the long beard and plain robe of the bard Torawc as he walked around the circle, chanting in a strange, melodious voice. Aurora struggled to listen, but the sounds seemed to blur together. In the back of her mind she seemed to know what Torawc was saying, but when she tried to remember, her thoughts eluded her, swimming away into the humming darkness. The bard began to scatter something on the dancers, and in his light robe he looked like a flame moving in and out among the naked painted people.

The people in the center gradually paired off as couples, and Torawc approached each of them. He took a small curved knife and carefully cut the wrist of each person. As the blood began to flow, the couples pressed their wrists together, mingling their blood. Aurora watched in awe. So, this was what it was like to be married before the old gods. As your blood was joined with your partner's, an unbreakable bond was formed between you. Gwenaseth had told her that the bond was eternal—even death could not break it.

The handfasting over, the couples took turns leaping over the large fire in the center of the circle so that the smoke would purify them and make them fertile. Aurora wondered if she would ever have the nerve to jump through the glowing flames, even if Maelgwn were beside her.

The drums began again, and the wedding participants gradually moved back toward the rest of the group ringing the fire. Torawc stayed in the center, moving around the fire and chanting. Slowly, very slowly, he lifted up his arms to the sky, as if asking the gods for something. Aurora felt a chill, like that of a cloud passing overhead on a sunny day. Torawc shouted up to the heavens, and Aurora jumped with fright.

At the same time, a dark figure leaped forward. At first Aurora thought it was a stag who had somehow stumbled into the circle, but then she realized it was a man wearing a headress of antlers. He was naked except for a leather breechcloth, gloves on his hands and a mask that covered his face. The stag man seemed huge, taller than Maelgwn even, and his body was sleek and well-muscled. Aurora felt a stirring of desire mingling with her fear.

The drum began to play a stirring rhythm, gradually growing faster and faster, and the stag man danced, twirling and leaping within the center of the circle with tremendous grace. Aurora held her breath; it seemed that she could see the stag being chased by the hunters, his huge rack of antlers flashing through the trees as the dancer veered into the crowd and then whirled back dangerously close to the fire.

Slowly Aurora realized that the people around her were joining the ritual. In the firelight she saw the flash of wild eyes and bright teeth. She was surrounded by strangers with savage, exultant faces. They had became the hunters—greedy carnivores, eager for their prey's blood. She moved backwards, away from the fire, away from the people crowding forward to join the chase. The stag still veered wildly within the circle of watchers, and sometimes he came so close that Aurora could smell his acrid sweat, the piercing metallic odor of fear.

The hunters chased the stag man harder and harder as he sought to escape from the circle of people crowding around. Closer and closer they came, until they could reach out and touch him. They grabbed him, clawed at him, tearing his skin until the stag man's smooth flesh ran with streaks of dark blood. He seemed to be tiring, and Aurora felt his panic with a deep despair. He was beautiful, spectacular, and Aurora did not want him to die, did not want the hunters to kill him. She closed her eyes to the escape the horror of it. She knew what would happen next—the stag man would be killed and his blood would stain the grass black.

When she opened her eyes, the stag man had fallen. The hunters crowded around, covering his quivering body. A cry went out from the watchers as the stag disappeared, and Aurora was surprised to find that her own voice joined the eerie lament. Tears streamed down her face as she watched the hunters carefully, almost tenderly, lift up the stag man's bleeding body and bear him away triumphantly.

As the procession moved out through the circle of fires, Aurora found the drained emptiness within her being replaced with a strange sense of peace. As if prompted by an inner voice, she suddenly understood the purpose of the ancient ceremony she'd witnessed. The stag man died, but the rest of the people lived. In dying he had somehow saved them, for his death ensured prosperity and fertility for another year. A deep feeling of gratitude filled her heart, and she thought immediately of the Christian teachings she had grown up with. Perhaps Christ was like the stag—for he, too, had died to save his people. Perhaps all gods were one and the same.

Aurora was moved, and she wanted to share what she felt with someone. But the people around her were beginning to pair off or move to the center of the circle to dance. Some of them began to chant; their voices made a low rumbling sound like the beating of birds' wings, filling Aurora's ears with a confusing hum.

The fire in the center of the circle seemed to grow bigger. The flames leaped and crackled fiercely, and Aurora could smell the dizzying sweet odor of cherry wood. As she stared into the flames, it seemed as though the licking orange tongues were reaching out into the darkness, reaching out to devour her. The pounding of the drums quickened, and Aurora's fear deepened. She did not want to be left by herself in the circle of fire. What if the gods were not satisfied with the sacrifice of the stag man? What if they wanted more? She was sweating, and the silk of her gown stuck tightly to her skin. She could feel her body begin to quiver with fear, and she backed away, trying to find an opening in the ring of people and fire.

Aurora reached the edge of the circle and stepped out into a cool, still world. The dew on the grass made her ankles wet, and the bright moon lit up the landscape with a solemn, ancient glow. Aurora shuddered. She did not know what to do—whether to return to Caer Eryri alone or go back into the circle. She did not want to go back, and yet she did not want to be alone either. She could hear the voices of the spirits all around her—the whisper of the wind in the grass, the smell of water in the air, the crackle of the consuming fire behind her. She stood still, waiting. It seemed she had turned to stone and would wait forever on this moon-chilled plain.

Her trance was broken when she saw a movement in front of her, and a dark figure advanced upon her. As the creature approached, Aurora saw the towering horns and gasped—it was the stag man. Aurora stood trembling, afraid to run. Was it a man after all, playing the part of the stag? Or was it a god, who had died and come to life again?

As the stag man neared her, Aurora saw the gashes on his body from the hunters. The wounds no longer bled, and the rivulets of blood had dried to black stains upon his glistening skin. Her eyes were drawn to the rest of his body. The breechcloth was gone, and Aurora could see the stag man's erection clearly. He was just a man after all, Aurora thought with relief.

The stag man advanced steadily, making no sound. Aurora tried to see his face, to discern the eyes that looked out at her from the leather mask, but it was too dark. Perhaps it was better this way, she thought, with the man unknown, faceless. Aurora could feel the fever of desire burning within her. She wanted this man-god. She wanted to lick his salty wounds, to stroke the hard muscles beneath his sweaty skin, to feel the crushing weight of his strong body pressing down upon her.

When he was but a few feet away from her, the stag man stopped and gestured toward her clothes. Aurora looked down at herself in the soft sheen of moonlight. The thin silk was saturated with sweat, clearly outlining the curves of her body. She might as well be naked—aye, it would be better to be naked. Aurora smiled. She wanted to please the stag man, to make him want her. She began to undress slowly, languidly, as he watched. She undid the tie at her waist and draped it around her neck. Then she slid the gown down her body, baring her breasts. She cupped them in her hands, feeling their silken fullness, caressing the nipples, which appeared dark against her fair skin in the full moonlight.

She slid the dress down further, pausing tauntingly at her hips. She stared expectantly at the stag man. She could not see his face, but she saw the trickles of sweat down his broad muscular chest and heard his harsh gasp of passion. The dress tumbled carelessly on the ground, and Aurora's body was bare, shining like marble in the pale light. She pulled her long hair forward, draping it over her, as if to cover her nakedness. The stag man shook his head, and Aurora smiled teasingly at him. She could not believe that she was doing this—it was as if the spirits had entered her!

The stag man stood still, his proud, battered body gleaming even in the half-darkness. The sound of music came hauntingly from the circle of fire, and Aurora began to follow the faint rhythm, swaying her hips slightly to the beat of the drums, then moving faster, her shoulders picking up the melody of the pipe player. The stag man didn't move, but Aurora could feel his eyes upon her, hot and searing. She moved even faster, turning now to display the shape of her buttocks as she writhed with the music, tempting him with the promise of the ecstasy she could offer him with her blazing, naked flesh. Her long hair twirled around her, wilder and wilder. She was on fire, she was aflame, and this man-god represented the watchers, the worshipers. Soon he would try to leap through the flames, and she would catch him, and pull him down into her fiery, passionate heart!

The stag man moved closer, close enough to touch her, but still far enough away so that she could not see into the eyeholes of his mask. He reached out to grasp her, stopping her furious dance with an ironlike grip around her waist. Aurora closed her eyes, waiting for him to kiss her—to take off his mask and let her see his face. No kiss came. Instead, he stroked her gently, moving his gloved fingers along her body. The texture of the leather on her skin made Aurora swoon. Now *he* was teasing *her!* She wanted to feel bare skin upon her own, and she pressed herself to his hard, sweaty chest desperately, burying her face against his skin, tasting him hungrily.

He seemed to take pity on her, for when next he caressed her, his fingers were bare, flicking over her in tense exploration. Aurora sighed rapturously, and moved to kiss him, but still the mask blocked her way. She reached up, as if to pull it off, but he took her hands firmly in his own and pressed her down—down, down, softly, onto the wet grass. She took him in, all of him, heedless of the mask and the dampness beneath her, unaware of anything except his powerful hardness within her. Her body seemed to split open in flashes of light, echoing deep within her. She was a cave of mystery, opened for the first time. She felt no fear, no pain—only stark, profound pleasure.

The thought of Maelgwn nagged at her, but she pushed it away. Aurora could hear the harsh breathing of her lover close to her ears, and felt the tension within him increase with each convulsive breath, each violent lunge within her. She reached to touch his face, and caressed bare, slippery skin—the mask was finally gone. But Aurora could not open her eyes and look upon her lover yet—the excitement was growing within her own body once again. Aurora spread her legs wider, desperate for the deep probing touch of the stag man, silently begging him to take her to oblivion, to pierce her heart with his passion. She felt her body exploding into another flash of white, hot light. This was it. . . . she had reached it . . . something . . .

Aurora collapsed onto the soft earth and lay breathless and still. She was afraid to open her eyes—to break the spell that held her. She knew the stag man was still there; his low, rhythmic breathing was very near. Slowly, Aurora opened her eyes. The mask was gone, and she could see the face of a man next to her. His eyes were closed in exhaustion, and his hair was wet with sweat. Aurora started as she realized she was looking at her husband.

Her eyes swept over the figure beside her. Why hadn't she known? How could she *not* have known? The lean, splendidly muscled body, the tapering, sensitive fingers, even the slight angle of his erection—it had been Maelgwn's body which filled her with such strong desire. No wonder it had been so good, a part of her mind seemed to say—he was the one . . . the one she loved.

Even as she watched him, Maelgwn's eyelids fluttered and he opened his eyes to stare back at her. His face wore the mask that she had seen so often before—cold, ironic, inscrutable.

"So, you prefer the god to the man," he said softly.

His mocking voice unnerved Aurora, and all tenderness and lingering desire left her. "You tricked me!" she said accusingly.

"Aye, and it was not hard to do. You were so eager for me to be Cerrunos—the horned one. You were so eager for me to be someone besides your husband."

Aurora stood up abruptly and began to look for her clothes. "Do not come to me as a god again," she said coldly as she pulled on her gown. "Do not come to me at all," she whispered in a harsh, choking voice.

As Aurora disappeared into the darkness, Maelgwn felt the sharp pain of regret. He had not meant to hurt her. Nor had he meant to trick her. After his part in the ceremony was over, he had wanted only to find Aurora before some other man claimed her. He had been so relieved to find her alone in the darkness, and she had stared at him with such awe and naked desire that he had forgotten himself and decided to play the role of Cerrunos a little longer.

It had not mattered that she surrendered to him thinking that he was a god. It had been his body which made hers quicken with pleasure, not the god's. What had passed between them was as intense and passionate as ever. But now she was angry, bitter, as if he had betrayed her. Oh, how he wanted to call her back and explain his feelings. But he dared not. He would not risk her mocking contempt again.

Twenty-three

Aurora guided the horse down the path past the village. She had forgotten her cloak and been soaked in a sudden rain shower as she rode in the valley. Even though she was in a hurry to get back to the fortress and change her clothes, she could not resist riding past the cluster of rude huts, hoping for a glimpse of the blond woman called Morganna.

Aurora sighed. She wondered if Maelgwn still went to Morganna. He had not shared Aurora's bed since before Lughnasa, and although Gwenaseth told her that the king slept on a cot in his office, she could not be sure it was true. Why did it matter? It was only a matter of time until Maelgwn sent her back to Viroconium anyway. The marriage was over. Maelgwn avoided her completely. She didn't even see him at meals anymore. Perhaps that was just as well—she wouldn't have been able to touch a bite with her husband in the room.

The sick longing began again in her stomach. It was true. She cared for her husband, maybe even loved him. She dreamed about Maelgwn almost every night. Sometimes she woke and cried when she found herself alone. She made excuses to go places in the fortress where she would see him—even though the very sight of him made her stomach pitch and her body ache with desire.

Aurora shook her head. It was too late. She had ruined things with Maelgwn, and she had no idea how to make things right.

"Good day, Queen Aurora."

Aurora started as an old woman stepped in front of her on the narrow pathway. She nodded back politely and flashed a warm smile.

The old woman did not move off. She remained firmly rooted, blocking the pathway. Aurora would either have to turn back or confront the old crone and ask her to move.

"My lady," the woman spoke in her strange voice again. "Your gown is wet—won't you come and dry yourself by my fire?"

"It is but a short ride to the fortress," Aurora protested, pointing up the track.

"Nah, nah, someone so young and pretty should not risk catching cold. Come, my fire is already blazing, and I will make you some warm broth."

Aurora studied the woman carefully. Her cheekbones had a distinctive, foreign cast, and her dark eyes were as bright as jet. But despite her riveting gaze, she seemed frail and sickly. Her body was tiny and stooped, her face, thin and weary. Aurora decided that there was no harm in accepting the pitiful creature's hospitality.

"I guess I could stop for a while," she answered.

She dismounted and tethered her horse to a tree, then followed the old woman across a muddy, offal-strewn clearing to a small wooden hut. Aurora felt a shiver of apprehension as she stared at the tiny door. She would

have to bend down to enter, and she could not help recalling childhood stories of ancient fairy folk who lured
unsuspecting mortals to the underworld.

Despite her doubts, Aurora pushed the hide door aside
and went in.

She was surprised to find that the dwelling was tidy
and comfortable. The room was furnished with a small
bed, a table and two stools by the fire. Aurora wondered
where the furniture had come from. Perhaps the woman
wasn't as poverty-stricken as she had appeared. Aurora
noticed that the walls were hung with bunches of dried
herbs and flowers, and she recognized some that were
used for healing. Perhaps the woman made her living
selling herbs, she mused. Then a darker thought crossed
her mind—the little creature might be a sorceress who
used the herbs to cast her spells.

The woman seemed to sense Aurora's nervousness.

"Don't be afraid, Lady Aurora," she said as she pointed
to a stool by the fire. She turned to tend to her cooking
pot and in a few moments held out a cup of steaming
broth.

Aurora took the offered cup and smiled back uneasily.
"What is your name?"

"Justina," the woman answered in her clear, bell-like
voice.

"That is a Roman name." Aurora said in surprise. "Do
you have Roman blood?"

Justina laughed. "Aye, you might say that. My grandfather was a Roman soldier who stayed behind when the
legions left Britain, and my mother grew up near Deva,
at the old Roman fort there."

"But why are you here? Most Romans left this part

of Britain years ago." Aurora stopped, realizing that her question was rude. It was none of her business where this woman chose to live.

"I was once in love with a man who lived here—a Cymry—and after he died, I decided to stay."

"I'm sorry," Aurora said sympathetically. "Did he die in battle?"

"Nah, nah, it was a fever that took him." The old woman's face had grown misty and strained, and Aurora thought it best to change the subject.

"And now you live here alone?" she asked politely.

"Aye—but do not feel sorry for me. I am free to do as I please—how many women can say that?"

"Not many," Aurora agreed bitterly. "Most women are little better than slaves to their husbands."

The woman smiled. "Aye, I had heard that you were not happy in your marriage."

Aurora got up abruptly, as if to leave, and the old woman made a reassuring motion. "Don't worry, I didn't ask you here to speak of your relationship with the king. There is something else I wish to talk about."

Aurora sat down nervously, wondering what this woman could possibly have to say to her.

Justina turned and poked at the fire. The embers flew like stars in the dim room as she stirred the ashes. Finally she spoke: "You went with the king to visit Cunedda of Manau Gotodin, did you not?"

"Aye."

"What was your opinion of the relationship between Maelgwn and Cunedda?"

"I don't know—they seemed friendly enough," Aurora answered hesitantly. "Why do you ask?"

"Because I fear that someone at Caer Eryri is plotting with the Brigantes to overthrow Maelgwn."

Aurora stared at the old women. "What makes you think this?"

"When you were visiting the Brigantes, do you remember a man with dark red hair who was close to Cunedda?"

"There were many men there with hair that color," Aurora answered impatiently. "What of it?"

"Because there is a man like that who has been staying near the village, hiding in the woods. I think he is here to spy on Maelgwn . . . and to meet someone from Caer Eryri."

"The man could be any one of a dozen men who were close to Cunedda. There was only one whose name I knew, and that was Ferdic, Cunedda's son. He is a very tall, handsome man with a lean, graceful build."

Justina shook her head. "No, it is not him. This man is lean and tall, but he is certainly not handsome. He has the ugly face of a snarling wolf."

"You have seen him yourself?" Aurora asked.

"Aye, I have seen him. He creeps around in the evening, so that no one will notice."

Aurora was growing impatient. "If there is a Brigante spy in the village, who is he meeting?"

"Can you not guess?" Justina said softly. "Who craves the power of the Gwynedd kingship for herself?"

Aurora let out her breath in a slow hiss.

"Esylt!"

Justina nodded. "Esylt has always been jealous of her brother. Now she plots to bring him down."

Aurora looked at Justina with narrowed eyes. "It is

very grave to accuse the king's sister of treason—what proof do you have?"

"My proof is here," Justina said emphatically, touching her withered chest. "I know that there is evil and danger surrounding Maelgwn. I also know what Esylt is capable of."

Justina looked deeply into Aurora's eyes. Her dark gaze was hypnotic, compelling, and Aurora found she could not look away.

"Do you know the story of Dinas Brenin?"

Aurora nodded. "It troubles me. I know that Maelgwn was very young . . . that he did not mean for it to happen . . . but still, it is so horrible."

"It was not his fault! It was Esylt who insisted that the fires be set. It was Esylt who sought to destroy their family so that Maelgwn would be the uncontested ruler of Gwynedd!"

"How could Esylt order the troops to set the fires?" Aurora protested. "Maelgwn was the commander—the men would surely never listen to Esylt."

Justina's mouth was grim with hatred, and the lines in her face seemed etched in bitterness. "She made him give the order by taunting him, scorning him. Maelgwn was very young then, perhaps sixteen or so, and when she called him a coward and a fool, he gave in to her."

"How do you know these things? How can you know what was said and done so many years ago?"

Justina smiled her faint, haunting smile. "Because I was with Maelgwn afterwards, and he told me."

"Why would he tell you? Why would he tell anyone?"

"Because sometimes secrets and guilt are too heavy to bear alone," Justina said with a sigh.

"I don't believe you! Why would he tell you—a poor old woman—something like that?"

"Because I was not so old then . . . and he was a man and I was a woman."

Aurora stared at her in shock. "You mean . . . You are telling me that you and Maelgwn . . . ?"

Justina smiled sadly. "Is it so hard to believe that I was once young and beautiful like you?" She sighed. "It is this disease I have—it twists my limbs and weakens my spine—if it were not for the herbs I know how to use, I would never be able to stand the pain."

Aurora realized abruptly that Justina was not as old as she had imagined. Disease had turned her into this wizened little creature. Aurora could not help searching Justina's face for some vestige of her former beauty. Her dark eyes must have been entrancing once, and her long gray-streaked hair was still thick, but the rest of it was gone—horribly distorted by the ravages of time and her crippling disease.

"You shared Maelgwn's bed?" she asked in a hushed, disbelieving voice.

"Aye. It was only for one night, but the pain and guilt was heavy upon him, and he told me what happened at Dinas Brenin."

Aurora was silent for a moment, her mind churning with thoughts. This conversation frightened her—if Justina's story was true, Esylt was even more wicked than Aurora had imagined. She had always suspected Esylt of treachery, but nothing so evil as this. She looked critically at the tiny woman seated next to her. Could she trust her? She looked like nothing so much as one of the fairy folk.

"Now that you have told me these things, what do you want me to do?"

"I want you to go to your husband and warn him of the treachery that is plotted behind his back."

Aurora gave a deep sigh. "I don't know if he would believe me. Maelgwn thinks I am just as untrustworthy as his sister, if not more."

"Can't you at least talk to him?"

"Why should I bother?" Aurora answered in frustration. "If Maelgwn is foolish enough to trust his scheming sister, why should I try to help him?"

"It's a pity you care so little for your husband. He is a better man than most, especially for a king."

"Oh, I well know how beloved Maelgwn is among his people—to them it would seem he is generous, even kind." Aurora's voice was harsh with sarcasm. "But with his wife he does not pretend—I know just how cold and arrogant he really is!"

The old woman sighed. "I see I am wasting my time. Apparently the stories Esylt has been telling are true—that you hate your husband and would be happy to be rid of him."

Aurora gasped. "Is that what she has been telling everyone?" She paused, thinking of how coolly the people of Caer Eryri treated her. She had thought they were scorning her because Maelgwn no longer shared her bed, but perhaps there was another, more disturbing reason.

"It's not true that I hate Maelgwn," she protested. "It is just that we . . ." Aurora stopped, suddenly confused herself. "It is just that we . . . we can't seem to stop fighting."

"And is he *all* to blame for that?"

Aurora blushed. Her temper was almost worse than Maelgwn's, and she was at least as stubborn as he was. It had taken both of them to bring their relationship to this terrible stalemate.

"Isn't it true that Esylt has spoiled all your chances to be happy with Maelgwn?"

Aurora looked at Justina in surprise. "What do *you* know of it?"

The old woman shrugged. "I have heard things. It is clear that Esylt wishes to cause trouble between you and your husband. The king's sister is like the weevil that fouls the grain or the worm that rots the ripening fruit. Everything she touches is spoiled!"

Aurora was startled by the vehemence in Justina's voice. It was strange to meet someone who hated Esylt as much as she did. Still, hate was not proof of treason.

Aurora shook her head. "It's not enough—if I go to him now, I will never be able to convince Maelgwn that Esylt is going to betray him. You have not even seen Esylt and this man together. How do you know that this stranger is anything more than an outlaw waiting around for the chance to steal something?"

Justina went back to poking at the fire. She seemed to shrivel as Aurora watched, as if all her power came from her voice and eyes, and the rest of her was just an empty shell.

"I want only to help him—to help us all. Maelgwn is a good king; he has brought his people peace and prosperity. I don't want to see him fall victim to the jealous treachery that has toppled the rest of the line of Cunodag. Even if you do not love your husband, Aurora, can you not see how important he is to his people? Can you not help him for our sake?"

Aurora pulled her eyes away and stared pensively into the fire. Doubts crowded her mind. There were too many things she did not know—too many riddles left unanswered. She looked up.

"If you were once close to Maelgwn, why don't you go to him and warn him?"

Justina laughed a bright, tinkling laugh. "Do you think he remembers me? A worn-out whore he spent a night with so many years ago? I think not! Even if he did remember, he certainly does not know who I am now."

"You were a *whore?*"

Justina almost giggled. "Did you think I was some lovely farmer's daughter sent to warm the new king's bed? No—he came to me because I was experienced, because I had a reputation for keeping men's secrets."

"But why . . . why did you choose to be . . . one of those . . . women? Were you poor? Did your father cast you out?"

"It is not so bad a life," Justina answered wryly. "You might say I was born to it—my grandmother followed the legions. There is plenty of freedom, except for worrying about babies and diseases, and my mother taught me how to deal with those problems."

Aurora stared at the tiny woman incredulously. She had been brought up to believe that women who had sex for payment were the most despised of creatures, but this woman was admitting to it freely, almost proudly. Aurora was shocked, but it did not take long for her curiosity to get the better of her surprise.

"Did you . . . like it?" she found herself asking.

"It is just another way to put bread in your mouth and a roof over your head. It takes patience and the willingness to listen—more than great beauty or skill in bed. Men want someone to confide in—someone to listen to their complaints and troubles."

Aurora sat very still, staring down at the rings on her fingers. "Your story is very hard to believe," she said softly. "But somehow I do believe it. Still, there is much that does not make sense. I know that Esylt is a greedy, power-hungry woman, but I am not sure she would ever betray her own brother—and why now, when he has been so successful?"

"You do not understand, do you, Aurora? It is because of you that Esylt is driven to treachery. She fears you—fears your power over Maelgwn. That is what has forced her to take such drastic action."

"The power I have over Maelgwn? He doesn't care about me at all!"

"Ah, but you are wrong, very wrong. Even though the two of you have fought bitterly, Maelgwn has not talked of voiding the marriage or sending you back to Viroconium. Have you never wondered that he let's you shun him from your bed and yet insists that everyone treat you as his beloved queen? His feelings toward you are stronger even than his pride."

"I still do not see why that gives me any power over him that Esylt might fear."

Justina shook her head. "Esylt is afraid that someday the troubles between you and Maelgwn will be over, and you will take her place at Caer Eryri."

Aurora gave a hollow laugh. "If only she knew how unlikely that is. She may think that Maelgwn cares for

me, but I do not. He has always been cold and cruel to
me."

"Always?"

Aurora looked away from Justina's questioning gaze.
"Well, no, there have been times when I thought he
might begin to feel kindly toward me. But something has
always happened—Esylt was always there to ruin it."

"This time Esylt will do more than ruin things between you and Maelgwn. This time she may well see
that you and Maelgwn are both killed, and Gwynedd is
once again torn apart by warfare!"

Aurora shuddered. "I am afraid, Justina. I want to go
to Maelgwn and tell him what you have told me, but I
am worried that he will not believe me. I need time—
time to sort out my thoughts and make sense of everything."

Justina nodded. "We have a little time, perhaps. This
Brigante spy does not have what he needs or he would
not still be here. But do not delay long, Aurora. If you
care for your husband at all—do not wait too long to
warn him."

Aurora stood up stiffly. "I should be getting back.
I . . . I am glad to have met you," she added, extending
her hand to the woman's gnarled and twisted one.

Justina smiled her odd, egnimatic smile. "Remember,
I want only to help Maelgwn—and all of us."

Aurora leaned down to squeeze through the tiny doorway. It was already twilight. The afternoon had vanished,
and she was nearly late for supper. Had she truly been
in Justina's house so long? Aurora felt goosebumps along
her skin. She could not help recalling the stories of people who went to fairyland for a few days and returned

to find that years had passed. As she rode up the hill, the fortress still looked the same, stolid and gloomy in the fading light. Aurora leaned forward and loosened the reins to quicken the horse's pace. She was anxious to be within Caer Eryri's safe walls. If Justina was right, there was an enemy lurking in the shadowy forest pathways.

Maelgwn glanced at the setting sun as Aurora rode into the fortress, roughly calculating how long she had been gone. He had not yet stooped to following his wife, spying on her to see what she did with her days, but he was tempted. She had been going riding alone in the valley almost from the first few days of her arrival at Caer Eryri, but she had never stayed away so long before. It was well past supper, and she had ridden in from the direction of the village. Had she met someone there?

Maelgwn decided that it was time to confront his wife. He greeted her at the door of the stables as she brought her horse in.

"Good evening Aurora," he said as he stepped out of the darkness.

Aurora gave a little cry of fright, and then seemed to regain her composure. "Good evening," she answered.

"Let me help you down."

It had been a long time since he had been close to Aurora. His heart pounded unnaturally as he reached up and helped her slide down the side of the horse. He had forgotten how slender Aurora was—he could almost clasp his hands all the way around her narrow waist.

Once she was down, they stood there, looking at each other awkwardly.

"Where have you been?" he asked, trying to keep his voice light.

A flicker of fear registered in her eyes. "I . . . I have been riding."

"Where?"

"Around the lakes, down near the priory."

"Alone?"

"Aye, alone. Who would go with me?"

They were so close—Aurora was but a hand's breadth away from him. Maelgwn sensed something different in her attitude toward him. She seemed more vulnerable, even shy somehow. He reached over tentatively to kiss her irresistible mouth, and she did not draw away. It was a long lingering kiss, both tender and uneasy. It was Maelgwn who first broke off their embrace by releasing her and stepping backwards. His feelings were too confusing and troubling to risk staying near his wife for long.

"You should get something to eat," he said abruptly. "Come, I'll walk you to the kitchen."

After he had left his wife off at the kitchen, Maelgwn walked aimlessly in the courtyard, deep in thought. He paused and looked up, scanning the heavens, making out the faint pattern of the stars above him.

"Are you making a wish?"

Maelgwn turned away from the sky to see the bulky shape of Balyn silhouetted against the fading light.

"If I believed that wishes on the stars came true, I might make one tonight."

"And would it involve Aurora?" Balyn asked in a soft, almost gentle voice.

Maelgwn sighed. "Tell me what *you* think? It seems

that everyone has a different opinion of Aurora, and I can't even decide in my own thoughts."

"How's that?"

"There are times when Esylt near convinces me that Aurora is a conniving, untrustworthy bitch, but then I look at her as she was tonight, and see only her beauty and gentleness."

"Surely you cannot believe what Esylt thinks—she hates Aurora."

"Aye, you are right, but why am I tortured by doubts? Why do I feel I can never be sure of her?"

Maelgwn could not see his face, but Balyn's shrug was plain in the darkness. "Perhaps it is the way of love—never to be completely sure of the other."

"I was not speaking of love."

"Nah, nah, you do not love her. No, you let her throw you out of your own bed, you keep track of her every move, you resist any man who suggests that you divorce her, but no, certainly you do not love her."

"I do not need your sarcasm!"

"Well, you did ask for my opinion."

"Ah, so I did, but now that I have it, it solves nothing. It is my own heart I battle with."

"Where is she now?"

"She is eating, and then she will undoubtedly go to bed."

"And will you go to her?"

"The gods know, I want to, but I do not know . . . I cannot bear to risk another battle with her like the last one."

"All the same, you have no intention of disavowing the marriage?"

"Why should I? I would have to relinquish Viroconium, or fight a war with Constantine."

"It seems it might well be worth it . . . for your peace
of mind."

"You think I would have peace of mind if I returned
to her father? Think again. I would dream of her for the
rest of my days."

"But of course, you do not love her," Balyn said slyly.

"I do not understand the thing you speak of as love,"
Maelgwn said wistfully. "There are times I think this is
a sickness, an obsession." He groaned. "Perhaps Esylt is
right—this woman is like a poison in my blood."

Balyn shook his head. "I cannot help you, my lord.
The Roman god, Eros, has never wounded me so fa-
tally . . . but then I never had a chance with a woman
like Aurora."

"Tell me," Maelgwn said softly. "Tell me what you
truly think of her."

"Aye. She is beautiful and full of passion. She is the
kind of woman men dream of even as they sleep by their
wives."

"But I cannot make her care for me," Maelgwn said
bitterly. "I can make her obey me, but I cannot make
her love me back."

Twenty-four

Aurora glanced up at the sky uneasily. It was already late morning, and she had not been able to depart the fortress yet. If only it hadn't taken so long to get the food for Justina. Convincing the man in charge of the food-stores that she had a right to a bag of grain and an amphora of oil had not been easy. It was infuriating. She was queen, but with Esylt overseeing everything, Aurora was reduced to begging for a share of her husband's property.

Hurriedly, Aurora made her way to the stables. At least the stablemaster was willing to take orders from her. Paithu should be saddled and ready by now. She found the mare and began to secure the food to the saddlebags. Hearing heavy footsteps behind her, she turned.

"My lord," she gasped out as she saw Maelgwn.

"Good morning. Are you going riding today?"

Aurora nodded, trying not to meet his eyes. Maelgwn was such a shrewd observer, she was afraid he would see her fear and misunderstand.

"Surely that is not all for you," he suggested, pointing to the bag of grain she held in her hand.

"No, no it is not. It is a gift for someone in the vil-lage . . . a friend."

"And who might this friend be?" Maelgwn asked,

moving closer to her. The slight smile he had worn earlier faded, and his eyes searched her face with cool intensity.

Aurora bit her lip, trying to decide. Should she tell him the truth? Lying would probably only make him more suspicious.

"Her name is Justina."

Maelgwn's dark brows went up in surprise. "That old crone? What business do you have with her?"

"I went to her for some herbs. We talked and became friends."

Maelgwn's frown deepened. "Herbs, what use do you have for herbs?"

Aurora struggled to think of something plausible. It was clear that Maelgwn guessed that she was not telling him all the truth.

"I . . . I wanted to make a certain beauty preparation."

Maelgwn looked startled. Then his face relaxed. He reached out and touched Aurora's cheek gently, his voice was vibrant with regret.

"Aurora, you do not need such things. You have more than enough beauty to break my heart."

Aurora held her breath, feeling the aching longing that passed between them. Then it was gone, and Maelgwn's voice was light and controlled again.

"Go then, Aurora, but do not come back so late today. I cannot have them keep the gates open for you every night."

Numbly, Aurora let Maelgwn help her mount her horse and led the mare out of the stable. As she headed for the gate, her whole body began to tremble. Maelgwn had not seemed cold and mocking this morning, but tender and concerned. Was it possible that he wanted to forget the past and try again? Was it possible that he truly cared for her?

The thought filled Aurora with yearning. Perhaps there was hope after all. A giddy, light-headed happiness nearly overtook her—until she remembered Justina's warning. Maelgwn's life might be in danger; she must try to help him. Aurora sighed. But would he let her? Even if Maelgwn wanted her back in his bed, that did not mean he trusted her or would listen to her.

She thought of telling Maelgwn about Justina's warning and immediately guessed his response. He would ask what Esylt would gain by conspiring to overthrow him. He would point out that his sister already had as much power as any woman in Gwynedd. Why would Esylt risk everything on the chance that she would have more authority and honor as Cunedda's consort than as Maelgwn's sister?

The tangle of questions made Aurora's head ache as she urged Paithu down the hill. It was obvious that she needed more proof before she went to her husband. She could only hope that by today Justina would have learned something more, something which might prove to Maelgwn that his sister was about to betray him.

Aurora rode past the village, too deep in thought to remember to look for Morganna. She cautiously approached Justina's hut, set back in a clearing away from the rest of the village. Everything seemed deserted, and for a moment Aurora wondered if she had only imagined Justina and the events of the day before.

She dismounted and approached the hut, holding her skirt carefully out of the mud. Lifting up the hide that covered the entrance, she saw a low fire burning in the fireplace. Aurora went in and set the gifts she had brought on the table, further reassured by the fragrant odor of herbs which filled the dwelling. She sat down on one of the stools, to wait beside the glowing fire.

It was not long before Justina entered with an armload of freshly cut plants. Aurora had forgotten how tiny the woman was—her burden of greens seemed almost as large as she was.

"Hello," Aurora said shyly. "I did not think you would mind my waiting for you."

Justina gave her little tinkling laugh. "Mind? No, of course I do not mind." She dropped her burden on the floor and looked at Aurora intently. "Have you talked to Maelgwn yet?"

Aurora shook her head. "No . . . I was afraid he would not believe me. I need proof."

Justina sighed. "Maelgwn has ever had a blindness when it comes to his sister. We must do something to make him see what she is up to. I have learned a little more at least."

"What is that?" Aurora asked eagerly.

"The red-haired man's name is Urlain, and he met with a man from the fortress named Grimerwyn."

Aurora frowned. "Grimerwyn was once Esylt's lover, but he fell out of favor when we returned from Manau Gotodin."

"Do you think that is enough of a connection to convince Maelgwn?"

Aurora got up from the stool and paced. "I don't know. If only he was more reasonable about his sister, if only he trusted me."

Justina brought her twisted fingers to her chin, considering. "I would think that a woman who looked like you would be able to convince a man of anything."

"No, that is not true," Aurora said in a pained voice. "I tried to seduce my husband once, and it only made him angry."

"Well, if you cannot use your beauty, then you must convince him with words. Or, there is another way I have thought of."

"What?"

"If Esylt were to die," Justina said slowly. "Then whatever she is planning with Cunedda would end there."

Aurora stared into Justina's ravaged face. "Are you suggesting that I murder Esylt?"

Justina shrugged. "I am a healing woman, and there are certain potions . . . well . . . if used correctly, no one can tell."

Aurora shuddered. "And I would be the one to give it to her?"

Justina nodded. "You are the only one who could get close enough."

"I cannot do it," Aurora said firmly. "I cannot kill anyone so cruelly, even Esylt."

"Aye, you are right," Justina sighed. "It is better not to fight evil with evil. You must go to Maelgwn . . . you must talk to him . . . and soon."

"I will," Aurora said decisively. "I will tell him what you told me."

"Of course, you cannot mention my name," Justina warned.

"Why not?"

"You are the queen—Esylt dared not touch you, but

me—it would be easy for me to die accidently while picking herbs."

Aurora stared into Justina's eyes. They seemed weaker today, as if a film covered their luminous dark pupils. "But if I cannot tell Maelgwn of how I learned these things, he will never believe me!" Aurora began pacing again, moving restlessly in the tiny room.

"If I could tell Maelgwn what you know, then surely he could protect you, surely Esylt would not be able to hurt you."

"No!" Justina cried in a frightened voice. "Esylt knows things—some of the ancient spells, the old magic—there is no way Maelgwn can protect me from her."

Aurora exhaled a shaky breath. She had always suspected that Esylt had evil powers—now Justina was telling her that it was true. Was there no way to fight her—no way to make Maelgwn see that his sister was deceitful and wicked? Aurora struggled to shake off the spell of fear. She must be strong; she must go to Maelgwn and make him understand the danger he was in.

"I will talk to Maelgwn," she told Justina resolutely. "Somehow I will make him believe me."

Aurora made a move to go—determined to face Maelgwn before she lost her nerve. Before she reached the door, Justina stopped her.

"Here you have brought me gifts, and I have given you nothing in return," she said, gesturing to the food Aurora had left on the table. "I must repay you."

Aurora waited while Justina went to the corner of the room and dug in the ground there. She returned with a little round jar made of bronze. She placed it in Aurora's hand, closing her fingers over the faceted edges.

"Here—in case you need it."

"What is it?" Aurora asked uneasily.

"It is the special mixture I told you about. No, do not give it back," she said as Aurora shook her head. "You do not have to use it, but you never know, there may come a time that you will need it. It only takes a pinch in a cup of wine or beer to make Esylt fall into the sleep that lasts forever."

"Thank you," Aurora said softly. She could not understand why tears came to her eyes. Impulsively, she gave Justina a kiss, and then hurried out the tiny door.

Aurora returned to the fortress, shaking with tension. She left Paithu at the stables and went looking for Maelgwn. She found him in his office in the corner of the barracks. He seemed to be studying something on the table in front of him, and he did not look up as she entered. For a moment Aurora stood quietly, looking around the large room. The table Maelgwn was sitting at was in the corner by the fireplace, and next to him were shelves with dusty maps and a few parchment books. On the other side of the room there was a pile of sheepskins and blankets where Gwenaseth said Maelgwn often slept.

Aurora couldn't help contrasting the room's sparse, ancient furnishings with those of her father's office. It had a lovely tiled floor, a massive desk instead of a table, and tall shelves stuffed with rolled-up books. It was heated with a beautiful bronze brazier, and there were several well-made couches and chairs for guests. It was odd, Aurora thought, but despite the beauty and wealth that surrounded him, compared to Maelgwn, her father wielded very little power. Perhaps it was true that the days of the Romans were over and from now on the land would be ruled by the hardy Britains.

Maelgwn looked up, and an expression of mingled surprise and pleasure crossed his face.

"Aurora! What are you doing here?"

"I need to talk to you."

Maelgwn got up and found an old stool in the corner and bade her sit down. He sat down again with the table between them. Despite the warmth of his greeting, his face was wary and his blue eyes blazed with deadly intensity.

Aurora cleared her throat. "I . . . I have something to tell you."

Maelgwn nodded.

"There has been a man down near the village who I think is a Brigante. His name is Urlain, and he has been seen talking to Grimerwyn."

There was no change in Maelgwn's face. No flicker of interest. Nothing.

"I am afraid that Cunedda is plotting with someone inside Caer Eryri to betray you, and this man is his spy." Aurora spoke breathlessly, the words tumbling out in a flood of emotion.

"Who is it inside Caer Eryri that you think he plots with?"

Aurora bit her lips, and her voice was barely audible. "Esylt."

Maelgwn made an expression of disgust and stood up.

"Well, does it not make sense?" Aurora asked anxiously. "Grimerwyn was Esylt's lover until recently, and certainly Esylt is close enough with Cunedda that she might do something like this!"

"Can't you think of a better story, Aurora? Esylt has many faults, I know, but it would be stupid for her to plot against me with Cunedda. What could she ever hope to be to him—except another one of his wives? She has much more power now than Cunedda would ever give her." Maelgwn looked at Aurora with narrowed eyes. "I should never have told you of my doubts about Cunedda. It seems I cannot trust you with any information."

"Perhaps I am wrong about Esylt," Aurora said in anguish. "But the part about the Brigante man and Grimerwyn—that is true!"

"Did you see them?"

"No, but the person that told me is very trustworthy."

"Who told you?"

Aurora looked away from Maelgwn's angry face.

"I cannot tell you," she answered miserably.

"Perhaps it was that old crone—Justina," Maelgwn said scornfully. "I am told that she is a crazy, that the herbal potions she takes give her strange and fanciful dreams. Perhaps this is one of them."

Maelgwn came around the table and stood directly in front of Aurora; he was so close he was almost touching her. "It's just a story, isn't it?" he asked her coldly. "It's just a lie you made up to try and turn me against Esylt."

Aurora shook her head and stood up. "No, no, it is not," she said defiantly. Somehow the fear was leaving her, and she was angry and very frustrated. "Why is it you believe Esylt's stories against *me?*" Aurora challenged. "I would think after Dinas Brenin you would have realized what a manipulative monster she is!"

Maelgwn had turned his back, as if to leave, but at her words, he came back to stand close to her.

"Who told you of Dinas Brenin?" he asked in a quiet, deadly voice.

It seemed that there was something stuffed in Aurora's throat. In her anger she had forgotten her promise to Justina. She did not know what to say.

"I must have overheard someone," she said in a voice that was little more than a whisper.

"Liar!" he hissed. "No one at Caer Eryri would speak of it to you. No one would dare. Tell me," he continued threateningly. "Tell me who told you."

"I can't," she answered in a quavering voice. "I can't betray them."

For a moment Aurora feared Maelgwn would strike her—his face was so full of hatred. He grabbed her, his fingers digging into her arms, then he pushed her away and backed toward the door. "Damn scheming witch!" he shouted. "Your face is so sweet and innocent, but you dared to keep secrets from me and throw the ugliness of the past in my face!"

"No! I did not mean to hurt you," Aurora begged. "I am trying to warn you, to help you." She reached out her hands imploringly. "Please Maelgwn, please believe me. I have not betrayed you . . . I . . . I love you."

"Love!" Maelgwn sneered. "What do you know of love except the favors your lovely body can earn for you. I am not some boy you can manipulate as you wish. I am a man, a king, and I have had my fill of scheming women for the rest of my life."

"Please, Maelgwn, please," Aurora begged. "Give me

a chance." Tears streamed down her face, and she felt as if something was breaking inside of her.

"No!" Maelgwn thundered as he reached the doorway. "You have used up all your chances with me!"

Aurora stood in the bare, lonely office and cried silently. What should she do? She had tried to help Maelgwn, to make things right, and he had rejected her more terribly than ever. It was over, she thought bitterly. Now he would send her back to her father. She was so alone, so completely alone. Gwenaseth and Elwyn were so absorbed in each other, they no longer had time for her. There was no one at Caer Eryri she could call a friend. No one except Justina.

Aurora wiped her streaked face on her hands and tried to pull herself together. It was still early. She could easily slip out the gate and go to the village. Aurora had a great need to see Justina—to reassure herself that the intriguing little woman was real. Already she had begun to doubt her memory. Could it be that she had thrown away her last chance with Maelgwn because of a crazy woman whose head was full of twisted thoughts?

Aurora hurried to the gate, not stopping for her horse. She would walk this time. There was no need to keep up the pretense that she was just riding in the valley. She no longer cared if Maelgwn knew she had gone to see Justina.

It was early afternoon—just a few hours since she had visited before. The air was quiet and heavy, and Aurora knew a storm was on its way. She should stop and get a cloak, but it hardly seemed important. Aurora walked rapidly down the track to the village. In the warm, calm air, she could smell the heart-breaking scent of the starflowers on the hill. It was late summer, and soon the flowers would be gone. It would not matter, Aurora thought bitterly. She would be gone, too, and Caer Eryri would be just a memory.

Aurora had not yet reached the village when the small hairs on the back of her neck told her that something was wrong. She went a few paces farther and smelled smoke. The odor was acrid, intense, but mingled with it was another, softer scent. Aurora was not even near Justina's hut when she began to suspect what she would find. She quickened her pace, full of dread. Her breathing was quick and shallow. Justina had known—that was why she had given Aurora the poison.

Aurora reached the clearing and stopped. She could go no further. Even from this distance, the heat was intense. It was not only the dry, ancient wood of Justina's hut which blazed so fiercely, but also the herbs which had hung along the walls—that was why the smoke smelled so sweet.

Aurora turned her head away. She did not want to watch the wicked yellow flames, and she did not have to approach more closely to know that Justina had been inside—that she had been murdered. Aurora looked around the forest nervously. If someone had seen fit to kill Justina—why not her, too? She bolted out of the clearing like a frightened deer. Big drops of rain were falling. She could hear them sizzle on the fire behind her. She ran and ran, breathless, gasping. It was not until she was in sight of the gate that she slowed her pace.

Caer Eryri looked so solid and ordinary compared to the tragic destruction she had just witnessed. The guard dozed inside the gatehouse. Woman were chasing a few

squalling geese into their pens, while errant children
played a game of tag, heedless of the rain. Aurora ran
to the tower. She was soaked. She was not chilled, but
steaming with panicky sweat.

The stairs had never seemed so steep. Aurora reached
the tower room with relief, and let herself in. The sky
outside the room was dark and threatening, and no lamp
or fire had yet been kindled. It took a moment for
Aurora's eyes to adjust to the darkness. As her eyes began
to make out the familiar objects in the room, her heart
flew into her throat. Maelgwn was sitting quietly on the
bed, watching her.

Aurora had not expected to see her husband again until
he came to her to tell her that the marriage was over. It
unnerved her to find him waiting for her. She did not
know what to say—she waited for him to speak.

Maelgwn said nothing, but stood and went to strike a
flint to kindle the lamp. The golden light flared into the
dim, gloomy room. Still he did not speak, but walked
back to sit upon the bed. He seemed to be cupping something in his big hand, and he played idly with the object,
turning it around restlessly so that it caught the glint of
the lamplight and glowed eerily within his fingers.

"What is this, Aurora?" His voice was calm, without
emotion.

He reached out his hand, palm up. The small round
object stood out clearly—it was the vial of poison that
Justina had given Aurora.

For a long while, Aurora said nothing, searching her
mind for some story, some explanation that Maelgwn
would accept. Nothing came to her, and she remained
silent, listening to the sound of her own strained, harsh

breathing. Maelgwn twirled the small bronze jar until the facets along its edges reflected dazzling patterns on the ceiling of the tower room.

At last, reason seemed to return to her, and she had her answer. "It is a beauty potion from Justina," she said in the coldest, most withering tone she could summon.

Maelgwn stared at her a moment, as if willing the truth from her. Then he carefully removed the lid of the jar and looked at its contents.

Aurora had not had a chance to open the jar yet to see what the poison looked like. That afternoon she had hastily dropped it on the table beside the bed before she went to see Maelgwn. Now she leaned forward, startled by the sight of the white powder inside the vial.

Maelgwn examined the contents carefully—even sniffing it—then he moistened a finger and dipped it into the jar as if to taste it.

"No!" Aurora shouted. "Don't!"

Maelgwn looked at her curiously. "Why not?"

"Because it is . . . it is . . ."

"Poison?" Maelgwn suggested helpfully. "I thought as much. Justina is not as clever as she thinks. I have heard of this concoction, and it is deadly indeed, but until it is mixed in liquid, its odor gives it away. Tell me, Aurora, when did you mean to give it to me? Did you plan to wait until we had a meal in the great hall, and anyone could be blamed for it?"

"Not you!" Aurora said in an anguished voice. "Never you!"

"Who then? Esylt?" Maelgwn's fierce eyes bored into her. "It seems that you are the one who schemes, Aurora. You are the one who can't be trusted."

"It is not like that," Aurora protested. "I was afraid . . . afraid for you. Esylt is evil—she plans to destroy you."

"It is funny," Maelgwn suggested, although he looked anything but amused. "Since I was a child, whenever anyone in my family tried to justify their actions, they used that excuse. Whoever opposed them—they were always the evil ones. I am so tired of this jealous hatred, Aurora. So tired. I want it to end once and for all."

Aurora slumped down on the stool in the corner of the room, weak with fatigue and despair. She began to twist her rings around on her fingers. Finally she looked up at Maelgwn. He was watching her with a disgusted look that frightened her even more than his anger.

"What are you going to do with me?" she asked in a quavering voice.

Maelgwn walked over to her and picked her up by her long hair, bringing her face very close to his. "What *should* I do with you?" he hissed menacingly. "Surely if I were wise, I would kill you now, and put us both out of our misery."

Aurora stared in terror at Maelgwn's deadly eyes. The blue was gone from them, and they were an empty, savage black. Maelgwn released his grip, and Aurora fell back awkwardly on the stool. He seemed to gain control of himself, and the murderous rage left his face.

"I don't know what I plan to do with you," he said as he strode toward the door. "I will have to think on it—in the meantime, you are not allowed to leave this room."

"You mean I am to stay here? A prisoner?"

Maelgwn nodded. "There will be a guard at the bottom of the stairs."

"I will not run away," Aurora begged. "Please do not lock me up!"

Maelgwn shook his head. "I can't trust you—you've proven that. I wouldn't be surprised if you went running to Justina again."

"Justina is dead!" Aurora gasped. "Her hut burned in a fire." The pain hit her sharply. Justina was dead—for a moment she had almost forgotten.

"Good riddance, I say," Maelgwn said coldly. "Can't you see how she entangled you in her plot? She has always hated Esylt, and in you she saw the perfect tool to finally wreak her vengeance."

"No! I don't believe you!" Aurora protested. "She was not like that—she was kind to me, and she was concerned for the future of Gwynedd."

"I do not want to hear your stories and justifications. I will let you know what I decide to do with you tomorrow. In the meantime, I will send Gwenaseth to see to your needs."

Then he was gone. The door shut behind him with a finality that made Aurora jump.

Twenty-five

Maelgwn found Balyn just leaving the great hall.

"I need to have you do something immediately."

"Of course, Maelgwn, what is it?"

"I want a guard posted outside the tower. It does not matter who visits Aurora, but I don't want her leaving there."

"By the gods, what has happened?"

"See to it!" Maelgwn barked. Then his voice softened. "Then meet me in the council room—I need to talk to you."

Balyn hurried away without another word, and Maelgwn trudged wearily toward the barracks. His head was spinning. He needed quiet and time to think. A few hours ago, he had been determined to try again with Aurora—to make things right with her. Then everything had fallen apart. First, there had been Aurora's awkward and obvious attempt to discredit Esylt with her story of the spy in the village and the plot against him. If that had not been bad enough, she had dragged up the old pain of Dinas Brenin and thrown that in his face.

But the final blow was the poison. Maelgwn sighed deeply. How had things come to this—how had the sweet young woman he married become so warped by hate that she would plot murder? Or, had Esylt been right all along? Had Aurora always been capable of treachery, and he had been too besotted to see her for what she was?

Maelgwn felt the cold pain twisting in his belly. Aurora had told him that she loved him. She had finally said the words he longed to hear from her lips. But it was too late. He could never believe her. He could never be sure that it wasn't just another clever attempt to manipulate him.

Maelgwn reached the office and kindled a torch to illuminate the large, nearly empty room. He knew what he must do. He must banish Aurora from his life forever. He sat down heavily. How would he find the strength? Even now all he could think about was going to Aurora, of holding her in his arms once again. He tried to hang onto his hate, his anger. It was futile. His love was stronger than those feelings would ever be.

Maelgwn turned as he heard the hollow echo of Balyn's footsteps.

"My lord," his friend said tentatively.

"Come. Sit." Maelgwn said, gesturing toward the stool that Aurora had sat upon only a few hours before.

Balyn settled his bulky frame upon the small stool. His big open face looked worried.

"Ah, Balyn. You have been right all along. I do love her."

"That is good news. So why are you keeping her a prisoner?"

"Perhaps for now she is locked up so she will be safe from me."

"I don't understand."

"Neither do I. I love her, but it seems she is poison

for me. Hah—poison, that is a good one!" Maelgwn said humorlessly.

"What has she done?"

Maelgwn shook his head. "She accused Esylt of treason and admitted she was planning to poison her."

"Aurora? Poison Esylt? I don't believe it."

"Aye, it is hard to imagine. I'm not sure she would have ever gone through with it, but in these things, intentions do count for something. I will never be able to trust her again."

"So, you have decided to send her back to Viroconium?"

Maelgwn nodded. "If I can find the strength to do it."

Balyn looked thoughtful. He rubbed his meaty hands together nervously. "Well, there is another possiblility, you know."

"What is that?"

"Get rid of Esylt." Balyn looked directly into Maelgwn's eyes. "It would solve your problems with Aurora. And . . . I've never really liked Esylt much myself."

"How do you propose that I get rid of her?"

Balyn shrugged. "You could send her away."

"She would go straight to one of my enemies and raise an army against me. What kind of a solution is that?"

"But she couldn't win."

"Are you suggesting that I fight a war over a *woman?*"

"It wouldn't be the first time—you've heard of Helen of Troy . . ."

"Aye, I've heard of her," Maelgwn interrupted impatiently. "But what kind of a king would I be if I did that—risking men's lives because I can't control my own lust?"

"Or you could have Esylt killed."

"That would make it tidy, wouldn't it? All of Britain already thinks I've killed off the rest of my family in my lust for power. Cadwallon's eaglets they called us— squabbling amongst ourselves until only one eaglet is left in the nest."

"If only one eagle is to survive, would it not be better for Gwynedd if it is you rather than Esylt?"

Maelgwn sighed heavily. "I do not know if I could do it. It is one thing to kill a man in battle, but it is another to murder a woman because she interferes in your life. I already take enough guilt to bed each night because of Dinas Brenin. If I killed Esylt so I could have Aurora, it would ruin something for me. I think I would always blame Aurora for forcing me into something so evil."

"It is odd," Balyn said softly. "Your reputation is so bloodthirsty and cruel, but you have always been a just king, a fair one. It does not seem right that you cannot have the woman you love, just like any other man."

Maelgwn leaned his head on his hands wearily.

"I never wanted to be king. But now that I am, I know that I am not like other men anymore. Sometimes the king is the stag, the sacrifice that makes the fields ripen with abundance and women's bellies quicken with life. This land does not yet demand my life, but it is time for me, no matter what the pain, to put aside my feelings for Aurora and do what is best for Gwynedd."

"You have decided then?" Balyn asked.

Maelgwn nodded. "I'll tell her tomorrow."

* * *

Gwenaseth rushed up the tower stairs. Balyn's weary, patient face when he came to tell her to go to Aurora had alarmed her, but not nearly so much as seeing the armed guard waiting by the tower entrance. It seemed Aurora was in trouble, grave trouble.

Gwenaseth felt a stab of guilt. She had not paid enough attention to Aurora lately. She had been busy setting up her own household and adjusting to married life. No, that was not true. The truth was that her feelings were hurt when Aurora had been so cold and distant after Lughnasa. She had been selfish, and now things were worse than ever between Aurora and Maelgwn. Gwenaseth sighed. If Aurora were sent back to Viroconium, she would never forgive herself for not doing more to help.

The tower room door was unbolted, and Gwenaseth barely knocked before opening it and hurrying in. Aurora was seated on a stool, staring into the lamplight, her face pale and stricken.

"My lady, what is it? What has happened?"

Aurora looked up with dull eyes, and her voice was empty and harsh. "I don't know Gwenaseth, truly I don't. I've tried, but it seems it is no use."

"Did Maelgwn tell you—did he say he was going to divorce you?"

Aurora shook her head. "No, he said he would let me know what he plans to do with me tomorrow. I would be grateful if all he plans to do is send me back to my father. I think he may have me killed instead."

"No! Maelgwn would not do such a thing!"

Aurora shook her head numbly. "He said it would be

best for both of us. He was furious—I am surprised he did not murder me then and there."

"What did you do Aurora? Why is he so angry?"

"I got some poison from a woman in the village. Maelgwn thinks I was going to use it to kill Esylt."

Gwenaseth gasped. "You were not, surely you were not really going to do it?"

"I don't know. I was desperate. I believed that Esylt was plotting to betray Maelgwn, and that I was the only one who could stop her."

"Did you tell Maelgwn that?"

"Of course. He called me a liar, as always."

Gwenaseth stared at Aurora's swollen eyes and pathetic face. What was wrong with Maelgwn? Why could he not see his wife for what she was—a lonely, frightened young woman? But it seemed he could not. For some reason Maelgwn was determined to punish Aurora. Would it be death? Death hardly seemed appropriate for Aurora's mistakes, and killing Aurora would bring war and bloodshed. It was not right—she could not let Maelgwn do it. But first, Gwenaseth had to be sure of his intentions.

"I'll take leave of you now, Aurora," Gwenaseth said softly. "I need to talk to Elwyn. But I promise you, I will not desert you. I will help you somehow."

Elwyn hurried toward the barracks, the blood humming and bubbling in his veins and his feet churning frantically beneath him. Even in battle, he had never felt so tense and desperate. He could hardly believe the story his wife had just brought to him—that Maelgwn was planning to kill Aurora. It defied reason—all of it. He could not believe that Aurora had planned to poison Esylt. Aye, Esylt was a bitch, and evil at that, but poison? It seemed impossible that the sweet, tender-hearted queen he knew could even consider such a thing. And then, to think that Maelgwn was planning to have Aurora put to death for her mistake—that was madness, too. Anyone could see that Maelgwn was being eaten alive by his passion for Aurora. Her death would solve nothing, except to destroy Maelgwn as well.

Elwyn reached the barracks and saw with a mixture of relief and dread that the light in Maelgwn's office still burned. Gwenaseth had sent him to find out what Maelgwn intended to do, and find out he must. Still, he dreaded this confrontration with his king. He could not help remembering the last time he had tried to intervene in Maelgwn's relationship with his wife. Elwyn took a moment to slow his breathing and steady his nerves before entering.

Maelgwn looked up as he walked in. The king was seated at the table as if working, but nothing lay before him. His eyes were dark and hollow, his face streaked with shadows. Elwyn had never seen him look so old. The proud, powerful warrior was gone, and in his place sat a weary, dispirited man.

Maelgwn said nothing. Elwyn burst out bluntly: "My lord . . . I was wondering. What are you planning to do with Aurora?"

"What do you think I must do?" Maelgwn answered in a dull, heavy voice. "She has plotted to kill my sister—that is treason, even for a queen."

"But she is so young, so frightened," Elwyn protested. "Surely you must take that into account."

"Don't you see, Elwyn," Maelgwn answered in a voice of utter anguish. "I cannot let my feelings interfere with my duty. I must do what is best for Gwynedd, for my people—even though it tears out my heart."

"But there will be war. Constantine will surely never endure such a thing without retaliating!"

"Maybe," Maelgwn agreed thoughtfully. "But I went to Viroconium expecting to go to war—there will always be war."

Silence loomed between the two men for awhile. When Elwyn finally spoke, his voice seemed very soft, very frail in the large, empty room.

"Maelgwn, I must tell you—I cannot go along with your decision. I can have no part in this."

"Very well, Elwyn, it is not your decision to make. Nor your burden to carry."

Maelgwn spoke no more, and the silence stretched between them again. Finally, Maelgwn looked up.

"If that is all you have come to say, you may go. I have several other decisions to make tonight."

Elwyn bowed curtly and left the room. It seemed as though his knees might give way beneath him as he hurried to the small house he shared with Gwenaseth.

"You were right," he blurted out as he stumbled into the darkened room. "Maelgwn intends to have Aurora put to death for treason. He says he does not want to, but he must put the good of Gwynedd first."

Gwenaseth gaped at her husband, and then her face turned hard. "Stupid man! He will never forgive himself. Doesn't he know that honor matters little compared to love? Well, we won't let it happen!" she added in a determined voice. "We will keep him from making the worst mistake of his life."

"How can you speak so?" Elwyn asked in a shocked voice. "How can you dare to defy our king's wishes?"

Gwenaseth shook her head. "You are a soldier, Elwyn, and you have been taught to obey, no matter what, but my father raised me to be a princess and to think for myself. This thing that Maelgwn intends to do is wrong, and we must stop him."

Gwenaseth smiled at the young guard as she opened the door. "I am taking the queen some clothes and food," she said, gesturing at the large basket she carried.

"So late?" the man asked lazily. "I can't believe you are still up. I know I would be in bed already if I were not ordered to stay here."

"When does your relief come?"

"Not for another hour or two," the soldier sighed. "I hope I can stay awake that long."

"After I get these things to her, I'm going to prepare the queen for bed. It should be quiet the rest of the night."

"Tell me," the soldier said with a conspiratorial wink. "Why does Maelgwn have his wife locked up like this? Does he think she sneaks out to meet someone else?"

"I don't know," Gwenaseth answered impatiently. "Men sometimes get strange fancies regarding their wives."

"I concede that Queen Aurora's looks could drive any husband to jealousy, but Maelgwn's means seem extreme. Wouldn't it be easier for him to guard her himself by sleeping next to her every night? It would certainly save us soldiers a lot of trouble."

"Perhaps I'll mention it to him," Gwenaseth said as she hurried up the stairs.

Aurora had barely changed position since Gwenaseth had been to see her earlier. She still sat on the stool, staring at nothing and twirling her rings endlessly around on her fingers.

"I sent Elwyn to speak to Maelgwn, Aurora," Gwenaseth said gently, kneeling down beside the queen. She laid a tender hand on her arm. "You were right. He does intend to put you to death."

Aurora gave an anguished cry. "I am afraid to die, Gwenaseth. I do not even know what gods are real—which ones will help me!" She shuddered, and her voice became breathy and strained. "What if he decides to burn me to death—oh, please, Gwenaseth," she pleaded. "Please beg him not to do that. It is an awful way to die . . . the smoke . . . the smell of the fire!"

"Hush!" Gwenaseth cried, giving the terrified woman a shake. "I'm not going to let him do it—I'm going to get you out of here!"

Aurora seemed to calm herself. "Aye. You are right. I must fight him. I must not go meekly to my death." She looked at Gwenaseth uncertainly. "But there is only one way out of here . . . and the guard."

"No, there are two ways out," Gwenaseth answered, pointing to the window.

Aurora stared uneasily at the window that looked out over the valley. "I don't know, Gwenaseth. It is like riding a horse is to you—I am very afraid of heights."

"Well, you'd better get over your fear, at least for tonight. I could get you out of the tower by distracting the guard, but I could not get you out the gate. The only way you can escape is to climb out the window and down the fortress wall."

Aurora looked toward the window and gave a shiver of fear. "How will I climb down?"

"With this," Gwenaseth answered, pulling a braided leather rope out of the bottom of the basket. "It is not quite long enough to reach the ground, but you can jump that far."

"How will I get away? On foot, I can never escape before morning."

"I have thought of that," Gwenaseth answered. "Elwyn has gone outside the fortress—he told the guard that he has to see about the fire in the village this afternoon. He will get Paithu and saddle her for you. She will come when you call her, won't she?"

Aurora nodded. "It is a brilliant plan, Gwenaseth, but I am afraid for you and Elwyn. What will Maelgwn do to you if he learns you have helped me?"

Gwenaseth shrugged. "He will probably banish us, but we can go live with my father. I could not stand to stay here anyway if you do not get away, and Maelgwn . . . does what he plans to do."

Aurora reached out for the tiny, red-haired woman. "Oh, Gwenaseth, what would I have done without you?"

"Nah, nah, there is not time for hugging and tears, Aurora. We must hurry. The guard changes in but a little while, and we must be done before then. The man down there now is so sleepy and lazy that I doubt he will notice any strange sounds or bother to investigate them.

* * *

It was well past midnight when Maelgwn left the office. It seemed that the rest of the fortress slept peacefully. Out of force of habit, he glanced up at the tower room. All was dark; Aurora must have gone to bed. Maelgwn flexed his muscles. He had been sitting so long that he was stiff. He looked up again at the tower, and a wave of longing washed over him. He let out his breath in a long, drawn-out sigh, and then began walking toward the tower.

"Is all quiet?" he asked the guard by the door.

The man nodded. "I just took over the watch a few minutes ago." The soldier looked at Maelgwn curiously. "Are you going up?"

"Aye," Maelgwn answered abruptly. "It seems I can't stay away."

Maelgwn took the steps heavily. He wished he was not so tired. He could not properly say good-bye to his wife if he fell asleep immediately. But would she even have him, he wondered? She had spoken of love earlier, but once she knew that their marriage was over, would she welcome him into her bed one last time?

Maelgwn paused at the door, wondering if he should knock. It was really his room after all . . . and his wife . . . for a little while longer.

He opened the door, and it creaked noisily on its ancient hinges. The room was dark. There was no sound of Aurora stirring. Maelgwn took his sword off and sat down on the bed to remove his boots. Aurora must be deeply asleep—usually she woke as soon as he came into the room. No doubt she was exhausted by the day, much

as he was. Perhaps for now they should just sleep together and find comfort in the presence of each other.
There would be time for lovemaking in the morning.

Still, he could not go to sleep without touching her,
feeling her warmth nestled beside him, the extravagant
luxury of her hair. He reached toward Aurora's side of
the bed . . .

Maelgwn stood up suddenly, groping for the table,
fumbling for the flint to light the lamp. She had to be
in the room—why could he not find her? His fingers
were trembling, awkward, and it seemed to take hours to
light the lamp. Once lit, he shone it around the room,
covering every space in the small round chamber. She
was not there; she simply was not there. Maelgwn looked
around again, feeling confused. His eyes lighted on the
windows, and a wave of fear engulfed him. No, it could
not be.

He covered the space to the nearest window in two
huge strides and looked out. The courtyard looked peaceful. It had begun to rain, and the smell of damp earth
wafted up to his nostrils. Still shaking, Maelgwn moved
to the window on the other side. Looking down from the
height of the tower seemed to make him dizzy. There
were no torches burning on this side of the fortress, and
everything was very dark. He squinted, looking for the
light color of clothes, the shape of a body. There was
nothing.

He stood there for a moment, feeling puzzled and confused. His hands touched the cool stones of the window
sill, and came upon the unexpected roughness of a rope.
He pulled it . . . and pulled . . . It was very long; it
seemed to reach to very near the ground.

Maelgwn threw the rope down impatiently and began to dress again. His hands were trembling, and he could not move fast enough. He took the stairs two and three at a time and came crashing out the tower door.

"She's gone," he said in a choked voice to the guard.

The man gaped at him in amazement. "How *could* she be?"

"A rope . . . she climbed out the window with a rope. Quickly, tell me who came to see her tonight."

"I don't know," the guard said in a frightened voice. "I just came on duty."

"Think! Did the last guard mention anything?"

"He said that Lady Gwenaseth had been to see the queen earlier, but that is all I remember."

"It is enough," Maelgwn said grimly. "It is enough."

It did not take Maelgwn long to reach the small house that Elwyn had built for his bride during the summer. Maelgwn did not bother to call a greeting, but pushed the hide door aside and stalked over to the bed. Elwyn sat up and stared at him with one arm draped over Gwenaseth protectively.

"What is wrong, Maelgwn?" he asked in a frightened voice.

"You know very well what is wrong. Aurora is gone. The two of you helped her run away."

There was complete silence. Finally Elwyn spoke in a low, proud voice. "I won't deny it, my lord. I . . . we could not let you do what you were going to do."

"It was hardly *your* decision."

Elwyn sighed. "I know, and I am sorry. But . . . I care for Aurora . . . I could not let you kill her."

"We both care for her," Gwenaseth echoed proudly.

"Kill her?" Maelgwn asked in a puzzled voice. "You thought I was going to kill her?"

Elwyn began to stammer. "But you said . . . you said you had to do it, that you didn't want to, but it was for the sake of Gwynedd."

"Aye. For the sake of Gwynedd I was going to send Aurora back to Constantine and end the marriage." Maelgwn looked at the young couple huddled in the bed, staring at him with wild eyes. "Did you really believe I was going to have Aurora put to death?"

Elwyn nodded. "Aurora thought so, too. She was so frightened. You should have seen her—she is terrified of heights, but she climbed down the tower anyway. She is going to try and ride back to Viroconium."

Maelgwn buried his face in his hands. "Oh, Jupiter, Lugh, Cerrunos—save me! What have I done to her!"

Gwenaseth climbed out of bed and went to Maelgwn. "You were truly not going to kill Aurora?" she asked quietly.

"No, no! Of course not! I love Aurora. I am not sure I can live without her. If I had any other choice I would never give her up!"

Both Elwyn and Gwenaseth were perfectly still. They had never seen Maelgwn like this, and they did not know what to do.

Gradually, Maelgwn seemed to regain his composure. "I must find her," he said abruptly. "I cannot have Aurora return to her father thinking that I meant to murder her."

Twenty-six

Why did it have to be such a dark, dreary night? Aurora leaned forward, clutching the horse's mane. She could see but a few feet in front of her, and tremors still coursed through her body, reminding her of the danger she had already faced. At one point during the climb down the tower she had been ready to go back and face certain death rather than endure the dizzying fear that seemed to paralyze her. But Gwenaseth had continued to whisper words of encouragement and gradually she had been able to slide down the side of the tower to the safety of the ground. There she found Paithu, ready and waiting. Sweet Elwyn had done more than saddle her horse; the saddlebags were stuffed with food and other supplies. Now it remained only for her to ride as swiftly as she could and get as far from Caer Eryri as possible before morning.

As Aurora rode past the village, the faint scent of smoke came to her clearly. Tears formed in her eyes. How hard it was to believe that only one day before, she had left this same spot with her heart full of hope, pleased to have found a new friend. She whispered a brief prayer for Justina and urged the horse on.

Aurora reached the river and rode beside it for a

while. She was still in familiar territory, but her anxiety
was increasing. Somehow she would have to cross the
river and find the pathway on the other side. She moved
close to the water. She was lucky it was not raining
harder. It did not take much rain to make the river a
raging torrent, but tonight it was still relatively low. It
unnerved Aurora to think of riding into the cold swirling water when it was so hard to see, but her only
other choice was to ride farther down the valley and
take the bridge across. If she did that, she was afraid
that she would have trouble finding her way on the
other side of the river. It seemed better to trust Paithu
to get her across safely.

Aurora braced herself for the shock of the cold water
and urged the mare in. The water was deeper than she
expected, and Aurora's borrowed clothes were rapidly
soaked, but the horse swam strongly and they soon
reached the other side.

Aurora shivered. The night was fairly mild, but with
her wet clothes and the constant rain, she felt chilled to
the bone. She squinted into the darkness, trying to make
out familiar landmarks. The forest was pitch black, and
Aurora's spirits sank. How would she ever find her way?
She could ride all night and find she had traveled in
circles. Still, she had to try. By morning they would come
looking for her, and Maelgwn would be even more furious now that she had run away.

Aurora suppressed a sob—what had happened to the
man who had once made love to her with such delicious
tenderness? What had happened to make Maelgwn

change? Even now she couldn't hate him. Justina was right, it was his awful sister who had made him so cruel and mistrustful. Aurora felt tears mingling with the rain running down her cheeks—silent, bitter tears for what might have been.

Aurora was so tired, she could barely stay on Paithu. She no longer tried to guide the horse, but gave the mare free rein. The heavy vegetation seemed to claw at her, threatening to pull her off the horse. She leaned forward until her head almost lay on Paithu's neck. In her exhausted, dreamlike state her mind wandered back to the delicious contentment and pleasure she had once known with Maelgwn. Her head swam with memories of his fierce, demanding body, the touch of his work-roughened hands on her skin, his warm mouth kissing her with delightful sensitivity. Slowly, almost imperceptibly, her thoughts became hazy and seemed to stop.

Abruptly, the dark world tilted upwards and twisted around, and Aurora was aware that she was falling. She tried to right herself but it was too late. Something bright passed before her eyes, and then everything went black.

"She came this way," Balyn called as he held the torch over the muddy river bank. The other riders gathered around, staring at the hoof prints in the wet earth, now filling in with water.

"It looks like she crossed here."

"Why didn't she take the bridge?"

"Perhaps she was too frightened to go any further" Balyn suggested.

Maelgwn cringed at Balyn's words and the startled looks of the men around him. Aurora had run away in terror, so panicked that she couldn't wait to cross the river and be away from him. The guilt cut into him. He had lost his temper with her and threatened her life. Would he ever be able to convince Aurora to trust him again?

"We'd better cross," Balyn said grimly. "The river is not getting any lower, and the bridge is too far away."

The men rode into the water, swearing at the cold. After crossing, the riders grouped wretchedly on the other side. They all felt groggy and irritable—it was hard to be rousted out of bed to go riding in the rain.

"We should split up," Gareth suggested. "We can't be sure what route she took through the forest."

"Aye, that is a good idea," Balyn agreed. "Gareth, you and Elwyn go to the left. Rhys, Evrawc—you go this way. Maelgwn and I will keep to this side."

As the other men headed off, Balyn reached over to grab Maelgwn's stallion's bridle. "Are you all right, Maelgwn?"

Maelgwn roused himself from his thoughts to look into Balyn's worried face. "Aye, I'm fine," he answered weakly.

Balyn shook his head. "You don't look well, my lord . . . don't worry, we'll find her."

"Then what will we do?" Maelgwn asked harshly. "She is terrified of me—she thinks I mean to kill her."

"I'm sure you can explain to her, Maelgwn. She does love you, you know, I can tell by the way she looks at you."

Maelgwn stared into his friend's eyes. "I wish I could believe you."

"Come, we'd better get going," Balyn said gently. "The sooner we find her, the sooner you can make things right with her."

The two men rode in silence, pushing aside the low branches impatiently. Balyn still held the smoking torch, and the light reflected eerily on the trees and cast weird shadows across their path. The forest was thick and almost impenetrable in places. Dead trees seemed to be everywhere, and more than once they had to turn around to take another pathway.

"Maybe we should get down and search on foot," Maelgwn suggested when yet another fallen tree blocked their way.

Balyn disagreed. "Since we have not found Paithu, it seems that Aurora is still riding. She may be far ahead, and we could never hope to find her on foot."

"Paithu!" Maelgwn said suddenly. "Didn't Gareth train Paithu?"

"Aye, he did, and she is a superb and very gentle horse."

"I seem to remember Gareth saying that he had trained the mare to come when he whistled," Maelgwn said excitedly. "Maybe he could try that now—if the horse were to whinny back, at least we would know what direction they went."

Balyn nodded. "It is something to try. I'll call the others back."

He gave a shout—it did not take long for the other men to come riding toward them.

"Have you found her?" Elwyn called anxiously as he saw their torchlight through the trees.

"Not yet," Balyn answered. "Where's Gareth?"

"I'm here, sir," the older man called.

"Maelgwn has a plan," Balyn explained when all the men were assembled. "He wants Gareth to whistle for Paithu."

"What good will that do?" Evrawc complained. "If Aurora is running away, she will surely not let the horse ride back to us."

"It's just an idea," Balyn said coldly. "Otherwise, we night as well wait until morning. The forest is too dark and treacherous.

"Aye, let me try," Gareth said. He brought his fingers to his mouth and let out a clear, shrill whistle.

The men listened. They could hear the wind in the trees and the sound of dripping water on the forest floor, but nothing else. Gareth tried again. Twice more he made the high, piercing sound as the men waited.

"It's no use," Evrawc said impatiently. "She is long gone, or maybe hiding. We should either keep searching as we were or go back to our beds."

The men looked at Maelgwn. He was their leader, and they expected him to take charge in his usual confident, authoritative way; they were puzzled by his silence and his blank, pale face.

"Wait! Do you hear it?" Gareth said excitedly.

"What?"

The men strained their ears. There was the soft sound of the rain . . . and another sound.

"It is Paithu," Gareth said excitedly. "She is trying to answer me!"

"It could be a horse," Balyn answered gravely. "But where is it coming from? Gareth . . . whistle again."

This time the sound was clearer, although still very distant.

"It is hard to tell . . . perhaps that way . . . back toward the river," said Gareth.

"She did not get far," Rhys said with a frown.

"Perhaps she left the horse behind after all."

"Gareth—keep whistling!" Maelgwn ordered.

The men set off again, moving in single file. The ground was growing soft and slippery, and they were all numb with fatigue and cold. They were retracing their steps back to the river. They could hear the dull hum of running water when Gareth called a halt.

"There, over there!

"I see the mare!" Gareth cried excitedly. "But where is Aurora?"

Morning was near and the darkness was thinning to a gray veil. Paithu nickered softly to them from among the trees. The reins hung loose, but the mare did not try to come to them.

Elwyn was the first to reach the clearing where the horse stood. "It is Aurora . . . she's hurt!" he cried in an anguished voice.

Maelgwn had been lagging back, full of dread, but at Elwyn's words, he leaped off his horse and ran to the spot where Elwyn knelt. The two men stared in horror at the body of the queen, lying among the wet leaves. Her skin was dead white against the black tendrils of her hair and the dark vegetation all around her, but her face was peaceful and uncannily beautiful.

Elwyn felt frantically for a pulse. Maelgwn had the

impulse to tell him to stop. It seemed to him that this was not his wife—it was some forest goddess who had dreamed in peace for centuries. It would be blasphemous to try and wake her.

Aurora moaned. Her full lips, bleached white by the cold, opened and emitted a soft sigh of pain. The spell was broken, and Maelgwn's disordered thoughts turned from awe to terror.

"She's hurt!" he gasped.

"Aye, but at least she still lives," Elwyn said with relief. "For a moment there . . ."

Maelgwn reached out to touch Aurora's cheek. It was as cold and pale as marble, but at his touch she stirred again and mumbled something.

"We must get her back to the fortress!" Elwyn said in an anxious voice.

"Aye, but first we must get her warm," said Rhys. The other men had reached the spot where the queen lay and were gathered around nervously.

"She may be hurt, but the real danger is that she is so cold," Rhys continued, as he leaned over to examine the queen gently.

The rest of the men nodded. Rhys had some skill in healing, and on the battlefield they knew he was next best to Torawc.

"I have a blanket in my pack—if it is not too wet," said Balyn. "I'll get it."

"Elwyn, help me take the queen's clothes off . . . and the rest of you—start gathering some branches to make a litter to carry her home."

The men jumped to follow Rhys's orders. Maelgwn continued to kneel at the queen's side and stroke her face lightly with his fingers. It seemed that no orders would be coming from him, and his men were glad someone was taking charge.

Only Elwyn hesitated. "I cannot . . . take her clothes off," he said in a low, shocked voice.

"You must!" Rhys said irritably. "Her clothes are soaked, and we must get her warm—she could die if we don't."

Rhys searched for the tie at Aurora's waist that held the too-big trousers up, while Elwyn tried to slide her limp arm through the tunic. Neither considered that Maelgwn would be any help at all. He seemed to be in a trance—staring at Aurora's face and whispering to her softly.

It was a struggle, but the two men were finally able to remove Aurora's outer clothes. She had not stirred. Rhys reached down and tore the linen undergarment Aurora was wearing in half and began to pull it off.

"No!" Elwyn said. "It is not right that we should look at her naked!"

"Would you rather look at her dead?" Rhys asked coldly. "I am telling you, these wet clothes are chilling her; we must get her warm quickly. Here, give me your cloak."

"My cloak?"

"Aye, you fool. I will need several cloaks if I am to get her warm. Better that we should all catch cold than the queen die, don't you think?"

Elwyn nodded numbly.

Do you think you could make a fire?"

"I did bring the flint, but everything is wet—I don't know."

"Well, try. Use some of your own underclothes to start it, anything that is dry. We need a fire if we are to get her warm."

"Maelgwn," Rhys said gently, turning to the king. "I need you to stand back while I wrap Aurora up. Would you be willing to give me your cloak?"

Maelgwn nodded. It seemed like a dream, he thought. It could not be Aurora who lay there so limp and death-like. Surely she was back at Caer Eryri, safe in the tower room. This was but a spirit, a wood fairy, looking as lovely and ethereal as a white starflower.

The rest of the men had returned with branches.

"How is she?" Balyn asked.

"She still breathes," Rhys answered. "But very shallowly. I am worried that she hit her head when she fell from the horse. There seems to be a lump . . . here," he touched the side of her head. "See how she moans when I touch it?"

"Aye, perhaps that is why she doesn't wake."

Rhys nodded. "Moving her may make things worse, but we have no choice. . . . How are you coming with that fire, Elwyn?"

"I've got it," the younger man answered. "At least it has stopped raining, but I need some wood, anything you can find that is partially dry."

"Maelgwn," Rhys's voice was patient, gentle, as if he were speaking to a child. "I need you to carry Aurora over by the fire. Hold her on your lap, and move your hands over her under the cloak—that's right. Try to get her skin warm."

Balyn returned from gathering wood and pulled Elwyn aside. "What does Rhys say? Will she live?"

Elwyn shook his head miserably. "He does not know . . . he is afraid her head is injured."

Balyn sighed. "I wonder what happened. Did the horse trip, or did she fall off in exhaustion?"

"It is my fault," Elwyn said in a trembling voice. "I helped her run away. I let this happen to her."

"You cannot blame yourself. You were trying to help her."

"Who can I blame then . . . Maelgwn?" Elwyn asked bitterly. "How could he let things go this far? How could he drive her to such desperation?"

"Hush! I'll not have you talk like that. If she does not live . . . Well, I won't even mention it. It is clear that Maelgwn cares *now*. It is up to us to make sure he has a chance to make it up to her."

"How is the litter coming?" Rhys asked.

"It is almost finished. Do you think she is ready to be moved?"

"Soon. She's getting warm, and I see a little color in her face." The two men stared at the king, holding his wife tenderly in his arms by the fire.

"And the king?" Balyn asked in a hushed voice.

Rhys shook his head. "Jupiter, I've never seen him go to pieces like this. If she doesn't live . . ." his voice trailed off.

"We can't think about that," Balyn said briskly. "She is young and strong. A fall from a horse and a night in the cold shouldn't be too much for her. After all she did climb down that tower by herself." The big man shuddered. "I don't know if I could have done that!"

"Aye, she is young. And the cold may have kept her head injury from being worse. She was near dead when we found her though. We are very lucky Maelgwn thought of having Gareth whistle for Paithu."

"We are lucky, aye. So far we are lucky indeed."

Twenty-seven

Gwenaseth watched the king with concern. Maelgwn had not rested in the long hours since Aurora had been brought to the tower room. He sat by the bed, holding his wife's hand and staring at her pale, still face. His handsome profile was ravaged by fatigue and worry, and she decided it was time to take Torawc's advice and give him some drugged wine so he would sleep. She went to the table, poured a cup of wine and surreptitiously dumped a small pinch of white powder into the dark liquid. She hastily swirled it around with her finger, watching Maelgwn carefully. His eyes never left Aurora's face.

"My lord, you should drink something," she said softly, walking toward the king with the cup.

Maelgwn shook his head, but said nothing. All his concentration was focused on Aurora.

Gwenaseth placed the cup in his free hand. "Drink, Maelgwn. Torawc said you must have some nourishment . . . he insisted."

Maelgwn sighed and grasped the cup idly. Then he drank it down rapidly, without looking at it.

Gwenaseth trembled as she took the cup back from him. Maelgwn looked worse than Aurora. Her face wore a look of eerie peace, while Maelgwn looked like a man who had been tortured for hours.

Gwenaseth went back to her stool by the fire to wait for the drug to take effect. She was glad she had been able to go back to sleep after the search party went out. She was tired, but much more rested than everyone else. It had been shocking to wake up and find Aurora so badly hurt, and she could not help feeling guilty. If only they had known that Maelgwn did not plan to hurt her, if only they had waited until morning.

Silently, Gwenaseth chastised herself for her regretful thoughts. It was just as she had told Elwyn and Maelgwn when she first saw their devastated faces—you could not change the past, so there was no sense brooding over it. The important thing was the future, and making sure that Aurora got well. Her words had gotten through to Elwyn, and he went to bed to sleep off his exhaustion. But Maelgwn—Gwenaseth could see that he was beside himself with worry, punishing himself with remorse. He greatly needed the oblivion of sleep to soothe his tormented mind.

Gwenaseth glanced again at the king. His eyelids were finally drooping. Perhaps she should call someone. If he collapsed in the chair, there was no way she could get him into the bed by herself.

Gwenaseth got up again and went to the door. Maelgwn took no notice of her leaving—he did not even look up. She hurried down the stairs and met Balyn outside the tower door.

"How does she?" he asked worriedly.

Gwenaseth shook her head. "She still has not roused, but she seems to sleep peacefully. It is Maelgwn I am worried about. I have given him some drugged wine so that he will rest. Will you help me make a bed for him on the floor?"

Balyn nodded distractedly. "Do you think it is a bad sign that Aurora hasn't woken?"

Gwenaseth sighed. "I know much less than Torawc, but it seems to me that if she breathes, there is hope. Come, help me find something to make a bed for Maelgwn."

Balyn and Gwenaseth went to the office in the barracks, gathered up some bedding and dragged the sheepskins and blankets up the tower stairs. They found Maelgwn slumped over in the chair. After laying the skins on the floor, they slid him off the chair and onto the makeshift bed.

When Maelgwn was taken care of, Balyn motioned to Gwenaseth to follow him back to the stairway.

"There is something else you should know about," Balyn said in a troubled voice. "Soon after we got Aurora back to Caer Eryri, a messenger arrived from Cunedda. It seems he is having trouble with the Picts again and needs Maelgwn to bring his army to help him."

Gwenaseth looked up at the big man in surprise.

"Does Maelgwn know about this?"

"Aye," Balyn nodded gravely. "But he told the man he could not leave until Aurora was safe."

"Do you think the request from Cunedda is genuine, or is it a trap?"

"A trap?"

"I thought you knew," Gwenaseth said impatiently. "One of the things Maelgwn and Aurora quarreled about before he . . . before he locked her up, was that Aurora believed that Cunedda had a spy in the village and that he was plotting with someone within Caer Eryri to betray Maelgwn into a trap."

"Someone within Caer Eryri? You mean Esylt, don't you?" Balyn asked with narrowed eyes.

Gwenaseth nodded. "Clearly Maelgwn did not believe Aurora, but since Maelgwn was wrong about other things, perhaps it is something to consider."

"I have considered it," Balyn said slowly. "But it is not my decision to make. We need Maelgwn back to his normal self, and we need it to happen soon!"

"I have been praying to the Christian God . . . and to the other gods as well," Gwenaseth said sorrowfully. "For now that is all we can do."

Balyn nodded glumly and left her; Gwenaseth went in and took up her watch again.

The room was deathly quiet. Gwenaseth got up and poked at the fire. Then she walked to the window and looked out. It was a gray, miserable day, and it was still raining. The air coming in through the windows was damp and cold, and Gwenaseth shivered. The rains of autumn had begun; summer would be over soon.

Gwenaseth went back and sat down by the fire again. She pushed the stool back against the wall, so she could lean back. It was so warm and cozy there.

She woke with a start, nearly falling off the stool. For a moment she couldn't remember where she was. There was the sound of moaning, an awful sound, and Gwenaseth's heart leaped into her throat. She stumbled toward the bed. The room was dark, and she could just barely make out the bed and Aurora's form upon it. The queen was thrashing about as if in pain. As she struggled frantically in her sleep, she called out in a faint, anguished voice.

"Help me! Help me, Marcus!"

Gwenaseth stroked her fevered brow and whispered soothing words, but they did not seem to reach Aurora. She continued to cry out, her muffled voice growing stronger. Gwenaseth glanced anxiously to where the king lay sleeping. She did not want him to wake up, she did not want him to hear the name that Aurora kept calling, repeating it over and over in a voice full of grief and pain.

It was too late. Gwenaseth saw the dark form of the king rise on the other side of the bed. He leaned over to grasp Aurora's other hand, to whisper words of tenderness to her.

"Marcus! Marcus!" Aurora mumbled in her devastated voice, still tossing uneasily. "Help me!"

Gwenaseth heard Maelgwn's sigh. He did not pull his hand away, but he stopped speaking to Aurora.

Gradually, Aurora's voice grew fainter and calmer, and her restlessness eased. It seemed she had slipped back into the peace of her dreams again.

Sweat was dripping down Gwenaseth's face. Even though there had been no danger near, Aurora's calls had been so heartbreakingly desperate, she felt as if she, too, had been struggling with a deadly enemy. She moved to light the lamp so she could check on Aurora more carefully. She had only taken two steps when Maelgwn's low, vibrant voice came to her from across the room. "Who is he?"

The pain was etched deeply in those few words, and Gwenaseth felt her heart sink. Maelgwn had heard clearly enough—he knew that Aurora was calling for another man. Gwenaseth considered what to tell him. Things left unsaid had made things so hard between Aurora and Maelgwn. If Aurora lived, she and Maelgwn would have to begin to be honest with each other if there was to be any hope for their marriage at all. Perhaps it was time that Maelgwn knew the truth.

"I'm not sure," she began slowly. "I believe that Marcus was someone she was in love with at Viroconium."

From across the room, Gwenaseth could hear Maelgwn release his breath in a painful, ragged sigh.

"But you must not hold it against her," Gwenaseth continued anxiously. "She said he was someone she could never marry, and that they . . . that they were little more than childhood friends."

"Yet she calls for him, instead of me . . . now . . . when her spirit is so near death."

"You must remember," Gwenaseth spoke softly, her voice little more than a whisper in the darkness. "When she left here last night, she was very afraid of you."

"How can I forget?"

The raw suffering in his voice was unbearable to listen to. Gwenaseth hurried to comfort Maelgwn.

"Hush," she said gently, touching Maelgwn's arm with her hand. "She will wake soon, and then you can tell her the things you wish to say."

"Are you sure? Are you sure that she will not just die in her sleep . . . never knowing I love her?"

Gwenaseth forced her voice to be calm. "Of course. That she struggles and cries out means she is getting better, does it not? Next time . . . perhaps next time she will wake, and you can talk to her."

Gwenaseth was not sure if Maelgwn accepted her words. She went again to light the lamp, sure that neither of them would be able to sleep.

Ah, the pain, the searing pain! Aurora struggled to escape—down, down into the warm comforting darkness. The light would not leave her alone. It followed her . . . like the pain. She awoke with a moan of agony.

The room was light—a gray misty light that suffused the air. It was cold as well. Aurora shivered under the blankets. She was naked and confused. Why was she in the tower room. Had she only dreamed of escaping?

Aurora struggled to lift her head—fighting the waves of nausea and dizziness that seemed to overwhelm her. She could see Gwenaseth dozing in a chair next to the nearly dying fire. She tried to call out, but her throat was so dry. Her voice sounded like the faint rustle of dry leaves.

Aurora heard a sound on her other side, and turned her head carefully, wincing at the fiery pain the movement caused. Maelgwn's face came vaguely into view. Aurora did not feel frightened—the pain in her head was too distracting, and Maelgwn looked so tired, so concerned. She lifted her hand, as if to reach out and touch him, then let it fall again. It was too hard; he was too far away.

"Aurora," he whispered. "Aurora, my love." Aurora tried to nod, but the small movement seemed impossible. She could only stare at the exhausted, dirt-streaked face of her husband as he watched her with a look of exquisite tenderness. He reached out to touch her face, and Aurora's vision faded as his fingers stroked her cheek. Her head hurt so badly! She closed her eyes, seeking the oblivion of sleep once again.

"She is out of danger then?" Balyn asked Maelgwn anxiously.

"Aye, Torawc says so, anyway. It is the medicine he gives her to block the pain which makes her sleep so much."

"Have you . . . talked to her."

Maelgwn looked uneasy. "I have tried, but she seems so weak and confused. I don't want to tire her."

"Or perhaps it is too hard to tell her how you feel?"

"What are you saying?" Maelgwn asked sharply.

"You know, there was a time, Maelgwn, when you would have given your whole kingdom just to tell your wife that you loved her. But now that she is mending, you make excuses for not talking to her."

"That is not true. I did tell her that I meant her no harm, that I had no intention of killing her. I have also made it clear that I won't be sending her back to Viroconium. The incident with the poison—that is to be completely forgotten."

"But, the other—your love for her—have you been honest about that?"

"What can I say?" Maelgwn asked defensively. "It's true, I love her, but that does not solve the problems between us."

Balyn shook his head. "I don't understand. I thought at last—if Aurora lived—things would be right with your marriage."

Maelgwn was silent, and Balyn stared perplexed at his king's moody face.

"Have you decided if we will go to Cunedda's aid?"

"Of course, as his ally I am sworn to assist him. It is just a matter of when. I . . . I do not look forward to telling Aurora that I am going off to war right now."

"How long can you delay? It has been at least a week since the messenger arrived."

"We will have to leave soon. I have already sent the word to Abelgirth and some of the other chieftains. No one is anxious to leave so close to harvest."

"Have you considered that this summons from Cunedda might be . . . ah . . . something other than an honest request for help?"

Maelgwn frowned. "Not you, too. Gwenaseth has already reminded me of Aurora's concerns. How can I know? Aurora did not see this Brigante man herself—all we have to go on is the word of a crazy woman, and now she is dead."

"I have wondered about that—Justina was considered peculiar by the villagers, but certainly harmless. Why would anyone murder her?"

"Who says it was murder? Perhaps her hut caught fire by accident. It was full of dried herbs. All it would have taken is one errant spark."

Balyn opened his mouth to speak again, and then closed it. Maelgwn's face had that look again—he did not want to hear any more troubling suggestions.

Maelgwn took the stairs to the tower room slowly, as though his boots were full of stones. He did not look forward to this talk with Aurora, but he had put it off as long as possible. His army was grouped to march, and if he delayed any longer, Cunedda would begin to suspect him of disloyalty.

Gwenaseth opened the door. She had spent nearly all her days in the tower since Aurora had been brought in injured. She had shown herself to be a loyal and devoted friend to Aurora. He had to remember to thank her.

Aurora was sitting up in bed. She had regained some of her color, but she still looked very thin. He could see the bones in her delicate neck clearly through the pale skin. But the pain and illness had not marred her beauty. As always, Maelgwn felt a pang of desire just looking at his wife.

She smiled uneasily at him. "Good day, Maelgwn."

"Good day, my lady."

Maelgwn sat down on the bed. He reached out for Aurora's hand and twined his fingers around hers. It was hard to be satisfied with so little of her, but he dared not even kiss her for fear he would hurt her.

"It seems you have been busy," Aurora said after a moment. "I hear all kinds of commotion out in the court-yard—horses and people coming and going."

"That is what I have come to talk to you about," Maelgwn said gently, looking into Aurora's face. "We are going to war."

"Against whom?"

"The Picts. Cunedda has asked for our help."

Aurora said nothing, but nodded slowly. The troubled look on her face was clear.

"I don't want to leave you now—you know that." Maelgwn's eyes pleaded for understanding.

"When *are* you leaving?" Aurora asked.

"In the morning."

Aurora gave a rapid sigh. Maelgwn moved his fingers along Aurora's arm, stroking the soft skin. At her shoulder he stopped—he dared go no further.

Aurora felt his uneasy, reluctant touch and gave another gasping sigh. Then she turned her face away, as though she could hide the fat tears that welled into her eyes and then coursed down her cheeks.

Maelgwn moaned. "Aurora, what is it?"

"You are leaving . . . and you don't even want me." Aurora choked out the words in a thin, devastated voice.

Maelgwn leaned over on the bed and began to kiss her passionately. "Oh, Aurora, I did not know if I could. I was afraid I would hurt you."

Aurora shook her head mutely and began to return his kisses.

Maelgwn savored the sweet nectar of his wife's mouth, and then lingered his lips over the fragile bones in her face. Perhaps it was better this way—he could prove to her that she did not have to fear him, that he would not hurt her. She was so frail. His fingers trembled over the sharp ridges of her ribs as he pulled down her gown. But her breasts seemed unchanged—they were firm and liquid in his hands, the nipples fat and swollen—and she responded with familiar eagerness as he began to suck them. He could feel Aurora's fingers twining in his hair as he played with her breasts. She was holding him close to her with a fierce possessiveness that set him on fire. Oh, to know that she wanted him!

The hunger that he remembered so well—even from the first time in her father's garden—was still there. He felt the pressure of her hips arching against him, begging for his love. He slid her gown down further and pulled back so that he could stare at her naked beauty. He knew now that he could indeed put his hands around her slender waist, and the tininess of it emphasized the alluring fullness of her hips, the hip bones jutting out slightly. She parted her legs as he touched the dark curls between them. There was soft fleshiness there in the soft V between her legs, an arrow pointing the way to even greater softness and delight.

Maelgwn braced his hands on her thighs and spread her legs even further apart, and then he glanced up at Aurora's face. Aye, it was all there, the beguiling beauty and mystery he had first beheld in her father's feasting hall. Aurora's blue eyes were both misty and bright with desire, the exotic lines of her cheeks quivered with rapt intensity, and her full lips were ripe and swollen with passion. Aurora sighed with impatience, and Maelgwn turned again to the pleasures his mouth knew how to give a woman.

Salty, sour sweet—like tears or the sea—or did she remind him of the dark wet forest, a scent both musky and wild. His tongue dove into her, feeling the quiver of life inside of her, feeling her firm, slender thighs push hard against him, and pushing back with his strong hands, feeling the spasm of release shooting down her whole body. Her voice rose in harsh whispers of pleasure, and then primitive cries and finally wordless, sighing screams.

At last she collapsed against him, and he pulled himself over her. Had he already worn her out? No, her cheeks were fiery with passion, and she moaned intelligibly, as she pulled his body to her own. It had been so long—he had almost forgotten the luxurious snug embrace of her body tight around him. He coaxed her to accept more of him, more and more, until he was buried to the hilt, her long legs tight around him, her nails silencing her screams, in his skin. He had forgotten, too, the breathless powerful creature they made together—a seething monster that shook them both with agonies of pleasure, rocking and roaming over the oceans and mountains, the clouds and the heavens—over everything.

It was over too soon. He held her tight, reluctant to pull away even as he felt himself shriveling inside her. Finally, he adjusted his body slightly so that her lovely face was cradled in the space between his chest and shoulder. He could feel her heart still pounding, and he could not resist one last delicious tug on a rosy nipple. Now, he thought, now he should tell her that he loved her.

There was a knock on the door. Maelgwn swore and threw the blanket hastily over them.

"Come in."

Gwenaseth and Torawc walked into the room together. At first, they both gaped with surprise, then Gwenaseth broke into a radiant smile while Torawc advanced to the bed with a scowl.

"Maelgwn! What are you thinking of? She needs her rest!"

Maelgwn could not help smiling mischievously. "I am a man going off to war—you would not deny me this. I might be dead on the morrow, and I need to make sure I beget an heir before I go."

"Dead! 'Tis more likely you will kill your poor wife with your coarse attentions—why her face is bright with fever!"

"That is hardly a fever that inflames her lovely face," Maelgwn said smugly. He got out of bed with an abrupt movement, forcing Gwenaseth to turn away in embarrassment while he dressed. Then he turned back to Aurora. He did not want to say good-bye this way—there was so much left unsaid.

"I'd better make sure everything is ready to leave tomorrow."

"Will you come up here to sleep tonight?"

Maelgwn looked at Torawc's stern, disapproving face. Perhaps the bard was right—he should be careful not to tire her.

"It will be late, and I hate to risk disturbing you . . . but I will try," he finally said before he kissed her lightly and left the room.

Aurora spent a miserable night. Torawc said that it was important that she begin to sleep without the sleeping potion, but her head still ached unbearably and her dreams were confused and frightening. She woke several times and reached out for Maelgwn, but he was not there. She finally slept peacefully near morning, and when she awoke, she could tell by the light that it was late. Maelgwn and his army were gone.

Gwenaseth came in to bring her breakfast and help her to the chamber pot. Aurora was surprised to see that her face was streaked with tears.

"What is wrong, Gwenaseth?"

Gwenaseth sniffed and wiped her nose. "I had my first fight with Elwyn."

"I am sorry," Aurora said sympathetically. "What was it about?"

"He wanted to go with Maelgwn, and I wouldn't let him."

Aurora nodded. If she could have stopped Maelgwn from going, she would have.

"I can't believe the things he said to me," Gwenaseth continued angrily. "He said I treat him like a little boy and not a man. He even brought up my father—saying that the two of us act like he is a pet dog whose purpose in life is to keep me content!"

Aurora could not help smiling weakly at Gwenaseth's indignation. In her sweet way Gwenaseth *was* always ordering Elwyn around.

"So, Elwyn wanted to go and fight the Picts?"

"Aye, he said he is a soldier, and he ought to be going with Maelgwn."

"Perhaps there is some truth to his words," Aurora suggested gently.

"But we need him here! Our house is not even finished and winter is coming. Besides, who else will guard us while Maelgwn's army is gone?"

"Please don't be angry with Elwyn," Aurora pleaded. "I don't want to see the two of you fight. I want *someone* to be happy in their marriage."

Gwenaseth looked surprised. "I thought when we found you and Maelgwn together yesterday . . . that you had . . . that everything was all right."

Aurora looked uncomfortable. "Oh, Gwenaseth, it is just the same as it always was. In bed, aye, *then* everything is all right. But the minute he gets out of bed, he is a stranger again. You saw how he mocked my desire for him in front of Torawc. And now he has gone to

Manau Gotodin—knowing how I feel about Cunedda, knowing that I am so afraid for him."

Gwenaseth watched the queen carefully. She was sitting up in bed, and in her excitement, her face looked flushed and almost healthy. Perhaps it was time she knew the truth.

"Aurora, I think I know why Maelgwn may be acting so strangely," she began.

"When you were first brought to the tower room after your injury, Maelgwn did not leave your side. I gave him some drugged wine to make him rest, and Balyn and I made him a bed on the floor. During the night you called out in your sleep. You were very frightened—you were calling out in terror. You woke Maelgwn."

"I don't understand. What does this have to do with anything?"

"Because in your fear, you kept calling out a name—you kept calling out for someone named Marcus."

Aurora turned pale again. "I did that? I called for Marcus?"

"Aye, and not just once or twice, but over and over."

Aurora's eyes were wide with fear. "What did Maelgwn do?"

"He asked me who Marcus was, and I told him that I thought that it was someone you knew in Viroconium."

Aurora sighed. "So he thinks . . ." She sighed again and raised her hands to her face.

"It is not so bad as that," Gwenaseth said consolingly. "He was hurt that you called for someone besides him, but he must surely understand that you might have had feelings for another man before him."

"But he is so jealous!" Aurora said wretchedly. "He

has always been afraid I loved someone besides him. Now he is gone, and there is no way I can prove to him that there is no one else!"

Twenty-eight

Maelgwn and Cunedda looked at each other wearily across the sputtering fire. It had rained almost constantly the last few days and now it was starting again.

"I wish they'd stand and fight like men instead of cowardly dogs," Cunedda said angrily. "But that is the way of the Picts—move in quickly and quietly to kill and burn and then sneak away into the shadows."

Maelgwn shook his head. "My army has been here for almost a week, and we haven't even seen the enemy. Are you sure they're still within your lands?"

"Aye," Cunedda answered in frustration. "How do you explain the cattle bodies we have found burned, the slaughtered people? Who else could it be besides the Picts."

"I don't like it," Maelgwn muttered. "There is never enough damage done to leave a clear path for the enemy. How many are there? *Where* are they?"

"It is almost as though someone wanted to keep us here, but avoid fighting," Balyn said thoughtfully.

Maelgwn and Cunedda both looked at him sharply. His words expressed their own thoughts, although they dared not say it. Were they being led into a trap?

"It would not be so bad if Ferdic did not have half

my army on the northern border," Cunedda mused. "This kind of warfare makes me nervous—to have my forces split and my people unprotected."

"Why did Ferdic go north when the problems seemed to be here in the south?" Maelgwn asked.

Cunedda shrugged. "He thought he could head off the Pictish armies there. He's such a headstrong boy, that one. There's no arguing with him when he makes up his mind."

Both men were thoughtful for a time. Maelgwn could not help wondering if Ferdic was unwilling to fight beside him after the incident with Aurora and the trophy head. It seemed unwise of Cunedda to give his son half his army. It made Cunedda entirely too dependent on Maelgwn's help.

Maelgwn stood up impatiently and flexed his legs. "I'm sorry, Cunedda, but I cannot stay and help you indefinitely." He pulled up the hood of his cloak. "I have my own lands to look after, my own worries."

Cunedda nodded. "Give me a week, Maelgwn. We'll cover one end of my lands to the other. We'll find those cowardly bastards and wipe them out once and for all."

Aurora put down her sewing and fidgeted. Forced inactivity was wearing on her nerves. Torawc did not think it wise for her to go riding or even walk much yet, and she was compelled to spend her time in the womanly crafts of sewing and spinning. Out of boredom and loneliness she had finally joined the other women in the great hall. They seemed to be growing used to her presence.

They carried on with their gossip as though she were one of them.

"Ohhhh!" Leian cried. Her baby was due in a fortnight, and it appeared to be a ferocious kicker.

"I'll bet it's a boy," said Wydian, Evrawc's wife. "Only a boy would make his mother so miserable."

"Actually, my daughters were harder," said Sewan. "I was so sick with them I wished I could die the whole time I was pregnant."

"If men had to have babies, they'd not be so anxious to get us in bed," observed Marna.

"Aye, it seems to be all they think of when they are home," said Sewan. "I am almost glad when they go off on campaign, and I can finally get some rest!"

"I don't put up with it anymore," retorted Wydian. "I told my husband to go see the village harlot if that was all he wanted."

The woman glanced uneasily at Aurora, and a few suppressed a giggle. The rumor that Maelgwn had shared Morganna's bed this summer was still going around.

"How can you say such a thing to your husband?" Gwenaseth protested. "It's your wifely duty to fulfill your husband's needs."

"Why should I?" asked Wydian coldly. "I have all the children I want, and Evrawc never pleased me all that much anyway."

"Now, Wydian," Sewan scolded gently. "You should not be saying these things to a newlywed like Gwenaseth. I imagine she is still very much in love with her husband."

"Perhaps it is easy to desire your husband when he is

handsome and sweet like Elwyn," Wydian said sourly.
"But he may not always seem so agreeable."

"Aye, Elwyn is nice-looking," Marna said with a smile
at Gwenaseth. "Next to the king, I think he is the handsomest man at Caer Eryri."

At the mention of the king, old Browdan roused herself out of her doze to join the conversation. "Few men
are as fair as the king," she said with a nostalgic smile.
"Maelgwn has his mother's looks, you know. His father,
Cadwallon, was as plain as an old ox—a big nose and
not much hair. Maelgwn and Esylt both take after Rhiannon. What a beauty she was—raven black hair, deep blue
eyes and skin like pure cream. But she was as evil as
she was beautiful."

Aurora stopped her fidgeting and listened intently. She
had never heard anyone at Caer Eryri speak of Maelgwn's
mother before.

"Setting her sons at each other's throats like that . . ."
Browdan continued with a frown. "Anyone could see that
it would turn out as it did—with the strongest one win-
ning and the rest dead."

"Why would a mother do that?" asked Gwenaseth.

The old woman shrugged and her cloudy eyes looked
unseeingly at the younger woman. "I said she was evil.
She wanted things it's not fitting for a woman to want—
power and a say in men's affairs. I guess she thought
that if she found the strongest of her sons, he would give
her that."

"Maelgwn is not much like her, is he?" Wydian observed acidly. "He is far from ruthless. I've heard even
Evrawc say that Maelgwn was too weak and conciliatory
with Constantine. He demanded only modest tribute—

grain, wine, foodstuffs and craftsmen—he left behind the gold and jewels we could all be enjoying."

The women in the large room held their breath, glancing at Aurora nervously. Wydian was clearly baiting the queen, challenging her to take sides against either Maelgwn or her own people.

Aurora concentrated on the needlework in her lap, trying to ignore Wydian's provoking words. But it was too much for Gwenaseth.

"How dare you say such things about Maelgwn!" Gwenaseth said in an enraged voice, standing up abruptly. "In making the agreement that he did, Maelgwn sought a lasting peace that would benefit all the people of Gwynedd." She fixed the other women in the room with a scornful gaze. "Or would you rather have piles of jewels to wear around your necks and wrists and then lose your husbands in war when Constantine seeks revenge?"

Wydian's eyes narrowed, and she swept Gwenaseth's small frame with a cold, withering glance. "I've heard that Constantine plans to seek revenge anyway. When he joins forces with Gwyrtheyrn and invades Gwynedd, we will all suffer because of Maelgwn's weakness. He should have crushed Constantine while he had the chance!"

The room was silent as the women looked at each other uneasily. This had gone beyond gossip or mere cattiness toward the queen. They were talking of things in the men's domain—the problems of alliances, warfare and treachery. None of them really understood it, nor did they want to.

Sewan rose from her seat by the fire. "I must go and

call the boys for supper. I have had enough of sewing for today."

One by one, the women followed after Sewan. At last there was no one left in the hall except Gwenaseth and Aurora.

"They're not all like her," Gwenaseth said softly, coming to stand beside the queen. "The women have begun to respect you, and I know many of them were very concerned when you were so ill. It is only Wydian who is so hateful. Now you know why Evrawc always looks so sour-faced and miserable," she added with an uncomfortable laugh.

Aurora looked up; her eyes were distant and troubled. "Where did Wydian get her information regarding my father's plans? Why would she think Constantine was going to betray Maelgwn?"

"She must have overheard something," Gwenaseth answered with a shrug. "She might even have started the rumor herself just to make trouble for you."

"No, I don't think so," Aurora answered. "Wydian isn't clever enough to think of something like that. She must have heard one of the soldiers talking—but who? Evrawc does not seem like the kind of man who would share his doubts about an ally with his wife. There is something wrong here, Gwenaseth, and it scares me. I think I should speak to Elwyn."

"All right," Gwenaseth said quietly. "I'll find him for you. Maybe you *should* talk to him. Revenge and betrayal . . ." She shuddered. "These are things for men to worry about."

* * *

Elwyn met Aurora in the tower room. "My lady," he said simply. "I'm at your service."

"Sit down," Aurora remained standing, pacing slightly. Elwyn thought she had never looked more beautiful, more queenly.

"I have something to tell you that may be nothing more than idle gossip, or it may mean grave danger for all of us."

"Aye, my lady," Elwyn answered, sitting up stiffly.

"Have you heard that my father has joined forces with Gwyrtheyrn and plans to betray Maelgwn?"

"Who told you that?"

"Wydian—she told not just me, but the whole hall of women."

"Wydian? How would she know Constantine's plans?"

"How indeed?" asked Aurora in agitation. "It makes no sense. Wydian is no different than most of the other women; she normally pays little mind to politics and war—unless it is to make sure she gets her share of the booty and plunder. She could not come up with this by herself. She had to have overheard it."

"It is possible that Evrawc said something to her? He was always convinced that Maelgwn was too soft on your father. Perhaps in a mood of frustration, he accused Constantine of disloyalty."

"Perhaps," Aurora said slowly. "But I don't think so. Evrawc might have criticized Maelgwn to the other men, but not to his wife. Did you know that she no longer allows him to share her bed? Aye, she told a whole group of women that. I don't think that Evrawc would trust a woman who brags so openly of her rejection of him."

Elwyn spoke a trifle impatiently. "What does it matter,

anyway? It's probably just a rumor. I can't imagine that your father would do something so foolish."

"But what if it isn't just a rumor? What if it's true!"

Elwyn looked at Aurora in surprise. "You really think your father would betray his agreement with Maelgwn?"

"I don't know. If he were thinking clearly . . . no. But I have learned these past few weeks that jealousy and anger can make people do very foolish things."

"What shall we do?" Elwyn asked Aurora in a worried voice.

"We must get a message to Maelgwn. What I heard may be no more than gossip, but it is important that Maelgwn know about it."

"A message? But how?"

"Is there no man here at Caer Eryri you can trust to send a message to Maelgwn?"

"Well, there is Owen . . . or I could go myself."

Aurora shook her head firmly. "No, if you went, it would be too obvious. This must be done secretly. No one can know of the message except you and me and the messenger."

"But who will write it?" Elwyn asked anxiously.

"Have you forgotten? I can write as well as read. I will write the message—I'm sure there is a scrap of parchment somewhere in Maelgwn's office."

"Why must everything be so secret?" Elwyn grumbled. Then recognition dawned on his face. "You suspect that someone at Caer Eryri is a spy—you think your father has been tricked into fighting Maelgwn!"

Aurora nodded. "I don't like to think it's true, but Maelgwn must know of the possibility."

Elwyn sighed. "Well, you are queen, Aurora. Just tell me what to do."

Maelgwn was in his tent, drowsing to the monotonous sound of the rain, when the message came.

"Maelgwn," Balyn called softly.

"Uhhh," Maelgwn groaned. "What is it?"

"It's a message, Maelgwn . . . a message from Aurora."

Maelgwn sat up suddenly. "A message? Who brought it?"

"Owen—he's been on the road four straight days."

"Well, damn it, light the lamp. Let us have a look at it."

Maelgwn unrolled the parchment with shaking fingers. The note was, indeed, signed by his wife. He stared for a moment at the scrawling script, fascinated by his wife's messy, but very feminine handwriting.

"What does she say," Balyn asked impatiently.

Maelgwn shook his head. "My Latin is too poor. I can make out certain words: "treachery . . . war . . . Constantine . . . but I'm not sure what she means."

"Who can we get to read it?"

"Rhys, of course. I doubt that there is another man for miles who can read Latin."

Rhys concentrated. His forehead was wrinkled with effort.

"So," Maelgwn said after a moment. "Can you make any sense of it?"

"Aye, I can make sense of it, and yet it does not make sense."

"Read it to me then," Maelgwn ordered. "Perhaps it is meaningful only to me."

Rhys began to read in a halting, rather expressionless voice. When he was done, he paused and looked at Maelgwn questioningly. "What is she saying—that her father is going to war against Gwynedd and she is trying to warn you?"

"She is not so sure as that," Balyn argued. "She said it's a rumor, something overheard among the women. But why does she write at all, why send a messenger so far if she is not sure?"

"She speaks of 'grave danger,' " Maelgwn said softly. "She is right. If Constantine were to march against us now, even without Gwyrtheyrn, he could move swiftly into the highlands and take Caer Eryri."

"Should we go back? What will we tell Cunedda?"

"I only promised Cunedda that I would stay a few days longer anyway. It will be easy enough to make excuses to get away. It is the other problem that concerns me now."

"What other problem?" Balyn asked.

Maelgwn's face looked cold and murderous in the firelight. "It would seem that there is a spy at Caer Eryri. Perhaps there is even a spy here, with us now."

"Wydian!" Balyn said suddenly. "Why would Evrawc's wife be talking about Constantine's plans?" He looked at the other two men in horror. "You don't think that . . . Evrawc? After all these years?"

"I don't know," Maelgwn said wearily. "I can scarce believe it either. But we can't take chances. No one else must know the real reason we are going back. No one!"

After the other men left his tent, Maelgwn lay down

again, trying to sleep. He had been wrong, he thought suddenly—and Abelgirth had been right—you *could* trust a woman. Aurora had sent him a message to warn him. She might have saved his kingdom . . . even his life. Even more amazing, she had chosen to be loyal to him over her father. What better proof could he have that she loved him?

But there was a dark side, too. If Aurora was right, that meant someone else at Caer Eryri had betrayed him. Esylt would never do anything to help Constantine, that was certain, so despite what Aurora might think, it was not his sister who plotted against him. But was it truly any better if it was one of his men? He had trusted Evrawc for years, long since he had stopped trusting Esylt. No, Maelgwn thought bitterly. It could not be Evrawc. There must be some other explanation.

Twenty-nine

It had been two days since Aurora had sent the message to Maelgwn—two days of agonized waiting and keeping secrets with Elwyn. At night, Aurora could scarcely sleep. She worried incessantly over whether she had done the right thing. If Maelgwn came back to find that her fears were just women's gossip—Aurora shivered with dread—would he ever trust her again?

But by the third day, it seemed that she had made the right decision. A rider from Viroconium came with news of a large army outside the town.

"Elwyn!" Aurora met the young soldier at the entrance to the great hall and grasped his arm frantically.

"Is it true that my father has made an alliance with Gwyrtheyrn?"

"Aye." Elwyn nodded grimly. "I was just coming to tell you. We can only hope that Maelgwn heeded your warning, and that he and his men get back before Constantine and Gwyrtheyrn march into Gwynedd."

"Oh, Elwyn!" Aurora cried in agony. "How could my father do something so foolish?"

"I don't know," Elwyn answered gently, putting an arm around the queen to soothe her. "You said yourself that anger and fear can make men do strange things."

"Is this not a touching scene?"

Aurora and Elwyn moved away from each other uneasily at the hissing disgust in Esylt's voice. She had come up behind them, and they turned to see her watching them with a leering smile on her face.

"How kind it is of one of Maelgwn's captains to comfort his wife as she receives the news that her father is a traitor," Esylt purred.

"Go away, Esylt. Leave us alone!" Elwyn said angrily.

"Should I leave you alone so that Aurora can betray Maelgwn just as her father has? You have always pined for the queen, Elwyn. Now you have your chance. I doubt that Maelgwn will want to have anything to do with her now that the truce is broken, so if you don't mind the king's leavings, you can at last have Aurora's sweet young body all to yourself."

Aurora looked around in horror. A crowd of people had gathered, and she saw Gwenaseth standing among them. She was staring at Aurora and Elwyn in shocked surprise.

Aurora moved close to Esylt, feeling the blood burning in her veins. She was not afraid of Esylt now, no, she was too angry to be afraid.

"You witch!" she shouted at Esylt. "You have used your lies to ruin things for me ever since I came here. I won't listen to you anymore. Get out of my sight—I order you to leave us!"

"Who are you to order me to do anything?" Esylt said viciously. "You are nothing more than my brother's whore, and now that your father has shown himself to be a traitor as well as a coward, you will no longer even be that! Perhaps we should send you back to your father now, and save him the trouble of coming to collect you."

Esylt took a step toward Aurora, as if she meant to grab her. There was the hissing sound of a sword being drawn, and Aurora looked down to see the deadly flash of a blade between her and Esylt.

"Enough!" said Elwyn in a taut, strained voice. "I'm sworn to defend Maelgwn's queen while he is gone, and I *will* defend her, Esylt. If you take another step, you will find my sword in your lying, evil throat."

Esylt moved back and laughed mockingly. "It seems the queen still has her champion. Will you defend the rest of us, too, Elwyn, when Gwyrtheyrn and Constantine come to burn Caer Eryri to the ground?"

Esylt walked away with proud, haughty grace, but everyone else stood in the courtyard as if stunned.

"Is it true, Elwyn?" Sewan asked in a fearful voice. "Are Gwyrtheyrn and Constantine preparing to march against us?"

Elwyn nodded. "It's true. I just received word from one of our men in Viroconium. Gwyrtheyrn is outside the town, and he has gathered a large army."

"The gods save us!" one of the old men cried. "Maelgwn is ten days away—he will never get here in time!"

The crowd seemed to panic. Everyone talked at once in excited, frightened voices, and as if on cue, even the children began to cry.

Elwyn held up his hand for silence. It took a moment, but gradually the crowd settled down.

"It may not be as grim as that. The queen sent a mes-

sage of warning to Maelgwn several days ago, and with
any luck, his army is marching home right now."

"The queen . . . but how . . . her father . . ." The
crowd had dissolved into nervous talk again, and Aurora
could begin to guess what was being said. It was time
to face her people, once and for all.

"I . . . I would like to speak." Aurora's soft, feminine
voice could barely be heard above the commotion, but
several people turned to her in curiosity, and eventually
there was silence.

"I'm sure you may well wonder how I knew to send
Maelgwn a message," Aurora began. "I didn't find out
that my father and Gwyrtheyrn had joined forces until
today, just as you did. I sent Maelgwn a message because
I heard a rumor among the women." Aurora looked at
Wydian coldly. "I thought it was but a rumor, but I decided that Maelgwn should know of it. That is why I
sent the message."

The people were talking again, but Aurora saw Sewan
and some of the other women nod their heads as if con-
firming her story. It seemed that they would give her a
chance.

Elwyn called for silence and then spoke again: "Perhaps it does not matter why the message was sent. The
important thing is that Maelgwn is very likely no more
than a few days away now. We must begin to prepare for
war, and we must be quick about it. Maelgwn has left
me in charge, and I will direct the preparations. I would
like the oldest male of each family to report to me now,
and we will begin to make plans."

The crowd began to disperse at Elwyn's words, as
women ran to tell others and the men grouped uneasily

around Elwyn. Aurora stood nearby, uncertain what she should do. She started at a touch on her arm.

"Gwenaseth!"

"Aurora, you were wonderful," Gwenaseth said with a fond smile. "You acted just like a queen."

Aurora smiled back uneasily. "Then you are not angry? You do not believe Esylt?"

"Of course not." Gwenaseth lowered her pale eyelashes in thought a moment, and then looked up at Aurora again.

"I know that Elwyn is infatuated with you, but he loves me. Even if he could have you, he would not be happy. I know that *I* can make him happy."

"Oh, Gwenaseth." Aurora reached out to touch Gwenaseth's freckled cheek gently, and there were tears in her eyes. "How did you ever come to be so wise?"

Gwenaseth laughed. "Now you sound just like my father!"

Aurora and Elwyn met later in the tower room.

"I wanted to report to you, my lady," Elwyn said formally as he entered.

Aurora nodded.

"I think we are ready—or as near ready as we can be. Now there is nothing else to do, but wait for Maelgwn to get here."

"And if he doesn't come?"

Elwyn shifted on his feet restlessly. "I have sent couriers to Abelgirth, Maelgrith and our other allies. I'm sure they will send men as soon as they can, but the timing is critical. Their men are scattered in the fields

for harvest and in fishing boats along the coast—it may
be a week before they can assemble an army and get
them here."

"How long before Gwyrtheyrn and my father arrive?"

Elwyn shrugged. "If they left shortly after the messenger arrived here . . . they could be here by tomorrow.
But I don't think they will," Elwyn added hastily. "I think
they are confident that Maelgwn is still a long ways
away, and they have plenty of time. I don't think they
have left Viroconium yet."

"Have you sent out scouts to find out for sure what
Gwyrtheyrn is doing?"

"Aye, they went out this morning."

"Good," Aurora said softly. "You have done well, Elwyn. Maelgwn would be proud of you."

"Thank you."

Aurora stood up, and began to pace. "Now that I am
sure everything is taken care of here, I can leave without
worrying."

"Leave!" Elwyn gaped at Aurora in surprise. "Where
are you going?"

"I've made up my mind—I'm going to see my father."

"But why? It's too late. He has already joined forces
with Gwyrtheyrn."

"No, it's not too late—I don't believe that!" Aurora
stopped her pacing and stood quietly before Elwyn.
"This alliance with Gwyrtheyrn—it does not seem like
something my father would do at all. I'm sure he was
tricked into it . . . or else forced."

"But why does that matter?" Elwyn asked impatiently.
"It's too late now. He has chosen the side he will fight
on."

Aurora looked at Elwyn, her blue eyes bright with anguish. "If I could talk to him, Elwyn, I know I could make him see his mistake. I might even be able to convince him to fight *with* us instead of *against* us!"

Elwyn shook his head. "It's too dangerous, Aurora. I can't let you go and risk your life. Maelgwn would never forgive me."

"How can you stop me?" Aurora asked defiantly. "Will you lock me in this room as Maelgwn did?"

"Oh, Aurora," Elwyn pleaded. "Please don't do this. I'm sworn to protect you."

Aurora's eyes flashed. "And I am absolving you of that oath! I will go . . . I *must* go."

"Then I will go with you," Elwyn said suddenly. "Even if Maelgwn does not get back in time, Abelgirth will be here by tomorrow, and he can direct what army we will have. I will stay with you and protect you. That is the least I can do."

"No, Elwyn!" Aurora cried, aghast. "What will everyone say? Already the people whisper that you are too loyal to me. I suspect that Gwenaseth is the only one who is sure you have not bedded me already! If you go with me, Esylt will make sure that Maelgwn thinks the worst."

"I don't care," Elwyn said stubbornly. "I can't let you undertake such a journey unprotected. If you insist you have to go, then I insist I must go with you."

Aurora sighed. "I'm going to get ready to leave now. Have Gwenaseth come to me. If she agrees to let you go, then I will take you."

* * *

"Well, the fortress still stands," Balyn said as Maelgwn's army reached the overlook above Caer Eryri and saw the stone towers gleaming in the waning sunlight.

"What do you mean by that?" Evrawc asked irritably. "We haven't been gone that long."

"Perhaps now that we are nearly home, it's time to discuss what we do mean." Maelgwn's voice was low and controlled, but his face was grim with tension.

"Is something going on?" asked Evrawc angrily. "Everyone is talking in riddles!"

Maelgwn pulled his stallion to a halt. Balyn and his other officers stopped, too. Maelgwn motioned the rest of the army to keep riding toward home, and then he dismounted and gestured to his men to do the same.

"Perhaps it is best if we settle this here, before we are within Caer Eryri's walls," Maelgwn said ominously.

"Settle what?" Evrawc asked with a glowering frown.

"I say we should get him safely within the fortress before we confront him," Balyn argued. The big man's usual sardonic smile was gone and his face looked deadly serious.

Maelgwn shook his head at Balyn. "A man has a right to face his accusers, and once we're home, there will be no way to talk of this without the whole fortress knowing that something is wrong."

"What is going on?" Evrawc asked in aggravation. "You have all been behaving very strangely since that messenger came. What was in that message anyway? I can't believe we left Manau Gotodin so abruptly without good reason."

"Aye, there was a good reason," Balyn said, his eyes

never leaving Evrawc's face. "Aurora sent word that she had heard a rumor that her father had joined forces with Gwyrtheyrn and was planning to invade Gwynedd."

"A rumor? Is that what this is all about?" Evrawc looked at Maelgwn doubtfully. "I can see why we had to return Caer Eryri, but that still doesn't explain why you are all acting so strangely."

"The rumor, Evrawc," Maelgwn said softly. "The rumor came from your wife."

"Wydian?" Evrawc looked thoroughly startled. "I can't imagine why she should talk about such things. Normally she has no interest in men's affairs."

Evrawc looked around at the dozen eyes watching him and laughed a short, mirthless laugh. "I see—you think that my wife might have learned of this 'rumor' from *me*." His mouth twisted into a cockeyed smile. "Let me assure you, if I told my wife that the sky was blue, she would be sure to tell the world that it was yellow. No rumor that my wife is spreading could come from me. We speak seldom enough, and when we do, she only contradicts me, *not* repeats me!"

Maelgwn sighed. "I believe you." He turned to face the other men. "We all know that Evrawc and his wife are not . . . shall we say, on good terms. Truly there is no reason to think that anything she says might come from him."

"That does not solve our problem," Balyn said uneasily. "There is a spy at Caer Eryri."

Maelgwn looked across the valley. The light was fading now, and the fortress was a drab dull gray again.

"Let's go home. If the rumor is true, then we are

needed there. And whatever we find at Caer Eryri—we will have to deal with it soon enough."

Abelgirth met Maelgwn at the gate.

"Seldom have I been so glad to see you, Maelgwn," Abelgirth said with a smile. "I was not looking forward to facing Gwyrtheyrn's army by myself."

"It's true? When do they march?"

Abelgirth shook his head. "We really don't know. Your man in Viroconium left there four days ago, and they had not set out yet. Perhaps since they think you are still in Manau Gotodin, they have grown overconfident and are taking their time."

"Good. I don't want their army anywhere near Caer Eryri when we meet in battle."

"You plan to march to meet them then?"

"Aye. We'll set out first thing in the morning, after my men have rested. With luck we can keep them to the lowlands and fight them there."

Maelgwn looked around, as though he had just remembered something.

"Where is Aurora? I thought she would be here to greet me."

"Ah, perhaps you should talk to my daughter about Aurora," Abelgirth suggested. "I don't understand it myself at all."

"Understand? Understand what?"

"Well," Abelgirth began hesitantly. "It seems she has gone to talk to her father." He nodded at Maelgwn's blank, dumbfounded expression. "Aye, I thought it very strange, too. First she sends a message to you to warn you of the invasion, and then she runs off to warn her father. But Gwenaseth assures me that it is not like that—

she says Aurora has gone to convince her father not to fight you. I suppose we ought to believe Gwenaseth's version though. If she trusts Aurora enough to send Elwyn with her, perhaps we should give your wife the benefit of the doubt."

Maelgwn gaped openly. "Elwyn, too! Of all the foolish, irresponsible things. This is utter madness! They will be captured—Gwyrtheyrn will show no mercy. Or worse yet, he will use them as hostages against me."

Abelgirth shook his head sadly. "I agree with you. It *is* madness. Still, you have to admire the girl's spirit. It seems she means to try and save you both—both the men that she loves."

Maelgwn looked uncomfortable. "I don't know about her love for me. I can't help wondering if she is not more concerned with saving Viroconium and the people she cares for there rather than me."

"Well, she certainly didn't have to warn you, did she?" Abelgirth asked pointedly. "Don't belittle your wife's courage," he added. "It's a quality that not many woman have . . . nor men either."

"Loyalty is not a quality many have either," Maelgwn said with a sigh. "You must excuse me, Abelgirth. I will meet with you later to talk about our strategy for the battle, but right now I must have some answers for the questions that are troubling me."

Maelgwn left Abelgirth and headed for Esylt's chambers. It was late, and she was already dressed for bed when she let him in. She wore a long loose white gown and her dark hair fell gracefully around her shoulders.

Esylt spoke lightly. "So, brother, you have come home to defend us."

Maelgwn scrutinized his sister's face critically. "You don't seem surprised that Gwyrtheyrn and Constantine have joined forces."

"Should I be surprised?"

"Don't play games with me, Esylt. I need the truth this time—how long have there been rumors of this war?"

"Rumors? There have been rumors since you left Viroconium that you were too easy on Constantine. Is it any wonder that the conniving, sneaky weakling has gone behind your back?"

Maelgwn crossed the room rapidly and grabbed a handful of Esylt's hair, drawing it tight in his fingers until she winced in pain.

"I will have the truth, Esylt, not more of your taunts. When did you first hear of Constantine's alliance with Gwyrtheyrn?"

Esylt's eyes were as bright and deadly as two blue flames, but she answered him matter-of-factly. "Like everyone else, I first learned of Constantine's treachery two days ago, when word came from Viroconium."

"Are you sure?" Maelgwn hissed, pulling his sister's hair more tightly.

"Aye, I am sure! Would you like me to make up a lie so you will stop hurting me?"

Maelgwn released his sister, pushing her away in disgust. He turned to look about the room distractedly. "It's strange that Aurora would hear of this rumor, and you—who usually have ears as sharp as a fox's—would not."

Esylt shrugged. "You know I don't listen to women's gossip—whose baby has colic and whose husband lost at gaming—I can't be bothered with their simple-minded babble."

"You can't tell me that Evrawc's wife and the rest of the women know more of what is happening in Viroconium than you!"

"All right," Esylt said calmly. "I won't tell you that. Perhaps I heard this 'rumor' as you call it. What does it matter? Why should I pay attention to it? Don't you think it's odd that Aurora heard the same things as all the other women, and somehow she *knew* that the rumor was true. If I were looking for a spy at Caer Eryri, I would look no further than your own bed!"

"That's absurd. Why would Aurora send a message to warn me to come home if she were in contact with someone from Viroconium regarding her father's plans?"

Esylt shrugged. "Perhaps she felt guilty, perhaps she was too cowardly to betray you completely. And now it seems she has gone to talk to her father—it is rather a coincidence isn't it?"

Maelgwn shook his head. "I don't believe it. Aurora may well be trying to stop this war in her own foolish way, but she didn't spread this story of Constantine's disloyalty. Wydian was the one who spoke of it, and she is no friend of Aurora's."

"It matters little enough now," Esylt said impatiently. "If you are done with your harassment of me, do I have my lord's permission to go to bed?"

Maelgwn longed to slap his sister's sneering face, just once, to see her recoil in pain. But he stayed his hand— he had too many other things to attend to.

* * *

The four men met in the nearly deserted hall. They sat down at a table by the fire for a late supper of sausages, apples and barley bread.

"So, Gareth," Maelgwn began when they were all seated. "What did Wydian have to say about telling the other women that Gwyrtheyrn and Constantine had joined forces?"

"Not much," he growled. "She said she overheard two soldiers who were gaming speak of an alliance between Gwyrtheyrn and Constantine—but of course she can't recall who the soldiers were. She claims she thought little of their words then, and it was only when she saw a chance to torment Aurora that she remembered."

"There is truth in that," Balyn said between mouthfuls of sausage. "I spoke with Gwenaseth, and she remembered Wydian's words exactly. She saw it as a deliberate attempt to humiliate Aurora in front of the other woman."

"Wydian must be lying," Maelgwn said thoughtfully. "But at least she didn't accuse Evrawc of telling her—I am glad to know that he is cleared from suspicion."

"What about Esylt?" Balyn asked pointedly. "You spoke to her—what was her story?"

"The same as always," Maelgwn said in disgust. "She claims to know nothing about the rumor, and naturally, she could not resist suggesting that it was Aurora who knew all along what Constantine was up to."

"Well," Gareth said quietly. "There is something to that. How *did* Aurora know to send you a message of warning?"

Rhys had not spoken yet, but now he pushed his plate away and faced Maelgwn resolutely. "My lord, I, too, would like to know—how do you explain that Aurora has run off to Viroconium with one of your captains?"

"*I* can explain!" Balyn interrupted. "I spoke to Gwenaseth. Elwyn tried to keep Aurora from going, but when he couldn't, he went with her to protect her. It seems to me that if Gwenaseth trusts her husband with the queen, then we should not suspect them of disloyalty either!"

Maelgwn sighed deeply and said nothing. The other three men watched him uneasily. More than ever, they felt the weight of responsibility their king bore. Each could not help wondering—if Aurora were his wife— would he trust her?

Thirty

Aurora looked sideways at Elwyn as he rode beside her. How could she ever repay him for his help? She had talked bravely enough before she left Caer Eryri, but the truth was that she would have never made it this far without Elwyn. Even in daylight, she could not have found her way over the mountains by herself, and the injury to her head still bothered her—she tired easily and sometimes grew so dizzy and sick she could hardly stay on her horse.

Elwyn caught her looking at him and smiled.

"Are you feeling better?"

"Aye," Aurora answered. "The mornings are the worst, as the day wears on, I begin to feel more like myself."

"We are almost halfway there," Elwyn said, his smile disappearing. He anxiously surveyed the frosty moors ahead of them. "I can't believe that we have not yet met up with your father and Gwyrtheyrn."

Aurora frowned, too. "It does seem like they're taking their time. I thought they would be advancing into Gwynedd by now. I wonder if the messenger from Viroconium could have been mistaken. Perhaps Gwyrtheyrn was there to talk to my father about something else. Perhaps they do not mean to make war on Maelgwn after all."

Elwyn shook his head. "I wish I could be so hopeful, but Maelgwn's man in Viroconium is an experienced soldier—he could easily tell the difference between a peaceful envoy and an army ready to do battle." He looked at Aurora critically. "Are you sure you still want to do this?"

Aurora held her head up stubbornly. "Aye, I must talk to my father."

"Do you know how dangerous this is, Aurora? If Gwyrtheyrn suspects that you are trying to turn your father against him, he may have you killed!"

"I know what a risk I'm taking, Elwyn," Aurora answered with a sigh. "It's funny, the young woman who left Viroconium barely four months ago would never have dared to do this thing, but after all I have been through with Maelgwn, I have to try and help him somehow."

"You love him, don't you?" Elwyn said in a soft voice.

"Aye, I love him!" Aurora answered with a gasp of emotion. "I have fought it and denied it, but it's true. Perhaps that makes what I have to do even harder. With Gwyrtheyrn, I will have to pretend that I despise Maelgwn, and that I have come to betray my husband."

"If he believes you, it might work. Gwyrtheyrn is a greedy, scheming man. He will not question that you would show no more loyalty to Maelgwn than that. Once we have his trust, perhaps we can influence things in Maelgwn's favor."

Despite Elwyn's reassuring words, Aurora suddenly seemed to grow pale. She stopped talking of their plans, and a short distance later she pulled Paithu to a halt and dismounted. She barely made it a few paces before she doubled over retching.

Elwyn watched her in concern. Was it the strain of the coming confrontation with Gwyrtheyrn that made her ill, or could it be that she had not yet recovered from her recent fall? He begged Aurora to stop and rest, but she stubbornly refused. It was past midday now, and she wanted to have her meeting with Gwyrtheyrn before nightfall.

Aurora noticed that the landscape was changing again. The mountains were behind them, and they had reached the soft rolling hill country. They were taking the same route that they'd followed when she'd left Viroconium for Gwynedd as Maelgwn's new bride. She guessed that they were about two days' ride away from Viroconium by now—surely they should meet up with her father soon.

Just before sunset, as they mounted the crest of another hill, both Aurora and Elwyn looked down on the plains below and gasped. A vast army was spread out on the valley below them. Gwyrtheyrn's standards were purple and gold, and in the light of the setting sun, the whole field seemed to bleed with color.

Aurora felt her throat closing up in fear.

"The gods help us," Elwyn whispered. "I did not expect this. Even Maelgwn will be hard put to defeat this large an army."

Aurora cleared her throat and sat up stiffly. "That makes what we have to do even more important."

They spurred their horses on and rode down the hill toward the army. It was growing dark when they reached the sentry at the edge of the camp.

"Who goes there?" the man cried, thrusting a torch up to peer at their faces.

Elwyn spoke up briskly.

"I am escorting Lady Aurora, daughter of Lord Constantine—she seeks refuge in her homeland."

They could hear the guards whispering among themselves in the darkness.

"Lady Aurora?" one of the guards said after a moment. "The Lady Aurora who was wedded to Maelgwn the Great?"

"Aye, this is she," Elwyn answered. "She comes east to seek protection."

There was more murmuring, and then the guard with the torch lifted it up even higher so that the smoke swirled into their faces. Aurora and Elwyn held their breath, but apparently the sentry was satisfied by what he saw, for he handed the torch to another man, and then grabbed Paithu's bridle.

"Come then," he said. "You can tell your story to Gwyrtheyrn himself."

They were taken quickly to a large tent near the center of the camp. There they dismounted and their horses were led away. Another soldier escorted them to the tent and then, with a few gruff words, presented them to Gwyrtheyrn.

Aurora looked into the shadows and saw a gaunt, feral face.

"So, you are Lady Aurora, or should I say Lady Maelgwn now?" the man suggested derisively.

"Aye, that I am."

"What are you doing here?"

"I've left my husband. When word came that my father

had joined forces with you, I decided I no longer had to endure my unhappy marriage."

"Your husband treated you unkindly?"

"Aye, he kept me almost as a slave, even locked me away at times. I have to say that I feared for my life at my husband's hand!"

"A touching story," Gwyrtheyrn said with a sneer.

He stood and moved out of the shadows, so that Aurora could see him more clearly. He was not a large man, but there was a lean, dangerous cruelty about him. Aurora stood as still as possible, trying to control the trembling of her hands.

Gwyrtheyrn walked around her, and his eyes inspected her warily, but at last he smiled. "I'm surprised that Maelgwn let such a beauty get away from him. Your account of things should help keep Constantine's army eager to fight for your honor. My men will escort you to a safe place. But your guard," he motioned to Elwyn. "He will stay with me."

Aurora moved closer to Gwyrtheyrn and tried to make her voice soft and enticing. "There is something else I would ask of you, my lord," she purred softly. "I have seen the standards of my father among your army. I would like to go to him and assure him personally of my safety."

"You may set your mind at ease on that account," Gwyrtheyrn answered. "I will go to him myself and tell him that you are safe."

Aurora moved even closer, hoping that Gwyrtheyrn would catch the scent of the sweet perfume she had hurriedly annointed herself with before they met the sentry. Then, with a subtle hand, she reached up to pull her cloak away from her face. As she did so, her loose tunic slipped down slightly, revealing the smooth, white skin of her shoulder. Aurora saw Gwyrtheyrn's fascinated stare and waited.

After a moment, Gwyrtheyrn looked back into Aurora's face and laughed. "You are a bold one, aren't you? Cover yourself up, woman. It is cold, and I have no desire to taste Maelgwn's leftovers—not when Constantine has two other lovely and unspoiled daughters to choose from. You will be taken to see your father when *I* choose, and not before."

Gwyrtheyrn dismissed them. Aurora had one last desperate look at Elwyn before she was led away, and then her guard shoved her roughly into small tent.

Aurora sat down heavily on the bare ground. There was no lamp, and no furs or blankets for comfort. She was a prisoner.

She tried to relax and think. Her heart still pounded unnaturally from her confrontration with Gwyrtheyrn. She could not help wondering what she would have done if Gwyrtheyrn had decided to take what she offered. Even if she had been able to see her father and change the course of the coming battle, would it have been worth it? Aurora shuddered just thinking of Gwyrtheyrn's clawlike hands swarming over her. No, perhaps she was lucky after all. Somehow she feared that even if she did it only to help him, Maelgwn would never be able to forget the image of her in Gwyrtheyrn's arms.

But what was she to do now? She was helpless, trapped in this tent with no way to reach her father. Even faithful Elwyn was gone. Aurora shuddered again. What if they hurt him? How would she ever make it up to Gwenaseth if Elwyn were killed?

Aurora shook herself, trying to clear her mind. She must not let her fears get the best of her—she must concentrate and think of a plan.

It was a bitter cold night in the highlands. Maelgwn's soldiers huddled by the fire and stomped their feet to get warm. Maelgwn was restless, as always before a battle. Would it be tomorrow or the next day? By morning, they would be in the foothills—surely they would meet with Gwyrtheyrn soon.

He walked quickly through the camp, stopping occasionally to give an order or share a word with a group of his men. He had almost reached his own tent when he saw a familiar figure, sitting alone by one of the fires.

"Evrawc," Maelgwn spoke softly. "So, you, too, are troubled by your thoughts tonight."

Evrawc nodded as Maelgwn sat down beside him.

"You know, Evrawc," Maelgwn began. "I want you to know how sorry I am about that business back there. I should never have suspected you of disloyalty."

Evrawc looked at the king. His face was even more careworn and angry than usual, but his eyes looked kindly, even tender. "There's nothing for you to say, my lord. I know that you are a king, and you must always suspect the worst of those close to you. I can't hold your caution against you."

"All the same, Evrawc—you've served me well over ten years now. I should not have thought . . ."

"It was natural enough," Evrawc interrupted in a dismissing tone. "No doubt most men do share secrets with their wives. But I . . ." Evrawc laughed bitterly. "It seems I share nothing with Wydian except anger and contempt."

"There are your two children—Ofydd seems like a fine boy."

Evrawc gave a snort of disgust. "Lately I have even begun to wonder about my children—are they really mine, or has Wydian kept a lover all along?"

"Wydian has a lover?" Maelgwn asked in surprise.

"So, it would seem. I just found out. As painful as it was to have you accuse me of treachery, it was even worse to learn that my wife had brought another man to our bed."

"Who is he?" Maelgwn asked impatiently. "It is not just idle curiosity either, Evrawc," he added hastily as he saw the man's troubled look. "If Wydian shares her bed with another man, perhaps she shares secrets with him as well."

"You think *he* is the source of the rumors about Constantine and Gwyrtheyrn?"

"It seems likely, does it not?" Maelgwn said excitedly. "You said that Wydian was not interested in men's affairs, but if a lover told her a story that seemed to make the queen look bad, she would surely remember it. What do you think? Could the man your wife betrayed you with be the one?"

Evrawc sighed and his face twisted with bitterness. "It was one of the soldiers left to guard Caer Eryri while we were in Manua Gotodin. Grimerwyn is his name."

"Grimerwyn? He is one of my sister's cast off lovers!"

"Aye," Evrawc said disgustedly. "It is bad enough that

my wife betrays me, but she must do it with a churl like that, too.

Maelgwn stood up abruptly. "I'm going to look for Balyn. I want you and him to go among the men and find this man, Grimerwyn. When you find him—bring him to me!"

It did not take long for Evrawc to hunt down Grimerwyn and drag him to Maelgwn's tent. As the man was brought before him, Maelgwn clearly recalled his swarthy face and thin, wraithlike form from the visit to the Brigantes.

The king stood, so that he towered above the prisoner, but he kept his voice controlled and impersonal.

"Do you know why we have been brought here, Grimerwyn?"

The man shrugged and glanced insolently at Evrawc. "It would seem it has something to do with that bitch, Wydian."

Evrawc glowered back, and his hands curled into fists, but he said nothing and made no move against Grimerwyn.

"Aye," Maelgwn said impatiently. "This has something to do with her—something to do with a story you told her."

Grimerwyn remained cool and arrogant. "I say many things when a woman is in the mood for talk."

"Ah, so then you admit that you told Wydian that Constantine was planning to invade Gwynedd."

Grimerwyn began to look around uneasily. His dark face seemed to grow darker still and the whites of his eyes shone luridly in the lamplight. There was the sickening rasp of a sword being drawn, and the sudden dazzle of a blade at the prisoner's throat.

"Answer me!" Maelgwn thundered.

The air of defiance that Grimerwyn had worn was fading. Those watching could see the beads of sweat begin to form on his face, and his voice was a harsh croak.

"Aye, I told her that—what of it? She did not even seem very interested—she was much more interested in complaining to me about the queen."

"How did you know? Where did you hear of it?"

Grimerwyn looked around at the grim faces staring at him. He stopped when he got to Maelgwn's still, deadly countenance and smiled weakly.

"It's odd about women, isn't it, my lord? They seem so weak and unimportant most of the time, but if they betray you, it hurts more than it does with a man. We are all fools when it comes to them."

"Explain yourself!" Maelgwn ordered. "Was it a woman who told you of Constantine's plans?"

"Aye, it was a woman, my lord . . . someone you would never expect . . . or would you?"

Maelgwn's calm mask seemed to crack, and his hand holding the sword wavered visibly, but he said nothing more, indeed, he seemed incapable of speaking.

Balyn moved forward to grab Grimerwyn's shoulder roughly. "Enough of your clever insinuations," he hissed. "Tell us her name."

Grimerwyn let out his breath slowly.

"It was Esylt."

"Esylt?" Maelgwn sounded stunned. "Why? When did she tell you this?"

"It was . . . I don't recall the time exactly . . . it was before you left for the north."

"Did she . . . she say how she knew this?"

There was a raw grating sound as Grimerwyn laughed.

"You still don't understand, do you, Maelgwn? Esylt told me—nay, she bragged to me, that she had made sure that you would pay for your mistakes at Viroconium."

The man paused and looked at Maelgwn with a mixture of pity and defiance.

"It seems she has spread a web of lies halfway across Britain, and you and Cunedda are to be the victims of her cunning deception."

"Cunedda?" Evrawc cried in surprise. "What does he have to do with this?"

Grimerwyn's face was bright with sweat and there was a wild cast to his eyes. "You see how shrewd she is? You still have not guessed, and by now you are too far away to help him. The Picts that you thought you were fighting—that was Cunedda's son making it look as though barbarians were ravaging Manau Gotodin. It was only a ruse to get you away from Gwynedd and to distract Cunedda until half of his forces had joined up with Ferdic. Even now, Ferdic is moving in to crush Cunedda and take the kingship for himself."

Everyone seemed paralyzed with shock. Finally, Balyn cleared his throat and asked the question which filled them all with dread.

"And Gwyrtheyrn and Constantine—did Esylt have any part in their joining forces?"

Grimerwyn flashed his ugly, ironic smile again. "Of course. Constantine would never have allied himself with a wolf like Gwyrtheyrn if he did not feel he had been sorely wronged. It was only when he heard that Maelgwn the Great had raped and beaten his beloved daughter that he even considered revenge."

He looked at Maelgwn with grudging admiration. "You had that one right, my lord. Constantine loves his youngest daughter dearly—he would make a pact with the gods of the underworld themselves to avenge her."

Maelgwn's voice seemed to come in a ragged gasp. "But it's not true! I love Aurora! I never meant to hurt her! I certainly did not rape her or beat her!"

"Ah, but you were not there when Constantine heard of your abuse. I, myself, carried the news to him. He was eager to believe the worst of you, and when several other soldiers reported that you struck your wife not two days after your wedding . . . well, he was enraged, so furious I thought he might have a fit and die right there."

The group of men in the tent waited for a moment in stony silence. Finally Evrawc spoke.

"I think we've heard enough, Maelgwn. Now that this foul scum has spilled his guts, I say we make quick end to his miserable, worthless life."

Maelgwn still seemed dazed. "What . . . I . . . No. We may need to ask him questions. Indeed, I have another question to ask of him now." He moved forward to look directly in Grimerwyn's face. His voice was soft, almost pleading.

"Why, Grimerwyn? Why did she do it?"

The man's face was scornful. "Why should I tell you? You're only going to kill me anyway."

"I have a right to know," Maelgwn said painfully. "I *have* to know."

Grimerwyn cleared his throat and spat nervously on the ground.

"It was Aurora, I think. Before she came to Caer Eryri, Esylt could feel that she had some control over you—that she could influence your decisions. But then you married Aurora, and Esylt knew it was all slipping away from her. Eventually, Aurora would truly be queen, and she would be . . . nothing."

"But now she is nothing anyway," Maelgwn said in an agonized voice. "Did it matter so little to her that Gwynedd might be destroyed, her own people slaughtered?"

Grimerwyn shrugged. "Ferdic and Gwyrtheyrn both promised her part of the spoils. I believe she hoped that they would even let her rule Gwynedd after you were killed."

Maelgwn sighed and put his sword away with a defeated gesture. The rest of the men watched him, full of pity. They didn't know what to say, or how to comfort him.

The king looked at Grimerwyn again, as if suddenly remembering him.

"Take this man away, and keep him safe. I don't have time to deal with him now. Then go among the men and pick out those soldiers who have any tie to Esylt—lovers, servants, whatever. Keep them under guard. I won't have any traitors within my ranks!"

Maelgwn's eyes lingered over his officers, and they all longed to look away from the suffering in his face, but they met his glance warmly, with compassion.

"And when you have done those things," he continued,

"try to get some rest. We may have a battle to fight in the morning."

After he dismissed his men, Maelgwn himself lay down. He had barely closed his eyes when the images came to him. He and Esylt playing as children. Her small brown hand resting on his own. Her face flushed with excitement. Her dazzling sapphire eyes bright with passion. What a waste, he thought bitterly.

Then Aurora's face appeared before him—enigmatic . . . exotic . . . beautiful. Even in a daydream, she made his pulse quicken. Had that been his mistake? Had he chosen wrong? Even now, Aurora was somewhere near Viroconium, trying to persuade her father not to fight him. If she did not succeed . . . if he did not win . . . he might never see her again.

Ah, but he felt her. Even across the miles . . . the lowlands that lay between them—he could feel her warm presence, hear her soft whispering voice. She loved him. She would not betray him. Maelgwn sighed in his sleep and thought no more.

Thirty-one

Aurora swooned in her sleep. She was surrounded by monsters—huge, with wings of molten metal that blinded her. The creatures beat their wings threateningly. The sound was deafening—Aurora could feel it drowning out her breath and the beating of her heart. She was terrified. She tried to move, but her limbs seemed frozen. She struggled against the invisible bonds that held her down. Her mouth was full of the bitter taste of bile.

Soft white things, like snow, began to drift down on her; they buried her lips and filled her mouth. She tried to cry out, to scream, but there was no sound—only whiteness everywhere.

Then she saw Maelgwn. He was calling to her, speaking soundlessly. The wind blew back his dark hair, and his blue eyes blazed like liquid fire. She saw him reach out his hand, and she reached out to him . . . forever . . . into an endless darkness.

Then there was a fluttering sound in her ears, and a familiar voice. The world came back to her with a painful, dizzying rush.

"Aurora!"

She woke and looked up into her father's worried face.

"Papa?"

"Aye, I am here. Your man, Elwyn, sent me to you. Thank God you are safe."

"It was just a dream," Aurora said uneasily. "I saw Maelgwn, but I couldn't hear him. I couldn't understand what he was saying."

"Hush, my love. He won't hurt you anymore. I promise you."

Aurora sat up, startled, suddenly realizing where she was and why she was there. She was still in the small tent, but a pallet of straw had been placed beneath her, and a lamp burned nearby. She could see her father's worried face.

"Papa?" she asked quietly. "Is there a guard outside?"

Constantine nodded.

"Do you think he speaks Latin?"

"He is a common soldier—I think not."

"Good," Aurora said, switching to the old Roman tongue. "I have something to tell you. Something which must not reach Gwyrtheyrn's ears."

Constantine looked startled. "What is it? What must you tell me?"

"I love Maelgwn." Aurora looked into her father's surprised face and shook her head to silence him. "Aye, it is true, and I have come to talk you out of fighting him."

"But it's too late!" Constantine protested. "I have made an agreement with Gwyrtheyrn. I don't understand . . . how could you love Maelgwn . . . after what he has done to you."

"It was all a mistake, Father. He never meant to hurt me. He loves me!"

"He raped and beat you, and now he tells you he loves

you! Oh, my sweet child—how could I have married you off to such a demon?"

"Maelgwn never raped me," Aurora protested. "He struck me once, but I'm sure he was sorry. We did have . . . misunderstandings, aye, but they are all over now. We love each other."

"But how can that be? One of Maelgwn's own men told me of his abuse. Then, a few weeks ago, I received word that you were badly injured, perhaps wouldn't live. Elwyn just told me that you had not completely recovered yet."

Aurora reached out to touch her father's arm with a patient, soothing gesture. "I fell off my horse, Papa. I was caught in a rainstorm, and I was so cold and tired that I fell and hurt my head. Maelgwn was there beside me as I recovered—he never left me. As for my illness now . . ." a smile lit up Aurora's pale face. "I think I am ill because . . . because I am going to have Maelgwn's baby."

"Oh, Jupiter," Constantine said in a ravaged voice. "What lies have I listened to. What cleverness Gwyrtheyrn has used to entrap me!"

Aurora sat up so that her mouth was close to her father's ear as he knelt beside her.

"It's not too late," she whispered. "You could still ask your men to turn against Gwyrtheyrn. In the heat of the battle, they could switch to Maelgwn's side."

"I don't know," Constantine whispered in dread. "If Maelgwn loses, we would be slaughtered by Gwyrtheyrn, and if Maelgwn wins . . . who can say if he will stay his hand against us."

"I will make him," Aurora said. "I know that he will do what I ask."

Constantine shook his head. "But Maelgwn won't win. Gwyrtheyrn is too strong, even for him. We will be well into Gwynedd by the time his army arrives from the north. We are less than four days' march from Caer Eryri now. We will crush his stronghold, and then we will cut his army to pieces before he can get reinforcements from the coast."

"No, Papa, I have warned Maelgwn. Even now he is probably waiting with his army between here and Caer Eryri. Nay, I know he is there. I can feel him."

Constantine looked at his daughter in doubt and confusion.

"I don't know what to do. It's too late to stop Gwyrtheyrn. He has come this far—he will not turn back without fighting Maelgwn."

"But once the fighting starts, could your men get away then?"

"Perhaps," said Constantine. "But there is no guarantee that our defection would turn the battle. And if Maelgwn lost . . ." Aurora could read the fear in his eyes.

"Papa, would your men change sides if you asked them? Would they abandon Gwyrtheyrn and fight for Maelgwn?"

Constantine considered. The lines in his forehead puckered in thought.

"Many of them are angry at the way Gwyrtheyrn has treated us. Viroconium has been like an armed camp these last few days. Gwyrtheyrn has seen fit to take the best of our cattle and grain to feed his men. Some of the women have been abused, and the men are afraid to defend them against Gwyrtheyrn's soldiers. For all that he humiliated us, Maelgwn didn't mistreat us so."

Constantine looked into his daughter's pleading face.

"I can only ask them, Aurora. I'm not a leader like Maelgwn or Gwyrtheyrn. My men respect me, but they do not fear me. I can't order them to follow me if they feel they would be better served by Gwyrtheyrn's protection."

Aurora nodded. "I know, Papa. Even though I love Maelgwn, I would not ask you to do this if I did not think it would be best for the people of Viroconium."

Constantine looked nervously toward the door of the tent.

"I must go now. I told the guard that you are sick, he will wonder that I risk tiring you by talking so much."

"Where is Elwyn? Is he safe?"

"Aye, he is safe, but very closely guarded."

Aurora smiled. "Elwyn has been a great help to me. How did he get away to speak with you?"

"It seems he knew one of Gwyrtheyrn's men—the man is a hired soldier who fought with Maelgwn once for pay. He brought Elwyn to me. Elwyn told me nothing except that you were ill and needed to speak to me."

"I'm so glad he found you. I was trying to think of a plan when I fell asleep." Aurora reached out for her father with an imploring gesture. "Remember what I said, Father . . . Papa . . . remember what I told you of Maelgwn."

"I will not forget, Aurora. Sleep now. You are very pale. I fear that what Elwyn says is true—you have not recovered from your injury. I will try to see you tomorrow . . . if there is time . . . if we are not at war."

After her father left, Aurora fell asleep again, but this time her dreams were unmemorable. In the morning she woke with a churning nausea in her stomach. It took all her willpower to rise from the pallet and shakily search for her pack of things lying in the corner of the tent. Someone had seen fit to bring it in when they brought the lamp and a jar of water to her. She was not quite a helpless prisoner, but oh, her stomach!

Aurora struggled to untie the package of barley bread she had left in her pack. She took a bite and gagged at the flat dry taste, but then took another and swallowed. She must eat—it was the only way she would feel better. When she was done, she drank the full jar of stale water. Now to attend to her appearance. Her comb was in the pack as well, and Aurora unbraided her hair and dragged the bronze comb through her thick tresses. She wished she had some water to wash with, but she had drunk it all. She moistened her veil with the last drops and rubbed it over her face.

Taking a deep breath, Aurora pulled the tent flap back and stepped out into the fresh air. The sharp chill of morning was in the air, and Aurora pulled her cloak close around her.

The guard outside looked at her suspiciously, but when she smiled at him, he seemed to soften.

"What are you doing?" he asked in a cautious voice.

"I just needed some fresh air," Aurora answered politely. "I don't feel well."

"Aye, the last guard said you were ill. He also said you had a visitor—Lord Constantine."

Aurora had trouble meeting the man's probing look.

She could only hope that her conversation with her father had not been overheard.

"Constantine is my father," Aurora answered coldly. "I just wanted him to know that I'm all right."

"Gwyrtheyrn was not pleased to know that you had met with Lord Constantine. He wishes to speak with you."

With that, the man grasped her arm roughly and led her to Gwyrtheyrn's tent. Aurora's heart was pounding. If Gwyrtheyrn guessed her intentions, she was doomed. At best, he would kill her outright, or even worse, use her as a hostage to control Maelgwn.

Gwyrtheyrn was having breakfast when Aurora was brought to him. For a moment she could not help gaping at the luxury that surrounded him. He sat eating at a table full of food served in fine pottery, bronze, even glassware. He was dressed in a rich purple tunic edged in gold, and his neck and arms were gilded with elaborate jewelry. She could not help contrasting this scene with the way Maelgwn normally took his meals while on campaign—squatting by the fire with his men, eating the same dry food as they, dressed in his old tunic and ragged leather trousers. It seemed that Gwyrtheyrn enjoyed the trappings of a king a great deal more than Maelgwn did.

"Well, well. Lady Maelgwn, we meet again."

Aurora met Gwyrtheyrn's cold, searching stare as levelly as she could.

"What do you want with me?" she asked him boldly.

Gwyrtheyrn frowned. "I understand that you disregarded my orders and met with your father."

"He only wanted to make sure that I was well."

"Aye, I was told that you were sick—what is wrong with you?"

Aurora tried to hold her head up proudly. No doubt she looked white and frail—she certainly felt that way.

"I had a fall from a horse only a few weeks ago. I still have not recovered. I was fleeing Maelgwn even then."

Gwyrtheyrn's eyes narrowed and then flicked over her suspiciously. "You look more like a woman who's breeding to me."

Aurora inwardly suppressed a gasp. How had Gwyrtheyrn guessed? She dared not let him know the truth.

She touched her flat stomach, and stared back at Gwyrtheyrn with an arrogant glare. "That could not be— I have not been with Maelgwn for many weeks."

Gwyrtheyrn grunted, and Aurora knew that it was time to distract him from this dangerous subject.

"While I'm here," she said briskly, "I would like to know your battle strategy against Maelgwn."

"What does it matter to you?"

"I have a strong desire to see you defeat Maelgwn," Aurora answered. "I want to see you grind him into the dirt."

Gwyrtheyrn laughed. "What a cold bitch you are—do you hate your husband that much?"

"Aye. You do not know what it is like to be married off to a brute like Maelgwn—he had his greedy hands all over me ere we were even wed. Besides . . ." she cast her eyes down coyly. "I have another reason I wish to see Maelgwn defeated."

"What is that?"

She smiled radiantly at Gwyrtheyrn. "The young man who was with me last night—he is the one I truly love. I thought that if I helped you, you might consider giving Elwyn a position of power in Gwynedd."

Gwyrtheyrn snorted derisively. "It seems that Gwynedd is infested with traitors—I almost feel sorry for Maelgwn."

"What do you mean?"

"His wife, his sister, one of his officers—it seems that Maelgwn the Great is hated most by those closest to him."

Aurora could not hide her surprise. "His sister? Esylt has betrayed Maelgwn? I didn't know."

"Aye," Gwyrtheyrn answered with a gloating smile. "She is as eager as you to see her brother dead. She thinks that I will let her rule in his place. Of course, I will make sure she has no real power—I would certainly never trust a woman, especially one who is a traitor."

Aurora tried to temper her shock. She had been right all along—Esylt was plotting against her brother! She composed her face carefully.

"Esylt—I'm surprised. When I was at Caer Eryri, she seemed completely loyal to Maelgwn."

"Aye, she is a treacherous one. It appears she has been plotting against Maelgwn all along."

Aurora tried to be flippant, although her heart was pounding. "In truth, I care little enough who rules Gwynedd—as long as Maelgwn is dead."

Gwyrtheyrn smiled again, like a cat that has cornered its prey. "If that is all you ask, then I am sure I can make you happy. I intend to slaughter Maelgwn's army and take his head as a trophy prize. Would you like me to save it for you—as a memento of your marriage?"

Aurora could not hide her disgust.

"No, thank you," she answered. "I never want to see him again—dead or alive." She pulled herself up stiffly, and tried to pretend that she was her mother—calm and poised. "You still have not told me your battle plans."

Gwyrtheyrn's gray eyes narrowed. "I will not share my battle plans with any woman—queen or not. Besides, whatever else you are, you are a traitor. Be glad that I need your father's support, or I wouldn't have tolerated the sight of you as long as I have."

With that, Aurora found herself abruptly dismissed.

"Come on," her guard said harshly as he grabbed her arm again. "You are to ride in a wagon at the end of the train."

"We are leaving, then?"

"It would seem so."

Thirty-two

Maelgwn was dreaming. Aurora was beside him. He could feel her warmth, smell the scent of her hair—rich, spicy, exotic. He stirred. It was still early, there was a chill in the air, and the light that glowed in through the tent flap was faint, tinged with rose.

He got up and dressed and put on his sword and dagger. There was a heaviness in his heart—the weight of sadness—but there was another feeling, too. The tingle of expectation stirred in his limbs.

He went out, half expecting the grayness of the last few days, but it was clear. The sun rose in the east, threatened only by a few fragile clouds of pink and lavender. It would be warm—the sunlight was already burning away the frost.

The rest of the camp was rising too. Men were building fires for breakfast. Tents were being taken down. Maelgwn stood for a moment, watching. He felt a surge of humble gratitude. This was his army; these were his men. He had trained them, inspired them. Today he might well lead them to their deaths, and they would follow him without question. He loved them.

"You are up early, Maelgwn."

Maelgwn turned to see the reassuring bulk of his second-in-command. Balyn wore his customary lazy smile, but a hint of worry lined his face.

"Did you sleep well?" he asked.

Maelgwn nodded back. "Aye, I slept well . . . I always do the night before a battle.

"You think today, then?"

"It would seem so. I feel it in my bones."

Maelgwn said no more, and Balyn felt a moment of discomfort as the silence grew between them.

"About last night . . ." he began finally. "I wanted to tell you . . . that I am sorry. It must be a grievous thing to be betrayed by your own blood."

Maelgwn sighed faintly. "Aye, it hurts. But you did warn me, and Aurora certainly tried to, as well. It was just that I hoped . . ." Maelgwn's voice grew harsh and strained. "I had hoped that the curse of Cadwallon was finally over."

"Perhaps it is now," Balyn said gently. "There is only one eagle left in the nest, and, the gods willing, he will rule for many years."

Maelgwn gave Balyn a quick, sharp glance, and Balyn knew he was thinking of the battle to come.

"So, my king, what is the battle plan?"

Maelgwn pointed. "We will march down into the valley and wait for them there."

"It seems risky," Balyn murmured. "With the foothills behind us, we will have no way to retreat."

Maelgwn shook his head. "There is no retreat. We either defeat them or we die."

Balyn nodded gravely. "You don't think we should wait for Abelgirth's other forces—the troops from the coast?"

"We haven't time. I don't want Gwyrtheyrn to enter Gwynedd."

"But the mountains have always been our best defense," Balyn argued. "If we waited for them here, we could cut them down little by little with small bands of men attacking all along the pass."

"But by then Aurora would be dead . . . I'm sure of it," Maelgwn answered in a shaky voice. "If he has not already done so, Gwyrtheyrn would use her as a hostage, or perhaps kill her outright."

"But if we go to meet him head-on in battle, he will think we have no chance to defeat him, and perhaps he will let her live," Balyn suggested.

Maelgwn nodded, and then he turned to Balyn with agony in his eyes. "Do you think me a fool because I risk everything for a woman?"

Balyn smiled. "Nah, nah, not a fool, just a man in love. It's all right. You deserve a chance for happiness, just like any other man."

"But I am a king," Maelgwn whispered painfully. "Am I putting my own happiness above my people's safety?"

Balyn patted the king heartily on his shoulder. "It could be argued either way, Maelgwn. If we meet them in the valley, Gwyrtheyrn will have the hills behind him as well. His men will not be able to retreat either. Since he has come this far and grown this strong, we must crush him now, once and for all, or he will always be a threat to Gwynedd."

Maelgwn smiled. "Thank you, Balyn. Ever since I met you, you have always known the right thing to say."

Balyn grinned back. "Now, if only Sewan were ever

so pleased with me. She says I have only to open my mouth and foolish words fly out."

"Come on, let's get ourselves some breakfast," said Maelgwn. "And order an extra portion for the men too; they will need it today."

The wagon lurched forward, and Aurora's stomach lurched with it. This was worse than riding her horse, she thought miserably. She still had not had a proper breakfast, and her nausea was agonizing. She crouched down, willing herself to feel better. Finally, she gave up and leaned back limply against the sacks of grain that were her companions in the wagon.

It was uncomfortable riding this way, but at least she was safe. Her bluff with Gwyrtheyrn had worked. He was willing to believe her story that she hated Maelgwn and would be pleased at his death. Aurora felt a pang of painful regret, thinking of her awful words. What if Maelgwn was defeated, and she did not live to tell him how much she loved him? Would he go to his own death believing that she had betrayed him?

Aurora forced herself to put her despairing thoughts aside. While she and Maelgwn still breathed, there was hope. But where was Elwyn? Was he safe? Had he been able to escape?

Aurora sat up and strained her eyes ahead to where the main part of Gwyrtheyrn's army marched. Surely they should meet with Maelgwn soon. She could see the gray and russet hills in the distance—if Maelgwn had come back from Manau Gotodin when she sent him the message, he could not be far away now. But what if he hadn't? If Maelgwn didn't stop him, Gwyrtheyrn would march into Gwynedd and destroy everything in his path. Aurora felt her agonized stomach convulse in fear. So much depended on whether Maelgwn had trusted her at last.

Aurora touched her stomach, feeling the deceptive taut, flatness of it. It was hard to believe that a baby was growing within her, but the signs were clear. When she had missed her bleeding time several weeks ago, she thought at first it was because she was so unhappy and upset. But now it all made sense—the sickness in the morning, the fatigue that lingered long after her head wound was healed. Still, she had not known for sure until she had the dream about Maelgwn; then she realized that she carried a part of him with her always.

Maelgwn's baby—what would it look like, she wondered? Would it have his beautiful blue eyes, his dark, nearly black, hair? She frowned. If it was a boy, it could look like Maelgwn, but a girl like him would seem too much like Esylt. Just the thought of her made Aurora shudder. She had been right about her sister-in-law, but there was no glory in it, no satisfaction. She thought of how hurt Maelgwn would be when he learned of his sister's betrayal. Aurora's heart went out to her husband. She did not want him to suffer again because of Esylt.

Aurora craned her neck to look ahead to where the long river of soldiers ended on the horizon. She must keep her wits about her. If the armies met today she would have to try and get away, to escape and find her way back to Maelgwn.

They traveled on—a bouncing, jarring, tedious ride. At midday, Aurora was able to coax the wagon driver into getting her some water. She drank it greedily and ate some dried meat and hard cheese from her pack. The food and drink soothed her stomach, but her heart was still gripped with icy fear.

The day was sunny and unseasonably mild. They had crossed a long stretch of hilly country, and there was no sign of the Cymry army. Aurora could not help feeling anxious as she saw that the army ahead was fast outstripping the supply wagons. They were being left behind, and it seemed her chances of rescue grew more and more remote.

It was well into the afternoon when—like a cry on the wind—word came that the battle was engaged. The two armies had finally met. Aurora waited, feeling terrified and useless. From where she was, stuck in the back behind the supply lines, she could tell next to nothing about the direction the battle was going. All that was visible ahead was a swarming blackness, accompanied by the dim, indistinct sound of violence. The wagon driver waited with her apathetically, and Aurora decided that he was a slave, and like Marcus, cared little who won and whether his ownership changed hands.

It seemed like hours that Aurora lay back on the hard, bumpy grain bags, praying to whatever gods she thought would listen. The sun beat down, and Aurora could hear the faint whistle of the wind across the frozen grasslands. If you ignored the distant battle sounds, everything around them was still and silent, and except for an occasional raven flying overhead to join the battle feast, no signs of life stirred over the brown and gray hills. Aurora could feel death in the air, and she imagined Maelgwn's face in her mind, willing him to live, to come back to her.

The sun was slipping toward the horizon and the line of stalled wagons cast long dark shadows across the hills when Aurora saw a lone horseman riding toward her. She sat up quickly, hardly daring to breathe—it looked like Elwyn. Then, in a second, Aurora left the wagon and went running toward him.

"Elwyn, Elwyn!" she cried. "What is happening? How goes the battle?"

Elwyn shook his head grimly. His face was white beneath the smudges of dirt that marked it.

"It is awful, Aurora," he said in an anguished voice. "The fighting is fierce, and neither army will retreat."

His breathing came in deep gasps. "For a long time I could not get away, and then the man guarding me was killed . . . it seemed to take forever to find you."

"Maelgwn," Aurora asked in a whisper. "Is he all right?"

Elwyn shook his head. "His banner still stood when I was close enough to see . . . but I don't know for sure."

"I hope I did the right thing, Elwyn," Aurora said faintly. "I tried to help him." She looked up at Elwyn anxiously. "My father's men—are they fighting for Gwyrtheyrn or against him?"

Elwyn shook his head again. "I can't tell. Everything is mud . . . and blood."

"What shall we do, Elwyn? Shall we wait here? I don't know if I can stand it."

Elwyn looked at Aurora again with his ashen, frightened face.

"I *should* take you away from here, back toward Viroconium, where you would be safe. But . . ." he smiled at her weakly. "I know that you would never leave Maelgwn . . . as long as he lives."

Aurora reached up to grab Elwyn's hand. "Take me to him, Elwyn. I cannot wait any longer. Even if I am to die by his side . . . I want to be there."

Elwyn dismounted and helped Aurora up on the front of the saddle. "It will be dangerous," he said softly into her ear as he climbed on behind her. "I may have to have you guide the horse so I can fight."

Aurora nodded, and they were off.

They rapidly passed the supply lines and moved into the swarm of soldiers. They saw frightened, dazed faces, a skirmish here and there, and dozens of wounded men. The horse shied and hesitated as they picked their way over bodies, and the warm, metallic smell of blood filled their nostrils.

Now and then someone would try and stop them, and Aurora held the reins in her trembling fingers as Elwyn wielded his sword, striking, chopping and stabbing at their pursuers. Aurora looked away, trying to concentrate on the way ahead of them. She felt her face being splashed with blood. At first it was warm, but then it grew colder as it dried on her skin.

Gwyrtheyrn's army was retreating. Waves of soldiers were running at them. Their eyes were glazed with fatigue and death, and Aurora cringed as Elwyn urged the horse through their ranks, slashing out brutally with his sword. There was no sign of Gwyrtheyrn or her father.

They neared the battlefront. There were more bodies, and the moans and cries of the wounded and dying were everywhere. Aurora wanted to look away, to close her eyes, but she dared not—she still guided the horse. She had never known such horrors existed as she saw: the tangle of mauve and purple intestines spilling upon the ground, faces slashed unrecognizably, bodies twisted into impossible shapes, and blood everywhere, coating the soggy ground with a foul slime.

But worst of all were the ravens. They were already devouring the fallen bodies, and with their pitiless, glassy eyes and short cruel cries of delight, they reminded Aurora of black-hooded gods of doom. Except for the ravens, this close to the battlefront it was a wasteland, and they rode on unhindered. Here no one was left whole to challenge them.

At last they reached the Cymry line. They saw wounded men being attended to, and there was some semblance of order. Aurora squinted, searching the horizon frantically for Maelgwn's standard of crimson and gold. It was dusk now and everything had faded to dark shapes floating in the eerie light.

She turned back to gasp at Elwyn.

"Where is he?"

Elwyn did not answer her, and they continued riding. Some of the soldiers stared at them with startled looks of recognition, but no one called out or tried to halt them. The men's faces were pale and expressionless, and Aurora began to fear the worst.

"We must stop," she begged Elwyn. "We have to ask someone—I cannot bear not knowing."

Elwyn halted before a young soldier who seemed to be guarding a pile of bodies.

"Maelgwn," he called. "Where is Maelgwn?"

The young soldier shook his head. "I know not—I saw his banner fall, but I'm not sure what happened."

"What direction was his standard when it fell?"

"Ahead of you," the soldier pointed. "If he lives, the king must be that way."

Elwyn whipped the horse into a canter. Aurora held on, feeling the wind sucking into her throat. They saw a tent and headed for it. As they neared, Aurora recognized Balyn and Evrawc. They looked exhausted and dazed, and as she and Elwyn rode up the two men stared at them as if they could not believe what they saw.

In an instant Aurora had slid off the horse and run to Balyn.

"The king," she shouted. "How does the king?"

Balyn looked terribly tired, but still he smiled.

"Come," he said. "Let me take you to him."

Inside the tent, Maelgwn was lying on pile of sheep-skins and blankets. His face was pale and drawn, but Aurora could see no visible wounds. As soon as he saw her, his eyes widened and he whispered her name and struggled to sit up.

Aurora went to kneel beside him. She reached with trembling fingers to touch his face, as if she could not believe he was real.

"Maelgwn, are you hurt?"

Maelgwn looked at her like a starving man who finds himself before a banquet.

"Aye, I took a sword wound in my thigh. I cannot sit my horse for now."

"But you are so pale," Aurora murmured.

"Ah, Aurora," Maelgwn laid a reassuring hand upon hers. "I have been to the spirit world and back these last few hours. We have lost many men—the army of the Cymry will be crippled for a generation—and until just a moment ago, I believed you were dead as well."

"Why?" Aurora asked, startled.

"We found Paithu, but there was no sign of you or Elwyn. I had my men search all around the area where Gwyrtheyrn was killed, and there was no trace of you. I thought surely he would keep you near him, as a hostage."

Aurora smiled faintly. "I don't think he thought you would want me back. I told him that I was running away from you, that Elwyn and I were lovers."

Maelgwn reached up to pull a strand of hair from her face with a tender gesture. "You are a clever girl, my love." Then he glanced toward the entrance of the tent.

"Where is Elwyn?"

"I am here, my lord," Elwyn said, walking in wearily.

Maelgwn's face became cool and expressionless. "I warned you once, Elwyn, about interfering in my marriage. It would seem you do not listen."

Elwyn seemed to cringe, and his hazel eyes were frightened.

Then Maelgwn smiled and his face became almost radiant.

"I never thought I would be thanking one of my men for disobeying me." Maelgwn held out his hand. "I will always be grateful to you for taking care of Aurora."

Elwyn took the hand that the king offered and nodded solemnly. Then he looked at Aurora. "My lord, I must admit that I once envied you your wife, but now . . ." he shot Aurora a mischievous grin, ". . . now I see that she is entirely too much trouble."

They all shared a moment of giddy laughter. Then it was Aurora's turn to become serious.

"My father," she said suddenly. "What has happened to him?"

Maelgwn reached up again to caress Aurora's face.

"Your father honored his agreement with me at last. When the fighting began, those men from Viroconium who could, fled Gwyrtheyrn's army and joined ours."

"And my father?" Tears glittered in Aurora's eyes—already she knew.

"I am sorry, Aurora," Maelgwn said gently. "He was cut down by Gwyrtheyrn's men."

Aurora tried to act like a queen, to be strong, but it was no use. She buried her head in Maelgwn's arms and wept bitterly.

Thirty-three

Maelgwn was meeting with some of his men when Aurora went to the door of the office and stood there shyly.

"Come in," Maelgwn said when he saw her. Aurora entered, and several of the men stood up. Both Evrawc and Balyn offered her a seat on the bench they were using.

"Nah, nah," Maelgwn said. "She can sit with me."

Aurora walked behind the table near Maelgwn, and looked at him uneasily.

"I won't hurt you?"

"Of course not!" he answered impatiently, pulling her onto his lap. "My leg is almost healed, and you are not heavy . . . yet." He patted her stomach and smiled at her indulgently.

Aurora blushed. She could not get used to this new Maelgwn. He could be so playful and familiar. The way he acted toward her in front of his men often embarrassed her.

"Now, where were we?" Maelgwn began again. "Aye, we were discussing what to do about the kingship of Viroconium—do you have any ideas, Aurora?"

Aurora was thoughtful. "I can think of someone who

would be strong, but fair, and well-loved by the people, too."

"Who is that?" Maelgwn asked.

"My sister."

"You mean Julia?"

Aurora nodded. "Why not?" she asked defensively as she looked around at the doubtful faces of the men. "She would be a good ruler. If she were a man, no one would question it."

"But that's just it," Maelgwn protested. "Viroconium needs a strong commander to defend the town."

"Perhaps we could marry her off to an appropriate warrior," Balyn suggested. "She is young and fair enough, it should be easy to find a man willing."

Evrawc cleared his throat. "I don't know whether this is appropriate, but I would like to suggest myself."

Everyone in the room gaped at Evrawc.

"You?" Maelgwn cried. "Julia is pretty, but she is as strong-willed and stubborn as a mule. I would think you would have had enough of overly independent women after your wife!"

Evrawc smiled sheepishly. "Perhaps I've grown used to being ordered around, and now that Wydian has gone away, I miss it. At any rate, I've always fancied the girl, and I would like to try marriage again . . . if she'll have me."

"Aurora?" Maelgwn looked at his wife questioningly.

Aurora shrugged. "Why not? If she gets to rule Viroconium, I doubt that Julia will mind our choosing a husband for her." She looked at Evrawc directly. "But mind yourself, Evrawc, Julia is a tyrant if you let her have her way all the time—you must stand up to her occasionally.

"I could not give you better advice in dealing with one of Constantine's daughters myself," Maelgwn said with a sly smile. Aurora caught his meaning and sat up indignantly. She made a gesture as if to slap him, and he grabbed her arm playfully and slid it around his neck so he could nuzzle her.

"Well," Balyn said cheerfully. "It seems that we are done here." He nodded meaningfully at the other men. "Perhaps the king and queen would like to be alone."

"Aye," Maelgwn said, laughing as he made Aurora squirm. "We are done for now. You are all dismissed."

Maelgwn's kisses turned from playful to serious after his men left, and Aurora broke away to whisper breathlessly: "Perhaps we should go to the tower."

Maelgwn smiled. "Aye, perhaps we should."

They left the barracks and began walking arm in arm toward the tower. Despite the dirty snow that was piled around the fortress—and the crisp, cold air—the sun was shining brilliantly and the harsh weight of winter was forgotten for a moment. Aurora slowed her pace to match Maelgwn's slight limp, and smiled to herself.

"It is hard to believe that you have just let a woman join one of your council meetings," she said slyly. "I would never have imagined such a thing."

Maelgwn smiled back at her. "It was hardly a meeting of my council—we were just talking."

Despite the jesting tone of his words, there was a lingering sadness in his eyes that Aurora could not miss.

"You are are thinking of Esylt, aren't you?" Aurora asked gently.

Maelgwn nodded. "It still pains me," He sighed deeply. "At least I did not have to have her put to death."

"You think she will stay safely out of trouble in Manau Gotodin?"

"Well, Cunedda has assured me that since he defeated Ferdic, most of his men have come back and pledged their loyalty to him. Ferdic and Esylt may wish to make mischief for us, but without an army, they are no great threat.

"I almost feel sorry for Esylt," Aurora said softly.

"You?" Maelgwn looked at her in surprise. "I thought you hated her."

Aurora wrinkled her forehead in thought. "I thought so, too, but somehow, when I found out Esylt had truly betrayed you, I was able to see things from her viewpoint."

She looked at Maelgwn meaningfully. "Women have so little power, especially among the Cymry. The bards tell us stories of great women warriors—like Boudicca, who defied even the legions of Rome—but now it seems we are little more than possessions of men. If she had been born a man, Esylt could have been a great warrior, even a king—but instead she was stuck here at Caer Eryri, worrying about the grain supply and whether you would marry her off to some dottering old chieftain."

"Esylt never tried to earn my trust or do anything but meddle in my affairs," Maelgwn protested. "She is an evil woman—just like my mother."

"Perhaps," Aurora said quietly. "But the lot of women is not an easy one here among the Cymry."

"Are you unhappy?" Maelgwn asked, stopping to stare at her.

Aurora looked back into her husband's face. Her eyes

caressed the proud line of his jaw, the delectable curve of his mouth and the hypnotizing blue of his eyes.

"No, I'm not unhappy at all," she answered with a smile. "I have everything I want."

Maelgwn smiled back with a radiance that matched the gleaming gold torque at his neck.

"Come summer, you really will have everything you want. I have spoken to one of the holy men from the priory to have him come and help us plant an orchard within the fortress next spring."

"And a garden?" Aurora asked breathlessly.

"Aye, and a garden."

Aurora smiled mischievously. "Then maybe someday you can fix the baths."

Maelgwn laughed. "You are still trying to convert me into a proper Roman farmer, aren't you Aurora?"

Aurora nodded. "I must if I am to make sure that our child grows up as a civilized Roman and not a barbarian."

"You vixen!" Maelgwn cried, catching her up in his arms. "Tell me that you love me as I am—a wild, dirty brute—tell me or I'll throw you into the snow!"

"All right," Aurora answered, laughing. "I love you as you are! Now *you* tell me . . . ," she said, sliding down out of his embrace. "Tell me that you will still want me when I am fat and heavy with your child."

Maelgwn's face grew serious and his eyes burned with blue fire. "Let me get you to the tower room, and I will show you how much I still want you."

They climbed the stairs in silence, with their fingers twined around each other's. When the door closed behind them, Aurora stared again at her husband's intense, passionate face.

"Take off your clothes," Maelgwn commanded, and Aurora hurried to obey. Her hands were trembling, and her breath seemed to come in short gasps. Would it always be like this, she wondered? Would he always make her feel so helpless with excitement?

Aurora lay down on the bed, and Maelgwn slid down next to her. He leaned over to take one of her nipples in his mouth, and Aurora moaned. "Be careful," she cautioned hoarsely. "They are so tender."

Maelgwn lifted his head up and smiled. "What a woman you have become," he said, gazing in awe at her engorged breasts and slightly swelling belly.

"Do you still find me . . . desirable?"

"Aye," Maelgwn answered solemnly. "You are more of a goddess than ever. Tell me something . . ." he asked. "The babe—when was it conceived?"

Aurora blushed and looked away. "I think, nay, I am sure—it was at the Lughnasa festival."

"I thought so," Maelgwn answered softly. "It should be an awesome child then, born of a goddess and a god." Maelgwn hesitated a moment, and then reached up to stroke Aurora's hair tenderly, smoothing it languidly into waves with his fingers.

"I'm sorry about that, Aurora. I didn't mean to come to you as Cerrunos. I didn't mean to trick you. But I felt the power move within my veins, and I could not resist you."

"It's all right. I understand now," Aurora answered. "I think it was meant to be. I wouldn't let you come to me as my husband, and so you found another way."

Maelgwn slid his fingers down her body, now caressing the fine, soft hair below her stomach.

"Tell me one more thing, Aurora," he whispered. "Tell me if it was better that night—tell me if the god pleased you more than the man."

Aurora sighed as Maelgwn pulled her close so that he could push himself into her.

"Ah," she moaned. "It is the man I love . . . the man I will always love."

Dear Readers,

Few settings are as steeped in romance and mystery as Dark Age Britain. The term "dark ages" suggests our scant knowledge of this time period and the lack of written history. In writing *The Dragon of the Island*, I was forced to rely on other authors' interpretations, as well as weaving the sparse threads of history into my own pattern of fact and imagination.

While Aurora is purely my own creation, there really was a Welsh warlord named Maelgwn the Great. The monk Gildas, writing in 643 a.d., referred to him as "O, thou dragon of the island," and denounced him as a tyrant and a terrible sinner. For all his bitter condemnation of Maelgwn, Gildas's work also suggests a complex and enigmatic king, a man who struggled with his conscience and had doubts about the value of worldly power.

Through military might, murderous intrigue and perhaps simply by the force of his larger-than-life personality, Maelgwn the Great eventually came to dominate much of Britain and reign as the ultimate symbol of Celtic preeminence. There are hints that he filled the void left by King Arthur's death and served as *Rex Britannia* for a number of years, and his sons held positions of power in what is now Scotland as well as Wales. Five hundred years after Maelgwn's death, Welsh princes from the region of Gwynedd continued to claim descent from his lineage.

Maelgwn's hold upon my own heart has been as compelling and passionate as his control of his homeland. Having created Maelgwn as a character, I found I could not easily abandon him and move on to my next hero. Halfway through *The Dragon*, I began planning two more books based on Maelgwn's life and times. I hope you look forward to reading the sequels as much as I do writing them.

Good reading,

Mary Gillgannon